MARQUIS AT BAY

MARQUIS AT BAY

A Novel by **Albert Belisle Davis**

La
Fic

Louisiana State University Press   Baton Rouge and London

Designer: Amanda McDonald Key
Typeface: Palatino
Typesetter: G&S Typesetters, Inc.
Printer and binder: Thomson–Shore, Inc.

Library of Congress Cataloging-in-Publication Data

Davis, Albert Belisle, 1947–
    Marquis at bay : a novel / by Albert Belisle Davis.
        p.   cm.
    ISBN 0-8071-1737-4
    I. Title.
    PS3554.A93128M37   1992
    813'.54–dc20   91-29369
                                                              CIP

Grateful acknowledgment is given to the Louisiana Division of the Arts for
its generous grant while this novel was being written; to Angela Davis for
permission to quote lines from "Landry Street Blues," copyright by Angela
Mary Davis; and to Carol Davis for the careful reading, both editorial and
emotional. All the books are for Carol Ann.

To my son, Benjamin Campbell Davis

The Lineman Tapes

(*circa* 4 B.C. –1 B.C.)

Platefuls of Connection

As close as I can tell, the grave was dug four years before there was a Carnival in town. I am certain now, after studying my husband's notes and taped interviews, his maps and photographs, that this account should begin at that hole in the earth in the small orange grove behind the house on Emerson Street in 1944.

I can picture that night: two men, a father and a son, waiting in a truck parked on the driveway beside the two-story house on Emerson. The father, a man known as the Lion of Landry Street, has left the truck and returned several times. The son, called Weasel then, has been sitting still in the truck cab, pretending to be asleep.

Finally, after an hour without a word, the father speaks to the son: "Main Street white people sure do like meetings."

What follows is my own transcription of the first taped interview my husband had with the son many years later.

That's just what my daddy's saying to me, "Main Street white people sure do like meetings." He's saying something else besides, about meetings, about how they seem to be the thing to do nowadays, everywhere, on Main Street and on Landry Street. And then he's talking about the reverend wars. Talking, talking, talking, you understand, while he's climbing back into the truck. I don't open up my eyes when he slams the truck door, don't even unfold my arms cause I

3

know that will make him repeat what he said and push hard and call me a lazy good-for-nothing.

The push comes, a stiff finger under my elbow. "Goddamn, boy," my daddy says, "don't you never, don't you never listen? This might be the most important night in both our life. Keep your eyes on that gallery behind the house there. They call that a 'patio' here on Emerson Street. Sit up. Pay attention. You lazy good-for-nothing, yes, boy."

I keep my voice calm and tell him not to call me that.

He says, "Don't you go and tell me what to call my own boy."

Sitting up slow, still without unfolding my arms, I listen to the screeching voice beside me and wonder once more why anybody would want to go calling my daddy the Lion of Landry Street. He's got the voice of a jay, the height of a giraffe, the teeth of a horse. Why Lion? My daddy, I decided for my own self long before that night, must've named his own self. I decided too it was him that got everybody to go calling me Weasel even though up to that night I never heard my daddy calling me that—he liked better to call me *boy, lazy good-for-nothing*, you understand.

Outside, from the house on Emerson Street, lights the color of the dull yellow of my daddy's gold tooth vanish from a second-floor window, then appear again seconds later between shutters on the bottom floor.

"Surely do like meetings," Daddy says again. "And all this time to decide on what? All to decide on what to do with a body. Know what that be, boy? Be civilization. That's what the New Reverend tell me. You got to meet and meet to have civilization."

I sit still, the word *body* livening up part my mind, the other part my mind wishing I could push *civilization* back into my daddy's mouth.

"What I just said, boy?"

4

I don't answer. I don't answer nobody's questions back then, you understand. Too much like giving.

Then Daddy says, "Goddamn it, boy." One thing my daddy don't like is me sitting there like I'm sleeping. It gets to him. And that's exactly why I like so much to pretend sleep, to kind of press him, you understand, to spark up the night. Just pretending back then, watching while I pretend.

He says, "Goddamn it, boy," again, and then: "Pay me some attention."

But he doesn't know all that night I been paying attention. Already that night Daddy and me, we've done two late-night moving jobs for the man wearing a Main Street hat. Took us two hours to haul away furniture, rugs, clothes, and jewelry from the house on Emerson, a half hour for the piano by itself. Took three hours more for me and Daddy to come on back and put everything back in place. Then another hour goes get took while we be sitting and watching yellow lights jump from room to room.

I tell my daddy all this taking too long and he brings up my stealing ways again, saying something like, "You like better be out stealing?" And then he's pushing with all his might against my arm. I don't move not a budge and the Lion of Landry settles like a heap of skin against the door.

It seems I been hearing that all my life, you understand, *Goddamn you and your stealing, boy. Boy, goddamn you and your stealing.*

Then, outside, the man in the hat starts waving at the truck from the shadows of the patio. I point at the man, and Daddy leaves, saying, "Meet, meet, meet," to himself, and "worse than the reverend wars."

Watching the silhouette of the two men all conferring like in yellow light, I can see that my daddy's taller than the man in the hat, but my daddy's thin and frail body curves to the words of the other man. You understand?

5

Then back at the truck again, Daddy's telling me that the man in the hat wants me to leave while Daddy gets started.

"Started with what?" I ask him.

Daddy ain't using the word *grave* or *bury*. He's calling it a *digging job*.

I ask him, "I leaving from here or what?"

"Ain't no way I going to be digging no hole for nobody. Body or no body, the Lion of Landry don't dig holes."

And Daddy tells me he told the man in the hat just that, and that he also told the man not to worry, that I'm going to dig and that Daddy's going to see to it that I sit still and quiet in the truck after I dig.

Then I exchange word for word on him. "Bury," I say. "You went and divide up that job into two—digging the hole and filling the hole. But it still burying, and ain't burying a body in some way worser than stealing?"

"Shet up," he tells me, and "shet up," again, all my life *shet up*. Then he quiets down, his voice, his screechy voice, and he says, "This a bad night for the Lion of Landry. But you just got to listen. And watch. Watch while I bury. Got that? Goddamn it, boy, got it?"

I unfold my arms and open up the door and I ask him where at he wants me to dig after I get the shovel out the back the truck. He says that ain't important, to dig anywheres, in the trees in the back, anywheres.

"It's after the hole been dug," he says. "Watch everything I do. Got me?"

With the shovel, I walk on into the rows of trees growing waist-high in the shadow of the backyard. There's enough space between the rows for any hole I need to dig, but I swing the shovel anyhow, swinging at the branches and trunks until two of the trees be gone. To spark up the night, you understand? When I sink the shovel through the fallen leaves and branches, I smell oranges.

Then back in the truck, I slouch, something like this, pretending sleep again, arms folded, watching the house through half-closed eyelid. I hear the patio door and recognize my daddy's skinny shape carrying a bundle toward the trees. The bundle's darker than white—maybe pink—and not heavy. Daddy's huddling it close to his body, from shoulder to waist. I think I see in his hand, before he gets to the trees, a plate, a plate catching the color of a yellow Emerson window.

I pretend sleep again when Daddy climbs on back in the cab, me peering through my lashes at him while he's hunching over forward and coughing with his elbows on the dash and his face in his hands. I smell oranges again and the fresh wet of Emerson earth.

Then pushing on my arm, the Lion of Landry he be cursing. He's grabbing on my shirt, twisting it in his hands. "Look at me when I talk, boy. Just this time, look."

I never look, then, you understand, into my daddy's face. I don't want to see what I hate most in life—his gold tooth.

Then Daddy's doing the first of his explaining that night, starting with "Goddamn you, lazy good-for-nothing. Don't you hear a word I tell you?" then going on to something like, "You got any idea what I done out there?" and ending with, "You got to remember this night."

I hate to say it, but Daddy, he was right. I should've been looking to remember. I remember now, of course, because of all that happen. But what I know now I had to relearn, you understand? Could've saved myself some trouble—all that walking I was going to have to do on the low flow, you understand. Yes sir, could've saved myself some trouble.

What I know now is that my daddy, he's telling me then, that night, them things I'd have to be relearning later. Telling me then, that night, that the man in the Main Street hat took a chance at stealing but he muffed it all up, that the man in

7

the Main Street hat needs our help now to fix up the muff-up, and that men like him pay men like Daddy and me for our help and then they leave us go.

"But he can't leave us go after tonight," Daddy says. "You understand, boy?"

Then he says something I remember clear, without relearning, something I can fish up out my mind from that night. Daddy says, "This night our connection with forever." And don't I know it for true now? Ain't that hole I dug the connection with everybody to everybody, me to the man in the hat, me to Daddy, even me to you? You understand? Shit yes you understand.

Then Daddy's telling me to start driving out quick. "Can you at least do that for me, boy?"

I sit still to his question. But after the direct order to drive comes, just before I reach for the key, I hear a woman-scream coming from one of the windows without light. When it stops, another begins, but a different voice, from behind the same window. By the time the yellow's lighting up that room, two women be screaming together in one long cry that will not die.

Then I hear the piano, the heavy goddamn Emerson piano.

My daddy makes me drive west away from Emerson, then north toward Landry Street to the Palace Bar. The bar's closed, but the gate in the tall fence around the sidehouse be open to all—to all colors, you understand—all the time.

I ask Daddy if he wants me to leave him there and drive on to the house. He ain't saying nothing. I ask him why we're at the Palace. Then he's wheezing and coughing and holding his chest with one hand, his throat with the other.

I tell him he shouldn't be out in the night air, and he tells me not to go telling him about night air, that it's not the night air going to smother him, but his own throat.

8

"Aw, shit, boy," he says, "don't you know yet what I had to do? It ain't just night air or throat or lung."

"We finish with it," I say.

"We ain't finish," he says. "The night ain't over. But tonight'll pay bigger than your stealing. So big you won't have to do no more stealing."

My daddy never did understand about stealing, about how it got nothing to do with money.

From between the buttons of his shirt, my daddy pulls out money wrapped in a bank band. He tosses the bundle on the dash, then puts his forehead on the dash, coughing again while he's clutching his chest.

I ain't seen money like that before, seen wads of it sure, but not a wad that big. When I reach for the money, he grabs my wrist, squeezing my hand with each cough.

I yank free, mumbling to myself, "Listen to the lions," before I ask if the money on the dash is payment for that night.

Stifling the edge of a shallow cough, Daddy wipes his mouth on his sleeve, like this, you understand? "It ours," he says. "But we ain't keeping it. We giving it to the Princess."

I ask him, "Why you want to give our wad to the whore that runs the Palace?"

"She ain't no whore!" Daddy, he's forcing them words out his lungs with what breath's left to him. I start to ask him if he's going to spend our hard-earn wad cattin' round, but he tells me to *shet up, shet up*, that the Princess is going to help us finish the job. The Main Street man didn't have enough cash money on him to pay us and the Princess both.

Then Daddy's using more precious breaths to tell me something I remember exact and clear. It's clear even to right now. I don't have to go fishing in the murk of my own mind to remember, you understand?

He says to me, my daddy says, "There ain't no connections no more, past to now, now to tomorrow. I found a old plate on the kitchen table on Emerson and I drop it in the hole you dug. I seen my mama do that at a burying long time ago. She told me it was a custom, maybe African. She couldn't remember. But she done it for connection. I dropped the plate in the hole and I heard it crack when I stomped on the dirt pile."

I understand now. You understand? Now I know what he was meaning back then by that. Things in the murk like dead fish come floating up sometimes.

But that night, all I say is, "What that got to do with us working free?"

"Goddamn, boy," Daddy says, "Don't you see? We made us a connection, past to now to forever, platefuls of connection."

"The man in the hat put the make on a lion," I say. "You feel your lips on his ass, that connection?"

Then the Lion of Landry, he's hitting me on the arm with all his strength, but I feel so little hurt you can't even call it hurt. "Goddamn, boy. Don't you realize what I had to go and do?" Then Daddy says something that I know now would come true. He says, "How I'm going to sleep now? How? How many voices going to call from how many graves? How many?"

And I know it for true now, true for my daddy, true for me. Them carrying the big burdens got the horriblest dreams.

But anyways, by that time that night I decide I had me enough. When I open the door to leave, Daddy takes hold of my arm with two hands trying to tug me on back in the truck. Then he's coughing again, his forehead on my upper arm.

I nudge him away and ask him what's left to do and what are we finally going to get from all this.

Shet up, shet up. Daddy takes off his shoes and puts them muddy-sole-down on the middle of the bench seat. He reminds me that it's almost time I'm going to have to take care of the family. Cause I be the oldest child, you understand?

10

But I heard that before, and heard it and heard it and heard it and heard it.

He says, "Stealing won't take care of nine childrens. And stealing can't pay the lease on no truck, can't help Angelle finish teacher school. And it sure can't fill our saving box." Then he's telling me about the saving box again, about turning it over to me and about me investing what we got, about learning a trade.

You can't help but be listening to a voice you hate, but like I said, I was good at pretending I ain't listening. Sparking up the night.

"Aw . . . ," Daddy says, "aw . . . drive us away from here. Down one of the five bayous. Away. I can't face the Princess without my strength. Drive us away."

How the Weasel Became a Lion

Before I introduce myself and answer questions, let me finish with my transcription of the first tape. After the words "Drive us away," there is a pause for approximately two minutes. During most of that time, all that can be heard is the sound of someone snoring; then the sound of what must be unfolding paper; then a loud snort as though someone has been startled from sleep.

What you asking me? Where at on this map I drive Daddy and me that night?

Here, see here? That's the Sugar Cane Experimental Station now. A left right here. Now-days the road's blacktopped all the way to the DuPetit Bridge. You know, the road with the banana trees and bamboo fence along the edge the golf course? And the DuPetit Bridge ain't there, neither, them days. And the long road I took that night along the Bayou DuPetit levee was all clamshell bed back then, all the way to the end.

11

Long fucking way to the end, you understand, and on both sides things growing only them that talk French can name.

Anyways, all that while I drive I be listening to my daddy breathing. He's laying quiet with his long body stretched over the seat and floorboard.

Then the Lion of Landry, he's moaning and kicking at a dream. Then a bare, cold foot of his be touching on my uncovered ankle. I go ahead and push my skin into the touch, which feels to me like the frigid air in my own favorite dream back then, my dream of the death of my daddy.

I didn't fight my dreams back then, you understand, just like I didn't answer questions. Lord, how things change. Way back then, you understand, I'd made kind of a deal with dreams. Something like I say, "Hey, dreams, y'all go ahead and prowl, prowl all y'all like into the deepest murks and flooded mines of my mind. Go ahead and steal what cache you will. I ain't struggling. In exchange, I only want to keep and remember only those dreams that are about my daddy." You understand? That ain't easy to understand. Let's just say that back then I didn't have to do no kicking at my dreams, snorting myself awake, taking my famous naps, stealing sleep when I can.

I brake the truck when I see the Dead End sign, and I leave the truck to take a leak. Standing in the glare of the headlights, I be smiling in my thoughts. Kind of like, *Here I am*, you know. Standing there in them *here I am* kind of thoughts. Like here I am under a plateful of moon in cool, before-spring air. Here I am, at twenty-two much too big for any army uniform, still carrying a name given me by my daddy. Here I am, a Weasel who dreams of his daddy's death, pissing a hole into the soft marsh while an old and scrawny giraffe with a royal name be wheezing, coughing, dreaming on the front seat of a truck.

Connections, you understand? Connections, spring piss to mud to moon.

Then Daddy's voice behind me. Then the word. "Good-for-nothing *nigger*," he says.

Before I can turn, Daddy's jabbing something hard into my spine. Falling to my knees, I'm muttering, mad, "You dying, old man."

Sitting in shell and sawgrass, shielding my eyes with my arm, I look up in the face of my daddy.

"What you just said, boy?"

I lean forward. I can see the jagged line of the branch in his hand.

"Answer me, boy. Answer me, Weasel."

Weasel? What's he saying my name for? Like I said, Daddy, he never says my name. The branch whips across my shoulder. Once, twice, I don't know. I feel a stun more by my name on his mouth than by the whipping. The third time the branch comes down, I dive at his legs. His knees pop and give. Rolling on my side, I grab on to his belt and drag the Lion of Landry closer to me through the shells.

I raise my hand on up and stare down into that face. His brown skin's shining in carlight and white dust. I look for the dull gold sheen of the tooth.

"Before you do it, boy, now I got your attention, listen to me."

I try to stop his mouth by talking back at him with as close as I can come to a shout without shouting. "No, you listen to me," I say. "Know what I dream of while you dream of being a lion? Besides your death, I dream of stealing your name, old man, just to even things out, a name for a name, old man."

Then he's telling me calm, calm as I was mad, "You can't steal everything, boy."

I remind him that I ain't never been caught, that I ain't seen the inside of jail or court, and he's repeating, repeating about my low notions, how he can see stealing to feed, how that is somehow a higher notion than mine.

He says, "That making do. I come close sometimes, maybe, to that kind of stealing. We was hungry sometimes. But we doing all right enough now. We leasing the truck, and money's still left for the saving box. Stealing won't keep that box full."

I ask him how a somebody digging graveholes for white people is going to understand about stealing. And he didn't understand. Nobody did. Let me try to explain.

Once, I saw a woman leaving her house with a photograph album under her arm. I saw her put the album on her car roof, and then while she went on back into her house to get something she forgot, I took her album, just to steal her album. Know what that means? Anything she thinks she owns, I can steal. I can even steal her past. You understand?

Where I was? Oh, yeah. I let my hand drop to the shells beside my daddy's head. "Know what I dream of, old man? I dream of you dying every night, your cold cold dying every night. I see Palo the mortician in his ice-cream suit and your cold body in a foggy ice-cream van."

Daddy says that he ain't cold yet, says it calm, and that makes me madder.

I almost shout, telling him, "That's just dreaming! I can steal now. I can steal your life if I want to."

I think I see a smile on the Lion's face—but I wouldn't know cause I ain't never seen one—and an expression like he's got me cornered, maybe just like an expression a lion's got when he's got you cornered and he's all calm with being certain.

Daddy says, "Your time coming to take, boy. And you can take it all. But first listen to me. What I'm about to say is your ticket. Bought by me for you. A ticket."

That's what he calls it, a ticket. He says he wants me to remember what he's about to say. But I'm so mad that I'm trying to forget a word as he's telling me a word.

Daddy tells me he wants me to remember two names, two.

The man to remember, he says, the man in the hat, his name is Roussell.

Already, laying on the ground, I'm trying to forget it, but the Lion's got me cornered.

"Say it, boy."

The Lion of Landry slaps me on the face. The stun again, you understand. My daddy never hit me in the face before. And it's kind of like the never-before's making me remember even when I'm trying to forget.

"You ain't listening, boy. Say it, boy. Roussell. Sound like burn-out flour, like roux. Roo. Roo. And Sell. He's a shop-keeper, a selling man. Sell. Roussell. Say it. Please."

Please? From where that comes?

"I say, say it, Weasel!"

Weasel? A stun again. A stun again like I be facing a real fucking lion, a stun like my own name is part of the lion power. I repeat the name once, twice, *Roussell, Roussell.*

"That's it, boy. Roo-sell. He wants to be important in town. Roo-sell. And in the house on Emerson. Two womens. They name is Belanger. B'lon jay. It sound like something belong to a jay, to a bird. B'lon jay. Say it."

The sting of his hand again, on my chin and cheek.

"Say it, Weasel."

I shout, shout the name, *Belanger,* lifting my hand from the shells. Shells stuck in the muscle of my palm fall to his face.

Then I ain't looking anymore at his face. I face up to the sky, straining to find the moon, anything. It's like I'm giving the lion my neck, anything not to have to see that fucking face, that fucking lion face. Bite, do anything, you understand, but don't make me look. Goddamn the power of a daddy on his boy, goddamn it be like the power of a beast with a cornered beast, name against name.

"That's it," he says, calm, calm, calm, calm.

And then I'm falling down toward the calm, falling like

down from the moon, with my neck to his mouth, Daddy, Daddy, you understand?

He says, "Those two names ought to carry you through the rest of your life. A ticket to forever. Roussell, Belanger. They connection. The hole we dug's always open to the past."

And then I'm listening with all the serene a choir must feel after going limp in a church pew, listening as Daddy tells me the connection between me, the Main Street man, and the two women name of Belanger.

Daddy says that the woman living in the house on Emerson, she's been crazy since her husband died and left her with a baby alone. Because she's crazy, she's got her a sister who's got legal charge of her and the baby. Roussell—the man in the hat—he's only been close to one of the sisters before tonight, to the one who's got legal charge.

And Roussell, he was trying to get money just for the woman he's close to and just for his own self. Daddy tells me that Roussell had us and our lease truck clean out that house tonight, that Roussell had a scheme to collect twice—once for furniture and jewels, once for insurance. Clean stealing, safe stealing. Cash money for his woman, cash left for building his business in town.

That's what Roussell thought, anyways. He had it all thought on out. He thought, too, that there wasn't going to be nobody home when Daddy and me got there to do our work. And that's where Roussell's thoughts downfall. The crazy woman and her baby, they be home when Daddy and me got there. She took her baby in the closet when she heard us. To hide from us. In that closet, she smothered her own baby hugging on it to keep it quiet.

The picture clear in my head then. I say, "You bury a baby, old man? Lord, you put dirt on a baby?"

Then I'm out of it, out his mouth, cause he says *Shet up* and *shet up*. All of the sudden, my head's clear as the sky, and

16

I take me a breath of the sky, like I'm feeding on my own clear mind. And I'm away from the Lion.

"What the whore of the Palace got to do with tonight?" I ask.

"She ain't no—"

"I say what she got to do with tonight?"

"At the Palace there's a baby about the size of the one—"

"Lordy, I can't believe this," I say. "You bury a baby and buy another baby all in one night? Lordy, just can't believe this."

Daddy says, "Believe it, boy," and then he's explaining about the ticket. He slaps my face again. But gentle this time. And I know then, I understand then, the spell of the Lion.

I feel shells cutting in the soft flesh around my belly under my belt. I sit up, breathing in my own clear mind again. "Don't never you touch me again, old man. Never."

He never would neither, never again.

Then he's telling me I ain't listening. But I am. He's telling me that I don't get what is significance. But I do. But it's like nothing is more significance than a man and his boy and a boy understanding finally, finally, how man and boy work, how Lion and boy work. And he's telling me I don't got to steal nothing again. That I can survive the family into forever without stealing. He's telling me things I know, but things that I know ain't as significance as the thing I'm starting to feel, feeling myself pulling away, up away from the Lion.

"When you need money, boy, for the saving box, go to man in the hat. Ticket in, ticket out."

I know that, know that now. But that night I be feeling all inside myself, the lion in the lion, you understand? Like a person is prey until he finally gets cornered. And then, cornered, a person really be facing himself, staring up into his own face, you understand? It ain't so hard to understand.

Calm as a lion now, I say to my daddy, "I'll decide what to do with the saving box. I'm going open me up a bar."

"That ain't a trade!"

"Know what I'll call my bar, old man? I'll call it Lion Man's. Spell it in big bent neon. L-i-n-e-m-a-n-s. What you think of that? Your name's mine if I want it. What you think of that?"

"I think it ain't no use," he says, the calm gone from him. He kicks at the shells like he kicked at his dream in the truck.

"You ain't listening, boy!"

"No, you the one ain't listening, old man."

The eyes on the Lion of Landry close. He coughs. He laughs. Does he know we be changing places? Sure he knows. But he gives it one last shot, kind of a last fight, last feast on cornered meat. "You can steal my life, boy. You can steal my name. You can steal the saving box. But you know the one thing you can't never have? Know it? My golden tooth. You can't never have my tooth. The future yours, but my tooth mine."

Looking down into his mouth, I see the gold tooth, a glimmer close to that like on the borrowed plate.

Raising my hand, I squeeze me a fist and I wait. I wait for my daddy to notice the fist against the black sky that always surrounds the moon. I say, "You listen to me, hear. Listen to me. It's simple. Nobody owns nothing. And there ain't nothing can't be stole. Everything mine. Even your tooth."

Then I'm bringing the fist down hard and I'm opening it halfway down. Then stop. I stop my open hand an inch from my daddy's mouth. The Lion of Landry shuts his eyes, but before he can shut his mouth the last of the shells from my palm drop to his tongue.

I say, "Everything mine that I want it."

The Cajun Spelling Lesson

Some questions I can answer now.

Who is my husband? Someone who wanted me to put to-

18

gether a written account, complete and whole, of the circumstances that led to a death in a south Louisiana town on Mardi Gras Day, 1963.

Who am I? By profession, I can be called historian. I was making a living by calling myself this as far back as the day my husband first met me.

Recently, I added another tool to help me with my task: a computer. It has not, as some people believe, replaced the other standard tools of my trade—the bulletin board, the desktop, reading glasses—but it has made the making of the final document somewhat easier.

I have at my fingertips commands like Cut-and-Paste, Merge, Insert, Delete, Append. When the time comes to transcribe, label, and file the scraps of information from my bulletin board and desktop, these commands help me to assemble these transcribed bits into documents, documents into larger documents, larger documents into a whole. I have a knack for assembling the experiences of others into this whole, have had it long before the computer made it into my room.

It is not difficult for me to do what my husband asked me to do—as I said, all of the scraps of circumstance are in front of me now in my husband's account, in the interviews and notes, in the photographs and maps. There is little for me to do but introduce, paste, summarize, append transition, footnote for the larger sense.

For now let me leave myself and return to my husband's interviews with the son of the Lion of Landry, to the second tape, which pertains to those years immediately following the 1944 Emerson burial and "the hole that is always open to the past."

First, some summary and transition:

The day after he threatened to steal his father's tooth, Weasel, "feeling all like a Lion," went right to work to become a man, "his own man and nobody else idea of man," by trying

19

to forget the names his father wanted him to remember. For three nights, Weasel woke sweating during dreams where his father appeared to him in a block of ice, clutching frozen blood like a blanket against his chest. The words his father spoke came from the deepest shafts of memory, *burning birds on the moon, flowers from the belly burning, stars from a woman's bayou, birds above her body, eat the birds that eat her body.*

As he lay awake, parts of him still in the dream, Weasel repeated the Emerson Street names to himself over and over— *Rouxsell Belongjay Burnjay Hersell Moonburn Bellyflower Eatburn Burnher Eather Longborn*—until within a week, even in the morning, he could not distinguish syllables from dream parts.

Within a month, Weasel had stolen the family's tin savings box and was busy stealing his father's name. He put the theft in writing, suspending a hand-lettered sign over the door of the old Ten By Ten Bar on Landry Street after he applied for and received a liquor license on his own, without the help of lawyers or Main Street men in gray hats.

The sign read Lineman's.

People started calling him Lineman instead of Weasel long before his father died nearly four years later. During those years before his father's death, Lineman went about what he would later learn was "the secret that moves the town": keeping a business open. The chairs and tables of his bar were filled every night, and on weekends, men and women sat and smoked on the two wood benches in front the bar as they waited to get in. He sold beer and wine easily enough until two o'clock in the morning, but after that—even though he stayed open past the legal limit—his customers staggered, laughed, and sang their way down the sidewalks to the Palace Bar and to the sidehouse adjoining the Palace Bar.

About a year before his father's death, Lineman built his own sidehouse—a fifty-by-fifty dance hall. When he opened his place at noon each day, the sunlight was broken into silver

20

stars by the nail holes in the exposed ceiling tin. Below his name on his sign, he wrote, "Where Your Day Is Always Night."

At first the sidehouse was never filled, even by the largest weekend crowds, but when Lineman hired a young singer named Zeema Steeple, four benches had to be built outside the bar to handle the Saturday night customers, the "excess that waited to spend while the inside spenders spent." Lineman gave credit for the new business to Zeema by paying him well. Although Zeema traveled often, sometimes leaving town for months before he returned, Lineman accrued profit enough to add a new product line, suggested by Zeema, that would cut into the Princess' past-two-o'clock clientele—a room for card games.

Also, during that last year before his father's death, Lineman went to school and acquired a trade, became what Zeema called a "mechanic"—a card cheat. Each day, before opening his place at noon, under the silver of a thousand tin-hole stars, Lineman practiced the skills Zeema had learned in army barracks across two continents: the pickup, the riffle stack, the overhand stack, the mechanic's grip, false shuffling, bottom dealing, nullifying the cut, crimping, peeking.

On Christmas Day, 1947, a week before the DA raided the place, Zeema taught Lineman the beauty, sense, and facility of dealing seconds. A second dealer, a number-two man, dealt the second card instead of the top card. Mouth open, Lineman watched as Zeema's long fingers worked in slow motion, the thumb of Zeema's left hand sliding the top card out, the right thumb taking the second card instead, the left thumb squaring the cards as the second card was dealt.

Now, my transcription of Lineman's own words:

Christmas night. After Zeema shows me about dealing seconds, I say to him, "Cards got to be marked for this to be good, right?"

Zeema says, "Something like that." He said that a lot back then. Those same words he'd use later in the title to his song that would become famous, "Something Like That."

According to Zeema, somebody dealing seconds is poison to a card game. Well, by that time I'm ready to be poison, you understand? So I tell Zeema I'm ready to open up my game table to the public that very night.

Then Zeema's warning me about what they say about proud men. Zeema, he's all full of sayings at that time, but I tell him that my schooling's over, that it's time for the final grade.

That's when I ask him to bring me somebody to take money from.

He warns me again. "There are things I haven't shown you yet."

After I tell him that two years of learning is enough for any man, even atomic-bomb makers, I say, "Bring the son of the Princess to me." I know the Princess of the Palace got her a son that Zeema was army-buddy with.

Back then Zeema rented him a room in the sidehouse next door to the Palace Bar. Back then they called that "living beside the Palace." Zeema went over with the crowds to the Palace every night after finishing at my place. I never had nothing to say about it or ask him nothing about it, you understand, even though information from the inside might've helped me with figuring out a plan to bump off my only competition.

Anyways, I say, "I want the first pot won in my cardroom to be like taking from the Princess herself."

Then Zeema's telling me again how I've still got things to learn and how I'll be learning from jail if I'm not careful. But I'm ready for that, too, you understand, cause I'm keeping some bills in my metal saving box. Just for cops if they ever come to raid on me.

"I think I know how things work," I say.

"Only something like that," Zeema says.

"Bring him to me. Bring me the son of the Princess."

The night after that, Zeema does bring me the son of the Princess, younger than me but bald, dressed in dungaree coveralls that smell new. His shirt buttoned up all the way to the collar, he's all tucked neat and wide-eyed like his mama just kissed him good-bye for first-day school. While Zeema's singing away in my dance hall, I win me eighty-seven dollars, every cent the son of the Princess has with him. The next night he comes again, on his own, neat and bald. Again, I take all.

Goes on like this till on New Year's Eve—or maybe early in the morning on New Year's Day—when three of the town's four patrolmen break through the door in the men's toilet that leads to the cardroom. I take the sergeant in charge aside and offer him three of the four one-hundred-dollar bills inside my saving box.

"You come a little late for your Christmas presents," I say. "But I been keeping them safe inside this metal box. Here, look inside. Here—"

"This ain't got nothing to do with boxes, no," the sergeant says.

I can tell immediate from the sound of the voice that this white man comes from a family that speaks French. In polite talk, the sergeant be called a "Cajun" around town, just like my family be called "colored." But in an argument, within the family and without, another word would come to the surface, in my family *nigger*, in the sergeant's *coonass*.

"What you mean, got nothing to do?" I ask.

"This here's a nigger-versus-nigger problem."

I'm certain, you understand, there's other accents around town, just as there's other white people who don't speak French. But I never spent time learning the difference. What matters in town, and still matters, is this: white people, including those tanned from the sun, is French or they ain't;

every other color—including those mixes of Indian, Negro, and white who could pass by daily laying blame to the sun—ain't white.

"The Princess," the sergeant says. "She suggested we close you down for staying open past the two o'clock limit."

"Then I'm reporting her, too," I say. "She stay open too."

"Not her bar business, *sha*. The curfew law says specific about the bar business."

"I said close down the Palace, too."

The sergeant, he's laughing now. I'm feeling spit on my palm and seeing gleams of it in his thin moustache.

"You one dumb nigger, *sha*," the sergeant says. I wonder, for a second only, what makes a five-foot-six French-talker be six-foot brave. Too much seafood, I guess. You understand?

"Answer me this, you," the sergeant says. "What your name, *sha*?"

I stand silent, moving the box from the Cajun's reach into the V of my arm. The metal lid be crimping and creaking in the join.

The sergeant, he stops laughing now. He's sweating now, moving a wet wrist to his mouth. He wipes his moustache with the crystal of his watch instead of with the back of his hand, then checks the time to cover his mistake.

"Be gettin' late, *sha*?" I say, kind of stressing the Cajun word, and then I ask, "What *your* name, *sha*?"

He tells me he ain't got to give me his name.

I tell him that his name's on his badge and I ask him can he spell it if I cover it with my hand? Just like this, I cover it. You see?

Now, my hand now, my hand's bigger than the sergeant's whole face, you understand?

"Get it off there," he says.

I close my palm on shirt and badge, saying, "How you going to get it off there?"

Then that Cajun be yelling, "I said, get it off, me, and I mean it!"

"Spell it first," I'm saying.

"Frank!" he's yelling. "In here. Bring Martin."

I've got me the badge ripped from his shirt by the time these Martin and Frank come in. By the time they've got it figured what's going on, I've got me another badge.

On the floor, I'm spelling the name on the sergeant's badge slow for the three men on me to hear, "T-h-e-r-i-o-t."

And that, that's how I finally got to see the inside of jail and court.

Sure Cop

Whenever I listen to Lineman's taped interviews, I realize how much is lost as I enter my transcriptions into computer memory. I have had to change words—verb endings and possessives, for instance—for the sake of my own sensibilities, into my own strand of English. Expressions like "Everything mine that I want it," though, are exactly as Lineman said them; a few words here and there—*sassy-frass, mollycools, Billy Rights, ray-dee-active, peer-ee-mid, rang-shackle*—are spelled phonetically to try to capture the flavor of Lineman's own strand. But how can I capture the speed and precision of Lineman's tongue when he makes "You understand?" into something like *yennerstan* with a heavily stressed first syllable? And how can I adequately describe the levels of power and resonance in Lineman's voice, a voice that is even more forceful when it is heard on recording tape in conversation with my husband, who had a voice that was especially striking in a courtroom?

Though the sound of Lineman's voice is lost to anyone reading my transcription of it, the voice of the singer Zeema

Steeple is, to this day, known to many people. The tape of Lineman's account of his first night in jail with Zeema and the son of the Princess begins with a description of Zeema singing softly at the screened and barred window of the warm cell on the second floor of the parish courthouse.

Zeema had "milky skin, white-man lips, an easy press to his black-man nose . . . big eyes, brown as the darkest African, lusters like lights off an old porcelain bowl." Zeema's voice was not at all like the voices of the other local singers Lineman had heard before, singers who were "Bible-school screamers, bouncing tones off the bone in back the nose." Zeema's song was "a smooth sink that made rounds somewhere down in flesh in his chest."

To Lineman, Zeema was "an example supreme" of what Lineman liked to call "a steal." The worth of Zeema's looks and voice exceeded any working wage Lineman could pay. Zeema was selling short whenever he agreed to take any amount of money in exchange. Thus, hiring Zeema, selling Zeema secondhand to the public was a kind of thievery that delighted Lineman.

But I have gone on long enough to feel the discomfort of my summary. Here are Lineman's words:

While I'm sitting there in the jail, Zeema's silhouette at the window be reminding me of my daddy's dark shape the night of the backyard burial on Emerson. Zeema's taller than me, but there's this same Lion Man type of frail and slim, a curve from the hips to the shoulders.

And I believe while I'm staring at Zeema, that's when I begin thinking about the night on Emerson for the first time in three-four years. About that ticket my daddy tried giving me. I start to understand what my daddy meant by that—a ticket out, a ticket in—and I'm sitting there wishing I ain't tried so hard to forget the names. I start trying to bring up the names again. Whitebird? Buyflame? But it ain't no use. I know I've got to get to my daddy as soon as I can. I've got to have the names.

Zeema walks into the shadows when the song's over, toward the other bunk, where the son of the Princess is laying, out cold after having him some kind of fit.

"What his name is?" I ask Zeema.

Zeema says I should've asked the man himself, and I say, "I know. You going to tell me I went too fast. You going to use one of your sayings like, 'The man that always take the shortest road to the dollar generally take the longest road from it.' "

Then Zeema's giving me a long talking to about how if you've got the skill and customers you can keep going forever if you don't get greedy. He's giving me an important lesson that night in jail. What I should've done with this son of the Princess is I should've won enough to make a profit, and let him win enough now and then to keep him coming back.

"Smart gamblers reinvest enough in the game for everyone to profit," Zeema says, and he says, "And for a change, on some nights, an honest game."

I sure did delight listening to the way Zeema went about thinking in the days back then. Throw in a little honesty— confuse everybody. That kind of thinking, you understand?

When Zeema lights him a cigarette, I can see him sitting in the corner, the knees of his long legs on the side of his face.

I ask him why the cops didn't take the matches from him, and he says, "Being in jail with you's like not being in jail. If they're too scared to search you, they sure ain't going to touch a friend of yours."

But scared of me or not, there I am, sitting in a jail. Without a ticket. I had to get to Daddy, had to have me that ticket.

Zeema and me, we talk about the son of the Princess for a while. Zeema says his name is Prince Albert Willis—that's for true, that name, but everybody calls him the Prince—and he fell over knocked out cold cause of a seizure. Prince Albert gets his seizures because of a head wound from the war. According to Zeema, the Prince says that a seizure is something like being in an iceblock.

When I ask Zeema about why the Princess shut me down, he says her son, the Prince, stole money from her to get into my game. According to Zeema, the Princess is connected to Main Street in some kind of way I ain't. I try explaining to Zeema then about how I could have connections, too—those names from my daddy, you understand.

But Zeema starts laughing to all that. "You? Connected?" he says. "Sure. And you also sell flowers to sailors."

Then we're talking about how a woman's parts resemble kind of like a flower—you know how talking goes, jumping from money to flower parts with barely but easy sense. And that's how I come to ask Zeema if that's why he goes to the Palace all the time, for a particular kind of flower. I tell him I heard he had him a girl that lives there and that I heard he favors Easter lilies just like his daddy did.

Zeema gets quiet. He's mad in his corner, I'm sure, but I can't see. Zeema's not the kind of a man to show mad, but when his temper goes, it blasts from all that storing up.

That night in the jail I might've wanted to see Zeema's temper blast just to get things happening in the dark, spark up the night, you understand? Or maybe I wanted to hear Zeema thinking out loud. Or maybe I wanted to know more of what worked the Palace and beside the Palace. I don't know. I know I kept on with pressing him.

Shit, everybody knew about Zeema's daddy, Ragtap Steeple, and his white woman he loved. Some still know. Some still say it was Ragtap that really wrote that famous Cajun song about a pretty blonde.

But anyways, a spark comes out of Zeema. "I could kill

28

you in the dark, Lineman. I could still have a knife on me just as well as matches."

I'm feeling so much delight at what he said that I want to laugh, but I keep on pressing. "Would you stick me?" I ask him.

He answers me, "My daddy would've. For what you just said."

I tell Zeema I believe he wouldn't stick me, knife or no knife. I tell him I'd bet on it. I tell him that I'd bet, too, that he would never cheat me, cause he's what I call an up-to-a-point man. He might cheat, but only up to a point.

Zeema asks me what that point is, and I tell him. I say, "Soon as a man trust you, you can't do him in."

"Which means," Zeema says, "you must trust me, because you don't believe I'll do you in."

I start laughing. Man, how I use to enjoy listening to Zeema think out loud. Sometime his thinking gets clear as his voice.

"And it don't take people long to start trusting you," I say.

"Which means," he says—and I'm really laughing now, even before he's finished—"which means, if I want to make a profit, I've got to make it fast."

Then I ask Zeema to tell me what the Palace has that my place doesn't have. "The sidehouse got whores in it, don't it, Zeema? It's a whorehouse, ain't it?"

"There might be some of that going on. Everything goes on at the Palace. But it's more a boardinghouse."

"What that is?"

"That's what they'd call it up North. My daddy . . . I used to stay at the Palace on trips between my daddy's gigs when I was a boy. The Palace was a place we could count on because . . ."

"Because of your daddy's blonde?"

"Things like that don't matter at the Palace."

Now—I think to myself—there must've not been too many doors open to a colored man singing Cajun songs dragging behind him a blonde and a boy.

"You telling me the Princess is a landlord? That people leave my place to go to the Palace to pay their rent?"

"Something like that," Zeema says, but kind of in a whisper like he careful not to wake nobody.

"You give me the right information, Zeema. You can help me close her down. I'll share with you. I'll build you a room next to mine at my place. You can move into a real Landry place."

"A boardinghouse is all. People from everywhere, Main, Landry, and all the perpendiculars. They come around, huddle together trying not to fight. I met Prince Albert during basic in Texas, and we came here on furlough. The Palace felt just as good as it did when I was a boy, everybody huddling close."

"You telling me there ain't some close, real close, smelly huddling going on?"

Zeema changes the subject by shuffling a deck of cards. "Come here," he says. "A game in the moonlight coming through the bars."

"That sound like a good song for you to write," I tell him as I move closer.

"Already been a song," he says. "But not by me."

We played poker in the moonlight for over an hour, I guess, talked and played. I found out some more things about Zeema—that he ain't never been in jail before either, though he's been everywhere, even to a place he calls Duke Elegant's Harlem, that he made friends with Prince Albert Willis in Texas because they both liked music and making songs.

And while I be learning more about Zeema, I be winning, every damn game, all the quarters and nickels me and Zeema dug up from the bottom of our pockets and the pockets of Prince Albert Willis, who still be out cold.

Once, as Zeema's shuffling for his deal, his hands stop and there's this long quiet. Then Zeema says my name, *Lineman*. And there's another quiet, not as long. Then my name again. "Lineman," he says, "My woman beside the Palace. She's the darkest pretty you ever want to see. I've been thinking of marrying her. She wants me to leave this town for good, go on over with her and our baby to Canton."

"You've got you a baby, Zeema? Shit. What color flower she is?"

Zeema smiles this daddy-pitiful smile. "The color of her mama, darkest pretty."

"That's enough. That's enough. And I'll take all y'all. All y'all can move in with me. Why leave?"

"Something's up around here. We've both got a feeling."

"Well, I tell you, Zeema. The Palace and what's beside the Palace be things of the past if I got my way. That's just business, between you and me."

"I believe that. I smell the asshole of a change. Landry and Main are both aiming down at the Palace."

"You know some people call it the Gumbo Palace. They say you can smell the bay and sassy-frass she got growing wild behind her fence. But now I know better what's in that name—that mixture of spice and flowers of all colors all together. Maybe there's a way I could steal that name from her."

"That's what we named our daughter," Zeema said.

"Shit, stop it, Zeema. You telling me you named a baby Sassy-frass Steeple or a Gumbo Steeple?"

We start laughing to that, and then Zeema starts to tell me her name, but I stop him from getting more pitiful.

"Well, who'd of ever," I said. "That's what Zeema Steeple wants? To get married?"

"To have the courage to. And to have the courage to leave the Palace when daylight comes."

I wait for the sounds of the deck again before I talk. "Know what I want, Zeema?" I say. "Everything. I'll even take the end of the world."

Then Zeema's laughing that laugh of his that makes you trust him more. Then we both laughing again and from the shadows the Prince himself is laughing.

"Know what I want, gentlemens?" the Prince says. "Don't want to die in no iceblock."

"Fool," I say to myself. "Neat, bald fool."

"He's got a Purple Heart and a medal for bravery," Zeema says. "Bronze or silver."

"I don't care if his pecker green," I say. "Deal."

After the laughing and the night kind of subside, I ask Zeema why, in the poker game going on, he's always got coins no matter how many times I win.

"Feel my palm," he says.

It's sticky.

"That stuff's called 'sure-cop,'" he says. "You put it on your hand to lift chips from the table."

I had to laugh again, low inside me and hard. "I was sure," I say. "Sure you wouldn't cheat me."

"Only something like that," Zeema says, whispering again.

Ten Cents' Worth of Technicolor

My husband and his family have a reputation as storytellers. They are comfortable with such words as *character* and *narrative*. As the reader eventually will learn, I was hired many years ago by my husband's family because of my abilities as a historian. The historian in me does not like to tamper with evidence—such as the Lineman tapes—for the sake of what my husband's family calls "story flow." But I find now that in my reluctance to edit the Lineman tapes I may have given the reader an incorrect impression. To correct this impression, I am going to have to use the words of the storyteller. It may seem at this point that the main character in this narrative is a man named Lineman. Lineman, however, will soon step away and someone else—my husband—will step up.

I say all this now because the next Lineman tape brings out my husband's first connection with Lineman, and with Zeema Steeple and Prince Albert Willis, in the courtroom the day after Lineman's second night in jail. In this tape, Lineman describes the courtroom and my husband—my husband at the time of that first encounter.

As I said, I do not like to tamper with the evidence for the sake of moving the story. But here, in my transcription of the next taped interview with Lineman and in the other interviews that follow, I have had to make important changes in Lineman's words. Lineman favors the present tense when he describes the past, as in the previous interviews. I have changed his verbs to the past tense because, on paper and screen, time gets difficult to follow if I do not make this change.

All my life till then, I had me this idea that being in a courtroom would feel like Sundays in church between the arms of my two fattest sisters, you understand, songs of dread and joy, waves and waves of wailing, sweating, and perfume filling every way out there was to run. Instead, I found my first courtroom to be more like the Grand Theater on Main Street.

The coloreds—me and Zeema and Prince Albert Willis and five other some-odd prisoners—we were sitting in these fold-down plywood seats of a vacant jury box staring ahead at ten cents' worth of Technicolor. Just like the balcony of the Grand Theater, you understand? At the Grand, I used to pretend to nap while flicking popcorn kernels into the White Only section below. Sparking up the dark. That morning it didn't take me long to figure things out, and this was what I figure: my first court time was going to be passed like Grand Theater time—watching, smelling, stirring up my own excitement.

My seat creaked as I laid me down and back. I sniffed. Murphy's Soap, lemon oil. I let my eyelids fall. My lashes, they subduing the light, you understand, so everything I saw was in a kind of shade, like looking through the black kerchief I stole one time from the Old Reverend's first wife.

I moved my eyes left, but not my head. In that shade my eyes made, I could see a wall picture above the entry doors: green blades of sugar cane; a purple-and-silver cane-knife blade; rolled sleeves of field hands, arms in all different tones of brown, even the white workers; an eagle, mad and mean as usual, in gold, with its talon in a horn of plenty swollen with parish products. Alone in the spectator's section, below the windows letting in blue daylight, I caught sight of my brother Emmon waving at me.

"Lord," I said to Zeema, "they send Emmon. Fourteen children ranging in smart from none to some, and they send the one don't register on the meter."

It was Emmon, you understand, took over Daddy's lease truck after I left home with the saving box. Took Emmon maybe a day, day and a half to lose that truck. Lose it, you understand. Couldn't remember where he left it. By the time he found it in Kaplan, the lease be gone.

Anyway, to my right, I heard a high voice saying, "There will be not a word from the prisoners."

I moved my eyes right and saw the pink, bald head of what got to be the judge showing over a wood plateau. "That the law?" I whispered to Zeema. "My first look at the law, and the law fat and got to sit on his feet on his chair to gaze over the table."

Then the judge was asking, "Who represents this man?"

That was the first time I ever heard your voice. You remember? You answered the judge, "I do, your honor."

34

I moved my eyes to where your voice was coming from. I saw you about three rows and one railing in front of Emmon. You were standing tall and neat in a dark suit. That was before you got all rumpled. Time rumple us all, I guess, some more than others, you understand? Shit yes. Even smiling, like now, you understand.

Anyway, back then you were something to see, in shade or sunlight. The silk sheen on your wine-color tie was more involved in the goings-on than the entire body of the district attorney, who was sitting at a next-door table trying to decide which of two penknife blades to use to slice into his morning mail. And behind you and the DA, there was my brother Emmon, pointing to you and grinning and mouthing the words, "He yours, he yours."

In a Technicolor world, if I had to steal a lawyer and fence him quick on looks and sound alone, I no doubt would choose the you I saw standing there with the high forehead and red-brown hair. That morning, even twenty feet away, staring at you through the darkest gauze-black of my lashes, I was seeing the greenest eyes I ever saw on a white man. Most men would've been confident having you on their side, like Emmon, like he was, waving proud and pointing. But even considering all of that and considering your voice sounding to me that morning like a dinner bell calling people in to feast on equal portions of justice and freedom, I shot up, out my seat to the rail in front of me: "Nobody talk for me."

That's what was coming out my mouth. And that's the trouble with court, you understand. People letting other people talk for them.

Well, that stirred things up all right, my words, *Nobody talk for me*. The judge started with knocking his hammer, you with apologizing for me, "If it please the court . . ." Then the judge be saying back, "Nothing would please the court more, Mr. Mar-kee, than to give this man a feel for the power of this court. But he is not one of the indigents you bargained for."

I'd never heard that word before that morning. *Indigents.* Funny-sounding, you understand. But what was funnier, I looked down at the seats next to me filled with the quiet, scared colored souls somebody was bargaining for. Well, I just had to laugh, but I kept it deep in my throat, a sound probably only Zeema on my left and Prince Albert on my right could hear. Just like at the Grand, sparking up the dark is sometimes as much exciting as stealing.

Then I was listening. First thing you were doing was trying to correct the way the judge said your name. "That's Mar-kwiss, your honor," you said.

But the judge knew something I knew from the night on the shell road with my daddy. A name be a man, a man be a name. Power, you understand? Judge said, "Proceed, Mr. Mar-kee," just like he said it before.

And I was listening close now. You told the judge that you were recently approached by the family of *this particular defen-dant*—that was me. And you told him you ain't had an op-portunity to *consult with any of the accused*—that was all of us on the bargaining block.

Let me see if I can imitate that high-voice, pink-head judge. He said, "And as you can see, Mr. Mar-kee, as we discussed, they are all Negro, mostly indigent, and you are here to save the court time, not to try our patience."

And you, your voice, not deep as mine, but close to Zee-ma's, you said back something like, "But still, as you know, your honor, not through any fault of the court or of myself, I have not consulted. I beg the court for a special amount of patience today, for me, and for this man, Mr. . . ."

And you looked at me, waiting. And court stopped. Zeema, he was tugging at my back pocket, saying, "I think he wants your name."

I turned to Zeema, said loud enough for you and all the

courts there ever was to hear, "My name something nobody can have." And I was still standing, remember?

The judge might've figured an order wouldn't hush me, so he tried a question. "Will you have a seat?"

Answering questions is like giving your name, you understand? I stood up taller to his question.

That was some tight time. Felt long. The cop Theriot was sweating in his moustache, figuring there was going to be a pileup.

Then, there you were, unblocking things. "May I approach the prisoner, your honor?"

"Please do, Mr. Mar-kee," the judge answered, "and do tell him what I can do."

After you walked up to me, you handed me a card, the letters all centered and raised to the touch. I got it in my memory that card. On the card, a name: James Peter Marquis. And at the bottom, other names—Sanderling, Sanderling, Marquis, and Sanderling—above a New Orleans address on Baronne Street. You gave a card to each of the other prisoners, too. Yes sir, that card be important later, and even later than that.

Zeema whispered the names on the card, then whispered to me, "Where your night and day are ours." And Prince Albert whispered, "Where we look on niggers with one eye, but on our pocketbook with two."

And you, you smiling along.

I asked you if you were the Marquis in all that sand. You liked that. You smiling, smiling, saying that the Marquis on the card was not you but your brother, but you were expecting to be on the card soon. You were saying, too, there was an address on the back the card you wrote if we needed to find you in town. Then you were saying how that address on back probably wouldn't be helping us too much seeing how you would be leaving town any day now. Yes sir, I got that in my memory, too, what you wrote on back the card. But ain't it something to know now how I didn't look the backside over? Wouldn't the backside've helped me save a few calories and walking time?

Anyways, there you was handing out cards. What the judge said to that? Yes, yes. *Solicitation.* He said, "No solicitation, Mr. Mar-kee."

"Let's be quick here," you said to me. "I've read the charges against you. You're not like the others here. You'll have to pay. But you need me more than they do. I'm your best chance. How about it?"

Zeema told you I don't answer questions, and Zeema told me: "Get him to work free for you, too, Lineman. A grand-opening kind of deal."

And you, smiling again. And I was studying your smile. What I saw? No meanness anywhere in the smile. Yes, that's it. That's what it was about your smile at that time back then. Was that what I thought would also be easy fencing? No, something behind the smile, a steal: a kind of confidence that did not know or need meanness.

Then the judge stopped the studying and the conversation. "That will be quite enough," he said. "Have a seat, Mr. Mar-keeee. Next word from a prisoner's mouth and every other word out of his mouth will cost him one hundred dollars or a day."

Why that judge had to say that? That started me wondering if my four or so one-hundred-dollar bills were still in my metal box. What four words would I choose?

"How about it?" you said to me. "A nod won't cost you."

And I said to you and to everybody in every court in all time everywhere, "Don't never treat me like a poor nigger."

"Five hundred dollars," the judge said.

Again you, smiling. "The judge miscounted," you said low to me. "You haven't known me ten minutes and you've saved yourself three hundred dollars. How about it?"

I sat, but only after waiting a few seconds for your question to vanish.

Though I took a nap through most of the rest of the court, I heard you pleading all of us not guilty. I also heard that the charge against Zeema and his friend Prince Albert was being dropped. And I knew where they were being dropped—they were coming plummeting down as added charges on top my head. Too, the judge ordered that my place be closed until after the trial, that the Alcoholic Beverage Commission be— what that word? *apprised,* yes—of the charges against me, that my parish and town business permits be suspended, that my bail be set at ten thousand dollars.

Rubbing my eyes, I mumbled to myself, "Say you welcome, Jay Pee Mar-keee."

But you were giving it back to the judge in Technicolor, stressing my presumed innocence under the law, asking that the court show mercy and not deny me my livelihood, and requesting my trial be put on soon as possible on the docket in the spirit of Billy Rights of the United States of America.

Oh, Mar-kee, Mar-kee, Jay Pee, what a show you put up that morning.

And I hope you don't mind me wasting space on your tape there by talking about something we both know. It's just got to be said out loud. Quite a show you were. And no meanness anywhere about you.

Look like your colors, they finally coming back, Jay Pee? How long it took your colors to come on back?

Anyway, the judge, remember, he told you he was a little bit familiar with Billy Rights, having heard of it he thought on his aunt's back porch. He set a trial date for six months later.

After that, before the town cop Theriot made it to the jury box, you and my brother Emmon came up to the box and spoke to me. You told me all I got to do is post bail and then I was free to go until the trial.

I asked where at y'all think I was going to get ten thousand dollars.

Then Emmon used the words. "Bail bondman," he said.

In my twenty-six years up to that time, I swear I never heard that name before. But as you started explaining the hows of the process, even I started smiling. Yes sir, I understood a word: bail bonding be stealing at its best.

Then you were telling Zeema and Prince Albert that they were free to go, and that the district attorney would probably be asking for their testimony against me, and I recall, I think, some questions about if I took a house cut off the proceeds of the card games. But all that wasn't changing anything in my life. I still had plans to take control of my life by having me a talk with my daddy. I'd be getting to my daddy and I'd be getting me a name or two and I'd be getting back my ticket to forever.

And I think I even told you I wouldn't be needing your service, didn't I? That somewhere in Louisiana there was going to be a man that didn't need the help of lawyers. And I might've said: *Imagine that, life without the need of lawyers.* You recall? Was that where we have that other talk? That little talk about how white men think that lawyers really are the best chance anyone can get. Even the white folks with sincerity in their heart believe it with the same kind of heart. Y'all say something like, *When you ready to climb out that ditch with your shovel, well, just give me a call. It's the onliest way, the best and lasting way.*

Wasn't that the time I was shouting while you were trying to calm me down, shouting about who was in the ditch and who wasn't and how you better not be trying to climb on down in the ditch with me cause all that was was the surest way to make me feel like a poor nigger . . . no?

Doesn't matter, does it? Because about that time was when Emmon said, "Daddy dead."

Sin Bravely

My husband, James Peter Marquis, gathered his details with care and sent all of his work to me. But there were a few holes in my husband's research that I had to fill in myself. In the Lineman tapes, there is such a hole.

Notice that everywhere in the taped interviews I have used thus far, although he senses the facts my husband is after, Lineman relishes relating details, embellishes his version of the story with what seems to be great pleasure. When my husband interviewed Lineman, more than twenty-five years after they met—and more than a decade after Mardi Gras, 1963—he recorded a Lineman eager to voice aloud these details: the sheen of a tooth, the black of the sky that surrounds the moon, the smell of a courtroom.

And that is why the hole is obvious. After talking about his first encounter with my husband and with court, Lineman goes on to summarize in ten or so sentences what happened in his dead father's room. He gives my husband the facts needed to move the story, but gives him no more.

For reasons that will become clear to the reader later, I got a chance to interview Lineman for myself in 1975. For now, let me say that when I eventually did get to town, I had this hole in the Lineman tapes in my mind. Lineman laughed at my notepad, the same yellow longleaf he said my husband had used for his notes as the tape had whirled in the recorder. Lineman said he preferred the tape recorder to the longleaf because the changing of the tape gave him more time to take one or two of his "legendary cat's naps." Lineman demonstrated how my husband sat in a chair listening, how my husband crossed his legs using his lap as a kind of desktop for the pad. And he told me to sit forward in my chair as my husband did, to use my own lap as my husband did. When I complied, he slapped his big hands together and laughed more. "That's it, that's it," he said. "It go on and on and on like we living over and over and over."

Taking my husband's place in this way, I asked Lineman about the morning he'd stood in his dead father's room. Lineman did not hesitate to answer my questions and gave me those details he had been unwilling to relate before.

What I am about to give now is an account of that late morning, after court, in a Landry Street bedroom. I have had to use my own words, paraphrasing from my own notes on my yellow pads. But even without my notes, it would be difficult to forget that picture Lineman gave me: a son, a father, a room where the living, quite awake, meet with the dreaming dead.

After making arrangements for a bail bond in town, Lineman, Zeema, Prince Albert Willis, and Lineman's brother Emmon walked to Landry Street. Somewhere along the way, Emmon told his brother about the death of the Lion of Landry. According to Emmon, his father had been one hour away from getting his final wish—to take his last breath in sunlight—when he died.

In the bedroom of the house on Landry Street, Lineman saw the body of his father lying naked on the bed, a handkerchief covering the loins, a handkerchief over the face. Lineman stepped from a parlor hot from three space heaters and a family that did not trust him into the icy room of his dreams.

Zeema spoke first, pulling his wool jacket tight around him and cursing the cold, and it was Zeema who shut the door behind him and behind Lineman and Emmon in front of him.

"What that smell and why the curtains on the floor?" Lineman asked Emmon.

"Camphor smell. Daddy put a salve under his nose help him breathe. The curtain he tore down hisself, to get and keep the full sun on the bed. Told us to take the top sheets away, too."

From the parlor, Lineman could hear one of his sisters screaming, "Thief!" It was Angelle, the oldest sister, who had been one year away from a teaching certificate when Lineman stole the savings box.

"Pay 'em no mind," Emmon said. "You brung the box back. That what matter. We can have Daddy buried. Palo the mortician on his way to talk to you."

Still on Lineman's mind were the two names—the connection—he had forgotten. "The Lion leave a message for me with anybody before he die? A word, just a word or two. A name?"

Emmon answered, "Not that I know, Weasel. I mean, not that I know, Lineman."

"Shit, Emmon. Who in here with him when he die?"

"The New Reverend . . . Reverend Bowman from Philadelphia. He been with Daddy a while. He the one turned off the heat. When he did, I told him he'd have to face you. He say that what he want *is* to face you. He coming here pretty soon, too."

Lineman ordered Emmon out of the room, told Zeema to stay. "Keep everybody else ass out, Emmon, specially women, specially Angelle."

Lineman walked slowly to the bedside with the tin savings box under his arm. He pushed a metal corner of the box into his biceps until he felt a pinch, then pain, and pushing harder still, at the pain, he reached for the handkerchief over his father's face. When Zeema shut the door again, Lineman retracted the hand as though the sound of the door had startled him from the movement toward his father's face.

The tin box fell to the floor.

Zeema bent down to get the box.

"Let it stay, Zeema. It empty. Know what emptied it?"

"The law I guess."

"Know what that word mean? More words. Words emptied that box."

"Something like that. White man use words when he should use his prick and his prick when he should use words. Know what, Lineman? I've never been in a room colder than this room."

Lineman wanted to laugh but could not.

"You aren't going to get what you came here for, are you, Lineman?"

"If it's true the Lion of Landry left without a word on his lips for me—without a name for me—then this here is like what they call the end of the line. Dead Daddy, empty box. What my family going to say when I tell them I don't have money to bury they daddy? Going to say, 'Hey, you, Bigshot. Bigchief. Bigthief. Your daddy told you you was a good-for-nothing.'"

"I didn't think you'd care what anybody had to say."

"It just that it look like somebody else was right about me. Like a question been answered whether I want it answered or not." Lineman felt hollow and weak, just as he did after eating a box of sweet rolls during a hangover. He held out his shaking hand for Zeema to see.

"Get out of yourself, Lineman. Maybe the dead can see. What if your daddy's looking up now to his first son's quiver?"

"Fuck him. Fuck his death even if it's cold as I want it. What he had to go die like this for anyway? Look at the lions."

Zeema spoke of the work of another thief, of death, of a stealing greater than Lineman could ever dream, *something like that*.

"Not so big a deal," Lineman said. "Me, too, I can steal your life anytime. I can cheat death by changing my mind and not stealing your life. That ain't what's terrible in here. What's

44

so terrible is the Lion of Landry lay down in the sun and said, 'Take. Go ahead, take.' Fuck him for the way he die."

After taking the tin box from the floor, Zeema walked to the window.

Lineman continued with his stare down at his father. He could tell by looking at the body what his father's last moment had been—a second or two of bone, skin, and weakness. The Lion of Landry must have tried with all his remaining strength to lift himself. Every bone—ribs, kneecaps, wrists— stretched the skin, but the skin held them down. That was how weak the Lion had been at his last live moment—like dead meat in an icebox, the plastic foodwrap of his skin had been enough to hold him down.

Looking to the small crater of cloth beneath the sharp outline of his father's nose, Lineman searched with his gaze for a glint of gold within the weave.

The door opened again. Again Lineman used the sound, this time catching hold to keep himself from falling closer to his father.

Emmon was at the door telling Lineman that the New Reverend was in the house. Palo the mortician had also arrived.

Turning, Lineman recognized Palo the mortician, who was also Palo the ice-cream man in the summer, by the white clothes—white shirt and pants, white shoes, white paper cap, and the white cape that also served as a bib when he stole desserts from himself. How many times had Lineman dreamed of his father's body lying stiff in the foggy compartments of Palo's van? But why was Palo wearing his summer suit? And why was this New Reverend standing in front of Palo? Lineman remembered that his father had sided with the Old Reverend in the reverend wars.

Never in his dreams had Lineman seen the sweet vision of the man taking small steps toward him now. Chuckling, Lineman called to Zeema, who was facing the leafless chinaball

45

tree outside the window. "Look, Zeema. The New Reverend. A splash of flavor in front the ice-cream man. Look. Cinnamon skin. Butterscotch suit. Is this what won the reverend wars?" Zeema did not turn.

Constantly circling the brim of his big hat in his hand, the Reverend Bowman continued his approach toward Lineman. Stopping within arm's reach of Lineman's chest, Bowman said, "Your father knew you would have a high time at his parting. What kind of brazen make a man stand so? Don't answer that."

Bowman's voice was high, the same grating tenor as that of the other minister on Landry. Where did God send the baritones?

Lineman summoned his own voice out of himself and spoke over the burnished, cinnamon-colored skin of Bowman's bald head, "Don't tell me what to answer!"

Palo stepped back. Zeema turned, arms folded and trembling in the cold.

Bowman's expression did not change, nor did he stop working the brim of his hat in a circle with his hands.

"You don't have to answer if the answer is known," Bowman said.

" 'Scuse me," Palo said, turning to the door.

"Don't move another drip, Palo," Lineman said. "I got business with you. And what you wearing your ice-cream uniform for?"

"It was your father's wish," the Reverend Bowman said. "Your father said he got the idea from listening to you."

"What you know about me and my daddy?"

"Only what he told me and what he told me to tell you."

Again Lineman exhaled in the cold air, again looking to Zeema. The Lion of Landry must have given the names to someone after all. Slapping his hands together, Lineman turned completely around once, nearly stumbling over onto

46

the bed in trying to stop his own weight. "Well, go on. Give it to me. What he told you to tell me?"

"That his way of dying was his own last gift to you. That all of what he was was left in you, as the son the father. And that you should carry the family on, as the family shares the body of one, as the family of Christ shares—"

"A name. Did he give you a goddamned name?"

"'Scuse me," Palo the ice-cream man said. "It too cold in here for me."

"Stand your piece of ground, ice-cream man," Lineman said.

"He give you nothing but what you see," Bowman said. "He couldn't talk at all at the end anyways. His throat was et up to a hole. Lift the cloth and look at what a man can suffer on this earth, look."

Lineman felt the cold room on his fingers and fumbled for his pockets.

"Lets hope that you come up with the same courage in pain when your number is called," Bowman said. "This man need Christian burying, and he told me you would have the family resources."

"We do business with the other church."

"Your father instructed me to instruct you to do your church business with me."

"I'd let Palo serve me to hungry children from his ice-cream van first."

"Then I'll leave you to yourself."

Standing at the window, Zeema came up with a compromise, a deal he thought both men could live with. The Reverend Bowman could help Lineman with the burial. In return, Lineman would keep his family in Bowman's church.

"The soul of this man on the bed already made the switch," Bowman said, the hat still circling.

"But his son's in charge now," Zeema said.

47

" 'Nother words, you want me to foot the burial?"

"Something like that."

"Guess I could see my way clear," Bowman said.

Zeema winked. "How about it, Lineman?"

"What I care about burying this heap of flesh? I don't deal. It's like answering a question. And I ain't setting foot in your rang-shackle chapel."

"You will be attending soon enough," Bowman said. "You will be regretting the delight you took from those dreams of your father. You will seek release one day. You will seek me out. Until then, sin bravely, my son."

"What the hell kind of preaching that means?"

"It means, son, that the greater you sin, the more it lights up the power of God's mercy. Sin play its part, son. Even sin."

"Don't never you call me son. I ain't nobody son. And how you know about my dreams?"

"Your daddy told me about your dreams of him. He was a man concerned with dreams. There was a dream he was having that pained him more than his throat. Dreams of babies screaming, babies—"

"You don't know nothin'."

"I helped your father find his way to peace. I will help you one day."

"Y'all do what the hell y'all want with this rotting flesh on the bed. And stay the hell away from me, Bowman. You and your circle of a hat go back to Philadelphia."

"What I should do?" Palo asked Bowman.

"Prepare the body for transporting," Bowman said. "The answers will come soon enough."

Lineman grabbed Palo's white cape and pulled. Palo gasped. "Let me tell you something," Lineman said. "I know all about how you steal from the bodies you prepare. I figure you figure anything that's on a body is what the Cajuns call 'lagniappe' for you. Things like gold teeth. If you got your eye on my daddy's gold tooth, Palo—"

Palo smiled, showing Lineman his sugar-rotted teeth.

"What's so funny?" Lineman asked.

"Tell him, Reverend."

Bowman put his large-brim hat on his head and reached into the inside pocket of his suit. Then he extended his arm, touching Lineman's chest with a matchbox he held between two fingers. "In here," he said. "Your father's last gift to you. You know what a gift is, don't you, son? Something that the receiver can never steal."

"I ain't nobody son, I said." Taking the box, Lineman rushed at the door. "Let's go, Zeema."

"Sin bravely."

"What's in the box?" Zeema asked.

"I said, let's go. I'm hungry."

The Great Perpendicular

In the notes I took on my yellow sheets when I interviewed Lineman in 1975, I reminded myself that Lineman pronounced the words *low floor* so that they sounded like "low flow." After leaving his dead father's Landry Street bedroom, Lineman said he prowled the "low flow," that "flat hard flow through the low valley" of his life, a plane in the valley he knew to be the lowest even as he moved through it, a plane he still considered to be the lowest even as he looked back on his life during my interview.

Later that same day he left his father's room, Lineman would rise above that valley, would stalk again, would make the connection he sought. But first he consumed.

Stepping outside into January with Zeema and Prince Albert Willis, Lineman headed for Palo's ice-cream van parked

49

on the Landry Street curb. Opening compartments, he pulled out fudge bars and banana bars and strawberry bars. Eating was all that mattered. Eating was like "stealing the outside world and hiding it inside."

For Lineman, everything he was "or could've been" had changed, had been wiped away by his father's death and by the words of a "cinnamon reverend with a always-circling hat." The two names Lineman needed for connection had died with his father. The metal savings box was empty— Zeema carried it out with him—and it looked as though it was going to remain empty. The deal Lineman had made with his dreams appeared lost also. What was going to become of Lineman now that the dream of his dead father had become real? Would his other dreams take over? Was he going to end up like the Lion of Landry, "all racked by his own dreams of dead babies, troubled enough by them to be nothing left but film of skin over bones?"

According to Lineman, all of this was low enough, but there was something lower. The "three great notions" Lineman had attached to himself were stolen away by the Reverend Bowman. Lineman had believed he could steal anything—someone's life, someone's past. But a gift, Bowman said, was something the receiver could never steal. And sin, what became of that notion after Bowman said, "Sin bravely"? The bigger the sin, the bigger God becomes. What pleasure was left after the notion of sin died? And answering questions, that notion. Lineman had never answered anybody's questions. But what was the use in that now? Bowman said, "You don't have to answer a question if the answer is known." What was left?

And so, Lineman ate, "and ate and ate and ate." He stuffed all of Palo's sweets into his mouth "till the whites and brown and red and yellows leaked to cascade" down his face. What was left?

There is another hole in the Lineman tapes, a hole even I neglected to fill when I questioned Lineman in 1975. After Lineman's short summary of what happened in his father's bedroom, the tape ends. Usually a tape ends with the sound of the "legendary Lineman snore" that comes while Lineman naps during pauses in any conversation. On this tape, however, there is only silence and the hiss of the tape following Lineman's last words, as though he is not finished talking. When I listen to Lineman on the next tape, he is describing the house on Emerson Street, the windows and grounds of the house where I chose to begin this story.

But what was it that got Lineman to prowl again across that flat and featureless valley from Landry Street to Emerson Street? What did Lineman tell my husband as my husband replaced one tape with another? I can only guess.

Did one of the other two men standing by the van say something? Zeema, perhaps? Something close to what Zeema had said before to Lineman—"Get out of yourself?"

Or had something happened strong enough to stun Lineman back to plane? Prince Albert Willis, perhaps—one of Prince Albert's seizures? Prince Albert's greatest fear was dying in the iceblock of one of his seizures. What could have been colder for him than the first aura of a seizure while eating ice cream on a January morning outside the coldest room on Landry Street? Did Prince Albert moan rather than excuse himself, as he usually did, "to find a safe place to fall?" I don't know. I know that Prince Albert, who was with them stealing sweets from Palo's van, is no longer with them when Lineman and Zeema stand on Emerson Street, under "trees that smell like Christmas," gazing at the orange grove and a new hole in the orange grove.

I do know that Lineman did move again from Palo's van and his father's house with Zeema following. And though Lineman might not have described for my husband during the tape change the walk through the low valley across the flat hard floor of the town as it was in 1948, I know the direction: south. I know because I have my husband's maps—the town in the late 1940s, the town in the early 1960s. I know the features because I have my husband's collection of photographs: the cypress fence around the sidehouse of the Palace Bar on one of the side streets perpendicular to Landry Street; the unscreened porches on that street and on Landry Street; the steps ascending to the porches; the black people on the steps and porches, sitting, moving from street side to street side even on the coldest days; the cathedral steeple, its point sword-sharp in the southeast sky above the tin roofs.

I know, too, because I have also walked the streets of that town. I have walked south from Landry down the streets perpendicular to Landry through the back of town, where people have no time to plan, and leaving the back of town have crossed Highway 90 into the trees and the carefully planned houses on Emerson Street and other streets like Emerson.

I know the changes builders make. I know the forty-five-miles-per-hour speed limit posted on the street where the Palace Bar used to stand, the street my husband and Zeema called "The Great Perpendicular," but which the townspeople call "The Boulevard"—that express through the evergreens and oaks and orange trees on one side of Highway 90 and through the back of town on the other; that four-lane express that comes upon Landry and then continues on, past the soiled ribbon of Landry, on toward the shopping mall two miles north of town.

And I know what has not changed.

Black, Green, What?

Me and Zeema, we ended up looking at the Emerson house. Zeema standing there beside me under trees that smell like

Christmas, questioning me out loud about what we doing there. "Why here?" he asking me. Then his questions getting closer to why my prowling brought me there. "Is there something here, Lineman, that has to do with the names you're trying to remember?"

I didn't answer. I looked. The house in daylight was bright with white wood siding. In the light you could see the trim you couldn't see at night—green shutters, green door, green window frames downstairs and up. From where I stood, too, I could see where my daddy and me parked that night in the driveway, and I could see the edge of what my daddy called the patio, and yes, I could see the orange trees, bigger, taller, all in line. I tried to figure out what tree and what tree had the path between them that I took to dig the hole inside the trees.

Then I saw, through the trees, a small brick house that wasn't there the night I dug. "What that?" I asked Zeema.

"What what?"

I remember both of us we had our hands stuck deep in our pocket, all four our hands frozen from Palo's van and January, too cold and heavy our hands to take a hand out and point. So I pointed with words and word-fog. "There, goddamn it. In the trees. That little house?"

Zeema be chuckling. But not enough to tighten me to being pissed off. "That," he said, "is a white man's everyday holiday."

That, that pissed me off, that. I thought of taking my iceberg hand out my pocket. Zeema must've known my unpatience was melting cause he said, "A swimming pool."

"Swimming pool?"

"Something like that."

Yes sir, a swimming pool. The first I saw.

What's that? You say it's the first swimming pool in the parish? No shit. Kind of a privilege, then, to be seeing it, now that I look back on it.

All historical? That's it. You're laughing and frowning at that word. But sure. All historical, the first swimming pool in Mondebon Parish.

"Know what that is?" I asked Zeema. "That's a big hole on a little hole. How you figure that big hole got dug without the diggers finding out about the little hole?"

Zeema didn't answer my question. I was sure he didn't understand what I was talking about. And he was sensing my unpatience, too, you understand.

"If you want something, Lineman, go and knock on the door. It's not like you to stand on one side the street when you want something on the other."

Zeema, I thought, was kind of right. It was like me to knock on any color door on any color street. After all, even court wasn't so all that bad. So the different ways to go start going in my head, you understand? Kind of like, *knock:* "What your name is lady?" *Knock:* "I know about what under your swimming pool, lady. I want a gift from you, something keep me quiet." *Knock.*

Then I remembered that terror scream I heard when me and Daddy drove away after the burying. And I heard it in my head, plain in my head. Let me see if I can do it for you. *Knock:* "What your name is, lady?" *Ohh-aiii Ooo-my aiii!* You imagine that? Listen: *Ah-ii my aiii, Oh ooo.* Wish I could do the crazy in that sound but I can't, can't get my voice that terrible high.

And I realized standing there frozen under the Christmas smell that it was no use crossing over the street. I think I realized it before we saw what we saw coming out the orange trees.

What we saw?

A child. I guess you call it that. Coming from the direction of the new hole on top the old where my daddy buried a child.

A child. Not a ghost or nothing. Even the ground was warmer than the air that day, so no ghosts be fool enough to rise up out.

A child. Without sleeves around its arms. I remember that first because that was what I noticed first, no sleeves. A girl, about the age for beginning school, no sleeves. Red winter-corduroy coat in one of her hands. The red of the coat trailing behind her.

"Look at that, will you, Zeema. How she stand the cold?"

"No," Zeema said. He took his hands out his pocket, both of them, and with both hands he pointed. "Wild," he said.

I started looking for what he meant, looked the way anybody would look, searching for wild. Then I thought I found it. In her other hand she was carrying an animal. A cat, tiger-goldish colored. She had it by the scruff. Not a kitten, not a grown tiger, but big enough, you understand, to claw. The cat was at her arm, wild with clawing at her arm.

"Yeah," I said, "the cat."

"No," Zeema said.

I moved my eyes from the cat to what the cat was clawing. And even from the distance I saw her arm. The scratches, the blood the color of the coat on the ground.

"Her arm," I said.

"No," Zeema said.

Then I moved my eyes again. And I was seeing the child-face, her looking at us while we looked at her, like their ain't no cat, no claw, no scratch, no reds.

I can tell you the exact words Zeema said next. I can tell you because the words are in one of his songs you played for me the other day. Zeema said the words right before I said, "Let's get the hell on out."

What he said? I'm going to tell you. Hold on.

He said, "Her eyes—black, green, what? She's standing in jungle looking out the jungle at us."

Just like that.

Sounds like one of his songs? Goddamn right. I told you it did. And that's where the words of his song come from.

What song?

Remember the other day we sat without your tape or pencil going, just listening to Zeema's records? I pointed to one of them records while we listened. You didn't notice then. I pointed with two hands just the way Zeema pointed that cold day, but you didn't notice. Remember how we talked about Zeema that day, about how Zeema said one of the bad things wrong with him was that he thought too much about writing songs to write the song? Remember? That he claimed he never wrote any of the words in any of his songs? Well, there's two songs I can kind of prove he wrote, two songs he didn't have to think about to write, two songs that came right out himself on the spots. Just came on out. One song came out of him in a turnip field—the "Half the World Is Magic" song. I'll get to that one later. The other song I can kind of prove he wrote came out of him that time we stood under the trees that smell like Christmas.

Yes sir, that cold day he said, "Her eyes—black, green, what? She's standing in the jungle looking out the jungle at us."

Then I said to Zeema, "Let's get the hell out."

And me and Zeema, we did.

Before going on to Lineman's escape from the low flow, let me give the words to the song Lineman was talking about:

Your eyes out the jungle at me, baby. Black, green, what? Ain't no blame come out the jungle, baby. Ain't no hurts but yours.

My husband knew at the time of that interview that these words were important. They are important to me, too, because I look back now after all the details are in, the details my husband never had. Isn't this—the irony of knowledge studied after all the details are in—within the historian's realm?

But I am filling a hole again. And I can only guess. That realm.

A-Whack-a-Whack-a

And so it occurred that Lineman and Zeema returned to Lineman's deserted dance hall on Landry Street. On January 2, 1948, the two men sat together at a table beneath the cold fusion of stars generated by afternoon sun and nailholes in a tin roof. For a while they did not speak. Lineman lay his metal box down on the floor beside his chair and emptied the contents of his pockets onto the table—a matchbox, a business card. . . . Soon Zeema would light a candle at the table to read the newspaper he had picked up somewhere on his journey from Emerson to Landry, and the two men would see each other and their shadows in that sparse new light. But there in the darkness, before the moment of new light, were strewn about the two men all of the atoms necessary to generate Lineman's future as it can be shown to have occurred.

And so it is with all of the histories I have helped the Marquis family to write: at some point beneath cold stars there is present the wastepile of facts that past events have generated; present also are items of chance—the business cards, the newspapers—and minds and hands capable of grasping. From my vantage point—the view of those who sit collecting and organizing the details of a past event—it is easy to recognize the generating rooms, the dark factories where futures seem to have been made.

And who has not wondered—as my husband did—what different futures would exist were one atom missing from the factory the day of generation. What if—for instance—the newspaper had not been there? Zeema might have left town within hours. What would his life have become without that two-week delay in departure? And Lineman's life? What forms would his prowling have taken along the low flow with an empty savings box in continuous presence?

In all of the jobs I have done for the Marquis family, and in my own books, I have never speculated in this way. Neither did most of the Marquis family, except on the night they spoke about these questions with Dr. Einstein—a night I will bring up later.

Someone in the Marquis family—my husband's great-aunt Veronica—wrote once of how the rotting smell of a speculative truth cannot be discerned as being different from the smell of despair or from the body odor of those who toy with circumstance. Veronica Marquis wrote also of the disinfectant smell of fact, of what can be shown to have occurred. One seeks that whiff of carbolic acid and bleach, she said, no matter how frightening the view.

The facts are that Lineman's savings box did get filled again, that Zeema did remain in town for the two weeks it took for him to become a king, that the two men did find my husband on the same day he was packing to leave the town.

But who has not wondered—as my husband did, as I have just done. And who has not asked the rotting questions?

Why the fuck you want to know that for?

Here I am about to lay on you how I climbed out the valley, how I got to be the parish first Negro bail bondman, how the names I forgot came on back to me, and you be asking me what come out my pocket on a table.

All right, all right, okay. Pack of cards. Always a pack of cards. Got that in my pocket even to now. Coins maybe. Maybe I had some coins left to me, an Abe Lincoln or two. A pocketknife—no, no pocketknife. Don't carry no pocketknife now, then, or never. The matchbox came out my pocket, matchbox with my daddy's tooth inside. Yeah, that for sure. And your business card you gave me in court—that had to come out, cause if it didn't, the story would end right there in the cold.

What you mean? Did I know Zeema had the newspaper before he lit the candle? Shit no. Where it came from I don't know. Maybe he picked it up in the court square, grabbed it off the wind. All I know is he lit the candle and he was reading and I was sick to my stomach from all the sweet. Then Zeema threw his own matchbox, the one he used to light the candle, onto the table.

In the candlelight, Zeema he started doing what newspaper readers they all do, you understand? Folding, unfolding, making creases that ain't there, making general paper noises that drive us folk that don't read or care about news-words nuts.

Then Zeema said, "Look a here."

How many big discoveries start with them words? Them white Spanish folks in silvered-metal suits on mountains looking at Indian cities, at oceans they think their eyeballs be first to gaze, what you think they said just before they staked claim? That's it. They said, "Look a here." Then they've got Indians for century, century and a half hauling treasure up to them Spanish boats.

Them white men in cinderblock back rooms with one eyeball flush up on microscopes thinking their one eyeball be first to spy God's own molly-cools, what they said before they staked claim? Yeah, that's right. "Look a here." Then they're hauling their atom-treasure over Japan and every eyeball in the place be syrup into sweet ray-dee-active soup.

Yeah, yeah, that's it. You understand. You're smiling on the edge of a laugh. Look a here, look a here. Yeah, I do love to see you laugh. Sure do now-days. You've got the saddest happy I've ever seen. But enough of that. Enough.

"Look a here," Zeema said. "You ever hear of Mardi Gras in New Orleans? Well, there's a bunch of businessmen in this town want to import Mardi Gras to here. To spruce up Main Street."

I'm kind of making up Zeema's words for you now, getting all like a conversation, close as I can get, you understand— except maybe forgetting a *something like that* or two—cause I wasn't listening quite yet to Zeema. I must've been fingering them cards that you and me just decided I probably had on the table.

I was still down in myself. But I can remember Zeema talking about the businessmen bringing down Mardi Gras from New Orleans. I can remember him talking about how the businessmen on one end of Main Street were having a dispute with some on the other end and how some were threatening to have the parade turn down Cathedral Street before it got in front of the business places of those that didn't want no Mardi Gras parade in town. A little white-man-shopkeeper, carpetbagging war, one of my favorite kinds of wars.

Then Zeema said, "Look a here," again. But this time he turned the paper to the candlelight and to me, and I saw what must've have been equal to a white Spanish looking at the ocean off an Indian's mountain. What I saw made me almost choke. I tasted curds of digesting cream on my tongue.

What I saw?

Saw a picture on a newspaper.

Hold on. I'm trying to come up with what's right with words to give you what was then.

When Zeema showed me the picture of the Main Street man that was planning to import Mardi Gras from New Orleans, something happened like you see in Bible pictures where the clouds got streamers of light shafting down on the world. I swear. Gold light came down in a shaft to the low flow I was on. I swear. I ain't storying. And it was like the shaft was on me and I understood for a second all the future, all the past, all together at once. All I'm saying really happened to me. I swear.

In the picture there was a man in a hat. And the silhouette fit right on over a silhouette pattern in my head. And my head be back on Emerson the night of the burial and the shaft of light in the present, on the low flow, be sheening off a gold plate, the gold plate I saw my father carrying in the past. The present shaft of light careened so hard off that memory plate it cracked it. I swear, you understand, in my head I heard a gold plate cracking with the light. Actual heard the sound. *Ca-thack-a-whack*. And then it be echoing through time *a-whack-a-whack-a-whack*. And I looked around at Zeema, at the cold room, the candle, the picture. And the valley walls around me and my soul, they were gone, you understand. And I was smoldering all smoky like my clothes be singed, *a-whack-a-whack-a*. And I shouted, "Roussell! Fuckin' Roussell!"

And Zeema, he said, "That's the name. How did you know that? It ain't written beneath his photograph."

I told Zeema never mind.

But Zeema, you know him, he's smart. "That's one of the names you've been trying to remember," he said.

I put my hand to my mouth. Something was coming up. Zeema must've seen it on my face. "You going to be sick?" he asked me.

And something sweet *was* coming up. I put my hand to my mouth to hold it back and not to let it answer Zeema's question. Held it back till my cheeks were brown balloons and my wet eyes were bugging out resting on them balloons. Then it came out.

Laughing. Laughing. You understand? Disgusting laughing came on out of me through my hands, and it must've blown into Zeema from over the candle cause . . . cause

61

next thing . . . cause then we be in the dark, both of us laughing. . . .

I heard Zeema searching on the table for the matchbox to light the candle again. I know that's what he was searching for. I heard him say "Oh, shit, man. Wrong box."

And I'm laughing again, disgusted with myself and my laugh and thinking about my daddy's gold tooth on Zeema's fingers, kind of a little nip-bite from the dead, who are a ways past sparking up the dark, you understand? But Zeema wasn't laughing anymore. He quit fumbling around in the dark on that table.

Zeema said, "We ain't alone, man."

Then I stopped my laughing, just closed my iron jaws and cut it off like lock gates on a river. "That true, ain't it, Zeema?"

"Something like that."

And ain't it? True, I mean. You understand? We ain't never alone. The dead can bite because they been ate by the mouth of the past and the past got the teeth. You understand? Sure you understand. Look at you now, all quiet in this here dimness we sitting in in the present time.

All right, all right. I'll go on on. Time bump you and you go on on. I understand. You understand.

I told Zeema never mind about the candle. Just to tell me what he read. And he related to me this information best as I can remember.

The man named in the picture was Nolan Roussell. Yes sir, burn-out flour and "sell," just like my daddy told me when he slapped my face that last time. Roussell was a haberdasher—my favorite white word, I think. You can see all those Main Street fools scurring, running around after something called "habers," can't you?

Anyways, Roussell, he was starting a club called the Mondebon Delos Main Street Carnival Club. Just like in New Orleans, with kings and queens and jacks and tens, like a deck of cards. With tourists and the twos and threes left in the town-deck scurring on the hard-pave street for trinkets that get thrown from floats by the royalty. Yes sir, just like New Orleans. Roussell he was even predicting in the paper the success of this—what they call it? Venture? Yeah, that's it, *venture*, his word exact. There would be a rebirth of Main Street. A rebirthing venture. More white words. Ain't that some shit, that? That's the history of this town, maybe of all-time white civilization. They always be trying to rebirth Main Street.

Why I use that word, *history*? I don't know. Maybe cause Roussell, he used it on me later. That's the first word . . . But that's the future. Stay where I'm at, stay where I'm at.

Anyways, Roussell, he says that the king will be called Delos. Still is to this day, ain't it? But that was way back then, you understand. We're talking about the first King Delos. I think now—no, I'm sure now—Roussell, he had his eye on the position, even in the article.

Zeema told me, there in the dark, that Roussell believed that Carnival was going to change the face of the town and the parish, *something like that*. Roussell said that everything before Carnival would be called "B.C." Everything after Carnival will be called "A.D." That's right, you got it: after Delos.

You got sad all of the sudden. I can see it on your face. Your my-mind-be-jumping-through-time face. I'm right? To A.D. 15, 16 or so? You're jumping to the Mardi Gras day you can't forget.

Oh yeah, now you're about to ask me a question, but I don't want to talk no more for right now about anything except that time me and Zeema were in the dark. I just want to tell you what I said when Zeema told me about this B.C. and this A.D.

I leaned on back in my chair, heard the wood creaking, almost cracking with what was me. I looked up at my stars in my roof and I said, "A.D. my ass."

Then I reached out my hand, like I was asking for the help

of all the ghosts and plates from my black-brown past to take over my arm. I thought of the plate my father buried. I ain't saying my arm got taken over, you understand. I'm just saying that in the dark there, where I couldn't see nothing on the table if I tried, there in the dark with all them things on the table, my hand came on down on you. On your business card. Now let your mind latch on to that moment. Then let your mind flash on through time all it wants. That's right. That's right. Let the tape go to the end and just . . .

Cheating to Lose

Now, yeah, back to Zeema and me and that table.

When the candle got lit again, I was staring down at your card, not the front of your card, but what you wrote on the back of your card. You wrote how I could get in touch with you while you were still in town, remember? What you wrote?

Now you understand what I'm getting at? When a person on the way up and out the low flow, like in a Bible picture of Jesus hovering up to heaven, everything around that person got a chance at going up and out, too. All those sight-see-ers in the Bible watching Jesus hover, they're all thinking, *If I can just latch on, just latch on.*

Anyways, on the back the card, you wrote *Office 6, Roussell Building, Main Street.*

That was when I made an important decision. No matter what I believed, I'd better do what they call now-days going with the flow. Seems I was being brought up out the valley on a plate and I'd better go the direction of the plate. Kind of like, if the plate says go to a lawyer, that must be the way to go. Who am I to go against that kind of power?

And that's how it happened. I knew I had to go to you. Some people call it "the signs," you understand? All the signs point that way. Me, let's just say I didn't want to fall off the fucking plate. Still don't. I'm a powerful man, you understand, but I ain't a fool. I don't go scurrying for trinkets thrown at my feet, and I sure as hell don't jump off no flying plate.

Laugh all you want. It never was disgusting on you.

So anyways, all this seemed like it got design instead of just happening scattered. Everybody around me, too, they knew it, too. All them if-I-could-only-latch-on people, you understand? Like Zeema. Like him sitting across from me must've known my change. He was silent. He'd been bitten by a gold tooth, remember? Zeema be watching miracles all round him. Even be watching a man who hated to laugh laughing with his guts all over the card table. He even must've seen me on my plate, rising. Zeema was a gambler, which is a doubter of top order. When Jesus turned the water to wine that wedding day, a gambler stepped out the crowd and whispered, *Hey, Lord, where you got the secret siphon-tube leading to the wine jar?*

Know what Zeema's face be saying? His gambler face? Know what it be saying?

Good guess. Zeema, he was past *something like that*. No, not quite *look a here*. What comes after *look a here*? His face was saying, *What next?* Because even the gambler in him knew it was all mine, that question, to answer. Maybe that's the difference between a white gambler and a black gambler. They're both doubters, you understand. But the white gambler asks, *Where the secret tube?* and the black gambler asks, *What next?*

But that's history again. And Roussell, he'll be coming along soon enough.

So I said to Zeema, "Go get your friend. Get the Prince. It time for an honest game."

And that's what we had, all that late afternoon, a game. Me and Zeema and the Prince played cards into the night. I told them both about my plans cause my plans were starting to come to me. I'd be going back to the lawyer, I told them. Be asking the lawyer to give this Roussell my demands. Prince Albert, he was slow to understand what was going on that night. He couldn't see the rising plate cause his eyes were on his lover, on the cards. But Zeema, his hands on his face, his hands alongside the easy press of his nose, he was listening.

During the game, I asked both men—Zeema and the Prince—what they wanted most in life. Cause what they wanted, I could get. None of that three wishes crap. That's what I told them, *three wishes crap*, you understand? The Prince kind of giggled, still involved in games. But Zeema, he was listening close.I told them anything and everything they wanted I could get.

They were snickering at first—the Prince saying things like he didn't want to die while he was having one of his fits, and Zeema saying he wanted peace of mind, a black woman, and black children. I hit the table with my fist. And when my fist hit, Abe Lincolns fly.

Zeema, he got quiet to that kind of power, just like I got quiet to the power of a question. But the Prince, bald and neat as ever, he was shitting on himself.

"Me?" Prince Albert said, "Didn't know you was serious. If I could have me anything, I'd like to be famous with the songs me and Zeema wrote together while we walk the army base and the town."

"Can't get you fame in a bayou town," I said. "Come on down to earth."

"Just in business with Zeema, then," the Prince said. "Something like that. That can be got in a bayou town. A business license."

"I told you I'm trying to leave," Zeema said.

"Then I want you to stay awhile," Prince said.

"I told you, don't be laying your trust on me," Zeema said.

"Shit, shit, shit," I told both of them. "Here I am offering you two the things of the world and you two sweet-tonguing each other's ears in public. What you want, goddamn it? I'm talking things, things."

I could tell both men, they weren't ready to take hold of what I meant. How many men are brave enough to take hold of wish granting except in dreams and tales?

I tried again with Zeema. "This is real, songman. What you want, songman? I can get it for you."

Zeema, he was getting pissed. He said, "That can't be answered, Lion Man. And if it could, there ain't no man could get me to say it."

"What you been trying to find in this town all these years, songman? What you looking for? A white woman like your daddy had? A kind of world where that don't matter? Or the courage it takes to have what you want to have in any world?"

That was the first time I ever thought Zeema would get up and leave a card game in progress.

"Make me a king, Lineman," he shouted. No—he kind of sang it with a shout. "A colored king in a two-color town. Then I'll make this son of a bitch a real prince. And y'all can both get off my ass!"

Now Zeema and me, we were both mad. The Prince was shaking with fear of me, but he still had his cow-sad look from what Zeema told him. Disgusting, you understand.

Then they're both shouting at me: "You tell us!" Now when a coward like the Prince start shouting at the Lion, I feel you've got people's attention.

"All right, you two bush-hoggers of Princess whores. Listen. I'm going to show you. Then we'll get down to the game. Things. Not dreams—things."

That's when I made my list. It came right on out of me. I call it my "plate list." I told those two the things I was planning to get for myself, and I told them they'd better latch on on.

Here's my list. Same list I had you write down for me the next morning, except you kind of did it a little fancy more. You called it my "freedom list."

I can't tell you exact what you wrote, but I can tell you still exact what I wanted.

I wanted to fill my saving box with no trouble, with the proceeds of my business. How you wrote that down? *Freedom to thrive.* Yeah, oh, words, baby.

I wanted to be a bail bondman. The first black bail bondman in town. I wanted that connection with a courthouse no black man had. What you called it? *Freedom to access,* oh, baby.

I wanted my sister to finish school and be a teacher. I know, I know, you called it something to do with dignity in the family, but I just wanted Angelle off my ass.

And I wanted the parish to extend the light poles over my roof. That way, when people looked at the holes in the ceiling of my place, they'd see stars all the time, stars in the daytime, stars at night.

I wanted to be the only Lion around, and I wanted Landry to be mine. I wanted to live without fear of anything except my dreams.

All those things might not be on your list, but I kind of started going off the end real deep there explaining everything to Zeema and the Prince, you understand.

"How you going to do that?" Zeema asked. He kind of dared me by asking a question. I almost showed him my power by answering. Almost. Then he sang it out without the question mark. "You can't even face a tooth in a matchbox."

"It's only gold, enamel, and pulp," I said.

Everybody at the table and everything got calmed.

Then the Prince said, "This getting spooky enough. Don't need long prayers when the faith strong."

"What the fuck that mean?" I asked.

"It means," Zeema said, "he'll give your ass a princely kiss if you can get those things you want. And a princely kiss a night for the rest of your life if you can transform gold, enamel, and pulp into something you can face."

"Something like that," the Prince said.

"Boys," I said, "Rake in your cards. Pucker your fucking royal lips."

And now you, you right now. I can see you've got one more question before the tape ends the night?

Good. You finally noticed. Zeema, he didn't use the words *something like that* when the Prince was around. I noticed that, me, too. I'd got around to asking Zeema about that before he left town. Let's save it for then. But you already know the answer, don't you? You just want it on the tape official.

Anyways, like I said . . . I think Zeema knew then, that night, I couldn't fail. Wouldn't fail for a long time. Long time. I was connected to all time to all things. And he was watching, even with his black-gambler brand of doubt, watching. And he saw me dealing an honest game. Yeah, I dealed an honest game. He watched me. And he saw that even then I couldn't lose. The chips and Abe Lincolns were piling in front of me. I had to start cheating again to give the Prince a share of the pile. And Zeema watched me and he knew. I was riding the gold plate up and out. I had to cheat to lose.

The Roussell Building

On January 3, 1948, a Saturday in what could be called the year 1 B.C. in the haberdasher Nolan Roussell's reckoning, Lineman, Zeema Steeple, and Prince Albert Willis walked south from Landry Street, turning east on Cathedral Street, which intersects with Main. The three men must have got an early start; in the tapes, Lineman mentions "a fool sun, all wobbly, staggering itself into the sharp point of the cross top of the Catholics' steeple."

To their right along Cathedral Street the three men had to

first pass the following: the red-brick schoolhouse that up to the years of the Second World War had been the parish's "new" high school; the graveyard behind the cathedral; the cathedral; then another schoolhouse, this one yellow—the parish's first brick high school; and finally the courthouse. Perhaps the three men sat on the green benches beneath the oaks in the court square at the intersection of Cathedral and Main, stopping to smoke, a preoccupation exquisitely pleasurable to most of the men out of that time, out of or near that war. From the court-square benches closest to the courthouse steps, the benches that face east, they would have seen—but barely—the building that was then called the Roussell Building, standing south of the large parking lot to the right of the post office.

I mention these details to make note of the research my husband did on the town. I have only to look at his maps and photographs—his own and those he found in books—to see what any person on a promenade might have seen while making that same walk at any time from 1900 to 1948. A quaint travelogue could be written using my husband's notes on the buildings alone.

Of all the buildings researched by my husband, more pages are given to the Roussell Building, a building that grew over itself out from its center, much as a pearl, in layers of wood, metal, brick, and glass. According to one local historian's book, the building was the parish's first opera house, "a wood, three-story edifice balconied with a six-sided tower on the southeast corner." Through the turn of the century, the building "accommodated traveling stock companies, lectures, school theatricals," becoming the town's first movie palace toward the end of the Great War.

If one can imagine this opera house—its belfry, balconies, and Roman arches—near an icehouse, both on a batture on a bayou with an outlet to the Gulf of Mexico, both with wharves for shrimp boats, oyster boats, and pleasure boats, both sharing an oyster-and-clamshell parking lot with hitching posts and—much later—parking meters; if one can imagine commerce and culture in a constant whir of boom-based change—the fur boom, the shrimp-and-oyster seafood-packing boom, the sugar cane boom, the oil boom, the tourist boom—one is imagining the backdrop of this town. If one crosses Main Street from the court square, as I did, and firmly clutches the telephone pole ten feet from the entrance to the Roussell Building, one is fixed at the center of what must have been for over a hundred years a constant bazaar.

On the concrete banquettes of 1948 in front of the Roussell Building, in front of the layer of display window glass and around the telephone pole that remains to this day, would be constructed in late winter the pine-stud platform used as the reviewing stand where the first parish Mardi Gras queen would toast the first parish Mardi Gras king. The deck of that same platform is the plywood floor one sees in the photograph that won three of 1964's top photojournalism awards, a photo as well known to Americans as *Life* magazine's image of the sailor's deep-bend kiss in Times Square on V-J Day, 1945.

Most who are reading this now understand suddenly where this chronicle is headed—to the colors of that famous emulsion, to the greens and purples and golds of the first day of A.D. 16, a Mardi Gras Day in the false spring of 1963.

The PS on the Freedom List

I have on file two descriptions of that early morning encounter between my husband and his three clients. One description is in the Lineman tapes—the meeting from Lineman's vantage point. The other description is from the vantage point of my husband, James Peter Marquis.

My husband, like most in the Marquis family, made written note of the experience of each day. He was packing his two suitcases when he heard the three men on the steep stairs of the Roussell Building. Later that night, on the train taking him back to New Orleans, my husband would write of the three men who stood in the reception area of his office. Two of the three, Lineman and Zeema, stood with "profound presence—one with a presence of occupation, of inhabited space, the other with the presence of grace and fair balance." The third man, "an animated and uncertain" Price Albert Willis, seemed to be "harvesting the energy around the other two even as he stood still and breathless from the climb." It was the biggest of the three, Lineman, who stepped forward, holding out my husband's business card as though it were, as my husband wrote, "a paid-for ticket of admission."

Switching vantage points now, to that of the Lineman tapes, one gets a brief description of my husband as he stood before the three men that morning. This description, I believe, is a markedly accurate rendering of James Peter Marquis as he was then: "a green-eye man with no meanness, an always-rested, always-ready, second-breath man."

Except for the eyes, Lineman here could have been describing any of the men in the Marquis family. Their second wind was, to all of them, a strength. To many of them, considering their rate of fiftieth-year cardiac arrest, their second wind was also a killer. Describe a Marquis, man or woman, and you are describing energy contained by an almost studied bearing and decorum. A Marquis offers his hand first because one always hesitates reaching out to a Marquis. With my husband James, the opposite occurred. One held the hand out to him.

"It's what you hated most in your white man of yours," Lineman would tell me years later when I sought him out. "That when you saw him you had to think hard about holding your hand back. Must have been them fucking eyes. On anybody else them eyes be take-a-advantage-of-my-innocence eyes. On him what a steal, what a tricky steal."

I have taken the time to mention all of this because I am thinking of my husband now, of the man who stepped from the train that next morning, of the delicate friction of his hand on my belly, of the openness and hope with which we walked. Later, when my husband began holding his hand back, one felt deceived in a way. Although everything else about him might have changed, the eyes remained the same. There was never any despair in his eyes.

There you were, Jay Pee Markee, remember? Shaking hands with Zeema and the Prince after they moved out front of me. I turned away from your hand, remember?

Was that the time we talked about black folks being in the ditch with the shovel, me saying about how you'd better never climb in the ditch with me, making me feel poor-niggerish? Yeah, yeah, that was the time, sometime that morning.

But not at first. First I asked you about Nolan Roussell. You smiled that green-eye shit and you kind of nodded us into your main office. You didn't ask me why I wanted to know. You must've remembered I didn't like answering no questions then.

In the office, I understood you were in a rush. Books be piled on your desk, pretty-color books. That's what I recall most about you in them days, colors, colors all round. Zeema, he walked to the books, handled them. That was Zeema, right? The Prince, he was looking for a place to sit, planning like he always did where he would fall if he went into a fit. I saw them books, too. They weren't law books, were they? I remember kind of the titles, Markee here, Markee there, all about Markees.

"You need me for something," you said. You *said* that, didn't ask me that, your voice lower than your courthouse voice.

"Need some things done, some things answered," I said.

"And I need me a deal cause I'm out of money cause your lawyering cost me."

You were sitting with one butt cheek on the edge of the desk in the Markee color pile. I opened up my saving box— empty except for a matchbox with a tooth inside—and set it down on the desk beside you.

"Tell me about Roussell," I said.

You told me what you knew. You rented your office from him. He—Roussell—had just bought him this building a year or so before and was making it over into a place to sell clothes and ties. I'd seen the scaffolds all over, and the display window frames. A five-and-dime, Zeema called it, a five-and-dime times ten.

All the while you telling me about Roussell, the Prince be interrupting, talking about a sword he seen hanging over the lobby door downstairs. "Man, that sword," he be saying. "Man, that sword." How many times I tell him, *shet up, shet up*?

Finally me and you got down to business. I told you I needed you to write me a white-man letter to the man named Roussell. "Use words like you do," I said, "important-sounding words, for all you worth. If you do it right, I'm in the clear."

"Connected," Zeema said, "Lineman wants to be connected to Landry and the Great Perpendicular to Main."

This letter, I told you, I wanted it to have demands on this man Roussell. I told you I'd made me a list.

The Prince be interrupting again with "How about adding that sticker sword to that list?"

Shet up, shet up.

You gave me the green-eye smile again, like you was liking the way I was talking. Got a feeling every-damn-body thought you liked the way they talked when you gave them that green-eye shit. Anyways, I gave you my list. List amounted to getting the charges dropped, leaving my business untouched, getting my sister a job, getting a position for myself like bail bondman, getting the streetlights pulled over my dance-hall roof for stars. When I say out loud the list now, I get the feeling to laugh. Must of sounded a far fetch coming like it did from a puffing man fresh off the stairs. But you didn't laugh, didn't even wink an eye. You knew when to laugh, when not to. Man can stay alive long time with that in his blood.

Then you said, "I assume you think that Roussell is in a position to get these things for you."

I said, "Why you think I be making the climb two flights closer to heaven with my awful weight if I didn't think Roussell in a position?"

Zeema and the Prince, they loved that. They be laughing. You be laughing. Everybody laughing but me.

Then you were explaining to me what you called "the secret that moves the town." Not elected people, but people who can keep a business open, move the town. Shopkeepers. These same people—car dealers, bankers, clothes men—they move on out their peer-ee-mids-like buildings sometimes, but only sometimes, to get somebody elected. Then they move on back inside their peer-ee-mids.

And while you were explaining all this, I heard your voice echoing off the walls in your office. No pictures anywheres. The walls, they were wood all over, but they were bouncing your words back like off of stone.

Yes sir, I liked the way you sounded. And I told you again I wanted you to use words like that in my letter, sometimes throwing in a word commonsense people can't find a head or a tail on.

You said you'd write it for me all right. And you said you'd give me a deal on the price.

"Address it to King Delos," I said, "care of the Mondebon Delos Main Street Carnival Club, the Roussell Building."

You told me you could hand-deliver the letter on your way out. I asked you what you meant by that, and you told me my letter would be your last official act in town. Was it the Prince that asked you where you were going?

"I'm meeting my wife tonight," you said. "We're having our second baby. I'm buying a house."

And that was when Zeema told you about how he wanted to leave the town, too. And about how he had him a woman and a baby of his own.

"Enough of that shit," I said. "If this the story in a movie at the Grand, I'd of walked out by now. Time too slow in here." And it was, slow piles of it like your color books. "Why the shit you here in town in court yesterday if you knew you was leaving?"

What was the words you said? Yeah, *pro bono*.

I remember those words cause you wrote them on back one of your cards. No, no, Jay Pee, don't remember what card, which card you wrote that on. Don't remember where you put that card, who picked it up.

Anyways . . . pro bono. Zeema and you explained it to me. It was like you were a servant to the people, put on trial yourself by your own law office to prove you were friend-of-men. That idea's no good, but I told you I liked the sound of the words. I told you to keep using them. To keep sounding lawyerish.

Yeah, wait. That was when we talked about the ditch, being in the ditch. It had a heat to it what we talked about, remember? You believed hard what you were saying about that Billy Rights. There you were about to be taking a train home to a new home and you were talking to three out-of-breath stair-climbing niggers about their rights.

Aw, shit, it didn't matter coming from you. Any black man talking to you would know you would be the last white man in front our firing squad. But anyways, I say it again, Billy Rights ain't got the teeth, you understand. Sure you understand. Takes more than Billy Rights and a green-eye smile to get the best of shopkeepers and crazy coonasses and God knows what else they got in this town.

Anyways, we got back to the letter. Zeema, he moved into your chair, reading. The Prince lay down sweating on your divan. You sketched out the letter for me, said it would have to be hand-wrote cause your typing woman be gone. And you put some flair to it, like you said, *freedom this, freedom that, Markee here, Markee there.*

When you finished writing, you told me I needed to tell you how you should tell Roussell to get in touch with me.

I said, "Don't want nothing to do with touching. Tell him I want to meet him in full daylight tomorrow, at noon, bright noon, at the corner of Landry and Main. No, the day after tomorrow. Make him wait. The end of the world always the day after tomorrow."

You told me the letter would cost me lowest it could be—free of charge. And then you gave me a suggestion, also free of charge. You used a lawyer word. And what was that word? Yeah, *im-pee-tuss.*

You turned to Zeema, still at his reading. Zeema said to me, "He means you need you something in the letter to get Roussell's juice going to where he feels he's got to do these things."

"Like a PS?" I asked.

You smiled to that.

"Well, PS this," I said. "You tell him, these words exact, from the new Lion of Landry. *There's a hole on Emerson always open to the past.*"

Bottom Boxes

The books Lineman spoke of are, of course, those eyewitness accounts known inside the Marquis family as "the chronicles," published by the same New York house for over one hundred years.

Someone asked a Marquis once if the Marquis children—there are many—are reared to believe not only in the Nicene Creed, but also in the notion that they will someday happen into a significant event that is destined to be recorded in every schoolchild's history book. The answer to that question appeared in the introduction to *Marquis at Appomattox*: "Yes, Marquis children are taught to take note of each day's experience. However, Marquis children are not led to believe, but *do* believe, that it is undignified and insincere to live a life expecting significance in an acquaintance or in a circumstance; that without doubt the so-called significant event will happen into them; that any Marquis child from the age of seven can open the proper Marquis chronicle to the page that proves that Marquises were not only present at the writing of the Nicene Creed, but also helped with the rough draft."

In the book section of the New Orleans *Times-Picayune* in 1919, a writer pen-named Quill called the chronicle published at that time—*Marquis at the Hall of Mirrors*—"Garden District pseudohistory, one remove from gossip." During my job interview with the Marquis family years later, I was told that it was that article that astounded the family into the "twenty-year-plus lapse" between chronicles. The idea of "being reviewed," they told me, of "having the Marquis style addressed," was offensive enough, but the writer's use of the word *history* moved them into a "cautious family hibernation."

I was also told that the Marquis family was interviewing applicants for a "ghostwriting team of history majors," not because the family now agreed with the use of the word *history*, but because they now saw that the "new-age" would not take any writing seriously unless it were labeled *A History*. Even though I had already, in my mid-twenties, published enough to substantiate my worth as a "genuine historian"—a discipline they still found offensive—my role on the team would be limited to what they called my "especial specialty," my "knack with the footnote." Footnotes would help transform their chronicles into "legitimate histories." The Marquis family detested the footnote: "Footnotes are stored in bottom boxes. One knows they are there; one might keep them—if one desired—as evidence that one knows deeply, but no more."

At my interview I was introduced to James Peter Marquis, on leave and still in uniform, who would be the family member in charge of coordinating the team. James married me while we were working together gathering and sorting the facts that would become the substance of his uncle's *Marquis at the Alcázar: A History.* Our first daughter was born within a year. The team was disbanded shortly after that when I became the principal ghostwriter. The last book James and I worked on together was his brother Berman's *Marquis at Nuremberg: A History,* which was published less than a year before Berman's suicide. My husband would not attempt his own chronicle until those years following the false spring before Mardi Gras, 1963.

A Spark in the Sun

Lineman, after leaving my husband's office that January day in 1948, went into his own hibernation for the rest of that day, that night, and the day and night that followed. In one of my husband's taped interviews with Lineman, Lineman says that he played cards with Prince Albert Willis and with Zeema Steeple, who had decided not to leave town for a day or two, "just to see what turtles crawled out on the log in the sun."

Also on that tape, Lineman says that his "legendary Lineman snores" began that first night after he left my husband's office. My husband interviewed several people who played cards with Lineman through the fifties and early sixties. All spoke of the rhythm of Lineman's naps. Some were certain the naps took place every ten minutes. Lineman's eyes closed, his hands relaxed almost to the point of dropping his cards, he snored once, and in the middle of the second snore he snorted himself awake as though he had never left the game.

Sure, sure, it's true. You know, Jay Pee. I take my naps everywhere. Anytime I ain't taking place in the talking, I take my cat's nap. I even take them now when you're changing your tapes. Ask my wifes and the women I coupled on top of. They learned how to satisfy themselves on the snake and the snore. I think I got me a way to get some sleep, but we'll talk about that later.

And where I was? Oh, yeah. The napping, it all began that day after I left you in your office. God, I needed sleep. But I didn't do no sleeping. I understood, you understand, that I'd broken that deal with my dreams. I expected them to return.

So I kept on playing cards, playing cards. The two men, Zeema and the Prince, they took shifts to keep up. Then it happened. I couldn't go no more. I surrendered just to see. My first cat's nap, you understand? Within seconds, I was dressed in red robes, velvetlike. No, didn't see myself like in a dream. Dreams don't work as if they *like in a*. I was the actual myself dressed in red robes standing front of a pregnant woman's belly. She smelled all dead and all funk at the same time. Could've been she was my mama, my sister, the mother of the child my daddy buried. Any of them women she could've been. I woke myself up before my sharp teeth, my sharp nails—God, you understand, the horribilities. That had to be why my father never ate nothing. What a man is when the mind of a man can draw up that?

I think I figured out while I played poker how many cat's naps a second, a second and a half long I needed to get enough sleep not to go crazy. I figured how many calories I needed to overcome the inside gnawing at my flesh that my dreams were about to do. I figured on hundred and hundreds naps a day. And I figured I would have to eat any chance I got. You won't believe this, but as much you've seen me eating during a game, I lost weight sometimes. The horribilities, you understand, the horribilities.

Anyways, I crawled on out the dark of my dance hall . . . Monday? That's right, a Monday. Still January? January five? I do like the way you keep track of my time, Jay Pee.

I crawled out the dance hall to meet Roussell on the corner of Landry and Main. I remember I had my saving box with me, because Zeema laughed before I left with it when I told him I'd be back with it full. Zeema, he said I had me a lot to learn.

I believe it was about ten o'clock when I left. I was hungry. So hungry I went to visit my brother Emmon. Emmon lived by himself but he always went over to see Angelle about ten, ten thirty, and Angelle gave him some meal makings, sometimes last supper's leavings.

Me and Emmon, we ate a loaf of bread and some cold potato stew. Emmon be eyeing the saving box all the while the consuming of the wheat going on. He told me the family was waiting before they bury my daddy. Palo the mortician still had the body, prepared and ready.

"Waiting for what?" I asked Emmon.

Emmon kept on staring at the saving box. I told him to tell the family I didn't want nothing to do with no funeral, Daddy or no Daddy, lion, giraffe, nothing to do.

Emmon gave me that what-you-expect-for-us-to-do look.

"Look," I said, keeping on my eating, "I might stop by on my way back from my appointment in town. I ain't saying nothing about no saving box, and being the oldest in the family and all that. I might stop back by with a full saving box just to shut Angelle up."

Then I asked Emmon what time it was and he said about eleven thirty. So you see I'm positive a hundred percent I had plenty time to get to the corner, plenty time. So it can't be I missed Roussell. I even checked the furniture-store clock, looking through the glass. I expected that son of a bitch to be there, you understand. Expected to see his hat and him. But there wasn't nothing on the corner but cars and people in coats and rocking chairs and divans behind furniture-store glass. Leaning on the brick corner of a furniture store, I napped, snored, woke, waited until past two o'clock.

When I came on back to my place, Zeema, sitting outside on a bench in the same sunlight, said something about how he knew that particular turtle wouldn't crawl out in the sun. I told Zeema I would've bet my life on Roussell showing. I knew things from this Roussell's past that could destroy him, you understand.

"Only something like that," Zeema said. Then he used your lawyer word again, *im-pee-tuss.*

"Fuck im-pee-tuss," I said.

Then Zeema reminded me it was my idea to use white man's words. "Trouble is," Zeema said, "you were playing a black man's game with him."

"You trying to tell me," I said, "Roussell call my bluff. But I can destroy him. You can't bluff off that."

Zeema tried explaining what happened like it was a game. What it come down to was something like this: Me and Roussell both bet words. I put all my money down on the word *past.* That's how a Landry Street man would bet.

"You should have bet the word *future,*" Zeema said. "That's how I figure this Roussell out. And figuring is everything."

I asked Zeema what exactly he was saying and he told me then about the one meanass plan he'd come up with while I was waiting in town for Roussell. I remember standing there, tired, the sun on my cheeks, while Zeema started telling me about the Zulu parades in New Orleans for Mardi Gras. Zeema said he'd heard that in New Orleans the black man's

Zulu parade with its black man's King Zulu was begun to mock the white man's King Rex.

"Let's do that here in town," Zeema said. "Let's follow behind their parade, the Delos parade. Instead of Delos, we'll have Zulu. Instead of trinkets, we'll throw painted coconuts. Instead of robes, we'll wear grass. Instead of marching in fine-order line, we'll dance, dance, dance."

In the sunlight, while Zeema talked, I took a fast nap, saw my mama's swollen belly, coffee-brown with a golden crescent of moon on the edge. When I woke, my eyes watering from the glare, I think I understood what Zeema was getting at.

I said the word out loud: *Zulu*. Then I said Zeema's name. How many days in a life you get to say two Z names on a cold January day with sun on your cheeks? Something like magic just in the sound, especially fresh out my dream. Little magic, you understand, just like the words in one of Zeema's later songs. Magic's easy to feel at night. Hell, anybody can see a spark at night. But magic was there in the light, just as powerful, but harder to see. Like a spark you can't see. A spark in the sun.

Then Zeema was telling me to wait. "Details," he said.

"Fuck details," I said. I was mad and hungry from my dream, and tired. Zeema told me to sit and listen. "I know you hate questions," he said, "but listen to these."

And Zeema gave me a whole string of questions. How were we going to get enough people to march? Who'd be making the costumes? Where'd we be building the floats, painting the coconuts? How were we getting some band to play while we march?

I sat to the questions, and to more questions that Zeema came up with. Then I asked him why the hell he brought up his plan at all if the plan's got so many questions.

"Because I think I have the answer," Zeema said.

"Then why the fuck you come up with the questions?"

Then Zeema said one word: *Bowman*. He waited. Then he said, "That new Reverend Bowman can get you all this. But you'll have to deal with him."

I started to say, "Fuck Bowman," but Zeema raised his hand. In the sun it was almost white. "Before you go fucking everything again," he said, "listen to me. Zulu will get you Roussell's attention in a white man's game. Bowman can take care of the details that will get you Zulu."

Zeema, he was the strangest mixture of magic and sense. But when he got them in tune together . . . he made me think what all niggers—God, why did Bowman make me hate that word?—Zeema made me think, *What we could've been if we'd been born with white hands white in the sun?*

I asked Zeema what a new reverend from Philadelphia could possibly know about Mardi Gras. And I asked Zeema how much I was going to have to pay.

Zeema told me we could go for the same deal he tried that morning in my daddy's room. "Bowman," he said, "he'd sure like you to make sure your family stays in his church now that he's got your family away from the Old Reverend's church. I'll tell him you've decided to give that to him if he buries your daddy and gets involved in the Zulu parade. Something like that."

I could see why Bowman might go along with burying my daddy. That was an equal exchange. But what were we going to offer him to go along with Zulu?

"I just think," Zeema said. "I think he'll go along. He's going back up to Philadelphia to a political convention in the summer. Something's cooking up there. I think he wants to do some cooking down here."

What's that, Jay Pee?. Any talk of what? President Truman? I don't know nothing about the Reverend and his connection to no Truman and no conventions. That's something you'd better find somewhere else. What I'm telling is what I know. I know I stood on up again, stood on up again, raised my hands again to the sky, closed my eyes. The sun was all warm on my face, you understand. And I was thinking of moving, eating, doughnuts and fudgesicles, and doing anything to stay out the low flow.

I asked Zeema if he really thought we were going to dance, and if dancing would get Roussell's attention.

"I believe so," Zeema said. "Something like that. Dancing doesn't get to them exactly. But colored dancing is something else."

"Then do it," I said. "Bet the future."

That's exact what I told Zeema. Bet the future. Then I said the two Z's again and I remembered what Zeema said he wanted when he was mocking me the other night. *Make me a king* he said. That's when I nominated Zeema for Zulu, while he was sitting there on my bench, me standing over him.

Zeema caught the connection and laughed.

"Go on," I said. "Tell Bowman I want you for Zulu."

What a steal, Zeema smiling with them white teeth sparking white in the white sun.

Before Zeema went off to talk to Bowman, me and him went to raid Palo's ice-cream van. But Palo was close by and Zeema had to pay for what we ate. Palo told me what Emmon had said, that the family was waiting for me to come up with this or that to bury Daddy. I told Palo we were close, just to keep the old man stiff and cold and smelling sweet.

Powdered Feet in the Pyramid

And that—allowing myself what the Marquis family calls "the blessed and quick transition"—is how the idea of Zulu began in that town south of New Orleans: the Mondebon Zulu Landry Street Carnival Club. Zeema bargained that same Monday. He bargained for a church burial, and the family buried Lineman's father before sunset.

That also is the longest summary I feel comfortable with now. I can see the Marquis family frowning and wincing as I continue presenting the evidence in the Lineman tapes. "Let the summary move," they would say. "Use your bottom boxes if you must, but move."

But as I said, Lineman's words will stop soon, and Lineman will become a secondary character in my husband's chronicle. For now, Lineman, Zeema, Prince Albert Willis, and cards at sunset:

I remember looking up at the holes in my ceiling, seeing them the dark purple they get before the sun leaves. I think I could hear Angelle wailing, even though the grave was miles away on the other side the Intracoastal.

Yeah, Bowman went along with Zulu, though I never knew why till years later. Kind of ahead of his time, you understand. Zeema told me that Bowman planned to tell his congregation about the Zulu parade the next meeting, and the cooking would start. All I had to do, Zeema said, was walk out to the corner of Landry and Main every day to see if we had us some turtle soup.

And Zeema, he was staying around town awhile. His woman had left without him for Canton and he was alone in his room beside the Palace without the courage to leave. Zeema wasn't official King Zulu yet, but he was a cinch for that. Who else would the people at that meeting lay their vote on? What a steal.

I reminded Zeema that he would need him a prince when the time came, and I reminded the Prince while he dealt a game of low-in-the-hole that he'd better start puckering up cause Zeema and him were about to be royalty just like they'd asked.

Then things started moving slow. Can you feel it? I prowled all them days on the low flow, got on a plate up and out the hole—and there I was, waiting, waiting. I saw myself going to the corner of Landry and Main, waiting, napping in the sun, playing cards, waiting, napping. What kind of life that is? What kind of sparks were left in the night? Even the stars be going purple above me.

Then I came up with the idea to spark up the night. Got the idea during one of my dreams. There was this blade in my hands with gold light on it and blood like strawberry jam, and anyways, I snorted and said, and this be exact: "I'm breaking into Roussell's building. I'm stealing Roussell's past."

Zeema said I didn't have to steal anymore.

"Shet up," I told him, and "shet up" again. "You sounding like my daddy. Stealing's my way. The nights is dragging by, dragging by, just like one of my daddy's all-night moving jobs. I don't even feel like a lion anymore. I'm stealing tonight."

"The sword," Prince Albert said.

"That's right," I said. "That sword we seen in the lobby. I'm breaking into Roussell's building and I'm stealing that sword."

"Yeah," Prince Albert said. "Oh, yeah."

Zeema told me he wasn't going along. But the Prince, he was game. Even his bald and neat head be happy. "Sticker sword," the Prince called it. And that's how the Prince—but I'm getting ahead again.

Anyways, the Prince asked me if he could have the sticker sword for his own self, for the parade, to kind of protect King Zulu. I granted his wish.

Just before me and the Prince left, I told Zeema he'd better start working on how the fuck he was going to get a truckload of coconuts in January.

Me and the Prince made the walk to Main and the Roussell Building. Oh, along about two, two thirty, three o'clock.

Didn't have to break in the building. No locks on the doors them days. That's what they're called. "Them days, them days." No bars, no locks, niggers on Landry, crackers on Main, no drugs, only alcohol to keep you stupid and put, crackers stupid and put in Main Street bars, us stupid and put in Landry Street bars—sweet, sweet time. That's what they call the past, right, Jay Pee—sweet, sweet. Shit to that.

Anyways, there was me breaking into a place wide open with no locks on the door. Me a man in competition for business with a woman called the Princess of the Palace. My accomplice? The son of the Princess. The little bald, neat, bravery-medaled, Purple Hearted son of the Princess of the Palace.

And this accomplice of mine, he was nervous and sweating, tiptoeing all gawky across the lobby floor like it was a hollowed peer-ee-mid in Egypt. And he be saying, in a tiny whisper, tiny-tiny mostly breath whisper, "Ain't going to make it, ain't going to make it. Got to find me a place to fall."

And this little accomplice of mine, I be telling him to climb up on my shoulder cause we can't find no chair. "Take off your shoes," I be saying. "Climb up," I be saying. "Take a hold the sword."

Then his shoes were off. And know what I saw? Saw in the dim light coming in from outside from the street, saw that this little accomplice of mine, his feets be powdered. Now this powder, it be all over his socks and my accomplice he be making little clouds of powder on the lobby floor everywhere he stepped.

"Take off them stockings and climb on up, Prince."

"Ain't going to make it, ain't—"

And then me, the new Lion of Landry, what I've got? Got this bald, homeboy little man with a bravery star from the war and powdery feets stuggling all over my body. His face in my belly, his foot in my belly, his belly on my face. Once he even be standing with his feet on top my feet and his face in my neck like we be dancing at the pharaoh's own party.

"Ain't going to make it, Lineman. I got to fall."

When the Prince said that, that meant he was about to have him a fit. And when he finally climbed on up my shoulders, them little feets and powdered toes wiggling under my nose, he fell off like a couple hundred pounds of beanbag filled up with crack corn. Landed just like a bag on the lobby floor. And along with him, came on down the sword.

Where it landed? Wish I could remember. Maybe on him, maybe next to him. Maybe even on his face. I know what you're getting to, but that's the future, Jay Pee.

Then I was reaching for the sword and I saw him. Still in a shadow, in a hat. Roussell. He'd been watching us struggling. And I was mad, powder feets by my nose, you understand. Me, the Lion, you understand?

So I slipped that sword out the scabbard. *Cree-sickkk*, it said, singing on out. And I said, my voice an echo like a roar on stone, "I'll cut your head fucking off, Pharaoh, you don't come out in the light."

Then Roussell was gone. Like into his shadow. And I was dragging a sack of corn and a sword out behind me into the night.

More Bottom Boxes

Most of the Marquis family I have met or have known through reading have been careful with their use of the word *history*. My husband's grandfather Richard Francis Marquis told me there was danger in the modern tendency to use the word's *life* and *history* interchangeably. There is a relation in the two, he said, because after all, the simplest definition of history is "a record of life lived." There is a relation, too, he said, because both life and history have "a smaller sense and a larger sense."

All Marquis chronicles before the twenty-year gap were records of Marquis experiences, and therefore could be called "histories"—but only in the smaller sense of that word because Marquises had never attempted to find patterns in their experiences that could be linked to larger patterns of events that are found "in every child's history book." They hired me and the other "research-trained, college-validated historians one remove from experience" to make that link.

A Marquis, I was told, would find that job distasteful. A Marquis does not go out seeking a link with history before or after an event, just as a Marquis would not sit at table with others calculating—before, during, or after—how the meal fits into the larger pattern of human dining. When Marquises write of their experiences, they write to preserve life in the smaller sense, days that were "freely and honestly" lived. The fact that a Marquis ends up being the center of the events usually found in every schoolchild's history book is only co-incidence. Even writing of these important events, a Marquis seeks only accuracy of detail, blended with the unmistakable, opinionated Marquis tone.

Before *Marquis at the Alcázar: A History*, the Marquis family found no need to relate a Marquis chronicle to any larger scheme or pattern of events. They simply recorded the details of an event as they had known them to occur, sometimes addressing the reader directly, all the while commenting, of course, on "good and evil and all those other most unobjective ideas one finds occasion to wonder about as one moves the narrative."

After *Marquis at the Alcázar: A History*, the family asked me to continue working as their sole ghostwriter because, they said, their apprehensions were "not soon going to retire." Indeed, they were certain now that the "new-age" use of the phrase *objective historical truth* had become so entrenched that readers would no longer accept as "truth" the writings of those who had taken part in the event. The family still wanted their chronicles to be read, to be considered with dignity "into the new age." But they were "permanently consigning the dreadful and dirty business of history," of a link to "the studied patterns of history in the larger sense," to me.

And so another question arises. Why is my husband, a Marquis, in the previous Lineman interview apparently trying to connect with history in the larger sense?

After the event on the reviewing stand in 1963, my husband went about the business of preparing his chronicle, tape-recording the people of the town, taking notes on his yellow pads, researching, drawing maps. But sometimes as he did, he attempted to make all of the connections he could between life and history in their larger and smaller senses, between the day-to-day and the history book. He also tried to include in his description of a person that person's awareness of these connections.

In the previous Lineman interview, for instance, my husband asks Lineman about President Truman. Lineman avoids or seems to break himself away from any knowledge that could be called historical in the larger sense.

In his notes, my husband labeled Lineman, by example and by Lineman's own definition, as being connected only to the day-to-day, living to eat, making what Lineman considers "enough money." There are many people like this in my husband's notes. There are others—like the Marquis family, like the Reverend Stillman Bowman—who seem to live life day-to-day, but who nonetheless are sometimes aware of their connection to history in the larger sense. And there are a few—like those whose faces are in relief on Lineman's coins— who come to a point where they realize that any of their actions are history-book actions, parts of patterns in the larger sense.

As my husband knew, by January of 1948—the month Lineman and Zeema were walking the low flow—President Truman's Committee on Civil Rights had released a report, entitled *To Secure These Rights*, that went so far as to say that equality of the races could not be achieved without abolishing segregation, and went further still to ask Congress to implement some of the committee's thirty-five recommendations, which included abolishing segregation in the armed services, in public conveyances, in public schools, in housing, and in places of public accommodation. The authors of the report said that "it is a sound policy to use the idealism and prestige of our whole people to check the wayward tendencies of a few of them," and suggested that federal financial assistance be denied to any public or private agency permitting race discrimination.

This report could have been just one of the many written by nonpolitical leaders—northern industrialists, labor leaders, a few southern liberals (such as the Sanderling family and the Marquis family), many editors, professors, lawyers—who were involved in what one historian has called the "mid-century assault upon the Southern way of treating the Negro." But Truman, the Democrat son of a Confederate soldier, in a somewhat militant State of the Union Address, followed by a "message a week" to the American people through the winter and spring of 1948, asked Congress to implement some of the provisions of the report in order to "realize the promise of the Declaration of Independence for all Americans regardless of race or color."

To the southern Democrat minority in Congress, the proposals were "the program of the Communists" and the northern wing of the Democrats was controlled by "an organized mongrel minority." Senator Sparkman of Alabama said that southerners were "so bitter" they would never accept Truman as a candidate for president at the Democratic Convention scheduled for Philadelphia that summer.

The chronicles of my husband's oldest brother, Geoffrey Marquis—the three books now called *The Southern Chronicles*—are an account of Geoffrey's experiences from 1948 to 1962 with the events that are a part of what is now everywhere labeled the civil rights movement in the South. The first of Geoffrey's three books, *Marquis at Independence Hall*, was the third Marquis chronicle to be subtitled *A History*. Written with footnotes and with the aid of another ghost-writer, it begins by detailing the "dump Truman" movement at that Democratic convention of 1948, and goes on to describe the nomination of Truman, his fighting acceptance speech, his special-session "dare" to the Republican-dominated Eightieth Congress, and the formation of the southern splinter party known as the States' Rights Democratic party, or the "Dixiecrats." Geoffrey was at that Democratic convention in 1948. Geoffrey also rode and sweated with Truman on Truman's "whistle-stop" train; Geoffrey got pelted with tomatoes while following the Progressive party candidates into Birmingham.

In the previous Lineman interview, Lineman did not respond to my husband's reference to Philadelphia and the Democratic National Convention. But there were people in the town who were connected with these larger events.

One, in his way, was Nolan Roussell. The other was the Reverend Stillman Bowman.

Though neither my husband nor I ever got to interview Bowman, my husband's research indicates that Bowman went to Philadelphia in the summer of 1948. My husband concluded that the "mysterious Negro with the circling hat" mentioned in Geoffrey's first chronicle is Bowman (Geoffrey saw this man at the convention and also on Truman's train headed south). My husband also concluded that President Truman got his idea to call the special session of Congress on Missouri's "turnip day" from a discussion the president had with Bowman.

One of my husband's first projects after he returned from the town to New Orleans in 1948 was to help Geoffrey organize the notes for *Marquis at Independence Hall*. My husband had missed the Democratic National Convention because he preferred to be present at the birth of our second daughter, after which I stopped being the "objective ghost of the family." My husband stayed in New Orleans to handle the day-to-day suits for the firm of Sanderling, Sanderling, Marquis, Sanderling, and Marquis, and together he and I lived life in the smaller sense, in the manner of a small family in our station with our station wagon at that time and that place.

Landry and Main

Interviews with Lineman, Lineman's brother Emmon, Lineman's sister Angelle, and Palo the mortician indicate that during the weeks before that first Carnival in town, the following occurred: Near noon every day after the theft of the Roussell Building sword, Lineman walked alone to the corner of Landry and Main. He was there, on the corner, when his family attended the next Sunday's services at the Reverend Stillman Bowman's church—an old warehouse in an overgrown field across the Great Perpendicular from the Palace Bar.

Lineman was still on the corner when, during the meeting following those services, the Mondebon Zulu Landry Street Carnival Club met for the first time in the Johnson grass and dandelion behind the church and officially elected Zeema Steeple as King Zulu I. Zeema, who was supposedly traveling to the French Market in New Orleans looking for coconuts, sent his "royal representative," Prince Albert Willis. Willis, with the Roussell Building sword scabbard in his belt, accepted the nomination for Zeema and then excused himself, making it back to Bowman's office with the help of Emmon and Palo; there he collapsed "down, cold-sweating down, into one of them fits of his on the ice-hard floor."

Bowman divided the tasks of parade making into committee work. In her interviews, Angelle remembers there were committees for cutting and keeping the field behind the

94

church; for gathering and dying feathers for Indian costumes; for the design and stitching of those costumes; for making flambeaux; for decorating Zulu's float—cardboard and bunting around a borrowed rocking chair on a borrowed truck; for drawing plans that designated positions for lining up behind the king's float.

And there was a committee, chaired by Bowman himself, for "retention of order throughout, lest we be judged out of order." This last committee had the assignment also of walking house-to-house along Landry letting everyone know of the parade, its route, and its "peaceable intentions."

Angelle does not remember having seen Zeema at any of the meetings, which were going on every evening as Mardi Gras Day approached. The Zulu Float Committee began sending anxious notices through Prince Albert that the throne was ready and Zeema was needed for a fitting.

Lineman continued his watch—napping, smoking, eating in the noon sun, and waiting for the "buckra turtle" Roussell.

Yeah, he came, Jay Pee, finally. He came.

I can't say how many days I spent standing and waiting. But I can tell you I expected to see a black shadow-ghost out the red-blood peer-ee-mid in my cat's-nap dreams. When he came, he was just another white man, but—

Hold on, Jay Pee, hold on to yourself. No, I don't remember the day exact. I was napping, leaning on the sharp corner of the furniture store with my face facing toward the oaks and the Roussell Building. I snorted. My eyes open up. And I saw this white man in a gray suit coming down the banquette. Gray suit, gray hat, strolling. Tipping his hat, you understand, to a him or a her. Closer he got, the more I saw just another white man, skin the color of those that live in shade, those that bring their shade with them under hat brims.

But not a ghost, Jay Pee, not a ghost, but neither was he one of the people he be passing by.

No, nothing special, you understand. No square shoulder, no round shoulder. Not tall, not short. Nothing worth stealing. No grace in the walk, no lumber in the walk, no shift in the walk. Hands out of pocket, in pocket. Nothing special.

"Mr. Lineman," he said, looking at me, smiling, not smiling. No, didn't look at me like a white man looks at nigger, colored, Negro. I didn't get that feeling, you understand. He would've looked at you and your white-Charlie face the same way.

Then he spell my name, "L-i-n-e-m-a-n," and he tells me, "That is how you spell your name on the sign outside of your establishment. But you are the son of the Lion of Landry. I remember your shape as you stood in the shadows."

There I was, ready to talk, but there was kind of a stun on me. We both knew ourselves from shadows. Equal, you understand? Stun.

"And I am called Roussell. But I am fond of 'Pharaoh' now."

He was waiting for me to talk, and I couldn't even get a *motherfucker* out my mouth.

"I do not want you to think at all about what brought me here to you," he said. "I have atoned." That wasn't the first time I heard that word, but we know what is significance about it for me now. Like how many people, Landry and Main, be walking at any given time, atoning?

Anyways, "I have atoned," he said, "am still atoning for that mistake I made that night on Emerson. I am taking great care of all those people who were affected in any way by that night on Emerson. I am taking care of this town, if you will."

If you will. There I was standing stun in daylight, listening to a man *taking care* and *if you will*ing.

And it was them *if you will*s finally helped me get a *motherfucker* out.

"You motherfucker," I said.

No, Jay Pee. He didn't react to them words. No shock. No not-shock. Kind of took the fun out of motherfuckering. He kind of was looking at me in the reflections of the glass window in front the furniture store. Then he turned and lifted his face. No marks, no red veins on the end of his nose. No big nose, small nose.

"Mr. Lineman," he said. "Both of us know how we arrived at this point. I know you want things from me. I am no monster as you may have suspected. I have watched over two families in my time. I outlived one wife who gave me a son. I married another woman and acquired all of her family in the bargain." Then he went into about his "second family on Emerson." How hard he'd been working to keep everything at order. He'd given them a lots, he said, and in the same ways he gave to them he could give to me. "I can give *things* to them, *things* to you," he said. "Shall we begin?"

Things. He said every letter, clear, maybe more clear than a usual person. And then we began, bartering on the corner.

He called us two businessmen. No, not white to nigger. Didn't get that feeling. Two businessmen. He could arrange to allow my *establishment* to reopen. He could *assist* in . . . *secure*? That's the word, *secure*. *Secure* its continuing. The bail bondman part no trouble either, he said.

Then he asked me if he had my *list* correct.

"Angelle," I said.

"Yes, your sister. You see, I did read your list. You want things for her, just as I want things for my family. My son, for instance, my son by my first marriage, will one day be king of Mardi Gras, just as I."

I said about my sister Angelle wanting to be a teacher.

"A school-board issue," he said.

"She got her a year in teacher school."

"A school-board issue, I said. I could arrange it with or without the teacher school. Simply a school-board issue, nothing to do with education. Anything else?"

I started to tell him I didn't answer questions, but we was in the sun now. Kind of equal in a way that made me feel creepy. What was this man? And what was it making me feel all of the sudden like the Lion?

I fought against this equal shit. Didn't want this kind of equal. We weren't really equal, were we? Not after all I knew about him.

"Emerson," I said.

"Mr. Lineman. That is not what has got me here. You must understand this. There is no hole, as you say, on Emerson. I have taken care to that—"

"The swimming pool? How you dig that big hole without nobody discovering what was in the little hole?"

"Shall we say I redug the little hole myself? I asked your father to do this for me, but he refused. I had to redig, had to carry the contents to my tomb in the cathedral graveyard. Then I had the swimming pool put in. As you say, a big hole. And so there is no longer any little hole. There is a swimming pool. There is you. There is I. There is this town."

Then he went on and on explaining about the town, using *kingdoms* as examples. He said the whole of our country, the U.S.A., is divided into two kingdoms: North, South. He said the South is itself divided into two kingdoms—he didn't have to name these two for me. Every town in the South follows this model. Every town in the South is also divided into two kingdoms. Okay, I'll say it for you, Jay Pee. Two kingdoms: colored, white. And that's how, through his explaining, we arrived at Main and Landry.

Then, following the same sense, he came to the Princess and the Palace. It was a third kingdom. Something that did not fit in the model. What it came down to was that both of us wanted the Palace shut, the Princess gone.

"The lines between the kingdoms—do you not see, Mr. Lineman?—support the model. The lines must be clearly etched. Landry, Main. Nothing in between. All of us on both sides must understand this. No gumbo kingdoms."

Funny, Jay Pee, but I was understanding him, like right

out my dreams type of understanding. What all of us understand. You know, North-South, that shit, you understand, but not the way you live it, but the way you talk about it. Just the facts of it. Not magic kingdoms. But how you talk about a magic kingdom the day after you dreamed the magic kingdom. A word makes it real. Funny, huh, Jay Pee? Even talking about it now I feel funny. This man, nothing-special white man, made me feel like we kind of were isolated apart from all the other walkers passing us by.

What you're asking that for again, Jay Pee? Trumans, Congress? I've got a feeling Roussell he might've known about all of that. But it was like all that not as significance as what we were doing, him and me, on the corner of Landry and Main. Or maybe the one was the other. I don't know, you understand. Don't want to know.

"And thus," Roussell said. "And thus, here are we, two businessmen in that frame. The little holes that we dig for ourselves each day are not as important as that frame."

Frame, he called it. I had a feeling he was choosing his words. But I didn't get the feeling he was talking down. What other feelings I got? Nothing from him, ghost, not-ghost, you understand? I don't know, you understand? Just the feeling in me that I was separate from all the passer-bys.

"And now for *my* list," he said.

Of course I was going to turn down the first thing out his mouth, Jay Pee, whatever it was. Still fighting him, you understand. Wanted him to know he wasn't in the listing position. But there I was, getting everything I wanted, and more than the platefuls of connection to Main my daddy was talking about, more than a full saving box. Kind of like a key to the kingdom, one of two keys. A dream key, Jay Pee, that was getting realized into a real key, right there in the sun. Shit, don't make no sense when I say it, but it was as much sense back that day as the sun.

Anyways, like I said, I was going to have to turn down the

first thing he asked for. Just to turn it down, you understand. But, but after that . . .

"The sword," he said.

"No," I said.

"That sword represents . . . it is not my sword. It came with the building. It represents those things that are more important than holes on Emerson, something that cannot be destroyed even when its origins are vaguely connected to us."

I was following, Jay Pee, believe me or not. Like I was fully attentioned and smart as anything. After all, I'm the man stepped on a plate for my daddy in a gravehole. Still feel the vibration of that plate on my foot-sole sometimes. Plate, sword . . . kind of smart, ain't I, Jay Pee? Thanks, man. I don't never take your smile as a down-to-me. We all smart in our way, right? Enough of this, enough. Don't want to get too romantic under the silvery nail holes here.

"No," I said again.

"So be it. I am willing to show you I am willing to give up quite a bit. But I must ask again."

"Don't ask. No sword."

"Very well."

And I got a feeling, here, Jay Pee: it *was* very well with him when he said "very well." And I got the feeling he figured I was going to turn down whatever he asked first, so he put the sword first, you understand. Then I had another feeling: whatever came next was his.

He took off his hat. Squinted to the sun. I saw little purplish beads of color in the eyeslits. His hair was oiled without a smell. He looked up at me.

"This mockery of Delos must be stopped," he said.

He said that kind of with the same tone as every other word out his mouth. But it was a shout, kind of, by the timing of how it came out his mouth, you understand? He put his words out in a certain order, like he'd been considering the order they would come out with every step he took from the Roussell Building to me. The beat in his walk was the beat of his considering.

I stood quiet.

"You may be needing some cash," he said. "A loan for reserves, for other necessities."

"Ain't borrowing money from you. Ain't answering your questions."

"Understood."

And it was like we had a understanding. I heard that word of his and no others. The way he said it, you understand. Like his teeth touched every letter his lung breathed up, *un-der-stoo-d*. Then he said, "But we must think on this. Go home, Mr. Lineman. If we have an agreement, we need see each other but rarely. I will know by your action if we have an agreement. I will send you cash capital. Not a loan, as we have agreed. I owe your father and thus you for a long night of work. I was not very good at that kind of work, I am afraid. It addled me for quite some time. I hope I never have to call on you again for work of—"

"Go on with the cash part."

"I will send this capital to you and something else, a sign, that will show you I am keeping my side of the agreement. The sign will serve as a shake of the hands and the sign will reassure you for the . . ."

"Future," I said.

Then again I stood silent.

He put his hat back on, put it right back at the angle and tilt with no accent of pressure on any finger, you understand. Then I saw his lips for the first time, tightening up, not enough to crease a cheek, but enough to be a smile. Comparing him to us, that must've been the same as us peeing on ourself with delight.

What you think he said, Jay Pee?

No, not *look a here* or nothing like that. He said, "history." And standing separate from passer-bys, shadow to shadow, I understood a word.

Pootin' and Bleedin'

I can picture that night: winter in south Louisiana; across the Great Perpendicular from the Palace Bar, a field behind a warehouse that would soon look like a church; in the warm mist between cold fronts, two men in shirt-sleeves. One of the men, the son of a man who had once been called the Lion, climbs onto the bed of a pickup truck and sits in a rocking chair decorated to resemble a throne. The other, the son of a singer named Ragtap, is peeling with a pocketknife the skin from what could be, in the diffuse light, an apple or an orange. Finally, after minutes without a word, the singer says, "Pootin' and bleedin'."

What follows is my transcription of the words on the next-to-last Lineman tape.

I came on Zeema in the field behind the Reverend's rang-shackle chapel. Sticky night. The Reverend, he'd been keeping the weeds tall along the edge of the field, you understand, like a curtain so nobody could see in to what the Carnival club was doing every evening. Before I came on Zeema, I came on two tracks through the curtain of weeds where the big wheels of a something like a dumptruck must've smushed the grass down. I followed the tracks to the middle of the field to the Zulu float—a rocking chair on top a pickup truck.

And this be fact, Jay Pee. Zeema, he was standing with his foot up on the edge of a pile that was tall as he was. A pile of round things. And he got one of these round things in his hand and he was making a long circle-peel.

I climbed on up the pickup and I sat myself down on Zulu's throne. Didn't say a word. By then I'd had my fill of words for all my life. In my mind, sitting up high above everything, that was like saying everything I had to say to Zeema. *The kingdom mine that I want it.*

I was hoping that Zeema would catch on to all this and he'd just take the smushed track through the weeds and disappear forever. But he didn't.

"Pootin' and bleedin'," he said.

"What the hell you talking about? What the hell you doing?"

Zeema started explaining to me he'd been in New Orleans, singing a few gigs. Between gigs, he'd been in the French Market trying to get a hold of a truckload of coconuts.

"Couldn't get coconuts," he said. "But I got some turnips."

Well, I rocked back with the force of my laugh, force kind of hitting me from the front, you understand. The rocker chair flipped over. My legs be flying. I be falling over the side the truck. All the while I be laughing, seeing in my head the Carnival Turnip Committee dabbing gold and silver paint, and the Lineup Committee making sure nobody got more turnips than the next man to throw to all the people lining up on Mardi Gras Day, and all the people lining up with their childrens on their shoulders yelling up at people on the float, "A turnip! A turnip! Throw me a turnip!"

And Zeema, he be laughing, too, eating turnips with a hand he'd cut with his own pocketknife. We be laughing cause we understood what's so all-sure ridiculous about living sometimes, fucking living. Doesn't take smart to see ridiculous when it hits you full force from the front. Then the laughter kind of calmed and I was sitting on the pile with Zeema, eating, not bothering to peel, devouring, tasting turnip, pepper and sweet, and tasting the dirt of some farmerfield, gritty and sweet.

"You made your deal, Lineman, didn't you?"

"More than I want. I can't explain it, Zeema, but all you

see around you, far as the eye can see, is mine. Landry mine."

"And you're taking it?"

"It's a steal."

"And the Palace will be gone."

"Take a sniff, Zeema. You smell anything? Bay leaves? Sassy-frass? The gumbo's good as gone."

"Or something like that."

I didn't explain it all to Zeema. He didn't want to know the details. Then I was asking him again to stick around, sing in my place. I could give him money he never dreamed. But Zeema didn't dream of money, living beside the Palace like he had.

"No," he said. "Time I leave. Daylight's coming. You'll have to settle with the Reverend."

"Got that figured. He's a greater-gain man. I'll offer him to remodel his warehouse so he got him one hell of a little chapel, maybe throw in a dump-truck, dump-truck-and-a-half load of clamshells to keep his back field smushed down. Something I learn from you, Zeema. Reinvest enough in every game for everyone to profit."

"Something like that."

"Where you going at from here, Zeema? Going to your woman and your child?"

"I hope."

"You ain't going to give me that courage shit, are you?"

Zeema didn't answer my question. He waited till a space long enough for an answer went by, and then he said, "You know, Lineman, it was close there for a while. You said once I was an up-to-a-point man. Soon as a man trusts me, I can't do him in. For a while there, it was close. The Prince was starting to trust me. In a few days the whole of Landry Street would be trusting me. Yes sir, close call, Lineman. Close as I ever came."

"Enough of this shit," I said. "In a while we be kissing each other on a pile of turnips making blood babies. I got a kingdom to run and the end of the world to wait for."

But look a here, Jay Pee: your tape's running out. You change your tape. I'll take a nap. Then we'll finish up for good.

Gold, Enamel, Pulp . . . and Two Diamonds

Zeema left town that night, stayed away for another fifteen years. My husband and Zeema returned to the town the same year, 1963—the end of A.D. 15 in another reckoning.

According to Lineman's brother Emmon, Lineman spoke to Emmon the same night he said good-bye to Zeema in the misty field. Lineman told Emmon that the savings box would be filled soon. He told Emmon to tell Angelle about the teaching job and to tell Angelle to make an offer to the Reverend Stillman Bowman about forgetting the Zulu parade in exchange for a contribution from the family that would go to remodeling the church. Bowman, in his sermon the next Sunday, explained "sacrifice" and "the greater glory" to his congregation. Soon the shells would arrive and the field would be "smushed," covering the spoor of Zulu for fifteen years.

Sometime during those days before the Reverend's Sunday sermon, Lineman received a package from Main Street. Emmon was eating with Lineman when the package arrived, by mail, addressed to "Lineman's Place, Landry Street." Inside there was money, and wrapped inside the money a policeman's badge with the letters T-h-e-r-i-o-t etched across the bottom.

What of the gold tooth in the matchbox? In one of my husband's interviews, Emmon takes a guess. Lineman did not attend the church services that Sunday the Reverend accepted Lineman's offer. Lineman walked to Main Street instead, telling Emmon before he left he was going to a "bakery, then a white jewelry maker." About two weeks later, Emmon says, shortly after the town's first Carnival, Lineman began wearing the well-known Lineman ring. From that day, the gold lion's head on Lineman's little finger glared with half-carat diamond eyes as Lineman napped, snorted, and dealt.

After that, for fifteen years, Lineman rarely left Landry Street. He stopped visiting the process parlor on one of the streets perpendicular to Landry and let the close ripples he combed over his head grow to a thick mane of black that he swept down and back over the sides of his head and neck. He hired lawyers whenever he needed to contact the world beyond Landry, and he never used the same lawyer twice.

For fifteen years also, Lineman's connection with Main Street seemed to work on its own. Each time the city cops closed his place on gambling charges, Chief of Police Theriot saw to it that the charges were dropped. Each time Lineman requested a sales-tax exemption, it was granted. The early morning raid on Lineman's only competition, the Palace Bar, came a week after he told the town council—in a letter worded and typed by a local lawyer—that the sidehouse beside the bar was a brothel, "unfit for any Street of any color in any place with children." Nolan Roussell and the other Main Street businessmen cosigned a similar letter.

Lineman had business cards printed months before he went to a lawyer to get the lawyer to do whatever it was lawyers did to get their clients permission to open a bonding company. Below his name, on each card, were the words "Mondebon Parish's First Negro Bail Bondsman."

The sign outside Lineman's place changed also. After the town extended the streetlights over Lineman's tin roof, the words "Where Your Day Is Always Night" became "Where Your Day and Night Is Always Night."

Doctor Einstein and the Fiddlers

One of the footnotes that I added to the fifth edition of Berman Marquis' *Marquis at Nuremberg* mentioned a visit from Dr. Albert Einstein to the New Orleans Garden District home of the Marquis family. I did not go into detail in that footnote, but I believe that the details are relevant now.

Though my husband and I would often talk about the "rotting questions," the implications, of what happened that night of Dr. Einstein's visit, my husband was traveling with his brother Geoffrey and was not present. I was present and pregnant.

My second pregnancy was uncomfortable and often painful for me, and I was upstairs taking one of my afternoon-to-evening naps when Dr. Einstein arrived. I learned later that it was Aunt Lucilla who greeted him at the door. He told her that Berman and he had been corresponding during the preparation of the Nuremberg manuscript and that they had scheduled to meet that day to "tink a little" and to listen to some jazz fiddling in the French Quarter. Dr. Einstein had waited for Berman in Jackson Square and was wondering if perhaps Berman had forgotten about the appointment. Aunt Lucilla called Berman's father down to the sitting room. It was he who gave Dr. Einstein the news of Berman's suicide.

Dr. Einstein politely refused several invitations to dinner until Aunt Lucilla promised him what he had come for—a long European-café night and jazz fiddling. It happened that Duke Ellington was in town, and it only took one phone call from Aunt Lucilla, a friend of Mr. Ellington's, to get Mr. Ellington and the fiddler Ray Nance to also accept invitations to dinner.

At the end of the meal, everyone gathered in what the family liked to call "the closest room to the table" for cognac, cigars, and fiddling. The bowing and laughing must have gone on for a long time because I woke to those sounds and listened in half-sleep for nearly an hour before I finally rolled myself from bed. It took me another hour to make myself presentable enough to walk the three flights down to find the room the family had chosen that night to be the "closest." By that time the music had stopped, Mr. Ellington and Mr. Nance had gone, and the speculation had begun.

The men rose when I entered. Aunt Lucilla introduced me to Dr. Einstein, who was tall—much taller than I had imagined—and robust and tanned. Aunt Lucilla also summarized for me the conversation up to then. She said that she had "trapped" Dr. Einstein into a discussion of the Marquis views on circumstance and history, and that the family had been trying to relate those views to Dr. Einstein's ideas on "scientific time." Somehow, she said, all of this had led to religion and to God.

As I sat, I asked if any conclusions had been reached.

"With your permission," Aunt Lucilla said, smiling at Dr. Einstein. "I believe, Molly, that we—the family and the good doctor—agree that after careful study an event can be known in every particle of its detail. As for God, well, we disagreed as to what that word stands for. Dr. Einstein prefers the idea of—Spinoza's God?—who reveals himself in harmony of all being. He does not much like our family idea of a God who concerns himself with the fate and actions of men. But regardless, even Dr. Einstein—correct me, sir—hopes that there is a mindful push behind the daily happenings of mankind.

"Hopes, yes," Dr. Einstein said. "Who would not hope that?"

"Dr. Einstein was also telling us that his belief in that mindful push, that belief in harmony is what is behind—"

I interrupted her here. I think perhaps my back had begun the deep hurt again. Judging from the way the smiles began to disappear, my tone must have been noticeably sarcastic: "Is everyone here saying that if the great phonograph record of life were played again, the notes would fall into place in the same order as they occurred during the first play?"

My husband, had he been present, would have understood the silence that followed my words. It was only the second time since my becoming a member of the family that I had spoken out during the Marquis after-dinner speculation. The time I had spoken up before was the night I had risen to confront Berman, the night of his suicide.

Aunt Lucilla answered, boldly, for herself and for every member of the family but me: "Yes, my dear, we *believe* this, but cannot *know* this. And I think Dr.—"

"But of course," Dr. Einstein said, "I too. To an extent. It is not certain to say if the harmony carries over into events. But—the word *hope* again. One can only hope this, should not one? As my first wife said often, God does not fiddle with the universe . . . or something to the effect of that."

It was Dr. Einstein who asked me to "ennumerate." Was I, he asked, supporting the idea of thorough randomness in the workings of history?

I answered that I was not arguing for coin-flipping, but that I was saying that beauty could be assigned to the idea of pure contingency in history, and perhaps in evolution too.

"Explain," Dr. Einstein said. "But I must warn you that I have something in me that fights such—Ah, yes, you are the Molly, the ghostwriter Berman mentioned to me?"

"Yes," I said. "I am that Molly."

"Explain," Aunt Lucilla said, comforting me with her smile, "and prepare for battle."

I explained that I agreed that an event in history could be known for every particle of its detail. And although I balked at linking Dr. Einstein's *relative scientific time* to speculations about *historical time*, I thought that some connections could be made in this regard. I talked, while everyone listened, about "atoms of history." I said that if the Einstein/Marquis belief in some manner of determined history were correct, then it fol-

109

lowed that atoms of circumstance would have to group in such a manner as to make the future inevitable.

"This is," Dr. Einstein said, ". . . to the extent that we are speaking . . . is what we must *believe* so, to some extent, even considering free will. You are saying you do not believe so?"

"It seems to me," I said, "that there exist only possibilities until there is the Event. Once there is an Event, then one can travel backward—only then—following cosmic trails. Until the Event there is no inevitability. There is only speculation, only scattered atoms and minds and movements of people. Indeterminate sequence and emphasis."

"But my dear," Dr. Einstein said, "we are born speculating. I speculate for a living. It is to find the proper pattern, the existing inevitable, that I speculate and study."

"But my dear," I said, "when we speculate, all we are studying is our own mind. Only the Event is absolute."

"In history, you are meaning?"

"Yes. And perhaps in evolution. And perhaps—"

"Are you saying, good lady," Dr. Einstein asked, his accent getting thicker as his conversation grew more animated, ". . . and I might agree to some historical extent . . . are you saying zat . . . there is no *is* until the Event?"

"Good gentleman Doctor," I said—a bit too sarcastically this time, perhaps, because Aunt Lucilla and three other Marquises flinched and sighed—"I am saying only that we are involved in fiddling, lovely fiddling, when we speculate before the Event. For us, as far as concerning the possibilities, there can only be the Event. And once the Event arrives it is absurd to even say we have found it. It always *is*. We see it once it happens. And only when it happens can we go back and say with some certainty *will be*. The Event makes time possible for the historian. It always *is*. Everything before it is past. Everything before it *will be*."

"Then, good lady, I say we are not totally out of agreement. All you are saying, for the historian at any rate, is zat only the past is knowable."

"Embarrassingly simple," Aunt Lucilla added.

"I am saying, good gentleman Doctor, these things: That the mind is embarrassingly simple and self-involved. That before the Event we study only ourselves, good lovely fiddlers all. After the Event, all is frozen for us, the 'us' who study. Then all the atoms can be known, but only in terms of the Event."

"And you are also saying, my dear," Dr. Einstein said, ". . . and here is where we are apart . . . zat if we play the record again, the chances are great that the music will be different, that the Event, that new outcomes . . ."

"Yes, my dear," I said, "I am saying that."

"And in history, surely you cannot also tink zat each new outcome is *worth* as much as each other outcome?"

"Yes, I can think this. And I think also that it is for us to struggle with putting worth—"

"Absurd, I must say, good lady. Yes, I must say that. Even I, who do not like to speculate publically of such, must say that. Thank God worth is not ours alone to assign. And as for the experiment of playing the record of our lives . . ."

"It is an experiment we could never attempt. But each alternative Event when traced back would be just as logical through cause and just as ready to be assigned its decency and beauty."

"I might, as a scientist, have not disagreed with tings you have said up to this point. But as a human being who has seen . . . like Berman . . . what have we to adhere to, outside ourselves? There must be that outside of ourselves to adhere to or— No, we cannot, good lady, assign that massive trust to man alone."

"Man and woman alone," I said.

The conversation ended there because Aunt Lucilla slipped

from the velour divan, falling with a thump to what she called her "derrière quelle abundante," taking blame—even before she made it completely to the floor, her snifter still in hand—with a smile for her "oblivious overindulgence." We laughed, all of us, and then listened as Dr. Einstein improvised on a fiddle—one of two Stradivariuses in the house—brought into the room for him. I remember, during the fiddling, as my baby moved in my belly, I winced aloud at the pain in my back. I remember also the release of joy I felt after having slept from afternoon to evening with the fear that the movements and pain would stop.

There was quite a crowd of Marquises saying good-bye to our visitor at the door. Aunt Lucilla was apologizing to Dr. Einstein again for "our usual and overbearing" eagerness. "We like to discuss such things as tonight," she said.

"As do I," Dr. Einstein said. "Tinking and fiddling together." Then to me, he said, "I can only hope that the atoms of circumstance do not try you to the limits of your tinking." Then, with his big moist eyes on my belly, he said, "It is not much of a world you have enumerated for us to be born into. A man is not so strong nor to be so trusted."

"We, men and women, are still born into it," I said, taking his hand, "and into the task and trusting."

It was then that my husband's father stepped from the crowd, saying, "Trust me, Doctor, she is a decent sort. She began as someone who was merely between hawk and buzzard in our house. Now she is part of us. And lends her fiber to us."

"Ah, sir," Dr. Einstein said, "I do not a minute doubt. And, sir, may I say it will remain a sadness with me I did not get to meet your Berman."

"It is a sadness for all of us," my husband's father said.

I have cited this conversation with Dr. Einstein because it is excellent transition into my husband's chronicle, into the worlds he would call De Plus En Plus and Second Chance after the atoms of circumstance had tried him to the limit of his thinking. For there was an Event on Mardi Gras Day, 1963, an Event frozen in an award-winning photograph. And the scattered atoms were all there on that day: green pills, a gold sword, purple specks on a pistol. And also, the minds and movements of people were there—fathers, daughters, sons, kings, queens, prisoners, moving moss.

The Last Lineman Tape

And there we were on the turnip pile. Remember Jay Pee? Just me and Zeema alone. Not even the smell of the bay and sassy-frass from the gumbo across the street was there with us.

And there on the turnip pile, I had this feeling. . . . I don't like to think about it. Kind of like Christmas, and I fucking hate Christmas. But there on the turnips . . .

I asked Zeema, "You got a question you want to ask me? I'll answer one if you want."

Zeema folded his knife and slid it into his pocket, standing up in the slimy night.

"You first," he said.

"Okay. Why you say *something like that* now, and when the Prince around you don't say it?"

"I'm worse a thief than you are, Lineman. I'm a stealing liar. Those are Prince Albert's words, *something like that*. I'm always stealing a song I heard somebody sing. Been stealing his words and songs since boot camp."

Zeema knew it was his turn to ask a question now. He could ask me anything, you understand, and I'd be answering.

"There was another place I felt safe in once, Lineman. It was as far away from anything as the Palace. My daddy showed it to me . . . Harlem, all the elegancies of Harlem."

That kind of pissed me off, you understand. Here I was, ready to finally answer a question for somebody, and what I got wasn't even a question.

"Ain't you heard, Zeema? Man, ain't you heard? There ain't no place called Far Away."

Then he asked me his question. And what he asked? Asked what got no answers. He put his hands in his pockets, stuck his face out like the mist was a warm washrag.

"Then what is this place, Lineman? Why do our people—anybody—climb out from the turnip fields to get together in places like this? They dance together till daylight and then . . . and what is any place? Half the world is magic, half the world is sense. You understand?"

Those are the last words I heard Zeema say before he left. He left a question, and he left walking away from it. And Jay Pee, those are your last, too: *You understand?*

So put your tapes away for good, now, and listen to me. I got an offer for you, a steal. I can see your colors returning. And me, I'm betting on the future, on teetering to a fall, a full fuckin' fall down to a sleep.

Yes sir, Jay Pee, a real sleep for me. And for you, a steal. And it ain't even the end of the world yet.

Jay Pee's Chronicle

(A.D. 15)

A Place Called Far Away

April 14, 1963
Molly,

 This is the second letter I have addressed to you. The first—the first, I will carry with me awhile. It is a letter you may never need to see.

 I have much to explain, Molly, but I am sure that I do not have to explain to you why I have not returned home, or written or phoned you in my months away. We both knew, didn't we, that I would leave your side sooner or later.

 I am tired of questions—and there is no question I miss you—but I must begin my explanation with one. Do you remember the morning I quit taking note of what my family calls "the daily experience"? I know you were watching me as you always did. I got up before dawn, as usual, two weeks after the funeral. I sat at the oak secretary but I didn't turn on the light; I returned to our bed but I didn't touch you. Taking daily notes was ingrained in me as a Marquis, so ingrained that it took two weeks for the habit to go away, although I quit being a Marquis—what my family defines as Marquis—two weeks before. The summer of 1961, was it? I have never looked back to see what I wrote for those two weeks before I quit. Details probably. Sensations I should have felt—the smell of salt and candles, the taste of the ham that awaited us on our return home. When I left you two months ago, I told you I had received a letter from a man named Stillman Bowman, a preacher in a town south and far enough away from New Orleans. I was leaving, I said, and I did not say when I would return.

When I got to this town, I began taking notes again. Rather than taking the jump everyone must have been expecting, I busied myself again. This should not be interpreted as a sign of hope—more as the idling engine slipping into gear. I will be using those notes and newspaper accounts and photographs and recording tapes to construct my own version of what happened after my return to town. Yes, Molly, call it my chronicle.

I can picture my father now if he were to see these words I have just written. He's been keeping himself busy ever since the night he learned of Berman's suicide. Father's been watching me closely I am afraid. But I can see him if he knew I mentioned a chronicle in a letter to you, his long silky hands tying themselves into knots of delight: I knew James would return to us! Meaning, of course, I knew James would compose himself. Meaning also, God send Berman back to us also, also composed.

But Molly you must not mention my chronicle to anyone, not to Father, not to Geoffrey. I am not sure they would approve of a Marquis chronicle being used as a form of blackmail. Tell them only that you have heard from me. My reasons for this will be clear after you have read.

All I am asking for now is that you do read the chronicle part by part as I send parts to you. Familiarize yourself with what has happened. Edit them for me, order them when they get confusing, tamper with the words at your will to get the distance right. You are very good at getting the distance right.

I have been living in a story, something a Marquis is supposed to be destined to do. The story seems to fit into history in the larger sense, into Berman's story, or one of Geoffrey's. I will send the first of what might be called chapters—unedited—as soon as I finish. For now, I am enclosing a photograph, which you have no doubt seen in many news magazines. Geoffrey, too, has seen it, I am sure, and will no doubt use it in one of his Southern Chronicles. *But Molly the story is not what it seems, although the larger sense may be accurate.*

I am a part of the story behind that photograph. Since the day that photograph was taken—Mardi Gras Day—I have left this town, have gone to Mississippi, have returned to this town.

Today is Easter Sunday. I sat in church, in the white of Easter-tide, sat in all the questions again, the larger sense, the smaller sense. The questions occupied me so well I forgot to do what I had gone to do. I had gone to church again (another Marquis habit I broke seasons ago; there is a beautiful cathedral here) to make an attempt at doing something that may sound absurd. I had gone to forgive God. I can see father now, untying the smooth long knots: James! That statement cannot exist by definition. James—

I had gone to forgive God, something of a promise I made to some-one you will get to know well after you read my chronicle. Had I succeeded, I could perhaps have returned to you, could have busied myself with you. But I walked out of the church doors—into oaks here—still carrying with me in the smaller sense what I understand Berman must have been carrying with him on the Huey Long Bridge after the Nuremberg story was completed.

I did not forgive God, but I did remember another promise I had made. And this promise seems to coexist with an old Marquis notion: to know an event in every particle of its existence, to find and to know no matter how terrible the vision.

I am going to busy myself with this, Molly. I am going to write my chronicle based on the notes on these yellow pads and the research I will be doing. I will send all to you, part by part, and we will sit together one day and make one account. (Remember the day we sat laughing, giving titles to the sections of Geoffrey's first book? Maybe again we can sit in the courtyard near the brick pond I built for—with—)

Molly, help me give this an accounting. I know you will call it an account and not a story. Call it what you will. But help me make something complete and whole.

I am tired of questions. Questions that rot, recrudesce, rot. Could anything have been different had one atom of circumstance been on holiday?

*Oh, Molly, holidays. The Gulf green beyond the beach. How I
have missed you. But I cannot face you yet, dearest.*

*Maybe after the story is over—after the recrudescence of spring—
Molly, dearest Molly—*

James

Mister Pro Bono

I assumed that the letter forwarded to me at home from the
firm was from someone named the Reverend Stillman Bowman. That name and an address on Landry Street were both
part of the letterhead. Undated, typed with difficulty, the letter read "Dear Pro Bono. I need your help. Meet me in court
square. Noon. Saturday."

A rusting paper clip at the top of the page held a foxed
business card with the firm address on one side and the
words *pro bono* written in my hand on the reverse. Using the
letterhead address, I answered immediately telling Bowman I
would meet him at noon as he requested, that I would take
the bus rather than the train. The train station, I remembered,
was fifteen miles northwest of town. I also remembered the
three men who were in the room with me at the time I wrote
those words on the back of the card. I did not take the time
to go through my notes for that period to find the names of
the men, but I knew Bowman wasn't one of the three.

Thus I returned to this town after fifteen years, arriving
late, 1:30 P.M., February 16, 1963, the day before Sexagesima
Sunday. When I stepped from the bus I was approached by
the chief of police, who greeted me without words by offering
his hand. He seemed hurt that I did not also make an offer;
then he uttered—in the flat French accent of those called
"Cajuns" by us who live outside—the first words I heard on
my return to town, *"De plus en plus,"* which can mean "more
and more" or "again," depending on how they are spoken.

Exhaled along with this man's shake of the head and falling shoulders, the words carried with them the burden and disgust of a task repeated, de plus en plus, "it never ends."

I read the name on the badge: Theriot. (Molly, see the enclosed list for pronunciations of common names in this parish; Theriot is pronounced Terry-O.) Theriot, still sulking from my absent hand, muttering "en plus en plus en plus," led me across the Landry Street Bridge, and without word I followed him over the half mile of Main Street one has to walk to get to the court square. Theriot stopped once to talk to a pretty woman in a feathered hat who mentioned the weather, the "false spring."

(Molly, later that day in my notes I would refer to this sidewalk weather report: *between the buildings on my left as I walked Main Street Japanese magnolia and redbud blooming above the banana trees on the bayou bank.* I will send you clippings from the *Times-Picayune* that give weather changes. Add these if you wish, for history's sake, but in my memory and my writing there is only one weather—this false spring, from the moment I stepped from the bus until Mardi Gras Day.)

Not counting Theriot, who departed seconds after the talking began, we were five beneath the twenty-four oaks in the court square that day I arrived. I had never seen Bowman before, although I think I'd heard of him during my pro bono stint in town. A wiry man, Bowman, in his early fifties I guessed, red tones in the umber of his skin.

The other two, standing with Bowman and me, I'd met years before: Nolan Roussell, my landlord, in his sixties now, I was sure, but looking much younger, white skin, no wrinkles; Lineman, a name hard to forget, taller than my six feet, closer now to three hundred pounds but still not fat, looking more like a lion than before, hair a thick black mane. And not with us but among us, slouched on the nearest bench, another man with what looked to be a scabbard and saber roped to his coveralls. I couldn't remember his name but remembered he'd been one of the men with Lineman in my office the day I left the town fifteen years earlier. Bald then also, neatly dressed, talkative.

Like me, two of the men wore suits: Bowman a shiny cinnamon-colored, double-breasted with pads extending like a five-inch shelf over his shoulders; Roussell a pressed gray tweed. Did they smell the bus-line diesel in my wrinkled black? Lineman had on claret-colored, gray-striped suit pants and a white shirt that had been ironed open at the second button.

Two wore hats. During the introductions Roussell's gray fedora with the peacock-green band did not leave his head. Bowman removed his hat, revealing a polished scalp.

Roussell's hand came out to me. I dropped my suitcase, kept my hand. Lineman moved to clasp his hands behind his back. Bowman reseated his hat, clinched his palms at his side.

And the man on the bench, animated, uneasy, watching us. His name?

I spoke first."Reverend Bowman, your letter said that you need help—"

"Didn't send you a letter. But I do need help. I'm the one who got a letter—from you. I sent out other letters—the National Association, *our* National Association, Civil Liberties Union. The only letter *I* got was from you."

"Regardless of how you got here," Roussell said to me, "the Reverend needs your help. He is familiar now with your family's reputation. I accorded him with a biography while we waited here. And you will do for him for now. He represents—"

"The Mondebon Zulu Landry Street Carnival Club," Bowman said. "I have written letters also to the town council and the police jury, the mayor, the sheriff, and the district attorney, as well as the other three Carnival clubs licensed to parade in this town—"

Smiling, Roussell interrupted, "Slowly, please. This must be done correctly so that it not be misinterpreted. I have been entrusted to represent these agencies of which the Reverend Bowman is speaking."

I remembered Roussell's voice from the last time I was in town. Moderate, pleasant. What was in the accent?

Bowman fidgeted but remained silent as Roussell went on. "And Mr. Lineman here beside me represents more than a few of the good people in our Negro community."

Bowman broke in, his grating tenor: "You are no more than a seller of clothes, and Lineman here, in my eyes and the Lord's, is even less."

"Don't you go speaking for no Lord," Lineman said. "You got my family cornered, but not the Lord."

"I stand," Bowman said, "I stand. I stand in representation of the Powerhouse of Salvation Church and the Mondebon Zulu Landry Street Carnival Club. I also stand, stand to represent this year's King Zulu, Ozema Steeple." Bowman turned to me. "And if you work for me, you will be representing all that I have listed and more than I may care to be listing."

I told the Reverend I would consider all of this, but there were questions. I told him again that I had assumed that the letter I'd received came from him.

"Who you?" Lineman asked me. "Something about you I know."

"I need legal representation," Bowman said. "I need it to get me my demand to parade on Mardi Gras Day."

I asked Bowman if Ozema Steeple was in town. I remembered the name *Zeema*. He'd been the third man in my office that day I left in 1948. I'd heard the name since then in the newspapers, on radio.

(Molly, see the articles I've found on Ozema Steeple's career in the 1950s.)

"He has not as yet arrived in town," Bowman said.

"Ain't going to arrive neither, you understand," Lineman said. "A little matter called courage, and that matter Zeema ain't got. Who you that you know Zeema?"

"This is the lawyer James Peter Marquis," Roussell said, "Of the renowned Marquis family of New Orleans." He pronounced the name properly, Mar-kwiss. I couldn't remember how he'd said my name years before. Something in the accent, I thought.

"Jay Pee?" Lineman asked. "That you, Jay Pee? What happened to you? Time got you and your suit all dull and twisted up. You a disappointment, my man. I remember you when you was a steal. You be careful, you hear?"

Of our four voices, I think Bowman's and Lineman's carried the farthest. Though much different in pitch and timbre, they were of equal volume, being easily heard I'm sure by the many people passing by on Main Street and Cathedral Street, both streets about fifty yards from where we stood. Many— on the sidewalks of the streets, the court-square sidewalks and benches—must have noticed us. If I remembered the town, no one listened. But one. On the bench with, of all things, a saber. His name?

According to my notes, I gave sleep another try at 2:45 P.M. that day. Too close to dreams to continue the attempt, I was up by 3:00, filling my notepad with the details of the court-square meeting.

I brought with me, besides my suit and notepaper, the sea-green pills my wife gave me the night before the funeral. I had tried one of them then because my wife handed me one. I remembered that their sea-green sleep came with depth, the depth below dreams. I'd put them away because I'd craved what they gave. I later found that fatigue, the tired past tired, worked just as well.

That first day back in town I craved also, more than I could have known, details, especially the details I was making note of on my yellow pads. Even though I'd had no success with my nap, I thought that I would try sleep again, soon and without pills. Perhaps even if I did dream, these new details finding their way onto my yellow notepad would find way into my dreams as well: oaks and bayou and icehouse.

In the court square I'd told Bowman I would get in touch with him when I decided what to do. I told him that I was familiar with his problem, as were others in my firm and my family, but I had come to town at someone else's request. I would get in touch with him soon. Bowman left without a word, then Lineman. Roussell lingered with me. He asked if I planned to remain in town now that it was obvious Bowman wasn't my client. I told him quite seriously that the Fourteenth Amendment of the Constitution of the United States was always my client.

And wasn't that as good a reason as any to give? Should I instead have said to him, "I've left my wife and and my house and my hand-bricked pond in the Garden District, trying to get as far away as one bus ride could take me?" No, the Fourteenth Amendment would be reason enough.

Besides tired, I was impatient. The last letter I'd read from Geoffrey (Molly, the letter is in the oak secretary; I'd wanted to bring it with me but left too quickly) mentioned that in the eight years since the Supreme Court's 1954 "all deliberate speed" decision, Louisiana had twelve Negro schoolchildren in schools that were once segregated. I used that number—twelve—with Roussell in the court square. (Molly, Geoffrey was of course correct; I've enclosed a photocopy of statistics from a Francis Butler Simkins book.)

I did not use the words *civil rights*. Geoffrey had reminded me in his letter that those words were for the larger sense only, for books, for the footnotes the family paid for, but not for parish consumption. Use *due process*, he'd reminded me, *equal protection under the law*.

"Very well, Mr. Marquis," Roussell said in the court square after we were alone. "Grasp your handle. Follow me." Again Roussell pronounced my name properly, but I started to correct him anyway. Something in the tone and color of his speech suggested an accent, the linger of an accent that remained even after he with apparent care and practice tried to abandon it—like the circle of darker gray that his hat left in his hair after he removed the fedora when we were inside Roussell's Style Shoppe in the Roussell Building.

Roussell offered me the same office I'd had during my previous stay, remodeled, he said, window added. There was even a blanket under the couch. A gesture. *Gratis*, he said. And *compromise*, he said.

"The Reverend Bowman may be an adversary, Mr. Marquis, but he deserves the best representation. Isn't that in your Constitution also?"

I asked Roussell how he'd known I'd be at the bus station. He said Bowman had read my letter to his congregation, had "cried my name out from the pulpit." My name, Roussell said, was "all around and about" Landry.

"And you," I said, "are all around and about Landry through your ally, through Lineman."

"Mr. Lineman is just an interested citizen, an interested Negro citizen who wishes to point out that not all of our citizens of color agree with the ways of Mr. Reverend Bowman."

Roussell then invited me to a party at the Senator's house (Senator Suthon, of course, but no one in Mondebon Parish needed or used any name for him beyond "the Senator"). "You can see the house from your window, Jamie. May I call you Jamie?"

Then I remembered. Jamie. He'd called me Jamie in 1947 and '48 also. Craft. I had to remember to be on guard.

I declined the invitation. I was too tired, but I didn't give a reason.

"Jamie, the Senator himself has asked me to invite you. Your name. I must say, Jamie, I was surprised when a Marquis—as busy as you must all be with the big cities of the South—consented to come here. I was surprised to see you approaching the court square. This town is too small even for the N-double-A people, *his* Association. May I ask why you are here, Jamie? Fourteenth Amendment indeed. Give us a why. Be completely honest with me."

"The office is upstairs?"

"Ah, but you are deeply tired, Jamie. It shows all over you. You are an honest man without even trying. Very well. But would you not be . . . interested . . . as it were . . . Yes, you might want to reconsider the Senator's party. It seems Mr. Steeple will be present, or so I have heard."

In my office, after my first try at sleep, after detailing my arrival in town on the yellow pads, I swallowed a sea-green pill. Before I slept, I closed my entry with these words:

Sleep will come now but what sleep? I must remember to read the name of this potion on the label. What sleep will come if one combines fatigue with the potion of these capsules? A dream of Molly, perhaps, young Molly?

The couch, blue-and-gold plaid. I must remember to keep clear of the anger, the waves.

I will not fail.

Come, young Molly.

I woke rested twice.

The first time I woke I was certain I was still in my dream. A girl—my younger daughter?—dark face, white lace on a white dress, called to me from the darkest green shadow: "Mister, Mister."

My daughter even in a dream would not call me Mister.

"Mister Pro Bono. I couldn't get to you in the court square. Too crowded. Me and Zeema be at the Senator's party. You work free like Zeema said, Mister?"

I turned away, into the gold-and-blue of Roussell's couch.

Was it the pill and fatigue together that made me feel part of my sleep, part of my sleep without fear of what I was part of? A dangerously desirable state.

It was in this state before I slept again that I first sensed the world I now call De Plus En Plus. I felt that in my life up to that time there had been two worlds. One world was the town, the town I had left in 1948. The other was the world that contained all that happened to me after that leaving. Now, reentering the town, I'd stepped into both worlds at once, or rather into the two worlds combined, two spheres fixed at some terrible point I could not comprehend to form my present world, De Plus En Plus. I felt also as though I had another chance somehow, as though I'd stepped back in time by continuing forward, and with one step forward I was blessed with knowledge of what was ahead. I felt this knowledge physically, in the strength returning to my arms and legs.

With me this time in 1963 in Roussell's office, there was one thing I had not had with me in 1948—my anger, the anger I had brought from New Orleans. On the couch in Roussell's office, before I slept again, I knew suddenly that I would have been better off had I carried anger with me back to New Orleans after I left this town in 1948. I should have led my pregnant wife away from the train station with the knowledge that what lay ahead for both of us would be as vile to me in the smaller sense as anything my brother Berman would uncover in the larger sense.

When I woke again I was certain I was not a part of my sleep. I smelled chlorine bleach. I saw the sky still cloudless and blue above the branches. I heard the voice before I saw the gun. And I remembered the name. *Prince Albert.*

Ruck and Rivel

"Prince Albert Willis. That's my name all right. You good, Markee. I hope you continue on good with your memory."

Clasping the gun with his hands behind his back, Prince Albert was turned partially to me, facing the window. I sat up and faced him. My eyes were having trouble adjusting to the light, but I could make out a white paper cap, white coveralls, the scabbard tied with a rope about the waist.

I pointed to the pistol.

"Call it protection, Markee. You'll learn soon enough. Things changed since you left here. Don't worry about this here particular protection. It ain't loaded. Don't think it could pass gas even if it was loaded. Know what I want?"

I mentioned the letter, assuming now the letter was from Prince Albert.

"Don't know nothing about no letter, Markee. Don't remember no card. Barely remember this office. This window here before?"

I asked what he wanted.

"To live on past tomorrow with lots of money. No less than nobody else. You always sleep in your suit now-days, lawyer?"

Prince Albert stepped back from the light. My eyes adjusted to the details. Shovel-faced. Black keen eyes, always darting. And now on his right cheek a swatch of white—gauze and tape—that had not been on his face when I saw him in the court square. Printed across the bill of his white paper cap, the words *Dugas Painting*. His shirt sleeves had been rolled up as far as they would go, about halfway up his biceps: veins on forearms popping. Specks of blue everywhere, cap and coveralls, veins, gun, and sleeves.

Trembling, he removed the cap, and blotted drops of sweat from his forehead with his sleeve. "This look like the face of a dead man, Markee?"

Then I remembered also: the other two men in the office with him in 1948 had talked about Prince Albert's *need to fall*. And I remembered thinking of this man later, years after my younger daughter had been born.

"Epilepsy," I said.

"Oh, you good all right, Markee. Doctor called it that once. The lepsy. I call it a iceblock."

I asked him what he wanted with me if he hadn't been the one who wrote the letter. My impatience must have shown in my voice.

"You not the Markee complete that I remember. Where you get your streak of mean?"

Prince Albert's knees buckled. He fell to one knee. Refusing my help, he stumbled toward the door. "You ain't as safe a place as I thought . . . to fall." As he leaned with his back on the door, his eyes rolled upward. He crushed his cap in his hands. When the irises dropped from behind the heavy lids, Prince Albert said, "Mosquitoes don't suit long prayers."

I knew what to expect next.

And sometimes, clearheaded, without the dull peace of sea-green pills or fatigue, doesn't one always feel a part of two worlds? This man in this world falling, my daughter in another world. And why, why in both worlds must one be reminded, no matter how hard one works at the opposite?

Alone in the room with Prince Albert I remembered my younger daughter, a seizure she'd had after church on Sunday. Still dressed for mass, she joins me on the swing in the courtyard. We talk. She closes her eyes. I lay her head on my lap and keep her warm, watching her until she wakes. She never remembers what happens during the twenty or thirty minutes away. But she accepts the place she wakes to and always seems delighted when she wakes to a face she knows.

Prince Albert woke smiling under the red blanket I found beneath the couch. "Hey, man, big blankets sure do make a man sleep late." He asked me how I knew how to handle *fallers* "without shoving things in they mouths like wallets and wood ice cream spoons." I told him something about first-aid courses I'd taken in high school.

"Yeah, school. You know, they got guys can teach you anything. That guy ever tell you what's it like being under? It's like being in a iceblock. Don't want to die in no iceblock. You writing about me on that yellow paper?"

After I told the Prince to be on his way, he said one word—*Zeema*—the last of the three men who could have taken my business card in 1948. I asked Prince Albert if he remembered Zeema's having taken the card.

"You and that card, Markee. Forget the card, and let's us talk just about Zeema. Things is cooking on Landry. But you know that. Zeema got as close to this town as he's been since 1948. He's been doing gigs in New Orleans. Know what got him that close? Me. Reverend Bowman, he's been sneaking up to New Orleans to talk to Zeema, trying to get Zeema to help him with resurrecting Zulu. You hear about Zulu?"

Prince Albert filled me in on the 1948 plans for the Zulu parade.

"Now why you think Zeema he agreed to come back to town to do this parade? The Reverend been writing to him for two years trying to get Zeema to be Zulu. Nobody answer the Reverend letter. It was me, me that got Zeema here. All my life I been following people. Following Zeema around town. Following Lineman's hands trying to figure out how he cheats me. Now everybody be following me."

I asked Prince Albert what his point was.

"I remember, Markee, laying on your divan years ago. It wasn't this pretty bluish-goldish you got here. But you sure made a man feel comfortable. What kind of a iceblock you been living in?"

Tossing a bundle of bills on the desk, Prince Albert said, "Here, sniff on this."

The money was rolled tight and held together with a rubber band. Each side of the roll had been dipped in the same blue that mottled Prince Albert.

"Yes sir, Markee. Don't know a lawyer that don't understand that. You take me serious now? I been collecting from more people than just Zeema. That cash wad just goes to show you some people taking me serious. Zeema, too, he taking me serious. Been writing letters to him myself, sneaking into his gigs in New Orleans. He's hard to get close to nowdays. Put a mulatto on horseback and he'll tell you his mama ain't a Negress. But it was me, my letters and my presence, that is bringing him back to town."

"Zeema's playing at the Senator's party," I said.

"How you know that? Lineman know that, but he got connection. Not even the Reverend know that."

I thought of my dream, asked Prince Albert if he had seen a girl, a teenager in a white dress on his way up the stairs to my office.

"Teenage girls, business cards. The whole world straining at the seam and you talking about that. Get your mind back on that cash on your desk. All of them bills fifties, twenty of them. This my playing roll for the game at Lineman's tonight. I got four more rolls just as pretty-wrapped as that. They safe in cedar. I could find it in me to give you some of that wad if you—"

I threw the money back to Prince Albert.

"Easy, Markee."

I said, "Go on. I'm listening."

"Fold my titty if you ain't. So listen. I'm leaving town. I'm pulling in money that's owed me. Some will be coming from Zeema just as easy as that wad come in from others. Yes sir, I been pulling it in a hell of a lot easier than I thought. But I got me a little more to collect that won't be so easy. Peoples after me now. I feel it."

I said the word: *blackmail*.

"I like the color of that mail, Markee. But you supposed to be listening. I heard all y'all talking in the court square. Negro this, white that. Might sound like Zeema being brave coming into town to be Zulu. Like he taking a stand or something. Zeema, he don't take stands, Markee. I got Zeema to come here to this town no matter what anybody tell you. Me. And I the one in trouble. Zeema owes me. You know his 'Calm John Wilbur' song, his 'Something Like That' song? He stole them from me. He owe me."

"You haven't told me yet why you're here."

"To be your first client. I started to tell you that till you jump back at me. I remember you work for some folks free. I need a lawyer maybe to get what is owed me from Zeema. That'd be the easiest way. Need you to get close to Zeema for me. Need you to help me stay safe. Kind of a charity case. I remember you was good at charity. But like I said, I be willing to unroll part this wad for your help."

I told Prince Albert I would never represent a blackmailer.

"And I can tell you serious about that. But I got a idea Zeema, he'll settle out of court. I also got a idea you holding something mean in you."

"Find yourself another lawyer. Anything else you want to tell me before you leave?"

"I can tell you what to do with yourself using your pet worm. But do everybody a favor and do a little charity work while you in town. I can get what I want without no lawyer help, but do a little charity. Tell Zeema something for me. The Prince be collecting for what was stole from him. Got that?"

"Tell him yourself."

"The Prince be collecting. Got that?"

"You're selling silence."

"Like the way you said that. Why not call it a settlement?"

"Most blackmailers are selling that. The songs you mentioned—Zeema's stealing. You'll go to the press?"

"The press?"

"Newspapers."

"Yeah, hey, that's a idea. Thanks for the free help, Markee. What Lineman call you? He call you Jay Pee. Something like that. I like that. Well, Jay Pee, do you got the feeling the seams in this place be swelling? You know what? I been trying to get to big stakes games all my life, for the big games in New Orleans. Open me up a place like Lineman's. This time I'm going to make it. To New Orleans, a real Mardi Gras with a real Zulu. I'm leaving after tonight."

I stood up with my anger, but I was sure I had control of the waves.

"Okay, Markee, okay. I thought you could help me. But do everybody else a favor. When you see Zeema, and I figure you will, tell him I'm leaving. Zeema's playing a gig at Lineman's on Landry Street after he finish at the Senator's party. Tell Zeema to meet me beside the Palace after that. Zeema, he'll know what that mean. Tell him be careful for my dog that chews on shoes and pants bottom. Tell him be there with the money I ask for. Tell him at the Senator's party for me. I'm sending others to him with the same message."

I told him that this business seemed to be between him and Zeema.

"It's about more than that. It's about more than the seams of this town. It's about me and my following all my life. See them bills here all dipped in ugly blue paint? I'm not just collecting from Zeema. I'm collecting from other people through my legacy my mama give me. A legacy she give to Reverend Bowman to keep safe for years and years. Know where my legacy is?"

I walked to the door.

"My legacy be safe," he said. "Safe in cedar."

I opened the door for him to leave.

Prince Albert pulled the blanket closer to his face. "Jay Pee Markee, you ain't a calm man no more. Don't make a man feel the same way no more."

I asked him to get out.

Prince Albert sat up. "One, one more thing. I been going under pretty regular now, just like you seen here on your floor. I know the warnings and I careful, but I cutting it close sometimes. I surely thought I'd feel safe around you like back in the old days. Too bad you don't know about Zeema's 'Calm John Wilbur' song. It come from a story I told Zeema about first week we was back in town, still in our uniforms. Remember the war? Japs and Germans. Calm John kill his wife and his baby child after he come home from Japs or Germans. Take away they calm, folks kill."

Prince Albert walked past me through the door. At the stairs he stopped, turned to me with his hand on the bandage on his cheek. "There's some crazy people out there in this town, Jay Pee. You remember the three of us—me and Zeema and Lineman—when we climbed these stairs to get to you long time ago? We going to all be together again, soon, but all of us different. All of us heavier. Heavier by the weight of how long—fifteen years? Things be popping at the Senator's party tonight. And me, I'm making the popping. I ain't following no more. But there's some crazy people out there in this town, Jay Pee, crazy. No calm anywhere about them."

It was just after closing hour when I entered Roussell's Style Shoppe from the rear door behind the stairs. I saw Nolan Roussell and a customer—a bayou Indian—staring at each other in a three-paneled mirror.

Roussell, a head taller than the Indian, had his right hand full of fabric at the back of a white sport coat the Indian was trying on. With his left hand, Roussell tugged down on the lapels and pressed them flat with his palm. To keep a snug fit, he loosened the grip in back and tightened as he adjusted the lapels. A practiced motion.

"Relax," Roussell was saying to the Indian. "It was I invited you inside."

The Indian turned and strolled down the aisle between the racks. Still holding the back of the coat, Roussell followed. At the front door, the Indian dropped his arms to his sides, leaned forward and ran, leaving the coat in Roussell's hand.

Turning, Roussell waved to me. "They make me feel such a gypsy, Jamie." He hung the coat on the rack marked *Sale* and walked to where I was standing. "What is in the air, Jamie. Is it revolution? You are a Marquis. I have read your brother's books about the situation. There are some who believe the uprising will come on the Fourth of July. The Senator believes this. But not in this town. I vote for Mardi Gras."

"You invited an Indian into your store," I said. "Your way to compromise? Are you ready to invite darker inside?"

"Ah, Jamie. Someday we will talk history. I might just be related to you Marquises. That would be an honor indeed. But making and plotting is for those more highly situated than I. I prefer a quiet hand on things."

Roussell hesitated, waiting for me to speak. I started to say something about how I would leave discussion of public property and equal adversarial rights to the hand of the court, something I had said many times before. I remained silent. I did not trust my control.

"Such a gypsy, Jamie. And Bowman is trying to disinter Zulu."

I could not stay quiet to that. "The Zulu Carnival Club has a right to a license."

Roussell smiled as I spoke. "The Mondebon Zulu Landry Street Carnival Club. And do you know the name of my Carnival club? The Mondebon Delos Main Street Carnival Club. Do you see the friction there, Jamie? It has little to do with *a* license, everything to do with license."

"Would Zulu have marched in 1948? Before there were licenses?"

"Ah, Jamie. You have done your research. . . . But enough. May I help you?"

I told Roussell I'd decided to go to the Senator's party.

"To see a man named Steeple? Is he your client, Jamie? Or will the answer to that take more research? But do you see, Jamie? Steeple, a Negro, will be at the Senator's party tonight. Do you see? Compromise already. Some in this town feel it is not dangerous to give in a bit. What kind of people do you think would invite the symbol of the insurrection into their houses?"

I started to ask if any other darker-than-Indian symbols had also been invited. Again I did not trust myself.

"Very well, Jamie, very well. But you do not need an invitation to get into the party, if that is what you are seeking from me. Just your name will do that for you. What history behind that name. But there is one problem: it is a formal affair, tie and tail."

"I would have said it was a costume party. I saw your sign outside that said you had a new costume section."

"Costumes. Yes, I am planning for the future. But I must clear my formal-attire section first. Good business. But things are slow here, Jamie. This is not New Orleans. You have things to learn still. Until then, you will have to trust me."

He laughed with tight lips and guided me with the almost imperceptible touch of morticians and haberdashers to the mirrors. Still laughing, he stood beside me. In one mirror I saw his profile, the arced nose and blunt chin, a profile very close to my father's father. In another mirror Roussell's gaze was resolute. In all mirrors his posture was without flaw, his skin without wrinkles. A Marquis indeed in the world called De Plus En Plus. Although I was taller and twenty years younger, my bearing lowered my unkempt red and gray head to the same level as the gray on Roussell's head. Before I turned away I saw the ruck and rivel beneath my own eyes.

"You have nothing to be embarrassed about, Jamie. You are a fine-looking man, a legendary Marquis and no less.

Who would think you would have such a poor reputation of late in the New Orleans courts?"

Had he found out about the incidents in New Orleans? I had let my anger work hard for me, work *at* people, judges, witnesses.

I tried to retain control of my expression. How much could Roussell see?

"That's all right, Jamie. I am quite on your side. Maybe you are in this town for more than the Constitution as we said. Maybe you will confide in me later. For now . . . costumes, yes. This is not New Orleans. I invented Mardi Gras in this town, knowing top-level locals needed nights of formality. I am not without motive myself at times. Would you care to step into the wing I call Roussell's Formals? I have a clearance going on. Next year, we will go for the costumes. Let me say that for you again: Roussell's Formals. I like the sound of that. The final esses. I will miss the sound of that. But into the future, Jamie. I will call the future Roussell's Pyramid of Costume."

I had time to try to rest after leaving Roussell. I tried it without the sea-green. I dreamed of my dream, of the teenager with the dark face. Then I was with her in the green that is close to black, and the waves woke me.

It was 10 P.M. I was going to the Senator's party in a tuxedo rented in a town somewhere south of New Orleans where the shades of brown progress geometrically generation to generation. Where Princes with sabers slouch about freely. Where sea-green waves . . . (Molly, I know you would caution me here about the poetry.)

I took two more pills. Not for sleep this time. But because the two spheres forming my world had bumped just slightly. Because I had a realization suddenly that this world of new chance was only present because I had knowledge of all that was past chance. Because dream had nudged non-dream. (Forgive me again, Molly.)

Before I left I made this entry on my yellow pad:

I will wrap the Constitution around my waist and stand with Marquis bearing. I will not dream of what I do not choose to dream of. I will not fail will not let the waves of anger wash me toward incident. I will not fail.

Ever again

Molly.

The Chicken and the Fox Paw

I walked to the party that night in my rented tuxedo. As I got to Cathedral Street Bridge I began to feel the extra padding of a sea-green stupor from the pills. But even in that state, as I looked past the bridge to the Senator's house, I could tell that everyone standing in line at the Senator's gate was wearing a costume.

It was as I took my place at the end of that line that I saw her for the first time, a young woman beyond the fence in the Senator's yard. As the line moved forward slowly, I watched her, on her knees beside a camellia bush in the light of the kerosene lanterns lining the stone walkway to the porch. She wore sandals and jeans and a velour pullover.

In the soft sea-green of my senses and De Plus En Plus, I remembered watching my wife in that position, my wife after a garden party, after midnight in wet spring, her dress at her waist, a breast uncovered. I remembered myself on my knees behind my wife touching the small of her back lit by lanterns.

Then in that soft sea-green, I could see my wife in the Senator's yard, could feel the excitement and debility of the need to push near. Then I could see my oldest daughter and my wife as one, and I was connected to my daughter and to my wife in what I can only describe as a single desire of a man husband to women. Then I saw my daughter alone, on her knees in the sand, herself a young woman, eyes on the sand, ear to the water. And I felt empty and sad in the distance only a father and daughter share. I saw these things as I thought them, and I had to sit on the sidewalk, my back to the wisteria wound into the Senator's fence.

When I looked again to the Senator's yard, the young woman was running toward the back of the house, and from there I thought I heard my daughter's name being called . . . Abby.

The cop checking invitations at the gate under the wisteria arbor yelled at me, "You drunk, you? How about standing up before I run you in."

I recognized him before I stood up as the cop who had greeted me at the bus station. Theriot. He recognized me as I stood up.

"Oh, *mais*, you again," Theriot said. "Look, ladies and gentles, at who we have us here. De plus en plus. Just stand your place in line, you, and I'll get to you." As the line moved again, slowly again, I could hear Theriot repeating "en plus en plus en plus."

Just before I reached Theriot, the line stopped. The guest ahead of me, a short man in yellow and white feathers, was having trouble finding a way into his pockets. Theriot told him to stand aside until he found his invitation. The man in the feathers did as Theriot ordered, then said, "But I'm Mayor Poule."

Theriot waved the mayor through without checking the invitation. Before I could say my name, Theriot also waved me through, saying, "Mr. Roussell told me to let you in without checking you. He said you were a member of the band. Why you didn't tell me that in the bus place? Me, I thought you was something, yes. Political or something. And here you are . . . go ahead, go ahead. Just remember your place."

Because I couldn't concentrate fully, I didn't understand what he was talking about, but suddenly understanding Theriot did not seem to matter to me. Some pressure at the back of my neck though, some slightly noticeable push toward my throat, did seem to want to get me to form the words that would tell Theriot about his own place, *checking tickets like a movie madam*, but I said nothing as I passed him and stepped onto the walkway.

As I neared the front porch, a tall man carrying a tambourine and a guitar case strode by. "Sure enough," he said to me, "whitest neck I ever saw." Zeema Steeple had not changed since that time I saw him in my office in town in 1948: strong frame on lean legs, hair relaxed and oiled.

The young woman I'd seen kneeling in the fallen petals near the camellia bush ran up to Zeema. She said her name was Alison. Her voice had the life and lilt of my oldest daughter's voice, a new woman newly out of the age of fun. "I've admired your work, Mr. Steeple."

With her back to me, the small of her back flat and wide, I thought of my wife again. I looked to the young woman's face, but her dark hair, full-wild and wiry, hid her profile.

"Work," Zeema said. "Baby, where you dig up that word?"

Alison grabbed the handle of the guitar case, and Zeema released his hold, touching her arm quickly with the tips of his fingers. Then he let his hand drop to his side. "Hold up, baby. Let's sit and have a smoke first."

Zeema and Alison sat on the edge of the porch, their feet dangling behind an azalea bush. Breathing, listening, I leaned on a green storm shutter. They spoke of Alison's clothes— Zeema called them "weary-traveler, folk-song clothes." Alison wanted Zeema to talk about a singer she thought Zeema might know. (Molly, though I didn't hear the name clearly that night, I have searched the album collection in the parish library. Using the bits of the song titles I recall hearing, I've come up with Bob Dylan.)

141

"Oh yeah," Zeema said. "Burnin'-'em-up kind of boy. Studying me and John Lee and Big Joe. Hell, we didn't mind him for it. That kind of boy. Girl friend name of Susie."

"In the Village? Gerdes Folk City in the Village?"

"You been there?"

"No. I've just heard, that's all."

"You know the words all right, baby. Village. Work. I thought I was the one telling you about the boy. What else you heard?"

Alison spoke of "Blowin' in the Wind," which she said was on the singer's first album.

"What's it about?" Zeema asked.

"About war in general and knowing better."

"Don't recollect nothing like that."

Then Alison mentioned a song she said she was sure would be on the singer's next album, "A Hard Rain's A-Gonna Fall," written, she said, during the "Cuban missile thing."

Zeema, shaking his head and laughing said, "All involved, ain't he, baby?"

"And there's one he wrote called 'Oxford Town,' Mr. Steeple. That's about the James Meredith thing in Mississippi."

"The who?"

"Not your style, right?"

Zeema laughed again as he flicked his cigarette into the azalea. "Style? That like smell? Let's go make 'em smelly."

The two of them stood up. Nearly as tall as Zeema, Alison turned to me and smiled. I saw her clearly for the first time in the light of the Senator's porch: a full mouth, her nose broad but small for her face, little makeup except for some blue on her eyelids. Again, I thought of my first daughter, old enough to shun her mother's makeup for her own selection. My daughter had spoken of the "freedom of the Jackie Kennedy look" on one of our last trips to the beach. She had spoken, too, of the Peace Corps, of "being involved."

"The band is setting up behind the house," Alison told Zeema. "In the patio there. I know where it is."

Zeema turned to follow Alison, and as he walked by me he handed me the tambourine and stopped. "You might be needing this, Jay Pee," he said. "The cop at the gate somehow got the idea you're one of the brothers in the band. You sitting in tonight?"

Because he called me Jay Pee, I was certain that it had been Zeema who'd written to me. I would talk to him as soon as there was time.

"I want to sit in, too," Alison said.

"I can dig it, baby. Got a cowbell somewhere."

"Hey, Mr. Steeple—"

"Call me, Zeema, baby. We close now."

"Zeema. I've got a weird message for you from a really weird cat. Something about meeting him at the Palace."

"Not here, baby. Well, Jay Pee. You got a decision to make about which door you taking. You following us to the back?"

I did follow Zeema. I continued to follow through the door of the mosquito-screened patio to the bandstand—a tarpaulin over the parquetry flooring. A poster taped to the nearest screen wall read Zeema and His Boys. Standing at the edge of the green tarp, I watched the band as they prepared to play. As I watched, I slowly realized that I was wearing a tuxedo identical to those of the band. I realized also that only I, Alison, Zeema, and His Boys were without costume.

Besides Zeema and me, there were six on the green tarp bandstand that night: sitting in on the cowbell and rhythm stick, Alison Belanger, whose skin retained the color of the kerosene glow; Bill Court, who could play clarinet and flute in addition to his alto saxophone—Zeema called him Scutter; Mack Simms, who had a crooked smile and stood behind a bass fiddle; the white-haired James the Same at the piano; Foots Leonard on drums; and singing backup, a girl of sixteen or seventeen in a white dress, whose skin was shades darker than anyone else's in the band.

Zeema called the young girl Laurel, and I did not look closely until I heard her voice answering him. Then, still in my sea-green stupor, I recognized her. She was the girl in my dream, the girl in the white dress with white lace, the girl in my office. I called to her. I thought she heard me, but she did not respond. Because she was the age of my younger daughter, maybe because of my dream, maybe because of the world of More and More, I felt a weakness, a familiar helplessness, and I called to her again. This time my voice was loud enough, louder than I thought, and most of the people on the bandstand turned.

Laurel smiled, "Later, Mister. Later."

During the band's first number, a lively "Honeysuckle Rose," a man dressed as a leopard entered the patio from the house and stood waiting on the parquet at the foot of the tarp. When the music ended, the leopard said to Zeema, "The Senator . . ."

Zeema slid his Gibson guitar over his hip and bent over until his face was closer to the leopard's. In the stark fluorescent light, Zeema's skin looked sallow, rough, and pitted. His fine moustache lent harsh outline, edge to edge, to his thin upper lip.

The leopard stepped back. "The Senator wants it to sound more like Mardi Gras."

"Any particular type Mardi Gras?" Zeema enunciated each word.

"Similar to New Or-leens."

"Hear that, Scutter? New Or-leens. Give this cat a Dixieland lick. They're paying for the spit."

Scutter blew some notes—a familiar swing—on his clarinet, then called to me, sea-green and calm on my stool between Alison and Laurel. "Hey, you. Since you can't keep beat on tammer-reens worth a shit, how 'bout carryin' us some drinks. Looks like the saints be marchin' in all the fuckin' night long."

After I walked into the house to get drinks for the band, I saw Nolan Roussell talking to a chef and a great white hunter. I recognized the chef as Senator Suthon, a man with a reputation as a Creole cook in Washington. The hunter, I overheard someone explaining, was Murphy Stalker, president of the Mondebon Bank.

After the three men posed for a photographer dressed as a silver space-traveler, Roussell joined me at the bar. He was wearing an Arab djellaba and smelled of tonic, the spice he said he'd bought in a rug man's tent in Jerusalem. He spoke with more of an accent now. "What do you think of my work, Jamie? I coordinated—yes that is the word in fashion—coordinated this fete myself, chose each costume for each soul here. Quiet control."

Roussell pointed to the entrée table, where Mayor Poule was taking brisk, short steps to the garlic grits. "Poule may be my best. With his nose, there was no need for a cardboard beak. And the Senator just told me Poule was once a bantamweight boxing champion."

Breathing deeply, I leaned against the bar.

"Some food, Jamie. You cannot forget to eat."

"You're a liar, Roussell."

"About the costume affair, Jamie? I could equivocate, say that all clothes is costume. But that would cause an argument. What is important is that I got you here. Quiet control. The control of those who understand history."

"What costume would you have chosen for me?" I asked.

"You do not catch on as yet. The one you have on, Jamie. I would have chosen the one you have on." Roussell abandoned the accent, but I still detected a trace of an older tongue resting somewhere in cadence. "With your background, Jamie, your family I'm sure would feel more comfortable with those on the patio outside. Am I not right?"

"I thought it was strange that the Senator would invite me here. He used to fish and hunt with my grandfather until—"

"And with the bayou socialist Covington Hall. Yes, I know. But we all grow older and find the line behind which we stand, Jamie."

"My name isn't Jamie."

Roussell laughed. "Eat, my friend. And leave us to our hurts."

According to my notes, it was eleven o'clock when the space traveler snapped pictures while the Senator spoke into the microphone on the bandstand:

"Mardi Gras, Mardi Gras is only a little more than two weeks away, my friends. Though our town's Mardi Gras is only fifteen years old—and let me stop here for applause for Nolan Roussell, our first king, our guiding hand. . . . Though our Mardi Gras is only fifteen years old, I'm willing to go on record in front of the popping bulbs of the national press and say it equals—that's right equals—any Carnival anywhere else in the world. And that includes our neighbor to the north, New Orleans. And I'm here to kill the rumor that says downtown is dying, that our businessmen are divided as to how our parish should grow. I've spoken to Mr. Stalker and to Mr. Roussell on this matter, and there is room for all kinds of growth, downtown *and* the shopping malls on the edges of our town, the past and future together. Yes, my friends, as long as there are oil rigs pumping, there will be blood flowing and there will be plenitude and security for us all."

The Senator turned to the space traveler and raised his glass to the camera. "Put that on your record, too."

The Senator went on about the "threat south past our shores," about how he had been the first to warn the Congress of "Señor Communist Castro." Then, with his glass toward the door that lead to the patio, he said, "And I am here in town for the duration of another threat, the threat of social change praying on the minds of those not fortunate enough to have the learning to avoid the Castros who live among us."

My grandfather would have stepped forward at those words to take a bow, then would have stood erect in front the Senator until the last word. I sat sedate, listening between my two girls on the bandstand. When I looked to Alison, I saw that she was staring at me. I waved to her and smiled, but she did not react.

That was the first time I felt worried for Alison's safety. I'd felt the same concern for my oldest daughter when I'd waved to her on the beach and she pretended not to see me, as though she were old enough not to need to see me.

The Senator introduced the captains of the parade krewes, Iris and Istrouma and Delos. It was past eleven thirty when he presented an award for the best costume of the night to Mayor Poule. I moved to the door to watch.

At the microphone Poule thanked the Senator from the "very very bottoms of my heart." He thanked the Mondebon Main Street Delos Carnival Club for considering his name for membership in their Krewe of Delos. "I realize," he said, "that the first year of my tender in office has been difficult for everyone concerned. But any mistakes I have made are of the head, not of the heart."

Poule caught sight of this year's King Delos in the audience and asked him to come to the stage. Nolan Roussell's son, Barron Palmer Roussell, dressed as an Army Air Corps officer, his pants tucked tight in his calf-high boots, stumbled with his drink to the bandstand. He hugged the mayor. They both crowed and clucked while the crowd of krewes clapped and laughed.

The laughter ended when Poule tried to coax Barron Roussell into breaking tradition by revealing the name of his queen that night instead of on Mardi Gras eve.

Behind me I heard Scutter say, "Even I know a fox paw when I see it. That chicken goose be cooked."

Sure enough, the king of Mardi Gras, Barron Palmer Roussell, Delos XVI, announced his choice for queen to an uneasy Suthon party. He chose the girl in jeans and sandals, Alison Belanger. Then, with his flight glasses slipping from his nose, he fell to his knees and passed out in Mayor Poule's arms.

Nolan Roussell the Arab borrowed a mask from the desperado Zorro to cover his son's face. With the help of a monk, a pirate, and a biblical peasant woman in a lavender shawl, Roussell carried his son out.

I can recount the details of the speeches accurately because Roussell's son was tape-recording the party that night, and I now have the tape. But on my own I remember little. I may have slept and dreamed in my seat. I do recall telling myself that I had to talk to Zeema, telling myself that I did not want to leave the town. And I recall wanting to stay close to the two girls on the platform.

By the time I collected my senses, I was outside in the cool air, following Zeema, Laurel, and Alison to Landry Street.

New, Daddy

Zeema shed parts of his tuxedo along the way, his bow tie on a court-square bench, his coat on the steps of the old high school, while prisoners on the third floor of the courthouse whistled down to Laurel and Alison. On oak roots in front of the cathedral, Zeema dropped his cuff links and studs. He left his cummerbund on one of the two statues of kneeling women beside the ten-foot crucifix in the cemetery shrine behind the cathedral.

At the shrine, Zeema turned right, heading toward Landry on a lane of St. Augustine grass between the tombs. I followed, keeping my eyes on Alison. I could hear her telling Laurel about an orange grove behind her house, and telling Laurel not to worry about anything while she was in town. Older girls, she said, should take care of younger girls. But what else could she say in the world called De Plus En Plus?

Zeema stopped at the last tomb before he got to the gate in the chain link fence. "Hey, you," he said to me. "You think you fooling somebody? You tailing us in your cog-nee-toes?"

The two girls giggled, and I laughed with them.

"Us girls invited him, Zeema," Laurel said.

"Let's rest," I said to Zeema. "I need to talk to you."

I took out a handkerchief that came as lagniappe with the tuxedo, and I dusted off the top of a concrete cross. Across the lane, Alison climbed on a tomb. She lay with her arms outstretched and her palms up to the night sky. She told Laurel that when she rose her body would leave an impression in the black mold on the rectangular slab. Laurel's hands were over her mouth and her eyes were open wide, bright as whitewashed brick in streetlight and moonlight. When Alison sat up, they both giggled again. I wanted to keep listening, watching, a most desirable state.

"Hey, you," Zeema said. "So talk. I got me a gig at Lineman's."

"How do you remember my name?" I asked.

"Dark singers can't have memory?"

"All right, Zeema. The letter. Let's talk about the letter. You asked for my help. You're my client. We've got a lot to talk about."

Zeema lit a cigarette, a Picayune, then leaned on a two-story tomb. When he spoke again he gestured with his hands low, and Alison called Laurel's attention to the orange tip circling Zeema's loins.

"I remember you all right, Jay Pee. The way you used to

be. There's enough of you left to recognize from the old days. But that was then. I'm kind of famous now. What are you?"

"Just a lawyer who needs a client."

"Know what it's like being kind of famous, Jay Pee? The old days, women used to crowd round for a chance to see a legendary cock. Now they crowd round hoping to see the cock of a legend."

I looked to the girls. Laurel had not covered her mouth shyly as I expected. Alison also had not seemed to notice the words.

"No need to protect Laurel's ears, Jay Pee. She ain't scared of words. That's the first thing she taught me."

"The letter," I said.

"Man, I don't know what you talking about."

"The letter."

"Ease off, Mister," Laurel said. "You'll end up finding out what you want to know. The answers, they close as Judgment Day. See how quiet everybody round you is, lying quiet waiting on some answers?"

"Write that down, baby," Zeema said to Laurel. "Write it down."

"I'm talking to this man. That ain't time for composing. Right, Mister? Wouldn't you be kind of pissed if somebody talking to you was thinking of writing down the conversation?"

"I come from a family that believes in that," I said.

"You want to tell me all about 'em sometime, Mister?"

"Forget his family, baby. There is one thing you'd better be writing down. You promised me you'd have a song for Lineman's place tonight. Simple, remember? Bluesy simple. You've been thinking about it?"

"Not really," Laurel said, "but I guess it's time. I'll keep it in my head. You and Scutter can cut to my lead."

"No, baby." Zeema reached into his back pocket and pulled out a folded sheet of paper. He unfolded the sheet and laid it flat on the top of a waist-high tomb. From a front pocket he took a pencil. Zeema lit a match and held it over the paper for light. I could see in the light that the paper was a page of blank staffs for sheet music.

"Make what's in your head permanent, baby. I can't do it, but you can."

Laurel scribbled on the page under the glow of Zeema's matches.

(Molly, I have that page of sheet music. In one of my pockets. Have not enclosed it. Not the time.)

I walked to Alison, who was still on her back on the tomb. One eye, her left, was open.

"Are you all right?" I asked her.

"I can take care of myself now, Daddy." She'd colored the words with sarcasm, and I understood in the cool air the intent of the words. But the last word, the last word echoed from the curved walls of all three of my worlds.

"And anyway," she said, "you're the smashed one."

"I don't understand."

"New dictionary coming, Daddy. You took something stronger than alcohol, right?"

"I took some sedatives, yes."

"You don't need to apologize to me. I took something, too. New apothecary's coming, Daddy. For me and you."

"Hey, you pretty good yourself," Zeema said to Alison as he refolded the paper and returned it to his pocket. "You hear what she said, baby?"

"I hear it, Zeema," Laurel said. "Now let's get to Landry."

Alison jumped down from the tomb and walked to Zeema. The two opened the gate and began singing one of Zeema's hit songs.

At the gate, Laurel whispered to me, "Mister Pro Bono. I thought that was what your name was. But I heard Zeema call you Jay Pee."

"You wrote the letter to me?"

"Sure did. Borrowed the Reverend's paper. I need your help, Mister. There's trouble for Zeema in this town. Strangers with swords."

"Prince Albert," I said. "He wants to meet Zeema tonight."

"Don't you think I know that, Mister? Some danger going on. Strange letters Zeema won't let me read. This Zulu business. I need your help."

In the darkness I heard the voice of my younger daughter. "You all right, Mister?"

"Yes."

"I need your help."

"Yes, I know."

"So I got it, Mister, or what?"

"You've got it. More than you know."

"Just so I know it's free."

Laurel ran ahead to Alison and I followed again.

The Pauper's Pussy

The chant "Zeema! Zeema!" began among the drinkers along the Landry Street sidewalk long before we entered Lineman's.

My notes to myself, written during daylight the next day, contain only a brief description of what I first saw inside: *Black light lit the bar. White shirts and teeth phosphoresced. Above me, pinholes of silver twinkled in tin. And suddenly everywhere the borders of bodies were etched with exactitude. Lost sight of Laurel and Alison. Decided to get to Lineman for some answers.*

In my notes I do not have an entry that might help to explain how, following the bartender's directions, I managed to make a way through the bar and dance hall to the back room where Lineman's poker game was in session. Nor did I note the time it took a tourist like me to complete the trip, although time and accountings for time would soon become the subject of most of the questions I asked before and after Mardi Gras Day.

I had already met two of the four men seated at the table: Prince Albert Willis, slouched in his chair, his saber poking through chair slats; Lineman, eyes closed, mouth open, napping. The two other men—twins, slender and identical—wore madras shirts of similar pattern but different hue; they sat leaning forward so their shoulders would not wrinkle the brown suit coats folded over the backs of their chairs.

Lineman snorted himself awake, looked for his cards first, then saw me. Eyeing my tuxedo, he puckered and kissed the smoky air. "Now ain't you the pauper's pussy."

Prince Albert's paper cap, the bill and band, was saturated with his sweat. The gauze on his right cheek was gone and I could see three vertical scratches that had dried dark but not deep on his skin. "The Lord be good, gentlemens," he said, "but I got to be going." When he pushed back his chair, an empty beer bottle lying on its side on the table near his hand fell to the floor without shattering. Using his saber for a cane, he lifted himself from the chair and hobbled toward me. "You cuts it close, Jay Pee. But I told them you might be coming. What made you change your mind from today? You going to be my lawyer after all?"

"I'm not working for you," I said. "But we need to talk."

"Hear that, gentlemens. He ain't working for me but he want me to talk to him. Snap a finger, snap a finger, hop a nigger, hop. Did Zeema write that one, Jay Pee, or did I? Listen, Jay Pee, don't feel bad 'bout not helping a poor nigger in need. It all moving on its own now anyways."

Mumbling to himself, Prince Albert reached for his face with his right hand. I thought I discerned the words *crazy* and *fall* before his hand fell to the top of the sword. Turning to

153

Lineman, Prince Albert said, "Would y'all mind if this here lawyer take my place at the table and play with my bills for me? I got a appointment."

Prince Albert took a step closer to me and whispered, "Got to get to my crib. To fall. You got me, Jay Pee? Lineman here don't let nobody go till the game over. I'm shitting in my pants scared about what's outside with the night, but I got to . . ."

"Prince be winning," Lineman said to me. "Sit."

Prince Albert left. I sat in his chair with the blue-edged bills before me.

"You thought about going at us, didn't you Jay Pee?" Lineman asked. "It was like you didn't care if we tore your limbs from your branches. Better be careful with that, you understand."

Indeed *that* had gone through my mind, but it was not what I would call a "thought" or a "consideration." It was more a *going up* than a *going at*, without thought, like the sensation of having floated higher as a wave crested beneath me, the entire body above the water while on the water, a seabird on a wave. After I sat at Lineman's table, however, I did have a thought. I remembered the face of the last judge in the last courtroom the morning of another cresting wave. He had adjourned immediately, and within the hour had called my father and my senior partners. The next day only one Marquis was left roosting with the Sanderlings.

Lineman shuffled the bulldog-backed cards. I noticed that the index finger on his left hand had been cut off at an angle at the first knuckle. I noticed also that the flat of the fingertip met perfectly the plane of the bottom card as Lineman dealt. On the little finger of his right hand the eyes of a gold lion sparkled.

"Know something about mechanic work, Jay Pee? You

looking at my hands like you know what I'm doing to you. Four of hearts bet. That you, Jay Pee."

I tossed a bill into the center of the table.

"That's your ante, Jay Pee. Now bet."

Another bill, a blue-edged twenty. "What's going on with Zulu?" I asked.

"I don't answer questions, Jay Pee. But you answer one for me. Where you learn to play poker?"

"My father, my brothers, my uncles."

"Yeah, yeah, a gentlemen game."

"My sisters, aunts, nieces, too. Any game."

"You know, Jay Pee, I got a family, too. I bet that where we both learn to fight and play."

"Tell me why you're helping Roussell."

"Tell you what, Jay Pee. I'll tell you anything you want to know after you prove to me you a winner."

Behind me, someone opened the door. Before the door shut, I heard Zeema harmonizing with Laurel.

"She almost better than Zeema," Lineman said. "Get more claps, too. The claps Zeema gets is for him, not his song. Why you think he goes for such a young gal? When you figure she be eighteen? His daddy went for white but not for young. Bet Jay Pee. No ante, freeze out, your king bets."

It didn't take me long to figure out that the twins were somehow assisting Lineman in the game. I do not know how long the game went on. We might have played for hours. Both Lineman and I napped and bet. I remember having the feeling, in the world called De Plus En Plus, that we both had the same trouble with dreams. I remember, too, eating, delighting in the taste of cornmeal hot tamales wrapped in paper and joined in fives by a rubber band. Eventually, Lineman won what was left of Prince Albert's money.

"I been watching you, Jay Pee. Never sat across a table

with a man got the same style nap I got. Tell you what, Jay Pee. You a loser big. Sometimes I take me big pity on a big loser. Ask me a question. Any one you want. But ask it without asking."

Without considering my words, I spoke, "Tell me about Zeema and Laurel."

"Shit. This town be brewing to a pop and you want to know that? Why you want to know that?"

"She reminds me of someone."

"Shit, Jay Pee. You notice what I just did. I turn the table on you, got you answering my questions. I take it all back. All I got for you's pity. Big pity."

Behind me the door opened. I heard someone tell Lineman that Zeema had left the bar. I rose from the table.

"Oh, no, Jay Pee." Lineman returned the blue-edged bills to me. A loan, he said. He also said he wanted to play an honest game with me just to see how big a loser I was. Lineman dealt a hand of low-in-the-hole. I folded without betting. Checking my cards, Lineman saw that I would have lost had I played.

"Pitiful," he said.

"I have to go," I said.

"You got that look again, Jay Pee. Like you don't care if you get tore apart. But I'm warning you now. Don't mess around with my Main connections, you understand? You better put some thought into getting out of here safe. Can you do that? How you going to get out of here safe, Jay Pee?"

I told Lineman I had to go to the restroom.

Lineman laughed. "Good, Jay Pee."

One of the twins at the table wanted to know why I would want to rest in a room that smelled like that. Lineman said to them, "Shet up, shet up, shet up," and then to me, "There's a window in there, Jay Pee," he said. Then he told me how to find the three-story sidehouse where Prince Albert lived. "Used to be a place by it called the Palace Bar. The Prince and his blind painter friend, they the only ones left living beside the Palace. The Prince stay on the first floor. I'd bet all my money his room was a ten-dollar whore crib."

In the toilet I climbed through the window over the urinal. I walked the two blocks to the corner of Landry Street and the Great Perpendicular. In 1947, in the conversations of a few of my clients, I had heard of the Palace, of a building of castle-like proportions. One of my clients had invited me once to meet him at the three-story sidehouse beside the bar. He described for me the six-foot cypress fence around the house.

That night, minutes after leaving Lineman's, I stood in front of that fence. I could tell that all of the Palace except for the house and fence had been razed years before.

Recalling Prince Albert's mention of a dog, I pulled carefully on the rope attached to the gate latch, walked the wooden planks leading to the front door. I listened for voices at the door, heard none.

Once inside, still standing by the door, I could dimly see a long hallway with three doors on either side. There were stairs straight ahead at the end of the hallway. Only one room, the last on the left before the stairs, was lighted. In that bedroom, I found Zeema and Prince Albert Willis.

Prince Albert lay on the floor. With his back to me and the door, Zeema stood above Prince Albert. I could not see Prince Albert's face. In Zeema's shadow, Prince Albert's hands clutched the fabric of his coveralls at his hips.

From that still mass at Zeema's feet came another shadow, a brush-wide stripe of black painted across the floor at an angle toward a chair in the corner to my right. I whispered Zeema's name. Zeema spun around. He pushed me into the chair, then fled down the hall.

157

I sat up and followed with my eyes the stripe of shadow that fell across my lap. In Prince Albert's mouth was the blue-steel saber.

Braying Near the Pole

I have gone through the notes I wrote on the day following that long Saturday night. The notes begin at 6:35 A.M., when I returned to my office in the Roussell Building:

Even God rested. Leave it to a Sunday to let us know we are done in.

One dead, someone I do not know. Another, someone I do know, inches away from dead.

I have two daughters again.

This town, as far away as I could get, has washed over me and thrown me back to this beach to this yellow pad.

But I am too tired to write. I will rest to take the edge of dream away from fact.

And I finally would sleep. I would sleep deeply and without dream. I would wake and try to record the details of what happened to me after I found Prince Albert. I would take care to list and chronicle.

But reading these notes again I see that there is still a nightmarish tint to all of my objective-Marquis listings. Now weeks and weeks away from that night, I am about to try again, but I am sane enough now to understand one of my brother Berman's embarrassingly simple truths: the word *nightmare* is also apt to describe the visions of those who do not sleep.

From my position in the corner chair, Prince Albert's face and torso were mantled in shadow. For most of my time in that chair, I was sure that the saber had gone through his mouth and neck into the floor. I cannot be certain, but I remember uttering a word. I would like to think that word was *Molly* but it may have been *God*.

I would like to think also that I'd have crawled to the body rather than flee the room, would have gathered up my Marquis fortitude to kneel beside what appeared to be a grotesque death to gather the details that might have been of some use to me later. Hadn't it been I who accepted the task of compiling and cropping my brother Berman's photographs for his Nuremberg chronicle? Hadn't I seen grotesque death in the larger sense piled en masse in wide angle and close-up through my grandfather's magnifying glass?

But in my mind now, as I try to recount for myself the time I spent in that chair, I want to flee the room and I cannot help thinking that I would have done this had I not seen an almost imperceptible twitching of the sharp edge of the silhouette that was Prince Albert's chest. That movement made me look to his face, and with my eyes more accustomed to the light I perceived that the saber had not gone through his mouth but rather had gone into the floor on the left side of his face after scraping his cheek.

I am certain now that I moved without thinking toward Prince Albert, but only after I was sure that he was alive—only after I was sure that what I would be facing would be far less than the grotesque scene of individual death that history in the smaller sense is capable of rendering.

The light in Prince Albert's room came from a low-wattage bulb in a lamp on the far wall past the bed and from the blue-orange flame of a space heater to my right. In that dim light, I knelt beside Prince Albert Willis.

From the expression on his face, I was certain he had been having a seizure when the point of the saber had been embedded in the wood floor and burlap rug beneath him. The paper cap was still on his head, and his eyes stared up without fright, as though someone had tried to force no more than a wallet, no more than an ice-cream spoon between his teeth.

I put my hand under his head and called his name. His head rolled to his right and he closed his eyes. The gash I saw must have gone through his cheek to the side of his tongue. Besides the blood that had seeped into the burlap under Prince Albert's neck, I could see that there was blood in his mouth covering his teeth and tongue. I called his name again and this time he coughed up the small amount of blood that he must have swallowed.

After pulling a blanket from the bed, before covering Prince Albert, I saw that the twine he had used to tie the saber to his coveralls had snapped. The scabbard lay perpendicular to his spine under the small of his back.

Then Prince Albert spoke. I thought I heard the name *Zeema*, but when I asked him to speak again, his breathing calmed and he began to sleep. It was then that I looked up and exhaled. The bleach I smelled burned my throat; I thought I would have to leave the room. But there were questions. And each question came with the assumption that Zeema had created the violent edge of the scene before me.

When I touched the saber near the burlap, I could barely move the blade. How had it been that solidly embedded? Had Zeema leaned full weight on the top of the hilt? The shaft would have snapped before penetrating that deep into the hard wood.

Had Zeema got on his knees and pulled down with his hands above his head? I reached up to grab the handle. The round knob at the top of saber felt rough. Standing, I felt a residue, raised blotches of a softer metal on the knob. In the light the specks shined like copper.

To control my nausea, I breathed deeply, slowly, and tried to concentrate on details. In the sparsely furnished room, the bed was made; the window above and to the right of the bed was shut, locked by a swivel hook to the frame. The panes were painted black. I saw a pair of red foam-rubber dice hanging from the round mirror on a vanity near the foot of the bed; on the stool under the vanity, a cedar box with an open brass latch; and on a chest of drawers below the window, a statue of a braying mule.

Stepping over Prince Albert, I reached and lifted that statue, which was at least five pounds of what looked to be solid copper. Even in the dim light I could see that the base was cracked through an inscription between the four hooves. Walking to the lamp I sat on the bed. The only words I could read were *hire another*. Turning the statue over, I found two craters the size of the saber knob on the underside of the base.

The saber that had sliced into Prince Albert's left cheek had been hammered into the floor with a statue of a braying mule.

When I think back now to that time in the room alone with Prince Albert, I can remember smells—bleach, perfumed powder, cedar, sweat—but no sounds, although the sounds were about to begin within the minute after I replaced the statue. But in that minute of silence that remained to me, I moved back to the saber. I had a feeling suddenly, suddenly clearheaded and away from my nausea, that the two worlds I had thought about all day were somehow fixed at the point of that saber. And with that feeling I knelt again beside Prince Albert.

The saber had a guard of bronze below the grip, strands of hide wrapped around steel under the round knob. A band of bronze had circled the grip once, but that had broken off, leaving a pitted and oxidized weld on the knob and guard. On the flat of the blade just below the hilt I saw a word, and below that the date 1888.

I tried to read the word, already eroded by touch, but could not. I could tell only that the first letter was an *M*. I tried counting the letters. If there were seven, wouldn't my suspicions be correct? Wouldn't this word and the two worlds fixed at this terrible point be my own nightmare, Marquis at De Plus En Plus? I stood to lift the saber from the wood to take it closer to the lamp.

Then the noise, the night.

The clamor began when I rose and took a step toward the cedar box on the vanity chair. I heard voices—distant shouts, singing, a siren. Outside below the window, a dog whined and pawed the house.

Behind me someone screamed. Turning, I saw Alison standing in the doorway, her hands over her ears, her mouth open. Her breath stopped short at the end of her cry.

I ran to her, tugged at her wrists to get her hands from her ears. She twisted her hands free and ran for the front door. Before I could get past the next door a white form bolted from the darkness of that room and knocked me to the floor.

A man in white coveralls crawled in the shadows at my feet. At my feet also, on the floor where the last of the lamplight met the shadows, I saw a roll of money and a white painter's cap. Sitting up I reached for the money; the man in white dived at me and wrapped an arm around my head. The wet undersleeve that rubbed into my face smelled like wild onion. With the money and the cap the man raced away, out the front door. I ran also, stopping on the front steps as he bounded and lifted himself over the fence.

As I stepped down onto the plank walkway, I heard shouts and singing, loud on Landry to my left. Near a cistern to my right, a tethered dog growled. I had just reached the gate when the dog thrust itself free of its rope or chain and took my ankle. I twisted to the pain, swung my forearm down on

162

the dog's spine, leapt for the top of the shoulder-high fence.

With my back safely against fence planks, I closed my eyes and slid down and sat on the sidewalk. I felt the nausea again, tasted it as chlorine falling into the stale depths of my lungs and stomach at the same time.

When I opened my eyes, I saw Lineman lighting a cigarette and leaning against a lamppost across the Great Perpendicular. The oil in Lineman's mane glistened blue in the mercury beam of the streetlight as he blew smoke and puckered to kiss the same false-spring mist that bathed my face.

All of this is still part of that long nightmare that clarifies itself, muddles itself in my memory to this day. That night, clarity came for me in interludes between nausea and breathlessness, just as in a long dream. And just as in any long dream, the interludes begin when a new character enters to create a new scene. That character could be the sun, a streetlamp, or a man with a lion's mane. The nightmare apparently ends with each new scene, but soon that scene too becomes a part of the longer dream, and one returns to the horror, to the nausea, continually deceived.

My brother Berman wrote that it must be accepted as truth that nightmares end. Otherwise there can be no hope. The nightmare I am describing does end, just as any other dream, in daylight, the daylight of the next day when I walked in the sunlight of a false spring with my new daughter, both of us searching for truth at any cost.

Seeing Lineman across the street ended the nightmare for me. The nausea left me as I felt the wetness of the night on my face, saw the streetlamp and Lineman's kiss. I breathed again.

(Remember, Molly, how we sometimes forgot to breathe while we made love? Then, back to ourselves, the air dropped into our lungs, and only then did we realize how long we had been away? We dive into the same sea, it seems, awake or sleeping, holding our breath, practicing for the deep dive . . .)

Sure that the nightmare was over, I got up and limped toward Landry. But as Berman said, I was being deceived by hope: nothing ends until the deep dive.

The Parish Seat

With his guitar neck-down behind his back, Zeema walked two steps ahead of a crowd marching down Landry. Beside him were Alison and Laurel. Laurel held his left arm; Alison, sobbing without tears, clung to his right.

Two police cars pulled up fifty yards ahead of the crowd, but Zeema marched on, singing, "Don't want no sugar in my coffee." The crowd clapped once in unison. Zeema sang again, "It make me mean, Lord," and the crowd responded, "It make me mean."

A woman who had stopped her car for the traffic light at the intersection of the Great Perpendicular and Landry, a white woman in a feathered hat, rolled her window up, locked four doors, and covered her face with her arms as the crowd engulfed her car. (Molly, this woman—Mrs. Frank Prevost—would be interviewed the next day by a reporter from the *Times-Picayune*. I used that interview to find her; by chance, she is the same woman that Chief of Police Theriot stopped to talk to as he led me to the court square my first day in town. I am enclosing copies of that article with this batch of research.)

Two more police cars blocked Landry to the rear. The space traveler I had seen taking pictures at the Senator's party jumped from a Jeep and ran with his camera to get ahead of the crowd. (Molly, maybe you can figure out how to get to some of these photos.)

Zeema smiled as I approached him. "Jay Pee," he said.

I stopped in front of Zeema. When he stopped, the people behind him also stopped.

"You'd better get out the way, Jay Pee. This here bunch of rabble, they be one animal with a mind to go down this street."

"How did you get these people to march?" I asked.

"The Reverend got them ripe. They were sitting outside Lineman's. All I had to do was say 'Let's go,' and damn if they didn't up themselves and let it go. Move, Jay Pee."

"Prince Albert told me you might try to kill him."

"Hey, Mister," Laurel said. "I know Zeema and I know kill ain't part of him. You supposed to be working for me. Protecting."

"I can't be a bodyguard," I told her.

"Don't want you for a bodyguard," Laurel said. "I want you for the full protection of the law."

"You heard her, Jay Pee. Looks like I be—what they call it—inciting."

"Looks to me as though it could be a diversion. Did you try to kill Prince Albert?"

"Nigger on the spot got to be the nigger doing the killing, right, Jay Pee? Move."

"Move, Mister."

"Listen to me, Laurel," I said.

"Ain't time for court, Mister." Laurel sang this time, "Don't want no jet-black woman." She took a step forward and I moved aside.

Walking forward in front of the marchers, the photographer aimed his camera. Laurel grinned and took up the chant once more, "Don't want no jet-black woman." The photographer's suit gleamed in the Landry lights.

Zeema lifted his right arm and covered Alison's face to the camera flash.

"Okay, Jay Pee. Time you went to work. This little black singing girl here is your client. Take her."

"What you talking, Zeema," Laurel said. "Don't you go little girling me."

"Don't talk back to me now, baby. Go with this man for now. Please."

I grabbed Laurel softly on the elbow. The wave of people behind her advanced. My grasp got firmer. "Please," I said. "We can help Zeema later. Come with me."

Zeema placed Alison's arm in my other hand. "And this one, too, Jay Pee. She be out of it for sure. Ain't her own eyes she looking through."

Laurel pulled her arm free and ran into the crowd and then disappeared. I called her name, I remember, but in the world called De Plus En Plus it may have sounded like another.

"Her name's Laurel, Jay Pee. And she be all right. For God sakes, man, take this one out of here. Keep them safe."

Alison followed me as I walked toward the police car behind the marchers.

At the police car, I spoke to the cop Theriot about Prince Albert. "That been took care of, Boo," he said, swinging me around. Theriot searched the pockets of my rented tuxedo. Minutes later, after the town's first "illegal demonstration," Theriot arrested Zeema and Alison and me.

The first interrogation—by Theriot—was not taped. I remember little about my time in the courthouse, but I remember Theriot called me "Boo" the entire time he questioned me. I think that I was also questioned by a sheriff's investigator. I *was* fingerprinted and booked—a matter of public record, which I now have—with "suspision (*sic*) of attempted murder and fleeing the scene of a crime." All of this, I now know, had to take place on the third floor of the courthouse, the floor that served as a parish jail.

(Molly, the jail is now part of the adjoining annex recently completed on the site of what used to be the school where Zeema left his tuxedo coat.)

Handcuffed to a green-marble bust of a judge named Butler, I waited for what may have been hours outside the second-floor courtroom for what Theriot called "emergency arraignment." Because the district judge, who had attended the Senator's party, could not be stirred from sleep, I was then handcuffed to the grating behind the Coca-Cola machine in the first-floor lobby where, Theriot said, I would have to wait until an assistant D.A. arrived.

Left alone there, I tried to sleep, but the pain in my ankle and thoughts of what I had seen in Prince Albert's room kept me awake. The nausea was returning, and I began to realize that the new scenery was part of the old dream. I probably had thoughts of the saber, of what I thought was my family's name on the saber, of two worlds pinned together like burlap and wood. I must have thought of Laurel also, of her becoming an indistinguishable part of a wave of people. I know I thought of Alison and worried over what had become of her. The scar I now have on my wrist came to me, I believe, from my attempts to free myself to get to Alison.

Scene change, quick as in a dream: the front door at the end of the first-floor lobby opens.

"Jamie, Jamie," Nolan Roussell says, locking the door behind him. He has changed from Arab silk to a suit of green tweed. He puts his keys back into his pants pocket and, taking his fedora from his head, stands before me and smiles.

"Jamie, Jamie," he says again.

"Does every haberdasher have a key to the courthouse?" I ask.

"Quiet control."

I ask for the time.

"You must learn to listen more carefully. You read history, Jamie. I know you do. There are some, like me, who get delight not from putting crowns on emperor's heads but from knowing that we, quietly, have got the emperor into the room where rests the crown. We get them there, then pull away. What happens after is history."

Roussell shakes his head as though I cannot comprehend what he is saying. "Down to a bleeding dog, Jamie. What would your grandfather—"

"There's a girl upstairs called Alison—"

"Would you leave us to our hurts, Jamie? You do not belong here."

"I have a client."

"We shall see." Roussell smiles again, strides away to the stairs. "Oh, Jamie, if your grandfather could see you now on the courthouse floor. But I hear you were heading for that in New Orleans."

Minutes after Roussell had gone, Theriot returned and removed my handcuffs. He escorted me to another interrogation—this one taped—with a bald, red-faced man named DeRoche. (Tape will be sent, Molly.)

DeRoche's French accent and the toothpick in his mouth made him difficult to understand. I stayed on my feet even after Theriot dragged a chair in from the hall for me. Except for the smell of Roussell's Jerusalem spice, I was left alone in the room with DeRoche and the moving reels of his tape recorder.

"Well," he said. "What it is you think I want out of you? Oh, they said you was tough. You don't look so all tough to me. You drunk?"

"I don't have to talk."

"Look, we don't want no trouble. But Sheriff Gautier, even the DA and the judge, they don't know what to do with you. They pass the buck. The buck flapped here. Me, I always stop the buck from flapping. Mar-kee. That your name?"

"I don't have to tell you a god—"

"Hush-a-bye. You look like you want to come at me, but you too smart a piece of baloney for that. Heard you discovered the nigger that was almost killed back of town tonight and you didn't report it immediate."

"I reported it."

"Look, just let me in on what you was doing over by the old Palace tonight. I'll call you a cooperative man."

"The charges."

"Fleeing the scene. I drop the attempted murder and failure to report since you about to cooperate."

"Must make my call . . ."

"Oh, shit, here it come. Look. . . . Never mind. I was told not to bother leaning on you. Just get you to sign that you didn't get that blood on your socks and wrist from anything we done."

"Won't sign."

"Listen, I was told you in the nigger-protecting business. And I was told to tell you we've arrested us a nigger for the attempted killing of another nigger. I was told to tell you that. I was told to tell you the nigger that almost got his *boudin* toothpicked to the floor is in protective custody. And I was told to tell you there ain't no business here for you. We got us a total of five—count 'em, five—niggers in custody, and there ain't one that wants to see you. If you don't understand get-out-of-town, you should understand supply and demand. I kind of like that explanation, don't you, Mar-kee comma Mister?"

"You know what I'd like?"

"Oh, oh, a flaring up."

The words I used in my comments to an assistant DA named DeRoche are all part of public record, as are my comments to one or two witnesses and a district court judge in New Orleans. That night in the Mondebon Parish Courthouse, I told DeRoche that I'd like to see him choke on that word *nigger*.

There were many people, judges included, I wanted to see and still want to see choking on that word and the thousands of words and combinations of words used in place of that word. *Vomit* is the word I'd thrown at the judge the week before I lost my partnership. *The same vomit*, I'd said after listening to his ruling from the bench. And then I'd gone on to describe the consistency of the judge's brain.

What kept me from a contempt charge, the judge in New Orleans said, was the name Marquis and the court's knowledge of my "recent plight." A Marquis was summoned to escort me home. Several Marquises, each familiar with my recent plight, arrived to take me home to my wife.

(Molly, the record shows that *puke* is the word I used with DeRoche that night. According to the record, I wished out loud that one day he would disappear into his own bilious puke. *Lump crab meat* are the words I used to describe the consistency of DeRoche's brain.)

DeRoche shouted for Theriot to come in again. I turned. In the doorway Alison Belanger was standing beside Theriot.

I must have made a move toward Theriot. His hand went down to his holster.

"Back off, Boo."

"Hold on," DeRoche said. "She's been napping in the judge's private chamber. She's all right. You in the escort business now. She asked for you. She called you her 'daddy in the tux.' But we all know you ain't her daddy. But again, she won't go home with nobody else. Sign here."

(Molly, I must have signed, as the enclosed document indicates.)

I asked, with the lawyer's mind still present, if there were any charges against Alison.

Reaching for the button on the tape recorder, DeRoche answered: "Roussell's niece. Who would charge against Roussell's niece? And more than that . . . she's the queen of Mardi Gras."

Theriot drove Alison and me to the address she gave on Emerson Street, five blocks east of the cathedral. Both Alison and I slept on the back seat. She had her head on my lap.

When I woke I expected an interval of clarity, the clarity that should have come with Alison's face, the cool air, the Emerson lights. Instead I sat up with the double vision of drugged sleep, sat up Marquis-erect to the single visage of De Plus En Plus, to Alison's face over the face of my oldest daughter.

My body convulsed and I collapsed to Alison's lap.

"That's it, Daddy," she said.

"Not on the goddamn parish seat, Boo!"

Daughter Wife Stranger

I walked without help from the car to the front of the house on Emerson Street, a two-story white wood-frame. As I reached for the doorbell, Alison said, "No. My mother. We can't wake her." I followed her around the side of the house: in the backyard, over and between black foliage, moonlight on water; the aroma of oranges, oversweet and rotting.

Alison took a key from under a ceramic rabbit on the patio and unlocked the back door. I followed.

After turning on a fluorescent light above the sink in the kitchen, she took an orange-half from a plate on the table and then walked into a sitting room at the front of the house. I followed.

She opened double doors, let in the sound of sirens, the odor of fresh paint. Again, the nausea.

I called her name.

"My name's Alison," she said. "Here, sit in this chair. She tore a slice of orange from the rind. "Here, eat this. I've doctored it. Not much. You can't have much. Eat. We'll take turns resting."

I ate the orange slice. I wanted to tell her I would be all right. Instead, I sat. I surrendered to my exhaustion, ready to sleep or to die.

(Molly, I must try to remember for you the interludes of sleep, death, or dreams I had in that house that night. So, a poetic footnote, my dearest, black and green.)

I open my eyes. Alison, after switching on a lamp on the fireplace mantel, sits on the bench at the grand piano. She has put her arms on the keys. She rests with her head in her arms.

I call to her.

"I said my name's Alison. Ali, not Abby."

I open my eyes. Alison is standing over me. Her eyes are brown, almost black. I look for my daughter's eyes in her eyes, green in the brown. I see green in the brown.

"What's my name?" she asks, and "Did I see a dead man tonight?"

I answer her with a name.

She laughs. "Prince Albert. I like that." Then her eyes open suddenly as though she recognizes me. I cannot find my daughter in her eyes. It is Alison crying.

I am walking toward the fireplace to read the mantel clock. I open my eyes. "It's after four," Alison is saying, "and you're bleeding on my mother's Persian. You know Zeema Steeple, don't you? Out of this world. I've got his records, upstairs. Do you want to hear? Sounds are a real gasser in our condition. God, I hope I look better than you, Daddy."

172

I see my daughter again. I close my eyes to die with her again.

I am talking, with questions."Why did you go to Prince Albert's house?" I ask, and "Did you see Zeema try to kill Prince Albert?"

"A bad scene. For both of us. I'm not with it yet. Hold on, will you? I took something."

"What did you take?"

"Something. You've never heard of it. You took some, too, Daddy. In the orange. Easy. I need company bad. You too."

I stop the questions to look into her face. In the lamplight, her skin has no sheen. She is looking at me. I see my wife, cheeks high and square to the jaw. She gazes back into my eyes and, like a wife, does not look away.

I close my eyes, rub them.

"You can look," she says. "I saw you looking before."

I try to tell her no.

"Look in my eyes, Daddy. New apothecary's coming."

I open my eyes. I feel a warmth, wetness on my ankle and bare foot. I smell the paint, see my wife in the paint. Quick points of black. I look away.

"What's the matter?" she asks.

I tell her about the smells, in her house, in Prince Albert's room.

"You want to forget smells? Smell me."

She holds the rest of the orange to her face, rubs the pulp on her cheeks and chin. She grabs my hand and puts it in her hair. She squeezes my hand until I am pulling her hair.

I can smell her, the orange. I look into her eyes again. They are sharp and shining, brown and green, daughter wife stranger, all many women.

I kiss her. Kiss her in three ways, daughter wife stranger.

"Now you've got the idea," she says.

I kiss her again, harder. Softer. I want my wife, want my daughter back. But I do not want anything.

173

"No," I say.

But I am still wanting. In three ways at once. I say something to her but do not hear myself.

"Yes," she says. "Don't you get the idea? This is how we will forget. This is the new way."

"It is not new, Molly."

"That is not my name. But my name does not matter. What are you smelling? Tell me what you are smelling. No, let me tell you. Here. Oh, take some, please. Thank God I'm alive. I'm alive. I'm alive tonight, thank God."

(And that's the word I woke to, Molly. I hated God again and my anger cleared my head. I put my hands on her shoulders. My daughter was gone, you were gone. And in front of me was a young woman trembling. I held her close to me, the way I would a daughter. She began to cry. She asked me to help her. I carried her to the couch near the fireplace. I looked for an afghan, some cover. But there was nothing around to keep her warm. "Upstairs," she said, "My bed." And I carried her, a father walking out of warm green water. I know you understand, Molly, what I am talking about: emerging, carrying a breathing body to a warm place. I understood this symbolic resurrection as I carried Alison up the stairs. And I was deeply grateful for it. And shouldn't resurrection, even symbolic, be the end? No, not in the world called De Plus En Plus, Molly, our world, Molly, the only world, where we are pinned longing to rise, where we sometimes rise, run at the green, dive longing, sometimes emerging de plus en plus en plus en plus.)

At the top of the stairs in the house on Emerson you face a double door that leads to a balcony. In the first light of morning you can see a small orange orchard, a pool. To your left, straight ahead no more than five feet, is Alison's bedroom. Inside, the glow of a television set throws light on yel-

174

low drapery, a four-poster, yellow carpet and wallpaper. If you turn right, you see two more rooms. The first is a bathroom about ten feet down, again to your right. Straight ahead another twenty feet down the hallway is another bedroom. Inside on a king-size bed are a red quilt and one pillow; on shelves over the headboard of the bed, framed photographs, twelve pictures in sequence. Each photograph is of Alison. In each she is wearing an Easter dress and is standing beside an orange tree. The dresses change in style and color as she grows older, left to right.

I laid Alison down, covered her with yellow, switched off the television set. Looking for a bathroom to wash my face, I walked down the upstairs hall. The door to the first room was half open. I could see fluorescent light on white tile. I stood by the door, knocked. The door swung, opened wider, but no more than a foot. I saw an arm, palm up over the side of the white bathtub. The tub was filled with water. The water was red. De plus en plus en plus.

The Bottom of the Gulf

This is what my father's father said to my father's five children one Thanksgiving when we five were alone with him in the Marquis study—the room closest to the table that evening— the evening after a long Thanksgiving meal: Observe everything, even if you close your eyes.

That night on Emerson Street after I saw the woman in the tub, I closed my eyes and ran to look for a phone to call an ambulance. I looked first in the bedroom at the end of the hall. I made my call, dialing 0 for an operator, on the phone beside the bedside table. I told the operator to get the police and an ambulance to Emerson Street, and because I did not know the address, I described the house and said I would try to be waiting in front. The operator told me that a report had been made and that help was on the way. She also told me that the report had been called in from the same house.

I went immediately to Alison's bedroom. She stirred when I touched her shoulder. "I told you," she said, "I told you we can't wake my mother."

"Alison . . . you called for help?"

"Yes. While you were sleeping."

"Why isn't anyone here yet?"

"Mother's dead," she said. "She's been dead. I found her a long time ago, hours ago. I called help and Aunt Elli and Uncle Nolan just a while ago while you slept, just before I washed your leg. They'll be coming. They're always helping. We can't wake her. Please, you can leave. My family . . ."

I lifted Alison up from the bed, gently by the shoulders, to face me. She did not open her eyes. "I will not end up like my mother," she said. "I must not. I have been fighting that all my life, trying to slice free all my life. Please leave now. But promise me you'll come back."

There was no need for me to promise.

Alison put her hands to her ears as I held her up. I saw her fingernails, chipped and dirty. Laying her down again, I took her hands from her ears and placed them on her chest, then covered her with the quilt.

"Turn on the TV," she said.

I did that for her, and I left the room, shutting the door behind me.

The woman I took to be Alison's Aunt Elli stood looking up at me from the foot of the stairs as I began my descent. I had seen her before, that night, helping Nolan Roussell and others carry Roussell's son from the party. She was still wearing her lavender peasant's shawl; unbleached muslin covered the skin on her neck and arms and legs.

"You don't have to explain anything to me," she said.

The skin on her face was drawn, tight.

"I called for help," I said.

"That is all being handled. Someone is coming who looks to such things."

"Nolan Roussell?"

"Where is she?"

"Alison?"

"My sister. Bethany."

"The bathroom."

Lifting her dress at the knees, she stared into my eyes and then walked past me up the stairs. "Leave," she said.

I did that for her.

Feeling fully awake at dawn, I walked out of the house on Emerson Street, retracing the path I had taken to enter: the sitting room and living room, kitchen, patio. Outside, looking up from the driveway, I saw that Alison's window, the shutters and outside frame, had been trimmed in blue, the same color blue that lined the edges of Prince Albert's money. Limping a bit from the ache in my ankle, I headed for the center of town. Over the rooftops, the sky behind the church spire was the color of a peasant's shawl.

Observe everything, even if you close your eyes.

This is what I had seen in the bathroom on the second floor of the house on Emerson Street:

I did not know the woman in the tub, but I was familiar with the colors and serenity of her kind of sleep. She was wearing her black hair braided, with an orange bead at the end of each braid. Her face was powdered thick with the color of flesh, and the blue eye-shadow on the closed lids had been outlined in black to a point past the end of each brow. The skin on her neck, shoulders, and chest was pallid. Just below the surface of the water, her small nipples were the color of dry blood, but except in the water there was no blood anywhere, not on the porcelain beneath the wrist nor on the tile on the floor beneath her hand.

That is what I saw and remember still.

And this is what I concluded that morning as I limped to the Roussell Building in the center of town:

One chain of existence—Zeema Steeple and Laurel and Landry Street—was connected to another chain—Nolan Roussell and Alison and Emerson Street. The link in that connection was Prince Albert Willis. Enveloping these, of course, was my world of De Plus En Plus, with all my daughters and with all my time fixed where the saber pierced the hard floor in Prince Albert's room.

As I walked I believed—no, I had faith, possibly for the first time in my life—that there was a purpose and pattern to the circumstances around me, a design, and behind that a mind, the mind of a designer, cruel, perverted perhaps, but a mind. I was certain, as I walked, that if I could get back to the saber in Prince Albert's room, I would find my name *Marquis* inscribed on the hilt. Anger and relief found their way into my steps at the same time, and I limped on.

(Molly, this sounds to me and may sound to you like the fogged logic one has at the moment of waking, when one not only believes but comprehends at the same time, when all worlds—faith and fact, dream and waking—are not working after all under different laws but are really an entity bound by a single but not singular physics. But as I walked in the springlike air that morning and as I sit now recounting everything, I believed and knew and believe and know again that the logic is solid and makes sense, in every chain of existence in every world.

And I was about to know something else, after I made it to the office in the Roussell Building and found what was waiting for me there: that if I were going to help Laurel and Alison, I would have to understand fully both chains—Landry, Emerson—and their connecting link, Prince Albert Willis.

What did I find, Molly, when I opened the door to the office? I found Laurel.)

She was asleep, her belly and chest on the blue-and-gold couch, both hands beneath her. Her long petticoat covered her legs; the hem of her dress had been brought up to the back of her neck for cover. The white of the slip and the dress absorbed the dirty-gold color of the dawn entering through a window that faced east.

I sat at the desk, my pen in my hand, and watched her. Her cheeks were rounder than my younger daughter's, the bones of her wrists thicker, but she woke the same way my daughter had, her eyes on me as though she knew where to find me. She smiled as my daughter often had, and squinting in the light brought her left hand to her forehead. Her teeth showed, white as my daughter's, in the shadow of that visor.

"Lord, Mister," she said. "Where at you been? You look a sight."

I smiled back at her, said nothing. Did I think then, as I do now, of the answer to that question? *To the bottom of the Gulf.*

She sat up. "This what made you all goofy?" She opened her right hand, revealing the amber-colored bottle of pills.

"Partly that," I said.

"I'll be keeping these with me. If you working for me I want you stone-cold not-goofy. Why you work for nothing, Mister? Zeema told me that's what pro bono means."

I shrugged my shoulders, smiled again, watched her. "Did you get my card from Zeema?" I asked.

"From an old old box of his with songs and other papers."

"There are a few things you have to understand. I'm only a lawyer."

"You say that like it's a problem, Mister. Doesn't a lawyer

179

got the right to snoop around, getting to the bottom of things?"

"A lawyer does, in a way. If a lawyer has a client."

"I thought we got that straight. I'm your client. You work for me."

"But you . . ." I tried to think of the words that would make her understand. I remembered my younger daughter asking me what a lawyer was, and I remembered how I had believed once that I would have time to explain everything to her, how there was time.

"Zeema then," she said. "He needs a lawyer."

"Zeema doesn't want me around him."

"Then we'll change that, Mister. We'll talk to Zeema about that this morning."

"I need to tell you some things about Zeema."

"About how he tried to kill that man with the sword? I heard already. Got the word from Landry before I came here. And even if Zeema did it—and he didn't—doesn't he have the right to the best lawyer he can get?"

I shook my head. There was some pride in her smile this time, as though she knew she was right, a young woman who had taken to heart a junior-high civics book.

"And if he doesn't want you for a lawyer," she said, "we still ain't finished. I been doing some thinking. Something's going on in this town we got to get to the bottom of before we can get to the top of anything. Zeema tells me a lot about his past, but when it comes to this town he gets quiet. I want to know everything about Zeema."

"What else have you been thinking of?"

"Of that white girl. Alison."

I thought of telling Laurel about Alison's mother, but I said nothing. I was beginning to feel there would be time.

"I like her," Laurel said. "In a protecting way. Something's going on, me to her. I got that feeling. And I got the feeling

180

that me and you, Mister, it's up to us to get to the bottom of things. You thinking that, too, ain't you?"

"That I am," I said.

"Then, starting today, we going to do some walking and finding out. We'll try to do it lawyer to client if we can. If that don't work we'll still do some walking and some finding out. And we going to breathe in the air that we find out about no matter what the stink. You agree?"

"That I do. My entire family would agree to that."

"Relations, Mister . . . we'll get back on that. But, answer me this first. What you call people who go around finding out the truth, poking their nose into other people's business even without clients?"

"Just average citizens," I said, and Laurel laughed at that. She found humor in more than my daughter had at her age.

I must have smiled in a sea-green, goofy way because she nodded as she looked at my face, and she said, "My, my, my."

I looked down to the notes on the desk in front of me.

"You don't mind if I skimmed through those words of yours, do you?"

"No."

"That's how I figured how we both want the same things, far as this town concerned. It's all foggy right now, what's true, what ain't. You a religious man, ain't you, Mister? In a funny way. I can tell that by your notes. And you love your family, don't you, Mister? I can tell that, too, by your writing."

"I don't know if I'd choose that word."

"Love? Don't be afraid to throw that word around. There's love and there's love, you know. All kinds. Real love don't mind you throw the same word around to other things."

"In that case . . ." I said.

"That's all right, Mister. You ain't got to say it. You a lot like Zeema regarding that. Yes sir, sure is foggy."

181

"And I do agree about that."

"And about relations, too, Mister. Sure is foggy. What's family, what's not. Know what I mean?"

"You're getting goofy on me," I said.

She threw her head back and laughed again. I watched the small, strong muscles of her neck.

"But I agree," I said. "One goofy to another goofy."

"I was about to ask from all this . . . don't you get the feeling sometimes, in the fog, that we all related?"

And in the world of De Plus En Plus wasn't that true? I thought of Prince Albert's epilepsy and of my daughter's, of Nolan Roussell's posture and my grandfather's, of Lineman's troubled sleep and of mine, of the sound of my oldest daughter's nickname *Abby* and of Alison's *Ali*, of one daughter's vigil as she watched over another daughter, en plus en plus en plus.

I remembered Zeema and his sheet of blank music paper in the graveyard. "Shouldn't you be writing that down?" I asked.

"What I just said? Hell, no, Mister. Excuse me with that. You and Zeema sound alike on that measure, too. Put down your pen, Mister."

I felt the cold silver of the pen for the first time in my hand, and I looked into her eyes.

"Mister, you look at me like I'm the opposite of a ghost."

Exactly, I wanted to say, but I said nothing. I felt sure there would be time.

"Know what else I figure, Mister? I figure we need some rest, both of us, if we're going to help Zeema and Alison. Put down that pen, Mister. Sleep."

I scribbled a few words on the pad: *Even God rested*. Then I laid my pen down and put my head on my hands. I slept, was nourished by my sleep for the first time in what must have been two years. I slept and my daughters slept with me.

Average Citizens

April 18, 1965

Molly,

That last chapter I sent you, if it can be called a chapter, took me months to write. You, the able ghost you are, know the trouble one has recounting the past accurately. I'm sure you know that the conversations I had (those without taped records) are close to what was said, but only as accurate as memory. And memory is the biggest traitor of all. The historian in you does not trust it. But you trust me. What a dilemma, my dearest, for you.

And you realize, as do I, that pieces of conversations that I have sent you are out of place—especially my talk with Laurel in the office. I remember that Laurel and I said these things to each other, but we may have spoken the words later. History works so hard at being actual; memory is poetry. And trust? I can see your eyebrow lifting now, my dearest. Deal with all of this as you will.

Looking back on all that I have sent you, I see that I have been away from you now another two years. But I am beginning to see the patterns now, to my life, especially my life in this town the second time around. I feel now for the first time that I may never see you again. I had hoped that I would finish this chronicle and we would sit labeling sections and chapters with the sense of humor we once had. But I have not found my sense of humor yet—

I begin to see my life in this town as having three sections. I have just finished the first. I thought of calling it "The Bottom of the Gulf," or "The Nightmare." And I can see you laughing now at another Marquis overstatement. But the nightmare does seem to end in that office that morning with Laurel. A new section began when we—Laurel and I—woke to the smell of turpentine in the bright noonlight. The walking we were about to do through town (the eight days before Mardi Gras), searching for facts, is another section.

There is a final section coming. Just as in sleep, one finds that any nightmare worth its name is in control throughout, all along *through the night, even in the interstices of those smaller dreams filled with light. I am not sure where that last section begins, where I finally realized that the nightmare had not ended. Maybe from your standpoint beside the brick pond on St. Charles you will be able to see it—that line I crossed, or should I say,* entered.

It is Easter again. Even now I have been deceived by what appears to be rebirth. I am about to attempt to write a new section filled with the same sense of—

I was about to use that word, Molly, hope. *I remember what you said to my grandfather when he asked you to be honest about Marquis writing. You said, "Overly poetic, wordy." Grandfather laughed, I think, because he knew you were right. Then he asked you if our writing had any saving grace. You answered, "It is tempted toward but manages to avoid abstractions."*

Forgive the poetry, my dearest. Forgive the near occasion of an abstraction. I miss you.

I started to say I am beginning the second of what seems to want to be three sections. I think perhaps we will one day label the chapter that begins the first section with the name of the town. This second section I would begin with Average Citizens. *And the third?* Into the Waves, *perhaps.*

Forgive the poetry, forgive—

James

Dugas, Dugas

Laurel and I woke to the smell of wild onions and to a painter standing in the light of noon flaring through the window. Once again the painter was holding a pistol—the same blue-flecked .22 I'd seen the day before—but this time the hands holding the pistol were white.

When I stood up from my chair Laurel said, "Easy, Mister."

"Well, well, and well," the man at the window said. He paused before he spoke again, but those few words were enough for me to discern the accent, the accent of Theriot and DeRoche. "Have a look at you. Me, I ain't tripped on your tuxedo since at the Prince's house last night."

"You were at the Prince's last night?" Laurel asked.

"Ask the man behind the desk, here, *sha*." As my eyes adjusted to the light, I could see that like Prince Albert he wore a paper cap with the words *Dugas Painting* on the bill. His hands and face had been blanched free of freckles and age spots by what may have been years of turpentine scrubs at knock-off time, the same turpentine that may have caused the white hair at his temples to turn sulfur-yellow.

"We got some questions for you," Laurel said to him, and then to me: "Don't we, Mister? He's kind of like our first average citizen."

"You're Dugas," I said.

"Yas, yas. You some lawyer all right. Sharp one, too. Can read a cap. And you say my name right. *Doo-gah*. You speak French?"

Laurel giggled. "Camptown race track five miles long, Doo-gah, Doo-gah."

Dugas started a slow pivot toward Laurel. I took another step to him. "You keep that pistol pointed to me," I said.

"Don't get jumpy, flamehead, no. I'll give the orders in here." He held the pistol with both hands, but oddly, the left hand braced over the top of the weapon, covering the cylinder.

I stared at the pistol and then at the painter's eyes. One eye, the left, had a dead lid covering all but a crescent of red. The iris on the other eye flowered like gray-green lichen on the pink ball. Each time Dugas blinked, his good eye seemed to lift half his face. With some blinks, his shoulder moved to the rhythm of the eye, lifting arm and hand and gun.

In my corner vision I could see Laurel's hand on her mouth, holding in her laugh.

"Ain't nothing funny in here," Dugas said.

"Keep the pistol pointed to me," I said.

"Or else what you'll do? I come for money." Dugas' left hand went to his face to wipe his mouth. Before his hand touched his lips, he let it drop again, quickly, to the pistol. His knuckles whitened as his fingers covered the cylinder. "And, me, I'm the one got the drops on you and I can point to any damn thing I want."

Again, a slow pivot toward Laurel.

I walked to the door, twisted the inside latch. "It locks from the inside," I said.

"I'll shoot you down dead, me, I swear."

"How dead?"

"Mister, calm down."

"How dead, Dugas?" I asked.

"You crazy or something, you?"

"Don't you think it's a question of degree—" I said.

"Mister, don't talk about degrees—"

"What the shit you talking about, lawyer?"

"—with an empty cylinder?" I said.

"Mister, please."

Dugas turned the gun to Laurel and I ran at him. The pistol butt came down on my shoulder as I pushed Dugas into the radiator under the window.

"You crazy, you . . . you crazy, yas, you."

On the floor, I grabbed Dugas' face, planting a thumb under the chin and a finger near each eye.

Laurel tugged at my shoulders, "Mister—" and I let the painter go. Together, Laurel and I knelt beside Dugas.

"Lordy," Laurel said, "He fainted dead away."

"Are you all right, Laurel?"

"Course I am. You know what, Mister? We going to have trouble getting information from average citizens if you killing all of them. We going to have to work on that."

While another painter rested beneath a blanket on Roussell's blue-and-gold couch, I added notes to my yellow pad and answered Laurel's questions. Her questions accurately led me to tell her about everything I'd seen in what was left of the sidehouse of the Palace the night before. After more of her precise questions, we spoke again of Prince Albert's contact with Zeema in New Orleans and of my talk with Prince Albert in the office. I described the roll of money he carried with him, the paint on the edges. When she asked me to describe the color, I pointed to the appropriate specks and splashes on Dugas.

I volunteered nothing. I complimented her on her questioning and tried to get her to talk about "lawyering," but she saw past my ploy and asked more. Eventually we were talking about the paint on Alison's house and the paint on Prince Albert's hands and gun. She caught the connection, was about to ask the question that would bring me to tell her about what had happened to Alison in the courthouse and on Emerson Street, when she saw someone's shadow on the opaque window of the office door.

"Want me to check on that, Mister?"

I told her I would do the checking for us. As I got up to walk to the door, Dugas started to come to on the couch.

"You watch him, Mister. I'll get the door."

Before I could tell her to stay put, she was running to the door.

"Be careful," I said.

I moved toward Dugas, who was heaving himself conscious. I heard him shouting something that sounded like

"Milk! Damn it woman, hang it!" Quickly I put the pistol that was lying on the floor into my pocket and walked to Laurel. I got to her as she was reaching for the door.

"You just like Zeema, Mister. You going to have to let me do."

"This isn't like buying M and M's by yourself at a store counter."

"And you going to tell me, I guess, what this *is*? I know this ain't M and M's. I know how mean people can be. I know that. But you got to let me do. Now let me open the door. Even a fool can see there ain't nobody there no more. You think I'm fool enough to open a door when there's trouble?"

"There might be trouble and meanness you don't understand."

"I been listening all my life about that. I studying what I listen to all my life. I listened to old women and old men. I'm good at listening and studying. But there come a time when you realize that you going to be an old woman yourself if you got to wait for the complete list of all the shapes trouble takes up in the world. Come a time . . . aw, listen, Mister, I'm opening this door. And you ain't stopping me. Get on back. Get back."

I let her open the door, but I did not get back.

Laurel found a tray of food on the floor outside and carried the tray to the desk. I locked the door behind us.

On the tray, there were mashed potatoes, a bowl of brown gravy, fried chicken, green beans and rice, a fork, napkins, and a note. The note read "Jamie, please vacate the office by 5 o'clock p.m. Leave the tuxedo on the couch. Leave Emerson Street and Main Street. Leave us to our hurts. N.R."

Laurel asked me about the initials and I told her about Nolan Roussell, his connection with Alison.

"Relations," she said and was about to ask me another question when Dugas sat up on the couch.

"Don't get up," I said.

"I ain't et for a day, lawyer. You almost try to blind me and you ain't going to give me a piece of chicken?"

"Let him eat with us, Mister. It's Sunday. Of all the shapes of trouble I heard of, he the funniest."

The Woman in the T-Bird

Laurel and I and a painter named Dugas sat to Sunday dinner at a desk in the Roussell Building. We ate, we questioned each other.

"Who told you I was in this office?" I asked Dugas.

"The Prince. Who else could of told me?"

"How much did he tell you?" Laurel asked. "Did he tell you why he came here? Why he's been following Zeema Steeple, talking to him in the shadows in New Orleans?"

"The nig—the colored singer?"

"You told me you came for money," I said.

"Wait, Mister, let him tell us about Zeema first."

"No, both of you just shut up with two mouths moving. Let the lawyer talk, gal."

"I ain't your gal. Ain't no man's gal. Don't you never again call me gal."

"Tell us about the blue-edged money," I said.

"That's better, lawyer. The blue-edged money. I like that, yas. You know the Prince has been collecting money he thinks is owed him. There's two separate bundles of money. One bundle's coming from the nig—the colored singer, Zeema. The other bundle—that's the blue-edged bundle—that's coming from somewhere else. But both bundles is mines. All that money's mines. All of it. Prince can't go around giving it when it's mines, can he? I know he said he was coming here to talk to a lawyer, and they don't make a lawyer don't ask for money. So any money he give you's mines. I know he paid you with it."

"He didn't pay me."

Dugas reached for the chicken bone Laurel discarded. She pushed his hand away. "That there's *mines*," she said, "even after death. My mouth was on it."

"You said the money belonged to you, Dugas."

"Tell her to give me that chicken bone. There's enough meat left on it to feed a family."

"Take the bone," Laurel said. "Just you keep talking."

"Like I was saying, any money the Prince got is mines. The Prince been working for me for quite a while, working *for* me, scraping and scrubbing houses. I been good out the kindness of my heart to give him advances on his pay. The black son of a bitch, I mean the colored son of a bitch, he gamble it away at Lineman's place. When he win, he don't pay me back. I got to take it back. Nig—colored people ain't responsible like us, lawyer. I'll say that in front of anybody."

"You say it in here," Laurel said, "and you putting your chicken at risk."

"Then just say that maybe you and your race, gal, is too proud to pay back. So I help him save face by taking what's mines."

"And I'm taking what's *mines*," Laurel said, grabbing the bone from Dugas' hands. "That's for calling me gal."

"Did Prince Albert keep his money in a cedar box under the vanity in his room?" I asked.

"Sure did, lawyer."

"Is that what you were doing in his house last night, breaking into his box for money?"

"Didn't have to break into no gotdamn box, me. I know where the key to the box is. And I belong in that house, live in it most the time. The Prince sort of expects me to break . . . open the box when he win. Niggers—"

"Don't you go niggering round here," Laurel said.

"Then give me the bone back."

Laurel let Dugas take the chicken bone from her napkin. "Now you tell this lawyer where Prince Albert got the blue money."

"Not wheres, but who, maybe. The Prince tells me lots, but I figure out lots."

"Were you working on a house on Emerson Street, blue trim?" I asked. "I saw the shutters. They're the same color as the blue money. Does Prince Albert's blue money have anything to do with that house?"

"We going to talk about that blue bundle of money first, lawyer? That how we going to do it?"

"Just do it," Laurel said. "There's a few greasy crumbs you can have on the tray if you look close."

"Start with the house on Emerson Street," I said.

"All right, all right. The Prince got us that job. You ever see such a blue for a trim job? It took a long time to scrape and wash that house, but the woman that owned it come across with the money every Friday, so there was no needing to finish all that fast. One Monday, the Prince, him, he was up the scaffold in front the woman's bedroom, up top. The woman was downstairs, at the piano, singing. She's crazy, her, loon, loon, loon. You should of heard it. Anyways, I went to the front door to knock and tell her we was starting the trim in the color she chose, and I knocked for ten, twenty, twenty-five minutes, until I was all knocked out. When I give up and walk around the corner of the house, the Prince wasn't on the scaffold no more. Next thing, the Prince climbs on out the bedroom window.

"'Just cause they named you after royalty don't mean they can't hang your black ass,' I say to him.

"I push the Prince off the scaffold and he lands in the amaryllis, flat on his back. I ask him what he seen up there.

191

"'Pictures,' the Prince say, 'pictures. My legacy.'

"I climbed up for myself to have a look and a see. I seen these pictures behind the bed, all of the same girl."

"Did Prince Albert say anything else about the pictures?" I asked Dugas.

"Easy, lawyer, for the sake of Christ. I'm still answering your questions, me. It's still the same question, ain't it? The Prince said something about how the face come before the photograph. But the Prince, him, he was full of sayings like that. He got up out the lily bed and walks up to the front door. The woman was still singing. When she don't answer his knock, the Prince crawls in through the first-floor window and falls headfirst inside."

"Lordy, Mister," Laurel said. "Alison's mama . . ."

"Prince Albert was blackmailing her," I said.

"That a question, lawyer? Or do you know everything?"

"Was Prince Albert blackmailing the woman at the piano?" Laurel asked.

Dugas lifted his cap, put his elbows on the desk and laughed. "Got the color correct, honey." His good eye watered; he wiped a tear that was glinting in the window light. "There's a million ways to say 'gal,' you know."

"And a million ways to choke on chicken," Laurel said.

"The Belanger woman," I said. "Prince Albert was blackmailing her."

"Belanger?" Dugas pronounced the name the Mondebon Parish way. "That name start with a *B*, don't it? I know *B*'s, me. But that ain't the name on the checks the woman give me. But leave me finish. After the Prince come out the house, he is still smiling, but smiling bigger and bigger. He ask me for a advance on his salary, which ain't not-normal for him to do. But he ask me for a complete hundred. He say he's good for at least that now. I give him the money, always did, because of what his mama the Princess done to save my last eye. I'd steal it back later anyways."

I asked Dugas for the name on the check.

"Can't tell you that. The Prince used to read for me. I can't even pee my own name in the dirt. I know *B* and *X*. That's all. And I know every Friday another woman drive up in a gray T-Bird car. I figure she the one makes out the checks."

"Who is that, you think, Mister?"

"The woman in the car," I said to Dugas. "Elegant?"

"Don't know that word."

"Classy? The skin on her face, tight, smooth?"

"Who is she, Mister?"

"Alison's aunt," I said. "Elizabeth Roussell. Remember the party last night? There was a woman in a lavender shawl."

"The woman helped carry out the drunk king?"

"Yes," I said. "She's Alison's aunt. She's married to Nolan Roussell."

"What he was, Mister? The leopard?"

"The Arab."

"You two just hold on," Dugas said, "just hold on. This getting haywire for me. You trying to get me haywire. A lawyer trick. Ask me another question and get me back on the tracks and get me back so I can follow what y'all say."

"Then back to the woman in the car," I said. "Classy."

"Yas, yas. That sound like her. Snooty and in the air. Wears long dresses all the time with her arms all covered and her neck all covered, like she was going to a dance with no intentions to dance at all."

"Did Prince Albert ever collect from the crazy woman?" I asked.

"Next day, that would be Tuesday, next day the Prince come to work late. He lost the advance. He climbs in the first-floor window, and he comes out cursing this time. He says the woman inside's too crazy to collect from. Then who you suppose drive up? That's right. The woman in the long dresses and sleeves. She go inside, stay awhile, and when she come out, instead of backing the T-Bird out, she sit in her car

193

staring at the Prince. Then she wiggle her finger for the Prince to come. The Prince walk to her car, and then her and the Prince drive off. When the Prince get back—he walked back—but he's walking with what I figure is a thousand or two. He roll up the bills and dip them in the blue-trim paint."

"Did he get more money?" I asked.

"The Prince say that that money was just a start, yas."

"Mister," Laurel said. "It's time we talk about Zeema. Prince Albert was trying to get money from Zeema, too."

"Hold up, lawyer, hold up. I'm doing all the giving here, and what I'm giving's worth more than a chewed chicken bone. Let's back up. You know they arrested the nig—the colored fellow that sings."

"Zeema?" Laurel asked.

Dugas laughed. When his thin lips separated they revealed two yellow canines. "Attempted murder, lawyer. They got him on attempted murder. Now how you figure on that? They got him for attempted murdering the Prince, and they got the Prince locked up, too, for safekeeping. And they got other witnesses saying the nig—colored singer did it."

"Zeema didn't do anything," Laurel said.

"Who are the other witnesses?" I asked.

"The most upstanding nig—colored man on Landry. Lineman hisself. Lineman told the police he saw this singer and me and you and that crazy girl running from the Palace. But they let everybody out but the singer. How you figure that?"

"Mardi Gras, Mister. They want Zeema away from Mardi Gras."

"Prince Albert told me that Zeema might kill him."

"Mister, I said—"

"He's just a lawyer, gal—I can call you gal cause you et up most of the tray, you. He's just being a lawyer. Lawyers don't mean what they ask sometimes. We'll get back to that question, lawyer." Dugas laughed again. The gums between the canines were red as his crescent of eye. "Well, well, and well. You two got it figured yet? All this time y'all been questioning me. And all this time I been leading you two. I know lots, me. I know lots, but I ain't really told you nothing, not a gotdamn thing."

"Did Zeema try to kill Prince Albert?" I asked.

"Mister—"

"I said I know lots, but I ain't telling you another thing, me. Not a snit. Know where I'm heading?"

Laurel said the word before I could. "Money."

"That's right. You can beat me till I'm black, lawyer. And you can take all the chicken, gal. But if you want more answers from me, you'll have to pay."

"Just maybe we can get all the answers we need from someplace else," Laurel said.

"Like I said, lawyer, nigger gal, I want my money."

I leaned across the desk to grab Dugas' coveralls. Laurel stopped me by touching my arm.

"I don't need a white man defending me against that word *nigger*," she said. "You don't know what it's like, so you can't be defending. But I tell you what, that other word, *gal*, that's just as bad. And you don't know what that's like either. No sir, Mister, you don't know. Somebody call you 'nigger gal,' they putting you as low as low is. You don't know, so calm down."

"He crazy all right," Dugas said. "But like I said. You can beat me all black, I ain't saying no more. You want more, I'll be at the Prince's house, the Palace, if you two get in a buying mood. Come at night."

"Over our dead bodies," Laurel said.

"Just so they covered with money, gal. Now give me my empty gun and I'll be on my ways, me."

I tossed the .22 onto the desk. Dugas took the pistol, rose, wiped his hands on his coveralls. At the door he stopped, and turning he said, "Let me give y'all some information free. I didn't try to kill the Prince. Not me. And Zeema, that nigger singer, he didn't try to kill nobody neither."

Laurel rose this time, singing and dancing about. "Camptown race track five mile long, Doo-gah, Doo-gah. I told you, Mister. I told you. He didn't try to kill nobody. Zeema didn't—"

"If Dugas's telling the truth," I said, "that's right. But there were three of us in the Palace. If Dugas's telling the truth . . ."

Laurel stopped her dancing. "Oh, Mister, this ain't going to be easy. Alison. She didn't do it, neither, Mister. I know she didn't. I just know it."

"I want to believe that, too," I said.

The Mossman

Before we left the office, I changed into my suit and wrote more of what I remembered on the yellow pads. Laurel and I talked about facts, about what could be observed as having happened. We agreed, both of us, about how facts are worth seeking. It was Laurel who brought up the abstraction—faith, belief beyond the fact. But that discussion led to confusion, and like average citizens we let our words about that subject fade and drop.

Eventually Laurel began questioning again, and that led us to Alison. I told Laurel about Alison's mother's suicide. Just before we left the office, I asked Laurel for my bottle of pills. She refused to give them to me, saying again as we walked down the stairs that she would "take care" of them for me.

That Sunday, Main Street belonged to the Krewe of Iris.

(Molly, the parade, called the "woman's parade" in Mondebon Parish, begins where Louisiana Highway 54 becomes East Main. The parade rolls west, turning south at Cathedral

Street two blocks before the Landry intersection. Most of the town parades share this route, and to this day all of the parades stop once along the route for the champagne toast in front of City Hall across the street from the Roussell Building.)

The reviewing stand across the street from Roussell's Style Shoppe was draped with the colors of Mardi Gras, green and purple and gold. On the stand as Laurel and I reached Main Street, the king of Iris, town officials, and guests of the krewe were awaiting the arrival of the queen's float.

In the last chair on the end of the last row, without costume, sat Mayor Poule. Laurel recognized Poule from the Senator's party the night before and mentioned Poule's feathers and beak. "It's a good thing he didn't wear that today," she said. "He'd have to fear for his very life when Dugas be stalking around hungry."

We heard the sirens and drums. The crowd began to claim their places on the sidewalks as we crossed Main.

One straggler, a man covered with Spanish moss with playing cards tangled in it, danced along the court-square curb and poked excited children with an oak branch. He took a playful jab at Laurel's ankles, and I grabbed the branch and jerked it from his hand. Laurel took the branch from me and offered it to the mossman by holding it up to him, but the man did not reach for it. He belched and I smelled beer. I saw in spaces in the silver-green moss the quick and primal sheen of the mossman's eyes.

(Molly, this mossman is the vision I had and still have in many of my dreams. I have spent a lot of time trying to identify this person, and I have narrowed it down, believe it or not, to someone who would be sheriff of Mondebon Parish one day. More on this later, if I have time. Just let me say for now that he seems to represent something less than what my family calls "evil" in the Marquis chronicles—a primal license and meanness that stops just short of contemplating

197

itself. Forgive the abstraction, Molly, and the diversion of my dreams.)

After we turned away from the mossman, Laurel handed me the oak branch—a cane, she said, for my sore ankle. I asked her if we should go to the courthouse and the jail on the third floor of the courthouse. "No," she said. "We got to get to Alison first. Don't you know that?"

I did know that. And in the world called De Plus En Plus, a sister moved to protect a sister.

Daughter Daughter

At a white wrought-iron table on the patio behind the house on Emerson Street, Alison sat in peignoir, painting the nails of her feet. The heel of her left foot was resting on her right knee, and her right hand supported the arch of the foot under the brush.

Without changing her position, she looked up as we approached. Her face showed no signs of the crying I thought she'd done the night before. Pieces of my nightmare came back to me as I saw the back of her thigh in the peach-colored light beneath the loose folds of her peignoir.

She looked at me first and did not recognize me. Then she saw Laurel and smiled, and when her eyes came to me again she knew me, also.

Laurel ran to her. The two girls hugged each other.

"I heard, honey," Laurel said, "about your terrible night. You all right?"

Alison did not speak. Tears began to form in her eyes, but she did not cry.

"You just got up, didn't you, honey?" Laurel said to Alison. "I brought us a lawyer. You remember him?"

"Jay Pee," Alison said.

"Honey, you got to eat something. Where's your kitchen?"

"No, sit with me. We all have to talk. Zeema Steeple's in trouble, isn't he?"

"You heard her, Mister. Sit, for heaven sakes. Put down your suitcase and your crutch and sit."

I sat across the table from the two of them and then laid the oak branch on the suitcase at my feet. "How much of last night do you remember?"

"You're hurt," Alison said. "Your leg . . ."

"You tell her what she's supposed to remember, Mister, and I'll find a kitchen and some eggs and anything else that look like breakfast. You be okay, honey."

Laurel left Alison and me alone and before Laurel returned I told Alison about the long night. Alison seemed to remember each detail as I brought them up.

"So one of us tried to kill a man named Prince Albert," Alison said. "Last night, I remember, you were certain it was Zeema Steeple. I remember what you said to him as we marched in the street."

"The painter who worked with Prince Albert said that Zeema didn't do it."

"Then you tell me, Jay Pee. Did I?"

"You don't remember anything?"

"Not clearly, Jay Pee. Wait, I called you Daddy. I remember I called you Daddy. Well, let me tell you, Daddy, with me there's always a chance. Ask anyone in my family."

"What are you trying to say?"

Laurel returned with a plate of food—eggs, toast, juice. Alison ate at Laurel's urging and continued to speak at mine.

"I told you last night, Jay Pee, that I wouldn't end up like my mother, my hand over the tub. I won't. I can't. I remember asking you to smell me last night. Know what you were smelling? Survival. After high school, I spent some time in the hospital in Jackson. You know what that's for? Uncle Nolan calls it 'rest.' Shock therapy, straps, then you rest. After I got out, I left this town, with Uncle Nolan's help again, for

199

California, for college and beach and books. I was going to be a great woman, physicist or anthropologist. I ended up, within the first month, in another rest home. In Bakersfield this time. Closer to a rest. They're more up-to-date with drugs there."

"Is that where you got the drugs you used last night?" I asked.

"Indirectly, Jay Pee. That's the drug they used on me at the . . . at the rest facility, all right. But I didn't get the stuff I used last night directly from them. I bet the letters *LSD* don't mean a thing to you."

"No."

"But you felt them last night, Jay Pee. In the orange. Don't worry. Not too many have heard of the stuff yet. Not too many have heard of anything yet. Oh, marijuana, sure. Pot. Even you, I bet. A friend of mine says LSD is going to change the way the world thinks of itself."

"Your friend gave you the drugs you used last night?"

"Her name's Pistil. Not the gun, but the flower. I met her at the rest home in Bakersfield. A rest, everybody calls it a rest. Crazy I call it. Certified. I have the papers to prove it. I stayed in there a year. Pistil helped me, then. Helped me out. When I got out I swore I would never need rest again. I would do anything to find what I was, and I was going to keep what I found, understand? And everything was cool. I was close to finding what I was looking for. I had done some good, trav-eled. Freedom rides, sit-ins. I was doing some good. Then I decided to visit home. Visit mother."

"That's okay, honey, that's enough."

"No, let me finish. I want you both to understand. I'm determined to find what I set out to find."

"And what is that?" I asked.

"Quit being a lawyer, Mister, and listen."

"I'm determined to find out who the hell I am. And I'm

determined not to end up like my mother. I want you both to understand."

"And we here to help you," Laurel said. "You understand that."

"You don't remember much of what happened at the Palace?" I asked Alison.

"A palace?"

"The place where Prince Albert lived."

Alison shook her head. "As of right now, that's right. As of right now, I'm saying I've never heard of a Palace. I'm also saying maybe I'll remember doing something horrible to that man you're talking about, to Prince Albert. With me there's always a chance. I have the papers, remember . . . to prove it. Certified. I can be—"

"Hush, honey," Laurel said.

"You must have met Prince Albert earlier that day," I said. "I remember you told Zeema at the Senator's party that you had a message for him. Do you remember that message?"

"Yes . . . I think. Keep talking about it."

"No, Mister, hush now."

"Are you sure you want to talk," I asked.

"Yes. With me there's always a chance."

"We don't believe that, do we, Mister?"

"Tell me about the drugs you're taking. Can you stay away from them until we clear everything up?"

Laurel reached into the pocket of her dress and pulled out my amber bottle of pills. "Look who's talking," she said. "Follow me, honey. I ain't never been this close to a pool and I want to get a good look."

Alison and Laurel walked toward a stone path that led into the orange trees. About ten feet into the trees Laurel stopped and called to me. She raised the pills over her head, shook them. "Alison said we can bury these, Mister." Laurel and Alison got to their knees near some fresh-turned earth.

After digging a shallow hole in the St. Augustine grass with their hands, they buried the pills. Then, together, two young women walked toward the edge of the water.

(Yes, Molly, as I sit here straining to put together bits of conversation that come as close to resembling life as it can be shown to have occurred, I know that you have begun to see by now my own connection to these two young women and the world called De Plus En Plus. I felt this connection earlier under the influence of the sea-green pills, when I wrote in my notes *I have two daughters.* With a clearer head, sitting in the shade of a patio in the midafternoon light as I watched Laurel and Alison returning from the water's edge, I remembered also the other words I had written: *I will not fail,* meaning of course *Again . . . again . . . I will not fail again.* Can you imagine, Molly, what I felt as I saw Laurel and Alison walking back toward me from the water? Yes, I know you can.)

After Alison went back into the house, Laurel and I decided that it was time to see Zeema. She walked with me down the driveway toward Emerson Street.

"Mister, you ever hear the song 'Motherless Child Blues'? Elvie Thomas sang it. In the song, the mama tells her daughter not to go and be like the mama was. You know, Mister, there's words to songs fit everything. Or is it maybe everything you live already been lived by somebody? Know what I be saying?"

"I'm following you."

Laurel stopped at the end of the driveway. "Then you must know what else I be saying. I got to stay here. You go see Zeema and clear this up. You still believe, Mister?"

I did not answer.

Then Laurel asked me if I had any children, and I answered her: "Two daughters."

Laurel smiled, "I kind of had me a hunch."

If Laurel had asked me their names, I might have answered her, might have formed the sounds for the first time in a long time. But she did not ask. She seemed to know better than to go any further—at that time.

"Give me your suitcase," Laurel said. "I'll take care of your yellow paper. You get to Zeema."

Ministers but No Martyrs

I got to Zeema's cell easily enough by saying that I was his lawyer, but others—the Reverend Stillman Bowman and Lineman—had also made it in.

When he saw me, Zeema laughed, strutted about the cell in his jeans and white T-shirt—the standard Mondebon Parish prison dress at the time—then put one foot on the closed toilet seat below the barred window. "Welcome to stage two of prison, Jay Pee. Last night they wouldn't let nobody in. Today they letting anybody in."

Lineman stood leaning on the bars with his eyes closed. Bowman sat on the bunk with his hat in his hands, the collar of his coat curving like a hood behind his small head.

"What line you give them, Jay Pee? Lineman here told them he was my bail bondsman. Bowman here told them he was my reverend. What you told them, Jay Pee?"

"I said I was your lawyer."

"You are no one's lawyer," Bowman said. "This is bigger than you."

"Jay Pee, I've moved on up from song nigger to symbol."

"Don't go using that word in here, Ozema," Bowman said.

I heard Lineman snort as though his own snoring had waked him. "We got the right to use that word we want to," he said. "Who else got the right we ain't got the right, you understand?"

"Look who is speaking rights," Bowman said to Lineman. "You, a man who would sell his rights and the rights of others for a diamond ring or a chip of gold."

"How about people who sell they rights for what they call a greater good?" Lineman said. "Like for a new church. What's the difference, reverend-man, chips of gold or new church?"

"All right now, my boys," Zeema said. "I be consulting with a lawyer here. I'm a symbol, Jay Pee. Best you hear about it now. I represent injustice done to an entire race of people. Bowman here has called the NAACP about all this. They have answered his call this time. I think he wants me to stay put here in jail awhile so that idea gets established firm. And Lineman here, he's brought me a deal. He wants me out of here and out of town. He's willing to spring me free if I get out. Imagine the honor of that. Being sprung free by Lineman himself, the town's first black bail bondsman. So tell me, Jay Pee, where you fit in all this?"

"Laurel," I said.

At the mention of the name, Zeema turned from me and faced the barred window above the toilet.

"She thinks I should represent you," I said.

"You shouldn't be representing a living soul," Bowman said. "You got the name all right. Big name. But Lineman here let me in on how you are now ineffective as an attorney. You have sullied your name in the New Orleans court."

"How did you find out about that?" I asked Lineman.

Lineman opened his eyes with a snort. "Connections," he said. "My favorite word, you understand. *Connections.* You can use it if you want."

Again I mentioned Laurel to Zeema. This time his arms went up to stop me. "Not till they're out of here," he said.

"Ozema," Bowman said. "This is more important than singing songs."

"That's the best we can hope for, Reverend," Zeema said. "Ain't it? Song nigger or ball-carrying nigger?"

"I said do not use that word, Ozema."

"Out of here," Zeema said. "Bondmen and reverends out. Lawyer stay."

The jailer, who had stood outside the cell all that time, opened the cell door. Bowman and Lineman left without saying anything else. But somewhere down the cellblock, Bowman's grating tenor carried through and into all the bars. "You gave us your word, Ozema!" I heard other prisoners stirring in their bunks.

When Zeema and I were alone, he sat on the bunk and patted the mattress with his hand. "Have a seat, Jay Pee. You a liberal southern sort. You sit next to us."

I sat beside Zeema, my thigh about a foot away from his.

"Now, Jay Pee, say her name again now we alone."

I felt a wave of anger lifting me. I grabbed the mattress with both of my hands.

"The Reverend's right, ain't he? You got something biled up inside. Spit green, Jay Pee. Spit at me."

And I did let the green out: "Don't you think Laurel's a little young to be carried around town to town? What's her mother think of all this?"

"Her mother's dead."

"Her father, what's her father—"

"Now, Jay Pee, I can tell by your words that even you liberal southern sorts got assumptions. Her daddy must not be hanging around the house, right? Nigger men screw and leave, right? Nigger singers take advantage—"

I rose and told the jailer to open the cell.

"Hold on, Jay Pee. You told me you were going to take care of Laurel. You been doing that for me?"

205

The door opened and I started to walk out. Then Zeema said something that got me to stay with him: "Jay Pee. If anything happens to me, could you keep her? Bring her with you to New Orleans? School her?"

I had not thought directly of that idea, of taking Laurel with me back to New Orleans, but after Zeema said those words I realized that I must have been considering such a thing somewhere, somewhere in the green Zeema had spoken of.

"You know what I'm saying, Jay Pee? All those niceties you liberal southern sorts assume she deserves but can't get from us colored unfortunates?"

"You in or you out, you?" the jailer asked.

I turned to Zeema. He moved to the center of the bunk, sat cross-legged facing me.

"That's it, Jay Pee. She's a calming thought, ain't she, Laurel? Stay a while."

"Alison . . ."

"You say her name just like you say Laurel's, Jay Pee. You in the saving business this month, ain't you."

"Did Alison go with you to Prince Albert's place, to the Palace?"

"I know she must've gone to the Palace. I figured that out when she came running down the street toward me during my now-famous demonstration. But, no, she didn't go with me there. I'm guessing that she followed me. While I was in the Prince's room I had a feeling some others were in the Palace rooms. There's so many of them—rooms on rooms. But there's so many ghosts in there anyone would get the feeling the rooms were full, just like during the war years and before that. Tell me, Jay Pee. Did she get a look in the Prince's room?"

"She did."

"Yeah, that was on her face. That . . . but that was on her

face all evening, Jay Pee. You going to watch over her, too?"

"Prince Albert told me he was blackmailing you. He said you stole some songs from him."

"Then let it go at that."

"Did you try to kill him?"

"The Prince be telling everybody I did. Swore to it in writing. Lineman put pressure on the Prince to put things in writing. That sure is helping those people who want me out of action until after Mardi Gras. They want Zulu out of town."

"You didn't answer me. Did you try to kill Prince Albert?"

"Got to think about the answer to that real careful, Jay Pee. If I answer right, Laurel might get her a decent house, right? If I answer right, that put everybody clear, right?"

"Laurel needs to know the truth," I said. "Everything. I have a feeling she can take the truth."

Zeema patted the bunk in front of him. "Would you sit one more time, Jay Pee? Just one more time for the sake of all that's liberal you and your family believe in?"

I sat with my feet on the floor.

"No," Zeema said. "Sit like me. Face me."

I swiveled, crossed my legs, faced him. Zeema moved closer until our knees were touching and he raised his right hand.

"What color you think that is, Jay Pee, that skin that covers me? Kind of coffee-with-too-much-cream brownish. I ain't purely what could be called a man of color, but . . . hold up your hand, Jay Pee."

I raised my right hand for him. Zeema grabbed my hand with his, interlocking the fingers. Then he squeezed and twisted my wrist. I lunged forward with my body and also squeezed until our hands were parallel again.

Zeema strained, trying to hurt me. "This kind of just like life, ain't it? What's the issue here, Jay Pee? You're a powerful man. I'm skinny but I'm powerful, too. Is that the issue? My hand darker than your hand. That the issue? We both hurting each other. You hurting like my hand hurting? Is that the issue? Who's going to let go first? Somebody got to let go first. Is that the issue? What's the fucking issue here, Jay Pee. Say it!"

I said Laurel's name again. Zeema's hand and arm went limp and my force pushed him backward before I let go of the hold on his hand.

"That's the issue, Jay Pee. Laurel. There's bigger issues, but I don't hang around for those. There's only one issue with me at this stage of my life, and that's what I love and what I'm facing at any one moment. I sneak away from the rest. Big issues is for other people."

I thought of my brothers and sisters as I stood up, of the Marquis notion of history in the larger and smaller sense. I kept my back to Zeema.

"What is your connection with Laurel?" I asked.

"You're using Lineman's word. But I guess he gave you copyright."

"What's your connection?"

"Oh, Jay Pee, Jay Pee. What assumptions in there with your bile? You thinking this song nigger got him some young meat?"

I turned to face Zeema, to run at him. Both of Zeema's hands were up, the palms to me.

"Hold on," he said. "You got me. Don't go beating on the symbol of an entire race."

I put my hands to my face and breathed deeply.

"Jay Pee, your eyes was so slitty I couldn't even see the pretty green in them. We both got the issue straight here. You take care of Laurel. She's more important than symbols. I think we both agree to that, don't we? And don't worry about lawyering for me. Bowman's got me a fancy lawyer coming."

As I took my hands from my face to look at Zeema, I heard

Bowman's voice coming in through the window. "Brothers and sisters, stand to the tune. Stand to the tune!"

Zeema left the bunk and stood on one foot on the toilet seat to look outside. "Come up here, Jay Pee. Get a look at this."

I walked to Zeema and stood on one leg beside him. Outside in the schoolyard the Reverend Stillman Bowman, standing on the long trailer of a flatbed truck, was organizing what looked to be a choir of about fifty in gold-and-white robes.

"Look at that, Jay Pee. I got one question for you. You got hold of the issues here. You know how far away from here Bowman's church is. Tell me, knowing all the issues and distances involved, don't you wonder, don't you wonder how that man found an extension cord long enough to power up that electric organ and that microphone?"

Zeema laughed and jumped down. I was still too angry to laugh with him. I stepped down from the toilet and walked to the door; Zeema sat on the bunk again.

"Bowman dealed Mardi Gras away once before, Jay Pee. He ain't doing it again."

I told the jailer to open the door. "Not till you sure," he said.

"He's sure," Zeema said. "Jay Pee, you keep on the track. The issue we both believe in is keeping Laurel safe. Safe even from big issues like symbols and such. We agree to that?"

I did not answer. After the jailer closed the door behind me, Zeema said, "Jay Pee." Then he said Laurel's name for both of us to hear and said, "I tried to kill the Prince, Jay Pee. It was me. My aim was a little to the right, but I come close to doing the job. That ain't no lie, Jay Pee. Take care of Laurel."

After the jailer closed and locked the cell door, I asked him if I could see Prince Albert Willis. He told me that the "nigger with the bandage on his face" was being kept downstairs in a special cell and did not want to see anybody.

As I walked through the cellblock, I heard the choir in the schoolyard singing "Every Time I Feel the Spirit." To my right some of the prisoners also sang; in the cells to my left some cursed because they had no windows.

I bought a cigar and the evening edition of the local paper at the drugstore at the corner of Cathedral Street and Main, and then with my throbbing ankle propped on a court-square bench I smoked and read through sunset.

(Molly, I've enclosed a photocopy of the one-sentence story with the one-column headline about Zeema—NEGRO HELD— along with the next morning's edition of the *Times-Picayune* with the three-column 36-point head—FAMOUS SINGER DE-TAINED. Also I'm sending an actual clipping from the obituaries I tore from the paper at dusk that Sunday evening: "Bethany Arcement Belanger, 42, of 207 Emerson Street, of a long illness. She is preceded in death by her husband, Raymond Belanger, and is survived by a daughter, Alison Elizabeth, and a sister, Elizabeth Arcement Roussell.")

After I finished with the paper, I watched Nolan Roussell, in his gray fedora, sweeping litter from that day's parade from the sidewalk in front of his Style Shoppe. He saw me, waved, and walked across Main to where I was sitting; he knew better by then than to offer me his hand. We spoke about Bowman and his "gold-robed agitators."

"How disappointed, Jamie, Bowman must be to have got only a citation. Ministers but no martyrs."

"My name is not Jamie. You know that."

"Ah, and finally that has flustered you. You look the flustered one, my son."

"And I am not—"

"Do not finish that. You are correct. But what has mussed up your noble nature? Tell us."

"Why was Prince Albert Willis blackmailing your wife?"

For the first time, Roussell noticed he had carried the broom with him from his store to the court square. Nothing else showed on his face. He turned from me, still without changing his expression, and walked toward his shop.

After Roussell left me, I thought of what Zeema had told me about taking care of Laurel, and I sat staring until the streetlights came on, at the phone booth across the street in front of the drugstore.

(Molly, this was the first time I thought of calling you. I have not as of yet, though I consider doing it each time I see a phone. Perhaps I should have walked across Cathedral Street that evening when I sat alone in the court square. What would I have said then? *Molly, there are second chances in the world. I will finish up here, will be home soon with a daughter for us. Isn't that the only way?*)

But I did not cross the street. And I am convinced now that it was then, as I smoked and thought in the court square, that all of the abstractions like hope and the world called De Plus En Plus that had been gestating since I arrived in town were born as one dangerous notion: I believed that the world around me had been made for me. I believed, as many before me have, that all sorrows and pain are a test and that each of us—in all those worlds made for each of us—must meet and bear. And I believed that I had somehow met and borne enough so that my losses were going to be returned to me. I believed that it would be too cruel even for the God I hated to allow me to lose those things again.

And it was at that same time as I sat thinking that a cab pulled up to the Cathedral Street curb. The cabbie got out to walk to the phone across the street. I read the name on the cab door and called to him before he was completely across the street.

"Hey, Fabregas," I said. I stood up and pointed to Nolan Roussell. "Do you know where that man lives?"

"I do if you pay to get there."

I left my oak branch where it lay and started the short walk to the cab. "I pay," I said.

The Flier, the Cartoon Caveman, and a Daughter of the House of Levi

Fabregas drove me three miles down the northern bank of Bayou Mondebon to the town's first subdivision, Heatherland. He stopped his cab in front of a yard where a man in a white shirt was hammering a For Sale by Owner sign under a mimosa tree. The man's stroke with the rubber mallet was sure, his torso imposing against the gray sky. When I saw the flight glasses hanging from the pocket of the white shirt, I remembered the Senator's party and I remembered this man, King Delos XVI, being carried out drunk in his Army Air Corps costume.

(Molly, if I were to cross the river into Hades, whom do you think I'd ask the desk attendant to ring for me? Yes, dearest. My brother Berman.

I ask this question now because, as you will see, the man hammering in the subdivision yard was to become, in my mind at least, the De Plus En Plus version of Berman. In no way, however, did the two physically resemble each other:

Berman the frailest and shortest of us Marquises; Berman with the reddest hair of any of us, the saddest face—do you remember Aunt Margaret at the funeral saying of Berman, "He took too much to heart?"

Nolan Roussell's son, King Delos XVI, was taller than any Marquis, a full six inches taller than I, taller even than Uncle Francis. He had a pleasant face, a face that today we would call a television politician's face, blue-eyed, full, and handsome. Like his father Nolan, though, he had not been marked

212

with the lines that would be taken for depth of character in a politician making a speech on a soapbox in the full light of the court square.

So what was it, Molly, about this man that reminded me of Berman? It may be that I was expecting—hoping?—to encounter my brother's double in the world called De Plus En Plus. I do not know. But as I said, in the gray light of dusk, the hammering man was an imposing image. I had often thought of my brother in such light. It may be that I had been thinking of my brother on the drive in the cab.)

I gave Fabregas one of the last dollar bills I had in my pocket—enough to cover the fare and a tip—and I asked him to wait.

"That's Roussell's son, that there," Fabregas said. "He don't live in the house with his daddy. He lives, him, in the second floor of that garage there."

Roussell must have overheard Fabregas. As he walked toward us, he said, "Barron Palmer Roussell, who does indeed live in the small garage-turret beside his father's Heatherland castle." He slapped me on the back and held out his hand to me. "In Mondebon Parish, we forge our royalty on our birth certificates, partner. Seems easier than taking the chance of being properly conceived, don't you think?"

Barron Roussell's eyes were blue even in the twilight of Heatherland.

(Molly, I sensed immediately—possibly because of my thoughts of my brother—that Roussell had also survived some long pain. You could see this, remember, everywhere in and around Berman's eyes. Barron Roussell's eyes, like his face, were unlined, but I sensed—but I may be coloring a bit now with the sense of memory and the knowledge of what happened to my brother and of what I now know about Roussell and what I now know lay ahead for all of us.)

Though I stared at his eyes for what should have been an

213

embarrassing length for two men meeting, Roussell did not look away. It was I who looked away, down, at the hand.

"Well, partner? Marquis, isn't it?"

I shook his hand. I do not remember his grip or the shape of his hand, but I know that it was then that I realized that I had not shaken anyone's hand for a long time, and again I may have stared too long at what I was doing because Roussell said, "Not the hand of a hammer-bearer is it, partner?"

"I'm just glad someone in your family pronounces my name right."

Roussell smiled but did not laugh.

(I do not remember, Molly, having ever seen him laugh. Even Berman laughed, rising with his joy. Remember, we defined the difference between delight and joy one night when we heard Berman laugh, out of the long pain.)

"I make it a point," Roussell said, "to get at names correctly. My father gets at them also, but with an opposite gyration. Are you familiar with this end of town?"

"Fabregas filled me in."

"Then he's told you the town is dying? My father—you know Nolan—my father's moving back to town away from this place. 'Stalker's field,' we call it."

Roussell put the mallet under his arm and pointed to the lights in the distance over the line of flat roofs across the street. "There's the melanoma, partner. Westside Mall. The banker Stalker was the first to begin moving the town piecemeal west. But you aren't here to discuss real estate."

"I'd like to see your mother."

"My stepmother. She's my age—our age—partner. You are here to see her about the Negro with the sword, aren't you?"

I asked if she was in. Roussell nodded. When I asked Fabregas again to wait until I returned, Roussell said that would not be necessary.

"I'll drive you back, partner. I think you'll be here awhile, and we'll have to talk after you're finished with Elizabeth, with my stepmother. I think we have much to discuss."

With his hand on the small of my back, Roussell guided me toward the house—what he called a 'typical, wide, one-story brick, Stalker-in-the-heather home'—that stretched from one end of the lot to the other. There was a light on inside, behind the curtains of a picture window. He also pointed to the garage beside the house, to the balcony on the second floor. His apartment, he said. I saw the green, purple, and gold cloth above the door, the bunting that marked the house of the king of Mardi Gras.

"Don't bother ringing the bell," he said. "She won't answer. Just walk in. Besides an aptitude for the piano and the lie, her family breeds the shut-in. When you're finished, walk around to me. I think we have much in common to discuss. I will not lie if asked directly. Luck to you. Luck to you, partner."

I knocked anyway. The lights behind the curtain went off. I hesitated, listened for a voice. Then I opened the door and stood in the cold entranceway. On a small table under a mirror on the wall opposite the door, I saw an empty box from Roussell's Pyramid of Costume. I heard the hum of air being forced through ceiling ducts. In the living room to my left, Elizabeth Arcement Roussell sat on a sofa with her back to me; she faced the blue-orange light of a television set. Two pianos—a grand and an upright—filled most of the rest of the room.

"I met you Sunday morning," I said.

She answered me without turning. "And I asked you then to leave. My husband has since asked you to leave, has he not? Tell me what it is you want from where you stand."

"I've come to talk to you about Prince Albert Willis, the painter."

"You will have to describe him better than that."

"He was one of the two men painting your sister's house."

"A colored man? I guessed that from the sound of his name."

I felt my anger with those words. I wanted to say her stepson's name, but I did not.

"Did he ever come here?" I asked. "To this house?"

"You must know the answer to that question or you wouldn't be here. You are a lawyer. My stepson is a lawyer. I know enough to know that lawyers do not ask questions the answers to which they are not prepared for."

"He was blackmailing your sister. And you."

I heard her laugh. There was no delight anywhere in that laugh. On the screen a second boulder fell on the head of a cartoon caveman.

"You paid Prince Albert," I said.

When she rose and walked to the television set, I could see that she was dressed for bed. Her hair—ashen, blonde, shining—fell to the waist of her long-sleeved gown. Before the screen went black she turned, pulling her collar in close around her neck. In the light of what was left of dusk filtering through the curtains, I could see that she was my age. Even with heavy makeup, her face was as lined as mine, especially under her eyes. As was mine.

"I suspect you are guessing," she said. "But even if what you say is true, it is no business of yours."

"It is Alison's business. She has asked me for help."

"I suspect, regardless, that you are trying quite hard to make it your business. Am I not right?"

"Alison—"

"Enough, please. My past is no business of hers, then."

"It is," I said, "if it affects her safety now. Are you saying your past does not affect her now?"

"I am saying what part of my past is mine is mine. And

whom I choose to give my money is my business. Next witness."

Before I left, I read the label on the costume box: A Daughter of the House of Levi.

As I stood under the purple, green, and gold bunting on the balcony of the garage apartment, I heard voices behind the door. I could tell that one of the voices was mine. I opened the door without knocking. Inside, Barron Palmer Roussell sat on a stool at an oak bar; his hand lay beside a glass filled with amber liquid.

The wall behind the bar was lit by the yellow and green dials of an elaborate sound system—amplifiers, speakers, but no radio or phonograph. The reels of a large, professional-quality tape recorder were spinning.

Roussell smiled as he listened to the conversation coming through speakers in each corner of the room: *"Are you saying your past does not affect her now?"*

"Bold, partner, bold," Roussell said.

"I am saying what part of my past is mine is mine."

"But that—that, partner, is a riposte."

Roussell got up from the stool and pushed the buttons that stopped the reels from turning. I saw that there were no pictures anywhere on any of the other walls, but on the floor I saw the backs of framed pictures ready to be hung.

"Interested in the pictures, or the tapes?" Roussell asked.

"Both."

Moving to the nearest picture, Roussell turned the frame. "My old squadron," he said. "They're all pictures of my time in the service. You served? I heard that all Marquises serve."

"I stayed stateside," I said. "But I had brothers . . ."

"Then you know, partner, some of us were . . . how shall I say it? It has taken some of us years to take our pictures out. I have been shut in since '46. Not bred to be a shut-in as with

217

my stepmother's family, but nonetheless. . . . Some of us encountered things . . . how shall I say."

"You don't have to say. I had a brother."

Roussell walked to the bar again and sat. "I did not mean
to get maudlin, partner. And before you ask me some questions, let me say something to someone who would seem
to understand. I have been shut in, living under my father's
care. My father always said that when I was ready to emerge,
he would make me king of Mardi Gras. I have emerged,
partner. You do understand that I will not go back to the
sepulchre?"

I said nothing, but I did understand, and there in the little
two-room apartment I thought of my brother and the world
of De Plus En Plus. In the small space I felt confined and close
to Roussell. I said nothing, but I did understand, and I did
long to see my brother.

"But on, let us move on, partner. This is a wonderment, is
it not?" Roussell made a sweep of his hand across the wall
behind the bar.

"Is this your way of trapping a blackmailer?"

"Good, quite good, partner. Yes, my father came to me
and said that we would be having a visit from a colored fellow
who was prone to that felony. It was he, my father, who told
me it was time to emerge. He needed my help. Imagine, *he*
needing my help. Who would not have emerged, having
heard such as that?"

(Molly, —Berman)

"At any rate, partner, I may have gone over the board a
bit. I called a friend of mine from the time I was district attorney. Another story, there. I tried emerging once before—'49,
I believe—with disastrous results. Took to the bottle. A familiar story there. But at any rate, my contact with a professional eavesdropper came as a result of my public service. I
called him and found to my delight that his business had pro-
gressed technologically and imaginatively. And to do the job

correctly, I bought all that you see before you. All of this is to your benefit, partner."

Roussell walked around and took a small, white machine from somewhere beneath the bar. I had never seen such a machine before, although I could recognize a handle, control buttons. After fumbling through what sounded like small boxes, Roussell also brought out a shoe box and a white microphone attached to a long white wire. Leaving the shoebox and microphone on the bar, he carried the machine with him to his seat.

"Read the labels on the buttons, partner. Take a guess at what this is. See? Fast Forward. Rewind. That's right, a tape recorder. My professional eavesdropper purchased this in the Netherlands. I'm not sure if it's even on the market yet."

After Roussell touched a button, a cartridge of some kind popped out into his hand.

"What do you think this will be called, partner? See the small reels in here. All of that technology behind me is encapsulated within this small device. This will easily fit into that shoebox. Of course you still have to contend with a microphone and that wire. But one day, can you imagine partner, a tape recorder that might fit in your coat pocket? Amazing what one misses of the goings-on outside the sepulchre. Whether one is amenable to the idea of time's passage or not, partner, sometimes one can be ahead of one's time. The world may well one day be completely tapped—*tapped* is the word, you know. And the tiny microphones I placed in the house are called *bugs*. I doubt if there is a method of fumigation in Mondebon Parish that can deal with them as yet. But what is more captivating is that I, Barron Roussell, would be considered ahead of his time. But you are not impressed."

"I need to know about Prince Albert Willis."

"And you shall, partner. I shall drive you home and we shall listen to two of these small tapes that I have made. But first . . . Alison. Why mention her name in all of this?"

"She has asked me for help."

"My stepmother is correct in one regard. Why have you, a Marquis, decided to aid my . . . my partial sister. She is the town's first beatnik. No, she is beyond that. In what direction would you say she is moving, partner?"

"I don't know. But my daughter. I believe she . . ."

"Yes, I understand. The younger ones all seem to direct themselves similarly. I understand also, partner, that you would want to aid the Negro singer who is accused of trying to dispatch the blackmailer. But my . . . Alison . . . is a sidetrack, it would seem to me."

"She was in the house that night, you know."

"Yes, yes. I know, the Palace. Thick as gumbo, eh, partner. Every herb in the parish floating up. But come, let me drive you."

"To Emerson."

"To Emerson, yes. May I say one thing about Alison before we depart? She has had problems. Some of us could not care less were we not bound by the idea of family, even legally bound, as in my case. She has had problems. Most in the gumbo pot of this town know it—her teachers, her . . . friends. And I now find myself in the position of having to protect her because I find myself in her family. Surely you can understand."

I did. A Marquis would. And in the world called De Plus En Plus, a father would.

"A drink, partner, before we go?"

After I shook my head, Roussell pushed the glass away. "And neither for me," he said. "Not again. Emerged, I have, eh, partner? Never to be reinterred. And you understand that?"

I did. A brother would.

Taking the shoe box from the countertop, Roussell stooped behind the bar. "I can get another box to carry my poor old shoes to the repairman," he said. He brought the empty shoe box, the tape recorder, the microphone with him as we left. Inside the shoe box, he said, was a gift from the king.

The Mother of Free of Charge

(Molly, Nolan Roussell's son showed me how to operate the tape recorder and then played the tape—I've numbered it 3—for me as he drove me back to Emerson Street. I've decided not to assimilate this tape into my narrative. I'm afraid this taping of matters renders a person lazy—not as lazy as Aunt Penny. But why wrestle with memory when actuality is just a button-push away? Didn't we Marquises get into trouble before with our memory method of recounting what some call 'history'? Weren't our chronicles branded 'unhistorical' because readers had to *trust* that our stories were *accurate*? So here you have it—proof, the accurate, the history. Fossils of circumstance that wandered too close to the tar pit of technology.

Forgive my tone, my love. How these corny metaphors used to make you laugh.

Here is the actual.

But where is the poetry, Molly?

Tape No. 3

Elizabeth Arcement Roussell: You are ill-at-ease, Mr. . . .

Prince Albert Willis: They call this a picture window. I can see now for my own self why they call it that. Sure is airish in here. You don't look too much like the woman you calling your sister. You think old man winter get the word he still got responsibilities and come on back?

221

Elizabeth: I have nothing against an early spring, Mr. . . . Want do you want from us?

Albert: That better. I won't call you ma'am. You don't have to call me like the visiting colored just cause I sat in your backseat.

Elizabeth: Why did you ask my sister for five thousand dollars?

Albert: Your sister can't seem to find her mind. She crazy.

Elizabeth: What is your name?

Albert: They call me the Prince.

Elizabeth: Well, Mr. Prince, what makes you think you can extort—

Albert: Extra tort? You mean like sour?

Elizabeth: Stop playing games with me!

Albert: You play both these pianos? Your sister got just one. That mean you twice as crazy?

Elizabeth: Please.

Albert: Okay, all right. I see you got better hold your mind than her. Didn't want to go wasting my time again. You ain't going to cry, either. That good, too. Bet you cry ice. Your sister, or whoever live in that house on Emerson, owe me money. By way of an inheritance, guess you can say. My mama, the Princess of the Palace, ain't around to help me collect debts no more, so it follow I got to be collecting myself. Your sister live in that house. She owe me. You take care of your sister, you owe me.

Elizabeth: I'll have to know more, please.

Albert: No pleases, lady. . . . That television pick up color? . . . I seen something while I was painting your sister house. Well, I don't actual paint. Dugas, he paint. You know, it don't take a prophet to recollect the past. I ain't no prophet, no chance, but I got a suspicion there's something about your sister past she don't want nobody to know about. What I know's what I want pay for.

Elizabeth: If I follow you—and I do, I do—my next

question should be—should it not?—what do you know, Mr. Prince?

Albert: No use acting like a all-innocent Miss Ann in your dark cold of a room looking out at spring through picture glass. I been in your sister bedroom. Nice room. Nice pictures of a fine daughter but . . . but your sister got a daughter that gots a daddy that never lived on Emerson. That's what I figured from my legacy. Don't know the details past that. But I figure what I figure's worth some money.

Elizabeth: You understand you are speaking blackmail?

Albert: Oh, yes, yes, *ma'am*. I am speaking five thousand. And since it appear like I going to have to be speaking and speaking and speaking, the price be going up directly. Just be calm and get this straight. My mama, the dead Princess, took care of a lots of babies at the Palace.

Elizabeth: No games. Evidence. Without evidence, what is your word worth to the public?

Albert: You, you in your fine Miss Ann gown in your cold room, you don't get it yet, do you? It ain't a question of what you call 'going public.' It's a question of whispering in private. A whisp here, a whisp there, and pretty soon a fine house fall. But you want proof. I got proof. The Princess left me proof by way of the Reverend Bowman when she die. He give it to me. She call it my legacy. My legacy brought me to Emerson Street. My legacy is proof. I don't need to know no details, do I? What I figure is whisp enough to make a fine house fall.

Elizabeth: It's all here. I won't pay more.

Albert: Ain't you heard? The mother of free of charge is dead. This money cover your sister debt. You want to buy the proof? You going to have to come with another envelope. But I be in touch—ma'am.

Elizabeth: Can I assume this business will be kept strictly between you and me?

Albert: You know, you really ought to get out in spring

when God gives it. It's airish and dark inside, Miss Ann, where you live.

Elizabeth: My name is not . . . be extremely careful, Mr. Prince.

The Fake Frenchman

(Molly, another nontranscribed tape, numbered 4, the tape of Barron Roussell and me on the ride back from Heatherland to Emerson Street the evening of February 17, 1963. This is not so much out of laziness, my dearest, as to get you to hear for yourself the voice of King Delos XVI. Listening to it before I mailed it to you, I wondered again why I connected Roussell so strongly with Berman. In Roussell's voice, there is none of Berman's lilt. There is a fine voice here, one that does well through speakers, but none of Berman's lively, anchored resonance.

I think of Berman often, Molly. And of you. And of others. Often.)

Tape No. 4

Barron Palmer Roussell: And there you have it, partner. The dirty business indeed.

James Peter Marquis: Your mother came to you about the blackmail attempt?

Barron: My stepmother, you mean? No, no. Her sister, Bethany, the lady you found in her tub, came to my stepmother. My stepmother came to my father, to Nolan Roussell. My father to me. That is the long chain of desperation as I have known it as long as my return from . . . you remember the war, partner? Out there, look, the town limit.

J.P.: What do you know of the two sisters, Bethany and Elizabeth?

Barron: I know that when I returned from the ETO— remember those initials, partner? Everyone used to know them. When I returned, my father had remarried. Elizabeth was my age. When he married, I believe it was to hold the center together for these two women. Why do human beings need gravitational centers, partner, to hold the diadems of phlegm together? . . . At any rate, he could not have one woman without the other. Or maybe he wanted three pianos. I do not know. I know Nolan Roussell is good at containing the centers, as you might have guessed. He held mine together for me until I could hold my own, so to speak.

J.P.: What about Bethany? Did you know her well?

Barron: Weller since I've listened to the tape here. I guess I always knew one needed a reason to be as crazed as Bethany.

J.P.: And her husband?

Barron: The purported nonfather of Alison? . . . Shall we take the boulevard through Landry and the environs? One day, I suspect, the banker Stalker will extend the boulevard all the way through the swamps and cane fields to the mall. . . . Can you visualize the future, partner? What will be as sad as a town without a mall? At any rate, concerning the purported nonfather, I know what everyone else in the town knows, partner. Raymond, his name was. Killed after he ran into the back of a rendering truck on his drive back from some oil field. His wife, Bethany, supposedly was pregnant at the time. And I know what my father knows about the finances. When Raymond was killed his money went—not a goodly bit—into a trust. Bethany was, of course, incapable of trust. My stepmother Elizabeth managed for her sister Bethany for a while. Then my father, after he married Elizabeth. Kept the pianos tuned, he did, built a pool. There, partner—the graveyard behind the cathedral. Tomorrow Bethany will be laid . . . have you ever waked in the evening, partner, from a nap, alone in bed, after you have been dreaming of the precious dead? Of zarf and antimacassar? Of the pale beauty of the women you remember seeing as a child? You're laughing, partner. A wholesome sound from you. A bit too poetic?

J.P.: My family's vice.

Barron: Laughing?

J.P.: Being poetic.

Barron: I used to do much of that myself when I was a drunk. Not laughing, but poetizing. I was drunk with it sometimes. With poetry. Now I know that a Marquis understands. I know also that a Marquis understands that I'm drunk with something else now.

J.P.: And awake.

Barron: But never far from sad and precious dreaming of the dead, partner. I have a feeling you understand that, also.

J.P.: What else do you know about your father and his connection to the Arcement sisters?

Barron: Not more than I said. This blackmail business is new to me also, I'm afraid. All I know is that my father asked me to help. Now a question for you, partner. I know Alison can seem to be in quite a fix. The town knows she's been in quite a fix all her life. But shouldn't you be a bit more careful with your tampering? . . . Oh, silence from you on that. Let me have another try. The colored singer, Ozema Steeple, has confessed to attempted murder. Soon he will sign a paper to that effect. I'd bet the precious dead on it. I do not know his connection, as you say, to the man he tried to kill, the blackmailing Prince—though I can see that man having been almost killed. Why are you continuing with the Steeple cause when everyone in town by now, everyone who understands both sides of the Mardi Gras issue, wants nothing to do with you?

J.P.: His daughter is my client.

Barron: Fine, fine. I graduated law school myself. No more of that. But is there some connection between my family and Steeple's family? Fill me in, partner, please.

J.P.: The only connection that I can see is Prince Albert Willis. He was trying to milk everyone.

Barron: Whole lot of lactating going on? You laugh again, partner. Maybe we are good for each other.

J.P.: Tell me about the Mardi Gras business.

Barron: Let me tell you what you have already no doubt construed, partner. My father and the Senator and the banker Stalker do not agree usually on much. But they do agree trouble's afoot. They are responsible for keeping Steeple out of action. They will continue on this path, I'm afraid. History, my father calls it. But no need to tell a Marquis about history. . . . But let me tell you—park here in front? Okay. Don't want to smash the St. Augustine—let me tell you something you may not have construed. You and I may be on opposite sides in the Mardi Gras issue, partner. Not because I am a southerner, or harbor . . . partner, I've been dead for over a decade now. But you understand. You will shake my hand again, won't you? There. I knew you would. I feel somehow honored. But what is your connection, partner, to my family, to the Steeple family? Surely not the Napoleonic Code of law we fondle here in Louisiana.

J.P.: Do you know what *de plus en plus* means?

Barron: I would be a faker if I told you I know more than *bonjour*. Partner, I agreed not to lie, but as I said, I will try to avoid. But do go on. . . . No? Well, at any rate, a gift. Take this tape recorder. I've been recording us, by the way. History. Take this as a gift, partner. And this shoe box full of blank tapes. No, I insist. But, partner, allow me to be honest, poetically. I haven't tried to guess at people for over a decade, but you seem hell-bent, desperately hell-bent. And the furnace of some hell has burned you to ashes and your ashes have been burned. And the hot wind from the open furnace

227

has blown your own ashes around you. Around you. . . . I've heard that a second rising is nothing to a Marquis. Our families have much in common, partner. I've had the ash-fog all around me, too, partner. But I see the world, now. No more hot wind, no gray. A limpid sight for me. But in your green eyes, partner . . . others might not see the gray for the green, but . . . at any rate, see clearly. Luck to you. There. I had you reaching again. What an honor to shake the hand of a Marquis twice in one day, in the gloaming of one day.

Two by the Pool

Laurel was smiling at me through the screen door as I walked in the light of the patio behind the house on Emerson Street. She asked about the shoe box first, and I told her about the tape recorder. Before she could ask me about Zeema, I asked about Alison.

"Come on in, Mister. I'm alone in here and a new house is strange enough just being new, not to mention people dying all over the place in it."

Together, we sat at the table. Laurel mentioned how impressed she was with the blue-pink glow of the fluorescent light. Then she smiled again, wiping away imaginary crumbs from the enamel top. Slowly her mouth moved to form what I expected would be Zeema's name.

"I asked about Alison," I said. "Where is she?"

"She's gone to a wake. You know. They came for her, a man and a woman. Alison wanted me standing with her when they walked in back here, but I stayed in the living room. Me and my brown face, you know. . . . Zeema, Mister."

"He's all right."

"Tell me you wouldn't lie to me straight out."

"Not straight out, no."

"You didn't talk about him straight out, so I figured you were trying to tiptoe round the truth. He's all right?"

"He's even got lawyers coming from cities bigger than New Orleans."

"But they still think he did it, don't they? You tell Zeema what that painter Dugas said?"

I nodded my head, waiting for her questions, trying I think to give her a chance to tiptoe with me around the truth.

"Give it to me," she said. "Straight out."

"Zeema said that he did what they say he did."

"Zeema lies," Laurel said, slapping the top of the table. "Zeema will lie to you straight out. He believes the highest freedom a man has is the right to sneak and fib."

"Why would Zeema want to lie about that?"

"Let me tell you, Mister—and this ain't faith talking—Zeema ain't got it in him to try to kill nobody. You're just going to have to take that on faith from me. Or if you don't want to bother with faith, just remember you're working for me and if—You still working for me?"

Her eyes darted away from me. She looked anxiously around the room for an object to focus on. I remembered my older daughter doing the same thing when she struggled not to cry. I remembered also trying to help her succeed, not by holding her—she was too old for that—but by giving her words to focus on. The words, I remembered, worked best if they gave her an excuse for crying or for fighting back.

"A man's got to make a living," I said. "You tell me what to do, if you know everything about everything."

Laurel fought back, as my daughter had.

"Then here's what we do, Mister. You brought your step-ins in that suitcase of yours?"

I laughed. Laurel smiled again. We were both tiptoeing now, straight out.

"We'll be staying here, at the house," Laurel said. "Alison suggested it. She offered me her mama's room upstairs, but I

229

thanked her anyhow, but no. I'll be sleeping on the sofa. For you, there's a place in the poolhouse. Cot, table, space heater. She brought your suitcase in there for you and turned on the lamps. Alison said it be musty, but we agree you be musty anyway. She said, too, that the lights on the side the pool be burnt out, so be careful when you walk not to fall in."

"I'll be careful," I said. "Anything else?"

Laurel wiped the table again, then looked into my eyes. "Stay working for me," she said.

"I'll stay."

In my first hour or so alone in the poolhouse, I arranged the cot, the end table, and the two lamps—the only furniture in the room—so that I could sleep and write. I lit the space heater to burn what dust I'd stirred up, and then I sat on the floor in front of the end table to try to take note of the details of the day.

I wrote, but with difficulty. I could hear Laurel singing in the kitchen of the house. I rose from the end table three times: once to balance the other lamp on the ledge of the window facing the pool; once to take a walk to the side of the pool to see if the light reached far enough into the shadows; once to take another walk into the orchard and call to Laurel to tell her to make sure she let her eyes adjust to the darkness before venturing out to the poolhouse.

"There's enough light," I said. "You'll be able to see if you just wait long enough."

"Mister, I don't know how stupid they grow people in New Orleans, but where I'm from we ain't as dumb as what you're describing."

As I wrote I continued to listen to Laurel's singing. I could smell her cooking—fried sweet batter. When I heard the kitchen door slam, I balanced the second lamp on the ledge and walked outside again to wait for her in case she was coming to the poolhouse. When I lost the noise of her, I called out to her again.

From inside the garage on the side of the house beyond the grove, she called back to me, telling me to try my best "at not being all totally such a goof."

Minutes later, hearing her on the path, I stood up until I could see her emerging from the darkness. She was carrying a basket with her.

"Over here," I said.

"Mister, you got the world lit up like a revival tent. Ain't no stumbling going to happen around here."

When we sat at the table, I asked about the basket.

"Know the best way to catch a painter, Mister? Fried chicken. We're off to the Palace."

"I'll go alone if you want me to talk to Dugas."

"Not on your life," she said. "I got the plan. I also got the money."

Laurel held up what looked like a bundle of bills. I thought I could see a rim of dark paint on the edges of the roll.

"Prince Albert's money," I said. "Where did you get that?"

"If it'll fool you, Mister, it'll sure fool that one-eye-fool painter. Newspaper. And while you were gone today, I rummaged through the garage. There's paint in there the color you and Dugas described to me. Lordy, what a color. What would you call that color, Mister? Some kind of sky color?"

"A threatening sky."

"Hey, that's it. Threatening-sky blue."

I told Laurel to wait while I went inside the poolhouse to get the tape recorder and a new tape. Outside again, in the lamplight with my shoe box, I answered Laurel's questions about the machine.

"Now let's go catch a fool and fool him into truth," she said.

"Okay," I said. "You want to write that down?"

"Your turn, Mister. To sing. Record it up on your tape machine."

I tried my best for her. I sang into the microphone: "You two standing by the pool, Doo-gah, Doo-gah. Go and catch yourself a fool, all the Doo-gah day."

Laurel laughed hard at that. All my daughters thought my singing funny.

Basin Street Woman

April 22, 1973
Molly,

1973. Ten years away from you. And how much a part of this chronicle you have become! And how much still—

In these ten years, much has changed. History has assigned names to objects and to people. Alison would now be called the town's first hippie—a word that wasn't quite around when I spoke to Barron Roussell for the first time. The small tapes he gave me have also been given a name—cassettes. The cassette recorders themselves can be purchased by anyone with a Sears credit card.

Can you imagine, Molly, what my family would have done with a tape recorder at Appomattox? Or in the courtyard in the shadow of the four towers of the Alcázar in Toledo in the late summer of 1936? The interviews of a trapped Marquis with José Moscardo while the walls were being coated with gasoline from outside, while from outside the hand-grenades and shells were being tossed, while the explosives were being set in hand-dug caverns beneath—can you imagine the sound of the tape-hiss over the silence of those 800 cadets and 1,300 other men, women, and children.

And can you imagine the tape-hiss over the silence of those in the camps in Poland and Germany that my brother Berman—

But how much of our store of Marquis notes would go if the tape recorder had been present? And how much of the poetry of remembering would go? Playing back a tape is listening to an exactitude.

One straps the recorder at one's side, one lives. Then later one listens. And one plays back de plus en plus en plus. And the tape-hiss covers the silences.

Forgive my laziness, Molly, if I allow the tapes to fill in more and more what should be my own account. I am busy these days working to earn money in ways other than attorney fees. I am not doing so bad a job. I can tell by the books that continue to be produced that you, too, are not doing so bad a job.

Soon, perhaps, Molly, soon—

And forgive me again, Molly, for my diversion. Fast-forward the tape numbered 5 past my singing and Laurel's giggling and you will hear the hiss over the silence of the sidehouse of the Palace the night that Laurel and I went to confront the painter Dugas with fried chicken and newspaper money dipped in threatening-sky blue. At the end of that long conversation, you will hear Dugas say, "I got the chicken, you got the dough. Hot hot damn, hot hot hot. Basin Street woman." Don't stop the tape there. Listen to the ten minutes of sound that follow—footsteps on cypress planks, the rustling of wild bay, my laughing, Laurel's giggling. Then continue to listen as Laurel speaks again and I, very slowly, begin to speak the words I had not been able to say with you—

James

Tape No. 5

Laurel: Lordy, Mister. What you smell?

J.P.: Cypress wood mostly. Mildew. And layers of wallpaper. Look at that, where the wallpaper's peeling. Flowers on every layer.

Laurel: Keep that flashlight pointed where we walking. What's that? The stairs?

J.P.: The stairs. To the left there, that's the Prince's room.

Laurel: Where you think that almost-blind painter be staying? This chicken smell should have him whining by now. I don't know I have the courage to go up three flights of stairs into three flights of spooky.

Dugas: In here. Open the door. Across from the Prince's room. Open the door. . . . Well, well, how y'all doing? Don't get jumpy, lawyer, no. And turn off that flashlight. It bothers my eye.

Laurel: Don't you dare, Mister. You keep us what light we got us.

Dugas: Here. I got a candle—kind of what's left of a candle anyways—in this here tin bottom of an old beer can. . . . Now that's enough light, ain't it? Even for perfect-sight people that should be enough. That's better. Y'all have you a seat at my table here. Welcome. Welcome. Welcome. You brung money, you? That what in the shoebox?

Laurel: Sure is. Take it out the box and hold it for this—hold it close to the candle, Mister. Show him.

Dugas: That's nice, that. Yas, yas. Look at the paint on it and everything. I thought y'all said you didn't have no money—

J.P.: You'll get your money . . .

Laurel: And your chicken. I brought you chicken, too. The lawyer here had me drop a piece for the dog outside.

Dugas: Dog's dead. How else you figure your ankles ain't brown ribbons? I'll eat the dog's piece of chicken, too. Later.

J.P.: We came to find out about Zeema. You said Zeema didn't try to kill Prince Albert.

Laurel: He didn't—

Dugas: Let's don't start that again. I'm still saying he didn't, and I got a surprise way to prove it to both of you if you'll give me that roll there. Drop the chicken and that money here on the table and I'll start talking.

J.P.: Talk.

Dugas: Same old gotdamn shit. It's time! It's time!

Laurel: Ain't got to shout.

Dugas: That's my signal for my surprise. Listen. Shush now, listen.

Laurel: Mister, there's . . . on the stairs. Mister—

Dugas: We ain't never none of us alone in the Palace.

Laurel: Mister—

Dugas: Don't get jumpy, lawyer. She ain't going to be hurt.

New Voice: Hello, Jay Pee.

Laurel: Mister. There's somebody in the dark. Turn on the flashlight.

New Voice: No need for that. I'll step in the candle. There. Hello, I said. Hello, little girl. I been watching y'all from the dark. I love to watch all y'all from the dark.

Laurel: Mister—

J.P.: That's Prince Albert.

Laurel: I know. That's the man been bugging Zeema.

J.P.: What's—

Albert: Hold on, Jay Pee. It's a gun. But I'm putting it away. Look. In my pocket. See?

Dugas: It's a shiny new gun, lawyer. The Prince bought it for us. And a box of bullets. The old one . . . I got the old one. Loaded it just before you came, but I unloaded it again. Here, I'm putting the old gun on the table here. And here, look. Bullets to fill it if you want. Gifts. You can have it all. Easy, now. You don't think I'm so blind to not see that that roll you got there ain't money. The Prince told me you didn't have no money after all. That's downright not honest coming in here with a fake roll of money.

J.P.: When did you get out?

Albert: Hour, hour or two. Zeema's out, too, Jay Pee. Everything kind of settle. We all bought out and safe. Me and Dugas, we leaving town. Heading up to New Orleans.

Dugas: Hot hot damn. We going to have us a time.

Laurel: Mister, Zeema'll be coming for me.

Albert: She don't know him too good, do she, Jay Pee?

Little girl, Zeema's out of jail, all right. He signed papers confessing he tried to kill me, so they let him go. Won't be no big old court case for the papers. He ain't going to be King Zulu this year. Some of us knew from the start he ain't going to be no King Zulu. That might of took courage.

Laurel: Don't go talking for Zeema.

Albert: She don't know him too well, do she? Little girl, most of what Zeema sings comes from me. He stole a lots of songs from me. But that don't matter. I got to talk to Zeema before they let him out. Shit, Zeema didn't make no money on them songs either. The record people, they be stealing from him. Ain't that something? Can't collect from a man ain't got nothing to collect from. But I got my money from the others, from my legacy.

J.P.: Roussell?

Albert: It was hard collecting, Jay Pee. Look a here. A bandage on my left cheek, scratches on my right. But me and Dugas finish with it.

Dugas: Hot, hot damn. Basin Street woman, here we come, us.

Laurel: Let's go, Mister. Zeema will tell us everything.

Albert: She don't know him too well, do she? Know what else I done, Jay Pee? Sold the Palace here to Lineman. It's all his now. He paid my bail for me and I signed over the papers. He's stealing from me, I know. But we finish with this town. Me and Dugas, we—

Dugas: Hot hot damn—

Laurel: Let's go, Mister. Zeema'll be looking for us.

Albert: She don't, do she?

J.P.: Just wait a second, Laurel. Let me . . . Dugas said that Zeema didn't try to kill you.

Albert: That's right. Zeema didn't. And that's all I'm going to tell you. You smart, Jay Pee. I'm telling you Zeema didn't. You going to have to solve the crime. I'm leaving—

236

Dugas: New Orleans!

Albert: —leaving with my money and with my friend, this here—

Laurel: Fool.

Albert: —for bigger games, maybe my own place.

Dugas: Calling it the Bronze Star.

Albert: But like I said, I'm leaving the evidence with you if you want to know the truth. No matter what Zeema signed or said. He didn't try to kill me. I'll leave evidence with you, and you can figure out the truth, and you can do what you want with truth. Look at these cheeks if you want to see what truth get you.

Laurel: Alison didn't try to kill you either. If you're trying to pin it on her, you can just stop.

Albert: I ain't saying what I'm saying, little girl. But I am stopping. How many were in here when my sticker sword sliced through this cheek? You was, Jay Pee. You was here. Zeema, he was here. Dugas, he was here. And the white girl from Emerson—

Laurel: Alison.

Albert: —she was here. In fact, she got here before Zeema.

Laurel: That's right, Mister. I saw her leave Lineman's before Zeema left. I saw it from the stage because I was keeping an eye—

Albert: Hush, little girl.

Laurel: I ain't your hot damn little girl.

Albert: Here, Jay Pee. Some evidence for you. Besides the old gun and the bullets, this is yours.

Laurel: What's that he gave you, Mister?

J.P.: A matchbox.

Albert: Don't open it. In this light, you wouldn't catch on. What's inside there, I took what's inside that matchbox from my poor dead dog's eyetooth. Died while I was in the jail.

How you going to feed a dog when you locked up? Dugas . . .

Dugas: I forgot. I was running here and there with my life, me, Prince. I forgot to feed him, Prince.

Albert: All right, all right. Dog be buried in the bay leaves outside. What's in that matchbox there, Jay Pee, might help you figure. And as far as my legacy, it's safe again with the Reverend. Go to him if you want it.

J.P.: Why don't you just tell me now?

Dugas: Because you two think y'all know everything. Question here, there. You and the nigger gal think y'all can know everything. So try to know it. Let's go, Prince.

J.P.: I could try to stop you.

Albert: We know, Jay Pee. All of us in this room know you got mean in you you got to let out. But I got a shiny something in my pocket I got my hand on. And you don't want that. I wouldn't go shooting on purpose, but things fly about by accident. And me and Dugas know you in the protecting business when it comes to this—

Laurel: Don't you say it. I ain't nobody's gal.

Albert: So just take the gifts, Jay Pee. Do what you want with them. And take some advice. There's a lots of mean around. I had to face it looking up into my own sticker sword on my own floor. Crazy, no-sense mean, Jay Pee. From behind faces. From places behind faces that there ain't no way of—

Dugas: Let's go, Prince.

Albert: Only thing I'm taking with me from the Palace is my mule statue. Funny, ain't it? Zeema give me that as a gift himself long time ago. Know what it got wrote on it? *Kill a mule, buy another. Kill a nigger, hire another.*

Dugas: Let's go, I said. Hot hot damn, hot hot hot! Basin Street woman—

Laurel: Please don't sing, Dugas. Shoot my ears with a shiny new gun, but don't sing again. Never heard such—

Albert: So 'bye, Jay Pee. And you too, little—you too. But

238

I ain't finish up my list when I was interrupted. Dugas was here that night. You was here. Zeema was here. The Emerson girl was here. And somebody else, Jay Pee. Somebody else. It was all crazy and close. Another person was here.

Dugas: Let's go, Prince. I got the chicken, you got the dough. Hot hot damn, hot hot hot. Basin Street woman.

Sherlock and Shayna

Laurel: You finished changing the tape? Now, smell this one. Hold these leaves up to the microphone. But that's one thing that machine can't do, is smell. This here's bay leaves, machine. One man's laurel is another man's bay. That's what Zeema used to tell me. . . . What's these leaves? Flash the light up there, Mister. Most the leaves on the ground, but some of them still holding on to the branches.

J.P.: Here, hold the flashlight. Smell the dried ones. Not the machine. You. Smell the dried ones.

Laurel: Ain't no bells ringing to that scent.

J.P.: Sassafras.

Laurel: Go on. No bells ringing yet.

J.P.: They—the people everybody calls 'Cajuns'—they make something called filé out of the dried powder of sassafras down here. You've heard of filé gumbo?

Laurel: Fee-lay? Yes, yes, yes. But ain't no Cajuns invented that. My people had something to do with that. Zeema told me that. Or maybe they all got together here at the Palace one night and came up with it together. What you think, Mister?

J.P.: I guess . . .

Laurel: Don't go little-girling me, Mister. You don't believe that for a second, do you? You can't lie to me if you try. That a family trait? Never mind. Let's move on to another kind of soup. We got Prince Albert on your tape recorder there saying Zeema didn't try to kill nobody. Ain't that all we need to clear

Zeema? And we got him saying somebody else was here. That clears Zeema and Alison.

J.P.: This tape doesn't preclude . . . doesn't beat Zeema's confession, if that's what you're getting at.

Laurel: What kind of lawyer are you, Mister? The truth's on that tape. I hired you—

J.P.: The dog's buried somewhere in here.

Laurel: Don't go changing the subject on me. I can take the truth if you can. You don't believe Zeema's coming back, do you?

J.P.: In so many words, he told me he wasn't going to stay in town.

Laurel: What else in so many words he tell you? I guess you going to tell me like Prince Albert that Zeema won't be coming for me.

J.P.: He told me that, yes.

Laurel: Then you fell for a fib, lawyer. Cause Zeema would never leave me behind. Never.

J.P.: Prince Albert thinks Zeema would . . . would leave to avoid the Mardi Gras.

Laurel: I said you fell for a fib, Mister! . . . So why you think Zeema would leave me behind? You better tell me, Mister, or I'll fire you as my lawyer, and I mean it. Why would Zeema leave me behind?

J.P.: He told me that if anything ever happened to him . . . he said that I should take care of you. Take you back to New Orleans with me.

Laurel: That sounds like Zeema, him and his French Quarter school. Well, hell and shit—excuse me. No, don't excuse me. Hell and shit. You two put me on the block and trade my flesh away? What you two think I am? I ain't a little girl no more. I'm just into seventeen. Girls younger than me's married back where, where . . . and even if I was a little girl . . . hell and shit. Hell and shit. You can't go trading off my flesh. You just can't. And Zeema can't either.

J.P.: Zeema agreed that the life he's giving you isn't enough. He doesn't have the right to be bringing you around from town to town—

Laurel: What you mean Zeema doesn't have the right?

J.P.: You're too young to be . . . to be with Zeema.

Laurel: Mister, what the hell and shit you think's going on! How the hell and shit your mind be working? Zeema's my daddy, Mister. Zeema's my daddy!

(Five minutes, fifty-three seconds of tape-hiss and silence)

Laurel: Mister, that word hurt you more than I've seen somebody hurt for a while. I'm sorry, I guess. I guess truth is for small bites, not for gulping. We better remember that. I'm a child of the Palace. I was born here. Zeema met my mama here. . . . Hey, we still partners, Mister. Detectives. We got us a crime to solve. . . . But he's my daddy, Mister.

J.P.: And if he doesn't come back? If he's the coward everyone who knows him says he is?

Laurel: You learn that trick in lawyer school? How to use questions to say things? And you saying mean things, Mister. Know what everybody who knows you is saying? Prince Albert said it. It's on your tape there. You've got mean in you, Mister. And it has to do with me, or something close to me . . . the opposite of a ghost. . . . Tell me about your daughters, Mister.

(Three minutes, ten seconds of tape-hiss and silence)

Laurel: You need all this truth in smaller bites? I'm sorry again.

J.P.: Two daughters. Abigail . . . Abby . . .

Laurel: Oh, Mister. I—

J.P.: And Jane Ann. Jane was the younger of the two. . . . I can't. I can't, don't want to describe them to you, if you don't mind. Abby used to watch Jane . . . carefully. Jane had the same trouble Prince Albert has, with seizures. Abby was

241

starting to worry that when she went off to college . . . worry about Jane. I used to spend weekends alone with them. My wife liked to stay home and write, so I could be alone with my girls. Abby and I were starting to have wonderful arguments. Things that you're saying. About being nobody's girl. I took them to the beach on Saturdays. We'd set up the tent, fish in the surf. A beach south of New Orleans on a bay. The Fourchon, it's called. A little rustic. The station wagon would get stuck in the sand every other trip. No big deal to us. I'd dig in the sand, the girls would walk the edge of the surf. I'd jack up the car, put driftwood under the tires, lower the car, then drive to the hard sand by the edge of the surf. The . . . I guess the jack slipped. But I don't know . . . I just don't . . . I'd never gotten that far under the car before. The jack fell and I was pinned. Nothing dangerous. Up to my . . . the car here, on my chest. I was in a ditch, low, nothing dangerous, but pinned. Abigail worked with me to get the car, somehow, off. She looked for driftwood. Didn't panic. I told her not to worry. She kept looking to the surf, the way she always had. I couldn't see the surf. I kept looking at her face . . . blonde hair, but I can't describe . . . if you don't . . . I looked to her face to make sure she wouldn't worry about me. Then I saw it there in her face. No, I saw her—Jane Ann—there in her . . . there in Abby's face. Sisters. "Daddy," Abigail said, not a scream, but I saw her in her face. Her sister in her face. "Daddy," she said. "Jane," she said. She looked to me, then the surf. I couldn't see the surf. I could only see her, both of them in her face. She ran from me. I called to her. "Abigail," I yelled. She came back. "Daddy, I've got to . . . Jane." Abby ran from me again. I heard her calling her sister's name, I think. I couldn't see. Then I couldn't hear her. But I heard the surf. I heard the surf for . . . for how long?

Laurel: I don't know for how long, Mister. But I'm sorry.

J.P.: For all my life . . .

Laurel: I kind of see, Mister. I do. I see lots better now. But

242

I—and you're going to have to gulp this down in one big bite—I ain't your daughter. And even . . . even if I was . . .

J.P.: I've had the feeling that—after I came back to town—that there was a purpose. That just as everyone says, things happen for a purpose. I would understand how that—something meaner than I am, I'll tell you . . . how . . .

Laurel: God, Mister?

J.P.: That I had lost, but he was giving it back. And I would learn the lesson . . . the reason.

Laurel: Mister, I don't want to hurt you more than you hurting now, but I've got to say a big-gulp word. That all sounds like pride to me. To say that the world works just for you. For anyone to say that—that there's a lesson in everything—that's horrible pride.

J.P.: How do you pray to something—

Laurel: Mister, forgive me again, but I believe in God and praying, but not in praying where you ask for something. The second you ask for something, even for world peace and controlling sickness, you ain't got faith. You're making yourself the center again. Praying for God's company's okay, I believe. . . . But, hey, Mister, you still believe in God, Mister. After everything, you still believe.

J.P.: My wife doesn't. But she never has.

Laurel: If she doesn't, how can she even begin—

J.P.: I don't understand her strength in all this.

Laurel: But you believe.

J.P.: I want my time in court. After I die and . . . one minute to speak my mind to that face . . . that . . . hateful . . . before they throw me down to hell. One minute of court time, recorded, official. . . . "Whatever the scheme," I'll say, "whatever you had in whatever it is a mind you have," I'll say, "you should never allow anyone to live on past his children."

Laurel: Mister, if all that you're saying is true, after all this is over, you're going to have to forgive God. Lordy, I got to

243

cover my mouth. What I just said! And here's the biggest gulp of all. You going to have to forgive more—

J.P.: I know . . . and get on with my life. I've been given that advice, heard it from everybody. Even heard from people who would know to call it the cliché it is.

Laurel: Hell and shit, Mister, you're getting me mad. I wasn't going to say what you said I was going to say. So don't interrupt me, please, before I finish. I was going to say, "Get on with yourself, Mister, get on with yourself." Don't go putting words on my tongue, cliché or not cliché, whatever the hell and shit that is.

J.P.: And what if . . . to go on . . .

Laurel: That's enough, Mister. You trying to say you need hate and anger to go on. That's like them that ain't got the courage to kill themselves, so they get this big something that eats to eat them up from inside.

J.P.: That takes courage, too. It's a choice. A way to keep on living.

Laurel: Excuse me again, Mister. I ain't never said this to nobody before, but . . . but this is one talk I don't want to take part in. It leads to cold nothing.

(One minute, twenty-three seconds)

Laurel: Hey, Mister. And some gumbo. We'll have us some gumbo after this is all over. You'll go to church, forgive God, and then we'll come here, pull us some bay and sassafras and make us one pot, one shit-hell pot of gumbo. Pot as big as a bay. Come on. You've got a matchbox and a shoe box full of evidence. Let's solve a crime. You go to the Reverend. He's having him a late meeting at his church. You go get the Prince's legacy and we'll smell us the truth. Just like we set out to do. You do that and I'll . . . Mister, where's that old gun?

J.P.: In the shoe box here.

Laurel: You give me that old gun, and I'll bury it in the backyard on Emerson with your pills. Where Alison showed me. By the pool.

J.P.: You can't walk around with a gun. I don't care how old you think you are.

Laurel: I ain't a little girl. You do what I just told you, and I'll get to Alison, make sure she's . . . oh, Mister. I understand what your mind's been doing now. But she ain't my sister, really. Come on. I'll wash your step-ins for you so you don't get to smell bad, and you be Sherlock . . . that it? Sherlock—a detective. And I'll be Shayna.

J.P.: Shayna? Is that a detective?

Laurel: I don't know. I just always wanted to be called Shayna. Now I got the chance, I be grabbing it. . . . You need to laugh like that more. Mister, when you laugh the world stops turning just to hear. You got to laugh more, give the world a rest. You mind if I say something else, Mister? It's a mouthful of truth.

J.P.: Go ahead. I'll chew it till it's paste.

Laurel: Even if I was your daughter. Even if I am Zeema's daughter. You would have to let me go. Zeema's going to have to let me go. You'd even have to let me go to have my own death if that's where I was headed. Because it's mine, not yours. You're going to have to let them, your daughters, have—

(end of tape)

Clarabelle

April 12, 1974
Dearest Molly,

I sent you the last batch of tapes almost a year ago. I have not been able to write new parts of my chronicle since I myself listened to the last tape. But I have thought of them often, have concentrated deeply on them since then. For a while I thought that I might not continue, but my life here in town has begun to speed along. It is Good Friday and I think this year I will be able to collect myself and make my Easter duties, do what I promised to do: forgive God and get on with myself. I saw a priest on the steps of the cathedral yesterday, his nose round and red as Clarabelle's—Jane's favorite clown. I think there might be some cosmic irony in kneeling before him to confess.

And you see, dearest, that I have written her name, one of their names—Jane. Abigail. The years begin to speed—

I am ready to ask Lineman if he would allow me to interview him. But before I do that I have decided to write until I reach what happened on Mardi Gras Day, 1963. (I will send the tapes to you—in order—for those times when my written words won't come.) I do not want to know what Lineman has to say until after that task—chronicling up to Mardi Gras Day—is completed. I do not know what knowledge Lineman will give me, but I have a feeling that I will want to put the pencil down after I've listened.

Molly, I am beginning to understand something else I know, something else I may have always known. I said my life is daily speeding on, that I have been learning how to get on with myself. I am offering my hand to people I meet on Main; I shake hands, converse. I have made my own new money without touching any of our savings. (I know you are using them well. And your books are doing well. What a name you have made for yourself! I think of you sitting at the symphony—you do still get season's tickets, I'm sure. I can picture you with your head cocked, eyes closed, eyeglasses on your lap as you listen to the movements you so love.) I seem to be directing all my anger to heaven now and leaving the daily world to itself. But I am beginning to understand something else also. After I've forgiven even heaven, Molly, I think that if I were to see you again—I feel now that I may be able to go on if I am not daily reminded of our sorrow. I feel that if I look into your face—

Molly—

James

246

My Pal Beggar-Mule

(Molly, you might have noticed how detailed and slow time is in the writing and tapes I have sent you. I have been sending you words, words for years now. Notice how many pages and how many tapes it has taken me to get to this point. I arrived in town on Saturday, February 16, 1963, and the last of what I have chronicled for you deals with the moment Laurel ran from me through the cypress gate of the Palace yard—at about midnight or just before on Sunday, February 17.

But time would—will soon speed on. Maybe because, as I said in my last letter to you, my life is beginning to speed on. But I have stopped for one last moment because I know what is coming, because perhaps that is too much to know.

So forgive me again, Molly. These words do more than digress. They forestall.)

I was alone in the bay and sassafras after Laurel left me. I must have thought about my daughters, about what Laurel said. I knew that all that she said was correct. I had known this every second of the days since the funeral. All of what Laurel said to me about getting on was wise and perhaps a truth, embarrassingly simple. These words were no less wise when they had been spoken to me by my father, my grandfather, and a judge. But I had had no control of what came from me.

Just before Laurel ran off, I thought I would get control again, become again what my grandfather called a "well-collected" Marquis. Standing with Laurel, laughing with her, I thought I would be able to forgive God.

But then she left. She left and I ran after her. I remember my journey from the Palace back to Emerson as no more than an instant. But if I concentrate . . .

I can remember searching the darkness for her at first, at first thinking that she was hiding from me, playing. I can remember facing the darkness as I turned, my eyes fierce on the darkness the way they would be if I confronted any threat to someone I cared for, the way they would be if I confronted the Gulf. I can remember tripping once on a mound of earth that could have been the grave of Prince Albert's dog.

In my memory, I see myself running immediately after her, across the Great Perpendicular to the back streets that lead to Emerson, but if I concentrate . . .

I can remember opening the shoe box to check for the pistol. I can remember seeing it in there. I can remember myself fearing Laurel's defiance of me—how she'd asked me for that pistol. I can remember fearing that she may have tried to take the gun sometime when I had set the box down. It was this fear, I know now, that made me check the box and then think of reentering the sidehouse to take the bullets from the inside table where I had left them. I can remember darting through the front door of the sidehouse. Inside, I did not find the bullets anywhere, not on the table, not on the floor. And it may be that this added to my fear in what seems to be, unless I concentrate, an instant—one instant of terrible care and concern alone in the bay and sassafras.

And still, now, if I do not concentrate, I feel it as an instant, and in my mind and in my memory I am running down those streets to Emerson. But now, as I run, I am asking the question: What if one atom . . . ?

Laurel was not anywhere in the house. I called to her in the kitchen and as I walked up the stairs. In the first bedroom I found the television on and Alison sleeping despite my noise.

Outside again, in the orchard, I called her name: "Laurel."

And then from the darkness by the pool I heard her answer.

"Least you got the name right. I turned off your lights. Be

careful, hear, for the pool. There's a chair here by me. Sit before your own breath chokes you."

Laurel: You smell like the beggar's mule. This how you turn this on? Oh, goodness, I think I turned this on. Testing. Testing. This is Laurel Steeple, and this here man smells like the beggar's mule. No white folk ever better tell me ever again about how my people smell, no sir. You got your breath?

J.P.: You took the bullets, didn't you?

Laurel: Sure did. You got the name right. It's Laurel. Not little girl. And Laurel doesn't do any nothing dangerous. Toting bullets when they're outside of guns can be safe, I heard. I put them away safe. Tomorrow I'll bury them in the yard with that gun in the box this recorder was in. I'll bury them with your pills, in the earth where Alison showed me. Lord, Mister, you all right?

J.P.: Getting to be more and more . . . we need to talk about Zeema. What if he doesn't—

Laurel: I won't hear any of that. . . . I'm okay about everything. I checked on Alison. She's sleeping upstairs. I been thinking about her. I got a feeling we—me and you—going to have to keep close watch, Mister. I think anything we find out going to have to be spoon-fed to her. I never thought I'd say the truth got to be hid, but . . .

J.P.: I never thought I'd say that either. My family might disown me. "Truth is truth to the end of reckoning." Do you know who said that?

Laurel: Nope. You down to talking about words. We were just now talking about Alison. You already know a lot about her, don't you?

J.P.: If Prince Albert is telling the truth, yes. Alison's father, the man she thinks is her father, is not her real father. Prince Albert knows about it. Prince Albert's mother knew and somehow gave him the information.

Laurel: The Princess.

J.P.: Yes. And whatever she and her son Prince Albert knew and know is enough to get Nolan Roussell and the Belanger family to pay.

Laurel: You got the matchbox the Prince gave you?

J.P.: In here.

Laurel: Lordy, Mister, you went and lost it?

J.P.: I must've dropped it in the yard at the Palace.

Laurel: You went to the Reverend? You got what Prince Albert called the "legacy"? You didn't, did you? How we going to solve all this, clear up the air, when you . . . why you didn't, Mister? Oh, I get it. Say my name again. Say it.

J.P.: Laurel.

Laurel: You got that right. And I'm all right. But Alison. Remember, slow doses for her. Mister, let me see if I can put this in words right. Care, Mister. Too much care is kind of careless. It's like spilling the coffee when you scared of shaking the cup.

J.P.: Shakespeare said something like that. "It spills itself in fearing to be spilled."

Laurel: Oh, now I see what you trying to do with all that business about how I know this and don't who said that. I know: you want me to say, "Shucks, shucks and gah-lee, little colored girl like me don't know that word. What is it now? Shake-here? Lordy, Lordy, too long for me. Take me back with you, please, to New Orleens and teach me about the world I never had."

J.P.: I think, yes, I might have been trying that. I don't know. My daughters and I would make a yearly trip, with my family, to the Shakespeare festival in—

Laurel: I follow you, Mister. I understand the connections in your mind, remember. And I forgive you. But don't go trying to think you know me so hell-and-shit well. I been to school, Mister. Zeema and my mama wouldn't let me not go to school. And I heard of Shakespeare. And I heard enough I figure to last me one-fourth to one-full-half my life. Zeema tried that on me, too. After my mama died—you know who my mama was? No? See, there's lots you don't know about me. Lots even a daddy can't know. After Mama—she died—and after, Zeema kind of had the ideas you got, and he won't let go. He wants me to go to a school in the French Quarter, behind a brick fence, in banana leaves with lots of nuns. Nuns and school for a long, long time. Now let's get you to bed.

J.P.: But if Zeema doesn't come back—

Laurel: He will, Mister. And all them things that Shakespeare said, they just words to me. Like Zeema says about his songs, prunes without pits.

J.P.: I just thought you could come to New Orleans for a little safety while you finish growing.

Laurel: And who decides on ready?

J.P.: That's just what my daughter asked me. Abigail, the oldest.

Laurel: She asked you that cause it was hers to decide. Would you have let her? Before, I mean, before what . . . before the sand and all?

J.P.: Yes. I was beginning to feel I could have.

Laurel: Then let me, Mister.

J.P.: Laurel—

Laurel: I know, Mister. The sand's always with you. And the sea sounds, they always with you. I know. That's why it's for this here child of the Palace to decide for herself. But we were talking about Alison. In lots of ways, she's younger than me.

J.P.: Yes . . . Alison, too . . . I was thinking . . . to New Orleans.

Laurel: Still panting, Mister? You going to drop you run full speed again through this town. You know, Zeema's coming back. He's like you before the sand: not quite ready to believe I'm ready. No, no, don't talk, Mister. Breathe, for God's sakes.

J.P.: Just a few words . . . that quotation I used from Shakespeare? A Marquis can't lie well. I'm not good at stretching truth either. All those words about spilling to be spilled . . . I think those had to do with jealousy and guilt, not with what we were talking about.

Laurel: You gave it your best shot. Hush. Breathe. In the morning we got a funeral and we got a crime to solve. But we got to take our time. For Alison. Lordy, you all right?

J.P.: Just stop a second.

Laurel: Put your arm around my shoulder so I can help you to the poolhouse and bed. Yes, just like that, arm around me. Just like pals. You think, Mister, you would've got to be pals with your two girls?

J.P.: Yes, I believe I would have.

Laurel: We in danger, ain't we, Mister? All of us, we in danger when we believe too much in . . . in breathing things. Maybe that's why there's God.

J.P.: Or a need for there to be.

Laurel: Promise me, Mister. After all this is over. Promise me you'll leave me alone. Zeema will have to leave me alone, too. Promise me you'll get on with yourself, get to church and forgive God. At least you believe in something. Promise.

J.P.: I promise, but just for you.

Laurel: For who?

J.P.: Laurel.

Laurel: For who?

J.P.: Laurel Steeple.

Laurel: Now you got it, pal. My pal, beggar-mule.

Molly-James

April 14, 1974
Dearest Molly,

    Just a note to let you know I did not make my Easter duties. Clarabelle a bit too absurd. Was there ever a Marquis who broke a promise? That's like a Marquis lying. Too absurd to consider.

    I feel I can get to Mardi Gras Day now, in the narrative at least. And I feel the end of a section approaching. Remember, I told you I sensed these breaks? The last section is approaching, love, with speed, soon, into the waves.

    But before that, a question.

    Was there ever a Marquis in all of the chronicles who solved a crime in three days flat? Yes, I know, many of the Marquises in the chronicles resort to snooping and sleuthing, but three days flat?

    I'm sorry, Molly, for the tone of those words. I'm afraid I don't know what stance to take, with my words. We Marquises have taken them all.

    I miss you, but—

    Molly—

James

Children of the Sun

Monday, February 18, 1963. I woke without a clock, the sun near noon in the sky above the pool. Woke to the smell of bacon and the sound of Laurel's singing coming to me from the house through the screens of the two open windows of the poolhouse. Cleaned and pressed, my suit pants, my white shirt lay on the end table near my cot. I dressed, listening to Laurel. I searched for but did not find my tape recorder. I wanted to record the fabric of that voice at that moment, the white ribbon of a young girl's—no, a young woman's—song. I sat at my notes with my pencil in my hand, but thought I would wait. I walked to the house while she was still singing. Three or four steps into the orchard, I saw a fresh mound of earth and a garden trowel at the base of a shoulder-high orange tree. When I stepped up into the kitchen the singing stopped, and I forgot my purpose. I watched instead from the door, Laurel sitting at the table sewing.

White thread, I remember.

Laurel: Testing . . . this a test.

J.P: What is this . . . a sling?

Laurel: That's right, Mister. A broke-arm sling that Alison gave me. She's at the funeral now. If we eat fast . . . there.

J.P.: To carry the tape recorder?

Laurel: That's right, look. Round your shoulder. This here hangs under the arm, or shift it back. Then when you put on the coat here—I cleaned your smelly clothes—when you put on the coat, the microphone fits in this here inside pocket. Still kind of heavy, ain't it?

J.P.: It's the latest though. One day these might fit in our pockets.

Laurel: The world's sneaky enough, Mister. I'm just doing this because I'm a detective for a while. Shayna, remember?

J.P.: I remember. Why don't you sing into this microphone? What you were singing before—

Laurel: That was real singing, Mister. Professional practice. Zeema told me—oh, Zeema's back by the way.

J.P.: When?

Laurel: You hear your voice on that *when*? Almost choked. No, he ain't back yet. But he will be. You sure got adjusting to do in your life, Mister.

J.P.: Adjustments have already begun. Just a little time, is all. Maybe I'll call my wife soon. . . . You buried the gun?

Laurel: Alison helped me. There outside, in the orange trees. We picked up all the rotten fruit, too. Gun's in the hole with your greenish pills, in some kind of canvas sack. I had a long talk with her this morning before her family came for her. She wants the truth. How much we letting out?

J.P.: Let me talk to her first.

Laurel: A bite at a time. Looks like we both got father troubles, me and Alison. Eat, Sherlock.

J.P.: Easy. Give me time to adjust.

Laurel: Love to hear you laugh. What's my name?

J.P.: Laurel.

Laurel: Nope. Shayna. And Shayna says that Laurel said to tell you Laurel doesn't sing into a microphone unless she gets paid.

J.P.: Testing. I have walked from Emerson Street to . . . testing. I am about to watch—

Laurel: The recorder on?

J.P.: Yes.

Laurel: You wasting tape. There ain't nothing here to catch but breeze and whispers, and I ain't going to whisper into your pocket. I'll feel kind of goofy doing that. Turn it off.

After I turned the recorder off, Laurel and I watched Bethany Arcement Belanger's funeral from beneath oaks on a vacant lot west of the cemetery behind the cathedral. For a while, I thought of doing for Laurel what I had done for my daughters when they attended their first funeral (Molly: Uncle Roland), giving Laurel—as a way of a quiet and private eulogy—more of what I knew of the life of Bethany Belanger. But what did I myself know of Bethany, other than the woman's being Alison's mother, other than the colors I myself had seen, threatening-sky blue, orange beads on the end of black Egyptian braids?

Each time I did make an attempt to speak, Laurel interrupted. Whenever she recognized someone she had seen at the Senator's party, she nudged me, and even though our voices had no chance of carrying to the cemetery, she whispered with her mouth close to my ear each time she spoke.

I could make out Nolan Roussell by his fedora; Laurel called him the "Arab man." Barron Palmer Roussell was wearing his flight glasses; Laurel called him the "drunk soldier." I reminded her that he was the king of Mardi Gras.

I pressed the two buttons that started the tape recorder resting in the sling beneath my jacket.

J.P.: Just before noon, Bethany Arcement's funeral, Monday . . . what's the date?

Laurel: Turn that thing off, Mister. Hush.

J.P.: No one can hear us. I need to make sure this works, anyway. If I do it right, I don't have to do so many notes. I can just go about my business. History will take care of itself. History, you know that word? We live forever, in a way, on these reels.

Laurel: You accept being a goof forever if you believe that, Mister.

J.P.: Nolan Roussell and his son Barron, the king of Mardi Gras, are leading four other pallbearers down the concrete lane up to the shrine—a crucifix scene, two women kneeling beneath the cross—in the cemetery behind the cathedral. They are lifting the coffin off the cart and . . . they are walking with the coffin after turning right at the hairless hollow under Christ's arms.

Laurel: Mister, don't you be blaspheming this close. We dangerous close, Mister. And I'm dangerous close to you if electrocution from the sky strike you in your—look, mister: Alison.

J.P.: Two women in front of the file of mourners. On the right, Alison, in a yellow-and-white dress. On Alison's right,

Elizabeth Roussell—Alison's aunt Elli—in a black suit that covers her neck and arms. They walk apart without touching.

Laurel: Look. There. Who's that? The only one with a handkerchief. Ain't that the chicken from the party?

J.P.: Mayor Poule.

Laurel: That kind of sad, ain't it? That he's the only one crying. Okay. Turn that thing off. This ain't right at this time. Respect, I mean, you know? And don't get carried away with that machine. We here to solve a crime. Ain't got nothing to do with history. Thought you said your family didn't believe in living to remember so they could record what they saw later.

J.P.: That's what I've been taught. We just find ourselves thrown in the middle of things.

Laurel: And then the wheels start spinning. How you know when you're in this middle of things?

J.P.: When the day-to-day life turns into something more important. You just know it all of a sudden. My family calls that "history in the larger sense."

Laurel: And this poor woman's funeral is the larger sense?

J.P.: I don't think so. It's the smaller sense.

Laurel: I thought so. We got a lot to talk about, Mister. That small-large proposition. When is respect and disrespect fitting into all that?

J.P.: That's what decent, average citizens have to talk about.

Laurel: Turn it off for now.

J.P.: And who was it made the sling?

Laurel: Trying to catch me with my own trap? Okay. I'm caught. Turn it off before it eats me whole.

J.P.: Just for now. Let's move to where—

Laurel: No. You go ahead, Mister. Some of them people might be looking for an excuse to get their minds away from all this. A white man and a dark teenager might be too easy an excuse for them to use. I'll meet you back at the house on

Emerson. You see that Alison make it there safe, okay? I saw some big red apples at the A and P I'm going to buy. Ain't no history in that, is there? Just apples. Maybe a worm.

I stood outside the gate of a chain link fence—what is called a "hurricane fence" in town—while Alison talked to Nolan and Elizabeth Roussell after the graveside prayers were over. The Roussells, I could tell, were trying to persuade Alison to come with them, but Alison refused, pointing to me.

Alison's skin was as dark as the most reverent sun-worshiper I had ever seen on the beach at the Fourchon. Her dark hair barely moved in the breeze.

As I stole looks at the skin on Alison's legs, I remembered my daughter Abigail in her two-piece swimsuit on the beach. I remembered our arguments about "showing skin" and the "gap" in our views about "obvious display." Abigail said that there was nothing wrong with displaying the body. I agreed. But I told her that skin signals many things to the human mind, beauty of form being just one. Then Abigail used the word *screwing* with an openness that embarrassed me. "Are you talking about screwing, Daddy?" she asked. "Because that's okay, too, you know."

And watching Alison, I remembered laughing on the beach and my daughter running angry over the dunes. In the station-wagon driving home, as Abigail sat and glowered, I wanted to apologize for laughing and to tell her that all Marquises before her also delighted in the "display" we had talked about and to the openness and abandon she had referred to as "screwing," but not publicly. I considered telling her too about how as a father I secretly wished for her that delight while at the same time I was sad about the approaching loss her sexual development signaled to a father. Before I said anything, Abigail spoke about the changing world, about the Peace Corps and "being involved," about the "new concern" among people. "It's going to be a wonderful thing

258

to see, Daddy," she said. I agreed with her, as a way of apology, and said nothing else.

(It was on that drive home with Abigail, while Jane slept in the back seat, that I considered the idea that there possibly *was* a change coming. I realized also that I might have to surrender both of my daughters soon to a freedom and casualness about their bodies that no Marquis before had publicly admitted. Though we—you and I, Molly—admitted to it privately, did we not? And often. But I drove on, letting Abby think that her ideas were completely for her and for her generation, as any decent father would.)

While I waited for Alison, Barron Palmer Roussell walked up to me on the sidewalk that paralleled the fence. He asked me if the bulge under my coat was the tape recorder he had given me; he chuckled when I admitted it was. Then he told me to press the buttons that made it record.

Barron: Partner, you are not made for the covert. But I have something here to help you with your job. I found it beneath the bar at my home. Here. This suction cup can be secured on a phone receiver; this jack—it is called a "jack"— can be plugged into the recorder where the microphone plug goes now. Do you see? At any rate, I hope you know that no one who believes he is innocent· would object to being recorded. . . . Have you spoken to Alison about what the Negro prince, the painter, said? On the tape I gave you?

J.P.: No. I'm not sure she's ready.

Barron: You do not know her as I do, as I said before. She will insist on knowing. I attempted to speak to her before the funeral, to find what she remembers about that night at the Palace. One can tell by looking at her face, and the way she looks back into a face, that she remembers little. You have not spoken to her, then?

J.P.: Not yet, but soon.

Barron: Remember, partner, she is maladjusted in many

ways, in ways maybe only a family and her pets would know. Even a foster family. Regardless, I have a bit of information you may find humorous. The sword, the saber that almost killed the Negro painter? It is now in my possession, surrendered to me by someone at the district attorney's office. I am going to use it as part of my costume for the parade on Mardi Gras Day. Paint it white, what do you think? Or silver, maybe.

J.P.: Have you looked closely at the saber?

Barron: Not as yet, I'm afraid. Why do you ask?

J.P.: There is a name below the hilt.

Barron: I'll be sure to peruse, partner. Next time we speak I will have that information for you. Be sure the reels are turning. Good day. Maladjusted, partner. Only pets and foster parents.

(Molly, Roussell left me as Alison waved and walked toward me. I reached to turn the tape recorder off, thinking of what Laurel and I had discussed. Then I thought of Abigail and of Jane and what I would give up if I had a tape of their voices. I let the tape spin on, knowing it was spinning, wanting to capture forever a voice.)

Alison: Why do you think he walks away so quickly when I approach, Jay Pee?

J.P.: He's not used to the sunshine yet.

Alison: Children of the Sun. I remember reading that headline in a California newspaper, a story about the beach. While I was resting. . . . Barron was a great disappointment to his father, you know. Nolan thinks that Barron should have walked from his bomber to the governor's office. But Barron's doing better now, isn't he? I heard from talk in the graveyard that he'll be running for DA again. You like him, don't you? Most people do, when he gets out. What's it like being son to a fath—I saw you staring at me.

J.P.: I was thinking about my daughter.

Alison: Is that how you see me? I'll have to remember. You're cute, you know.

J.P.: Are you all right, about your mother?

Alison: I don't seem upset, do I? But did anyone seem upset? We were all well rehearsed for this. The Carnival club was hoping she'd do it before Mardi Gras so they could practice walking a straight line. . . . I'm sorry. But it was like a parade, wasn't it, Jay Pee? Barron Palmer Roussell, the king of Mardi Gras. And Nolan, the father of the club.

J.P.: Don't forget the queen.

Alison: They told me about that. Palmer wouldn't say much to me, but they talked about how drunk he was. Yes, I remember all that still. The Carnival club is going along with my appointment, now that mother's . . . I remember this place well, too, walking through here with Zeema and Laurel and you. It's time we talk. Laurel told me this morning that you two were on the trail of something big. She said that you found out that Zeema didn't try to kill that man.

J.P.: Prince Albert.

Alison: Yes, the man painting my house. What else did you find out?

J.P.: Let's walk first.

J.P.: Do you remember more now about Saturday, about the Palace?

Alison: Yes. I'm beginning to remember. It isn't pretty, Jay Pee. I told you before that I'm beginning. I don't want to, but I will. It won't take much effort. It's right below the surface, ready to be dug up. We'll talk. Maybe an orange . . .

J.P.: None for me.

Alison: I know. I remember our orange. You're cute, but I'm a . . . more like a . . . tell me, Jay Pee, what's it like being father to a daughter? . . . I'm sorry. I shouldn't have asked that. Laurel told me about your . . . children.

J.P.: I'd like to take things slow with you. Let me lead.

Alison: My father . . .

J.P.: Did Laurel tell you anything about your father?

Alison: No.

J.P.: Let's not talk just yet. . . . Wait a second. This thing's getting heavy.

Alison: Is that the tape recorder? Laurel told me about that, too. She was making a sling. Are you recording us now?

J.P.: Do you mind?

Alison: Why should I? Isn't it like a snapshot? A family album. After leaving a cemetery, who doesn't feel like part of one family. You dig? I'm sorry. Bad joke.

J.P.: You were talking about your father.

Alison: Yes. About my father. I think Prince Albert . . . I think Prince Albert was my father.

Laurel on the Roof

(Molly, I ran out of tape and turned off the recorder minutes before Alison and I made it to Emerson Street. So the hiss on the rest of that tape represents the silence of my walk with Alison. But had the recorder remained on, had I brought an extra tape with me, there would be recorded forever the sound of Laurel's singing coming to us from the house on Emerson Street. The song might have been "White Rider, White Rider," but I cannot say.)

Alison and I stopped for a while on the sidewalk in front of the house to listen to that song, and she commented about how the piano sounded *joyful*—her word—even with the *sorrow* Laurel sang about. In the patio behind the house, Alison made an attempt to try to describe what the piano had sounded like when her mother sat to play, but she had to wave the words away: "You had to have your ears there, Jay Pee. Not even the mechanical ears on your white box here could capture what came out of those keys. Did you see the color of the paint she chose for the house trim? What color would you say?"

"Laurel and I call it threatening-sky blue."

"Yes. Good, Jay Pee. Imagine that in your ears."

Standing in the patio, Alison told me to bring my tape recorder up to her mother's room. She wanted to tell me a story, she said, about the color of the sky, and she wanted to listen to herself after she was finished. I told her I had to go to the poolhouse to get another tape, but I would not be long. I also reminded her that we had decided to go slowly, and she smiled.

(Molly, in the green light from the translucent panels on the patio roof, I looked at her smile, the sorrow in her eyes and in that smile, and I thought of Abigail. Would Abigail have returned to me—after I set her free to her new world—with such a sorrow on her face? Abigail even in her saddest moments had a green joy in her eyes—the Marquis green, we called it, do you remember? What would it have taken from the world for the world to work at and into the color of Abigail's eyes? Are these the questions you asked yourself, Molly, when you stared into my eyes those long months after the funeral?)

In the poolhouse I sat with my pad briefly and wrote about my thoughts and Alison's words. I forgot then to take note of the words of Laurel's song.

Laurel: Mister, where you going with that recorder tool?

J.P.: Alison wants to talk.

Laurel: Easy, remember. Shit hell damn.

J.P.: What's the matter? Where are those apples you went after?

Laurel: Never mind, Mister.

J.P.: Just for the record, where did you learn to play the piano like that?

Laurel: You really don't know who my mother was, do you? She's Daddy Jazz's own daughter, Mister. Some people know her as famous. Shit damn hell. Who knows anything. Sometimes . . .

J.P.: What's wrong?

Laurel: It's just that . . . Zeema says I should hold my tongue. Just hold it. Some people, the darker they are, the more tongue they got to hold. Shit damn hell. I got a feeling I ain't going to be the kind to hold my tongue. You know the Reverend Dr. King, Mister?

J.P.: Sure do. My family has had him over for dinner.

Laurel: No kidding? Lordy. Big family, Mister?

J.P.: Big. Just my brothers on one side of the table. Berman . . .

Laurel: Go on.

J.P.: You were talking about Dr. King.

Laurel: Me and Alison talked about him. You know about that march going to be going on maybe in Washington this summer, and about Birmingham?

J.P.: My brother Geoffrey will probably be right in the middle of it. He's in Birmingham right now.

Laurel: You know, Dr. King, he's kind of what you were talking about. History in the big way. But you know what lead up to the big way? Apples. There's going to be world peace, Mister, in a big way before one person can face another over a back fence. Know what I mean?

J.P.: What happened, Laurel?

Laurel: Don't go wasting tape worrying about me. Alison needs you now.

J.P.: Let's waste some tape. What happened?

Laurel: At the A and P. I had the apples in a bag and I was ready to leave. I was by the manager's office—plywood, a glass window. I saw this water fountain, two signs, White, Colored. Behind the window, the woman manager was watching me. I heard Zeema's voice in my ears, telling me about what *is* and *got to be*. About how to get to tomorrow. But I'm going to have trouble getting to tomorrow if it means swallowing my tongue. I drank from that fountain, Mister. Drank one big gulp on down past my tongue. Then I drank again. The woman behind the glass, she said, "Hey, you, girl. Can't you read?" I answered, "I done something, Lady, make you doubt it?" She said, "You can't drink that." And "Look," she said, "that sign. Look. That's white water." I said, "Lady, I ain't never drunk colored water in my life." And, Mister, I put them apples down and walked out. Should I be feeling good or what, Mister? About talking back, I mean.

J.P.: That's hard to answer.

Laurel: Not easy being on the witness stand, is it? Sorry about your tape. Look, it's—

After I walked back to the poolhouse for another tape, I found myself suddenly tired. I took a nap with all the windows open, dreamed of my daughters, but was sad only when I woke. I had enough courage to make note of half of one dream before I left the poolhouse.

In the house, I found Laurel and Alison lying beside each other on the living room rug. Both wore faded jeans—Laurel, jeans with a borrowed gold sweatshirt; Alison, the same jeans and velour pullover she had worn the night of the Senator's party. Each had her eyes closed, her hands at her sides. Alison's hair had been cut to resemble a softer version of Laurel's "natural" and had been curled and combed around her face.

Watching them, I sat in the armchair near the fireplace. Alison opened her eyes slowly and smiled. Keeping her eyes on the ceiling, she said, "Look now."

Laurel opened her eyes. "Well, I'll be . . ."

"See it, Jay Pee?" Alison asked.

I saw a band of color on the textured ceiling directly above Alison and Laurel.

"Every Mardi Gras," Alison said.

265

"Just like she said, Mister. A spectrum. The sun through the beveled glass on the double doors."

"Relax again now," Alison said. "Feel the parts of your hand. Surrender to the parts."

Laurel closed her eyes again.

"Mind if I tell him, Laurel? Jay Pee, I'm teaching her to relax. You ever hear of the curse? Of course you have. Your daughters. Laurel calls it 'falling off the roof.' She hurts. I'm showing her how I learned to live with that hurt. Outside my mother's closet, I taught myself. How to relax and surrender. You might want to give it a try, Jay Pee. And, Jay Pee, would you give us our time together? We're learning about ourselves. Give us the rest of the day. You and I can talk tomorrow. We'll record the story about the color of the sky tomorrow, okay?"

I did give them the rest of the day. And I gave a big part of it to me. I lived alone with myself, napping, catching up on my notes, walking the town, feeding myself. I tried to think of nothing, which is a grave difficulty for a Marquis.

And I had to give the next day to them, also. Laurel and Alison and I were together only for the two meals we shared. Both girls wanted to hear me talk about Dr. King. It was after dinner that Tuesday, before they left for a walk through town, that they told me about their plans to go to Birmingham together after Mardi Gras.

I said no. I said it without thinking. I did not apologize; they did not throw the word back at me. But we sat without another word for the rest of the meal.

Alone in the poolhouse, I thought of Alison and Laurel, Abigail and Jane. I knew a daughter from a daughter. I knew also that, whether a world of second chance had been created for me or not, I had no rights in this town. And had Abigail and Jane lived long enough to tell me of similar plans over a dinner table, would I not have let them go on their journey, whether I claimed a father's rights to reluctance or not?

But they had not lived.

And I could not sleep.

For a while I tried to find sleep by lying with my arms outstretched, trying to feel the parts of my hand as Laurel and Alison had. By three o'clock that morning I was considering digging up the orchard for my green pills. Instead, I practiced my angry summation to an imaginary final court of appeal—a fatuous and biased winged jury—until Wednesday dawned and I slept again.

Pistil Among Azaleas

Laurel woke me at noon and we ate together beside the pool. We did not talk about the night before. After we ate, Laurel told me that Alison was waiting for me and my tape recorder in her mother's bedroom.

When I got to Alison, she was sorting and boxing her mother's clothes in the walk-in closet of the bedroom. From the size of the dresses, I could see that Bethany Arcement Belanger had been tall and long-waisted.

Alison: You ready now?

J.P.: Yes. Are you sure you want to do this?

Alison: Are you sure? You're doing it for me. Where should we start? About my father?

J.P.: No, not yet. Tell me more about your return to town.

Alison: Remember I told you that I met my friend Pistil in Bakersfield? She was a social worker there, kind of a guide for me with the therapy. When I left, she left, too. We lost track of each other for a while. Then I met her again at a sit-in. In Georgia. She'd made the stop on her way from Connecticut to New Orleans and Mardi Gras. It was ironic, she told me, that she should meet me. She'd just met someone who was experimenting with the same drug I'd been using.

J.P.: This LSD?

Alison: Right, right. I ended up driving with her heading toward Mardi Gras. Pistil and me in a Volkswagen with two guys—younger, barely a beard between them. She'd run into them in Connecticut. We were going to Mardi Gras, and then we'd double back to Birmingham, whatever was happening there.

J.P.: Happening? Now? You could drown in a stare.

Alison: Hey, that's for later. Now my story. When we got to New Orleans, we registered in a hotel—Pistil has a supply of money from her family. While we were unloading, I remembered how close I was to town. I asked Pistil to drive me here. I don't know why exactly. We spent the night in the court square. I remember walking home. No one was home when I arrived. I crashed. In my bed. I woke at sunset, startled by the—dissonance? Downstairs.

J.P.: Your mother was home? At the piano?

Alison: Know what I did immediately, Jay Pee? I ran to the bathroom and threw up. It was like Pavlov and his pooch when I heard that piano.

J.P.: You must have seen the scaffolding outside. Did you speak to your mother about the painters?

Alison: Hold on. That was quite a jump. Let's hold on.

(Molly, I turned the recorder off here. It was perhaps five minutes, no more, when Alison turned the recorder on again herself. She was sitting cross-legged on the red quilt on her mother's bed. Beside her was a box from Roussell's Pyramid of Costume.)

J.P.: Can you tell me about Saturday?

Alison: Yes. Did I get here on Saturday? Let me go back

now—I might have to do that a lot. Saturday. We got here on the day . . . no. It might have been as far back as Thursday. Whenever it was, the four of us spent the night on court-square benches. Smoked pot. We watched azaleas all night. There I was, back home, and I couldn't remember if azaleas and spring arrive this early every year. The next morning, Pistil and her boys and I got yelled at by city cops and we dove into the Volkswagen. I told Pistil I'd changed my mind about staying in town. We drove Highway 90 awhile, stopping to eat in Des Allemands. That's when I asked if they'd mind taking me back to town. Should I tell you why? Don't answer that. I'll have to think about that one. . . . But it had to be Friday. Yes, I'm sure now. I didn't get here until about three o'clock that day.

J.P.: In the court square again?

Alison: Yes. They let me out in the court square. I told Pistil I'd see her after Mardi Gras at the hotel. She said she didn't believe I'd come, and she gave me some of the LSD, already measured out in distilled water in little medicine bottles. She said I'd be safe with it as long as I remembered what we'd done with it in Bakersfield. She said there was enough, just enough, she said, for a night or two if I needed it. Then I walked home.

J.P.: Can you remember what you saw now?

Alison: Yes. The empty paint cans, the scaffolding. And the color of the shutters. Threatening-sky blue? And I noticed . . . the oranges. Mother hadn't picked them this year. She had always managed that. They were rotting on the ground in the orchard . . . trouble, you know. I crashed, turned on the TV, unappointed myself, and crash.

J.P.: Is that another California word? Unappointed?

Alison: No. That's a word my Aunt Elli uses. Houses aren't furnished, they're properly appointed. As soon as I discovered . . . you know, myself . . . my body . . . I call it unappointing myself. Oh, I've embarrassed you. You're cute when you're embarrassed.

J.P.: You slept all that night?

Alison: Yes. Then Saturday struck. There's no getting around it, is there? I didn't leave my room all morning. Downstairs mother was up, was lucid. She didn't need drugs or drink to fly. I heard her conversation on the phone, all to Aunt Elli. They were speaking about me. But I'm not sure. It was weird. I could tell there was some sort of problem. But it was my mother who was trying to calm Aunt Elli down. Does that make sense?

J.P.: Yes. Prince Albert spoke to your Aunt Elli. But go on.

Alison: I came down to lunch. Mother and I ate oysters on the shell. It was as though I'd never left town. Mother was sparkling. Do you know the mad can charm? The mad can act sane but the sane cannot act mad? I've learned these things, an expert you might say, you know. And mother was sparkling, Jay Pee. She told me about the Senator's party. She said she had to be sure to make herself go. She had to *require* herself to go. And then she was down . . . crash. In the middle of explaining what costume she was wearing to the party, she got up and walked to the piano. With her first note, I felt— betrayed? Again? Charmed again, you know? And I felt the oysters in one wad in my throat.

J.P.: You took the LSD?

Alison: Yes. I had the three little bottles in the refrigerator. I put one dose in what was left of the wine. And I pushed the oysters down. Now, please . . . I'm going to have to explain some things, some things you might understand better than anyone else because of what you felt when you . . . because you took some of the LSD with me. I had taken it many times before, but I never liked it. I had never found that inner space Pistil described to me, that white light of discovery she described. But Saturday, for the first time—I guess it was about an hour—I measured my room with the breadth of my arms. I measured the bed. The door, me. Me, unappointed without having unappointed myself, you know? I did a marvelous job of calculating area, area, in cubic breadths. Then I saw a black man at the scaffolding outside my window.

J.P.: Prince Albert.

Alison: Yes. The same man . . . the sword. When I saw him, I had a feeling he wasn't real. He smelled like bleach and beer and the sun was solid, a block of solid light behind him. And my curtains were yellow, solid. I thought I had created him. I thought that, because his volume fit so well into the rest of my room . . .

J.P.: You said you thought he was your father. That was a feeling also?

Alison: Yes and no. You will see. But the feelings make me sure.

J.P.: Did you talk to him?

Alison: Yes.

J.P.: About?

Alison: I think about Zeema Steeple. We sang some of Zeema's songs. The man at the window—Prince Albert—he told me he was Zeema. No, that the songs that were Zeema's were his, not Zeema's. And something else. Yes. He knew my name.

J.P.: You're sure?

Alison: Yes. I turned away from him once. To . . . I heard the piano again. When I turned to him again he was gone.

J.P.: Did he have a bandage on his face?

Alison: Bandage? No . . . I . . . after the painter left the window . . . I took a nap. When I woke it was still daylight. I didn't know who I was—no big deal for me. Then I heard . . . oh, God, Jay Pee. Oh, God. If you knew what I have to tell you now . . . are you running out of tape? Almost, look. Let's play this back. Will you? Let me hear how well I've done. Let me hear me. Me. Then I'll have to tell you, Jay Pee. I'm going to have to tell you . . . Mother. That was when I found Mother in the tub, but not dead.

Alison

Mother was calling, Jay Pee. Calling me. It was odd because I rarely heard her using my name. Weird, I know: a mother who doesn't use her daughter's name. No, I'm okay. I told you before. I'm okay. I think that's why I came back to town. I knew I could be okay.

I walked toward her voice, into the bathroom. The water in the tub. Not red yet. There was a green towel around her head. Her face had been made up—exaggerated. For the costume. Mother was lucid again, charming. She said she wanted to tell me something and she wanted me to listen. I should *require* myself to listen.

And she clarified some things for me while I listened. Some things I guess I'd always known. But never tried to guess, you know?

She told me that Raymond Belanger, my father . . . he was not my father. But I already knew that, didn't I? Felt that, you know. All my life. Things my mother had said, all my life. I stood there relieved because I had been right. My feelings right, you know.

Then she told me, she told me. She said that my *real* father might have been a Negro. But hadn't I guessed that all along? Too, guessed. The texture of my hair . . .

Mother's eyes closed. I didn't want to move to her. All my life I had not wanted that. But I looked into her face. Closely. I could see the makeup. On her face, it had begun to cake. Into patterns. Fine-lined mosaic. She said my name again. Maybe I was listening too closely to my name. Or maybe the drug. You understand? Her hand, her arm came out of the water. She rested her hand on the rim of the tub, her palm up, limp, over the side. Like this . . . I saw . . . I saw the water was . . . not red yet, but red.

I looked into her face again. She was looking at me, not into me. She had always looked at me. And I knew then. I understood then. She did not know me.

I wanted to move to her. To cry. I had wanted to do that all my life. She must have felt this. But she stopped me with her face, *no*, with her face. Do you understand? The way she always had. And I understood. Then, I understood.

She did not know me, she was not my mother.

And she was saying with her face. *Give me my death*. And I did. All my life, I had seen her face say, *Give me alone*. Can you understand? And I did. Give her that. All my life.

And I gave it to her again, left the room.

As I was leaving, she said, "This is for Alison." But she said it as though she wasn't giving to me.

I may have slept some. I know I went back to the room, in and out of the room. I remember searching the medicine cabinet, rummaging through her many pill bottles. I remember taking some. Once when I went back into the room, I saw the painter again. Prince Albert. He was on the scaffolding. Not a vision. Really him. And it was then I was certain he was my father. How else would he know my name? He was singing. Smiling. He told me to tell Zeema to meet him that night. And I went to the window and I scratched his face. This hand— I'm left-handed. Like this. On his face. *Alone, give me alone*, you understand?

Then he was gone. My father, he was gone.

The last time I went back into the bathroom—Wait, I took off my clothes first. All of them. I left my clothes in my room. I brought my backpack with me to the bathroom. I used the towel from mother's head. I wiped the floor beneath her arm as much as I could. I made sure there was no blood anywhere on the tub, on the floor. I stuffed the towel in the backpack. I left the house, naked.

I buried the backpack in the orchard, somewhere in the orchard. In the soft dirt. I had seen mother digging in the orchard often, with a small garden spade. It's one of the things she did when she flipped out, you know. She played the piano, or she dug in the orchard, or she locked herself in her closet—locked me out. I used to sit outside, waiting for that door to open. Till I found my hand. Till my hand found me and I could unappoint myself. . . .

After I left the orchard, I went back to the house, to my room. Measured myself without unappointing myself. Gave myself alone.

The Girl in the Box

Alison did not speak for a while. I turned the recorder off, and I watched her lay out her mother's costume: on the quilt, a green robe piped in gold, gold sash at the waist.

J.P.: You don't have to.

Alison: No. I want it on. Haven't you guessed? All my time in the—rest home, you know? In Bakersfield. I got quite used to talking while this kind of machine made circles. But I never could talk before. And I'm all right, really. It's as though I was supposed to make a stop here in town so that I could be okay. The words came to me finally. And it's like her death has released me, a sacrifice. Isn't that . . . like in the mass at church. That maybe she was giving me that. . . . No, mother was not like that. But I'll have to take her gift as that. How about you, Jay Pee? You all right?

J.P.: I don't like seeing you . . .

274

Alison: Hey, Jay Pee. Maybe you were sent to this town to help me out, right?

J.P.: I want that, yes.

Alison: I know. And you have. You and your turning circles here. And you can help me more. I'm ready to know everything. I really am. Listen to me. Something crystallized for me that night. The sight. Mother in the tub. The red. The green. The white tile. The sight did something for me that a year in a wicker room in Bakersfield never did to me. It was a solid encounter. Yes, solid. A fact, you'd say. I realized that what I was seeing wasn't coming from inside me, from the black bits eaten and reshaped by drugs. What I saw was obviously a piece of a world that worked without me. I wasn't making the world up as I went along. There were facts outside of myself. Can you understand?

J.P.: Yes. Especially fact. Something to turn to. Yes, I understand.

Alison: And as I said, I'm ready now for more. Listen, please. I had been inside myself for so long, I realized. In a space no bigger than Mother's closet. I came out of myself Saturday. I looked at myself for the first time, for the first time from the outside. I saw myself alive, no more than that, a part of a working world, solid as crystal, solid as fact. After I buried the backpack, I forgot what I had seen for a while— Mother, the red—but that feeling, that feeling. I left the orchard calm. And I met you. . . . Do you want me to embarrass you again? I wish you weren't seeing me with a father's eyes. I'd unappoint you. Right here. In this room. We'd be alive together. Screwing while the circles turn. Does that word embarrass you? You're smiling.

J.P.: I've heard the word before.

Alison: And you're hearing me the way I think a father would. And that's why I haven't jumped you. I think I want you to look and hear me. You understand? After what I've just said . . . and I'm okay, Daddy. I'm okay. Tell me everything you've found out, about that . . . that man. Prince Albert.

J.P.: I will. But I need to know a few more things.

Alison: About what happened at the Palace? You think I could have tried to kill him? I did scratch his face. They say I tried to kill my mother once. The first time Uncle Nolan sent me to the first rest home. But I was only at the closet with some scissors. I don't think I would . . .

J.P.: No, I can't believe that.

Alison: About the first rest home? That's a fact, Jay Pee.

J.P.: No. About the Palace. Albert said there was someone else there. I'm close to finding out . . .

Alison: The facts? And Zeema didn't do it.

J.P.: No, I don't think that anymore. Tell me why you went to the Palace. Do you remember?

Alison: It's weird, but after I say it, I do. It's like the talking is keeping the hole open. Do you understand? We'd better keep talking, right?

J.P.: Yes. But only if you want to.

Alison: I'm tired. But I have a feeling you have some things to tell me, some facts.

J.P.: Yes. Things are starting to fall into place. How did you get to the Palace?

Alison: After you left me that night, at the bar. After, I listened to Zeema and Laurel. You should have heard how marvelous they were, Jay Pee, their voices together. Father and daughter? Then Prince Albert walked up to me at the bar. I laughed. We laughed together. He told me he felt as though he'd known me all his life.

J.P.: Is that exactly what he said?

Alison: Yes. All his life. Wait. And he said he had seen my pictures, the pictures in my mother's room. Of me, you know, these pictures. And I remember wanting to look into his face, but he walked away. He walked away and I followed. He must have seen me following. After he opened the gate, he waited until I was inside. Yes, to hush the dog. How's your ankle? Laurel told me the dog bit your leg.

J.P.: It's all right now. More shoe than flesh gone. But think carefully now.

Alison: The house was stuffy. No circulation anywhere. Not a sound. Anywhere. There was a light on, coming from a door at the end of the hall. I felt choked immediately. I closed my eyes. I had to put my arms out, on the wall, to steady myself. He . . . Prince Albert told me to wait. I could hear him walking down the hall, unlocking a door. He came back for me, took my hands from the walls, guided me to his room.

J.P.: Did you hear anyone, anything coming from the other rooms?

Alison: Yes. No. I had a feeling we weren't alone. Still have that feeling. I may have heard movements coming from the other rooms as we passed. I stopped outside the lighted room before walking in. I doubled over, gagged. When I went in, he was sitting on his bed. He looked as bad as I must have. He had a box on his lap.

J.P.: A cedar box?

Alison: Yes. Wood box. It was wood. He said—I remember now—he said, "You were in here." That's it. "You were in here." Can you imagine what that did to someone after LSD and Mother's—no, she isn't my mother—and Bethany's pills? He put the box down somewhere. Then he had his head in his hands. The room was thick, thick, and the smell . . . chlorine? He pointed to the window over the bed, motioned for me to open it. And I did. I let in the air for us.

J.P.: Did you see anyone else outside when you opened the window?

Alison: No, I—

J.P.: Was there a dog barking?

Alison: Jay Pee, come on. A man I took to be my father

told me I had been living inside a cedar box. Do you think I'd notice a dog barking? There, that smile again. You're beginning to think I'm all right. And I am.

J.P.: I'm watching you close.

Alison: Thanks, Daddy. Just keep me out of boxes and I'll be okay for a long time. . . . Another crash, Jay Pee. After I opened the window. I ran out of the room. I just stood there in the darkness at first, hoping to God I had left all my senses in the room with the light. But it wasn't dark enough in the hall. I found a dark room somewhere. I remember putting my face into a pillow. Yes, feverish, sick-flesh smell of a pillow. I can't remember how long it was. . . . When I ran back into the room, I saw him. On the floor. And you. Kneeling. When I think about it now, it's funny. You, muddy, in a tuxedo. I should have known my imagination could not make up something such as that. You had to be real. . . . You think someone else was there?

J.P.: I believe it now.

Alison stopped the recorder but did not listen to herself on the tape. She was tired, she said, as was I. She said it would be nice if we were to take a nap, and then she lay on her mother's bed, pulling the green cloth of the costume over her for warmth. Before she slept, I told her all I knew, confident that she would be able to accept all that I had to say. (Molly, in the world called De Plus En Plus, I was confident also that my daughter, that Abigail would have also been able to accept the facts as truth.)

I told Alison about Prince Albert, his hometown extortion of Zeema; about Zeema, his stolen songs. I told her about the tape with Prince Albert's words, about how Albert said that Raymond Belanger was not her father. And I told her about what had happened to Laurel and me at the Palace as we tried to get to the answers to the questions that came from that night of terror and smells when a saber grazed a cheek and ended up embedded in a wood floor.

Alison's eyes closed partially, and sometimes she stared at me dreamily. But when she spoke, when she asked questions, I felt that she understood and accepted all.

"What was Prince Albert's legacy?" she asked. "In that box. What?"

"I'll find that out soon," I answered. "A man named Bowman can give me that answer."

"Do you believe what Prince Albert said about . . . about my first father? About Raymond Belanger?"

"We must believe at this point. Your family paid Prince Albert. No one pays for a lie."

"Was Prince Albert my father?"

"I don't know that he was. But I'll try to . . . to answer."

Before she slept, Alison told me that she had taken some papers from the downstairs safe. She had looked in the closet for more, but had found none. The papers she did find were in a small manila envelope. It was in her room, on her bed. She thought that the papers might help me with the answers she wanted. She had hoped there would be a birth certificate among them, but she had been too wary to make that search.

"Would you make that search for me while I sleep?" she asked. "And tell me what I've come to town to know. What am I besides a little girl prowling the orchard on Emerson Street? Where did I come from? Why am I here?"

I didn't answer those questions for her because she fell asleep.

(Molly, some of those questions are age-old, aren't they? And some day she would know, as all daughters shall know—for some questions there are no answers. An embarrassing cliché. But, as Laurel would have said, true nonetheless.

And, Molly, before I moved again I stared at Alison and I thought of Abigail. I was not sad. Again I kept the two girls

279

separate in my mind. But somehow, still, I was holding to the hope that there was a purpose to the world as it unfolded for me in this town. That in this town, I would be able to get along with myself again. That I would be able to think of my daughters again and not wish, not wish to die with the thought.)

While Alison slept, I made the search. Before I went to the papers on her bed, I looked at the pictures on the shelf behind her mother's bed—that yearly record of a girl's growth taken of the same girl standing in her Easter dress beside an orange tree. In her hand in each picture, she held a basket with what looked to be oranges rather than Easter eggs. Then I walked to Alison's room, turned off the television set, and sat on her bed to read the documents from the manila envelope.

When I returned to her mother's room, Alison was sitting up. She had taken the pictures from the shelf and placed them on the bed, sequentially, over the green cloth. One of the pictures—the first—had been removed from its frame.

"I've found some answers on my own," she said. "But you go first. What did you find?"

I explained what I knew from the papers inside the envelope: Bethany Arcement and Raymond Belanger were married in 1940, got a mortgage on the Emerson house the next year. Raymond Belanger was pronounced dead on April 2, 1942, by a Plaquemines Parish coroner: injuries sustained in an automobile accident.

"That's it?" Alison asked. "No me?"

"No birth certificate, if that's what you mean."

"But look at this, Jay Pee." Alison handed me the photograph from the first frame. "It's been tampered with. Prince Albert, do you think? No, look at the back."

On the back, printed in a circle similar to a postage stamp cancellation, was the date 1944. Below that were the handwritten words *Alison Elizabeth, 1 yr. 3 mos. 13 days.*

"Do you think this is how Prince Albert knew my name?"

"I don't know. It's possible. But tell me, are there any pictures of you at all before this first one."

"No."

"Are you sure? In any albums anywhere? In the house?"

"No. I noticed that many years ago, though. That there weren't any baby pictures of me. And you won't find pictures anywhere of my mother, Jay Pee. The day Uncle Nolan took me to the state hospital in Jackson, I gathered up all of mother's pictures, sat in front of the closed closet door. And with mother inside, I cut up every one of those pictures. That's when Uncle Nolan found me."

Alison sat up. One of the pictures fell to the floor. Then Alison folded the green cloth over the other pictures and tossed the bundle from the bed. "Tell me, please. What do these pictures mean? And the missing birth certificate?"

"This is a conclusion and a belief," I said. "You and Laurel are both children of the Palace."

(Molly, my words to Alison are easy enough to write. I hesitated saying them. I said them, though, and waited, waited perhaps to hold her as she cried, to give her any comfort, to even tell her, if I had to, that there are no answers sometimes. But she put her hands behind her head, stretched her arms toward the ceiling, stretched, and laughed with a face as happy as I had seen on any daughter in the warm sun on a fair day at the beach. "I am being born," Alison said.

And in the world called De Plus En Plus so are, so were we all.)

Children of the Palace

Downstairs, Alison and I explained everything to Laurel, who became more and more delighted, especially when Alison talked about the Palace and our conclusions about Alison's past. Laurel asked Alison if she was feeling all right, and Alison assured her that she was. Then the two girls hugged each other and danced circles.

(And I must tell you, Molly—having known my brother Berman, knowing for myself the full definition of joy and its connection to pain—that I also danced, in a circle, in my heart, as I sat and watched from the piano bench. And Molly, as you compile with me my chronicle, know that I was my happiest here, as I was my happiest on the beach watching my daughters in the surf before the accident. But I did not think of the past or its connection with the present in the world called De Plus En Plus. I was watching two girls named Alison and Laurel. I sat apart, happy for a joy that existed outside of myself.)

When the dancing stopped, Laurel sat Alison down beside me. Laurel looked to me as she spoke: "Now let me get this straight. She was adopted in some way by the people who lived in this house, here on Emerson Street?"

I answered her by saying that we could conclude that, but the conclusion was not certain. As both girls giggled at my seriousness, I told Laurel also that I believed Prince Albert's legacy, now in the Reverend Bowman's possession, would probably indicate just that—that Alison had been taken from the Palace, had been in effect adopted by the Emerson family.

Laurel continued to look at me as she asked another question: "But why wouldn't anybody tell her this before?"

I looked to Alison. Alison seemed to be smiling for me, to reassure me. "I told you, Jay Pee," she said. "I have waited a long time to understand the fit, the nonfit, the looks I got from my mother." Then she turned to Laurel and gave her the same smile. "My family wouldn't tell me any of that, and *that* fits. My Aunt Elli, my mother, my Uncle Nolan . . . they are not the kind of people who would tell me that."

"But they got to tell you now," Laurel said. "If you want

to know for sure. And this man here. He's our lawyer. He got him the right to ask that for you if you want. If you want to know for sure."

"For certain," Alison said. "For an end. Aren't we close to an end, Jay Pee? Don't you feel it?"

I did not answer. I did feel it. But a shadow fell over my thoughts, the shade of the world called De Plus En Plus, of Alison's worlds inside and outside of herself, of Laurel's world and what she carried from her world into ours, of connection, of balance, of waves and undertow, of chance, of circumstance, of terror. And I thought, in the shade, that I knew better than to answer. I watched the two girls, and I listened as Alison told Laurel that Mardi Gras was beginning, the real Mardi Gras. A practice and a formal dinner would be taking place later that night for the krewe. I listened also as Alison told Laurel that there were formal dresses in her mother's closet that would fit the two of them, that she felt that they—the two girls from the Palace—could change the town.

"I'm taking Laurel with me to the dinner," Alison said.

"I don't believe so," I said.

"Mister, we ain't—"

I could have finished that sentence for her, *ain't your little girls.*

"I mean I can help you," I said. "My family's gone to many parties. It has to be done with care."

"Drown in a stare, Jay Pee?" Alison said.

"Hey, Mister. Forget all that. You glad, ain't you? For all of us?"

I shook my head and tried with a smile to reassure them. Because I *was* glad. For all of us. Even in the shade of my thoughts.

"Well," Laurel said, "what you waiting for? Git. Git that legacy."

"And the matchbox," Alison said.

"Lordy, you know about that, too?"

"Everyone in this room," I said, "knows all there is to know at this point. But you two wait until I get back."

Laurel took a few steps toward me, her arms opening. Then she stopped. "Git, Mister. Let's finish up here."

"And bring your recorder," Alison said. "We want to know everything."

Into the Waves

I did bring my recorder with me, swaddled in my sling. And I brought more blank tapes. I would get to use them again soon. I got to use for the first time also the most recent gift from Barron Palmer Roussell—the microphone that attached to a telephone receiver.

(Molly, I am not certain what made me turn right at the end of Emerson Street rather than left, what made me make the big circle detour in the direction of the cathedral and the court square rather than the direct route to Bowman's church and the Palace grounds. It must have been that for the first time in a long while I allowed myself to be carried by a wave created by my own swell of what Berman used to call the "beneficent-munificent contentment that follows joy," that tongue-twisting feeling that does nothing toward advancing or retarding society, but that nonetheless is the ultimate reward of history both in the smaller sense and the larger sense.

I had felt this lifting swell of contentment first in my life after those dinner debates with the family when we had argued, trying to answer the questions that our experiences brought to us; when with my father and brothers and sisters, aunts, cousins, and you, I had walked pleased and without consideration of worth or values from the table to sit with cigars and cognac and thoughtlessness in the closest room.

That feeling, Molly. It must have been a similar carry as I walked from Emerson. I bought a cigar at the drugstore and I smoked and I thought of nothing, absolutely, as I chose my bench and sat beneath the oaks. And when a thought finally came to me, it was of you. I remembered your eyes, on me, and your breast uncovered and the small of your back in amber light. And there were no questions, just the absolute nothing-but-living of desire. Then I crossed the street to the phone booth.

I was going to call you. I dialed the operator first. I was going to tell you that I was coming home soon, after Mardi Gras. I would get Laurel and Alison to return with me, not as replacements for my daughters, but as two girls I had met on a journey south to the watery part of the world, a journey I believed would soon be over. They could stay with us, have a place to push off from when they decided to leap. I would sit with you, Molly, eventually, beside the brick pond I had dug and built for our daughters in the courtyard. I would sit beside you and think of nothing, absolute nothing.

Then I heard the operator's voice. Maybe because it was not your voice—or maybe because I realized suddenly what hearing your voice would do to the wave—I put the receiver down and looked up the number for Nolan Roussell in the local directory.)

J.P.: Mrs. Roussell?

Elizabeth: Yes. . . . It is you, the lawyer. Mr. Marquis.

J.P.: Yes. I've just finished talking to Alison. I am recording this conversation. Do you mind?

Elizabeth: Nolan! What do you mean recording. To what end?

J.P.: There are some things Alison wants to know from you. She has asked me to call you, to represent her. She is close to certain that her father was not Raymond Belanger, that she was taken from the Palace in 1944 and brought to Emerson Street. If she was adopted, legally or not—

Elizabeth: Why are you doing this to me? Oh, God. It never—we paid that man, that Negro. Nolan!

J.P.: Alison feels that she was adopted. She wants to know now. She feels, as do I, that she has the right to the truth.

Nolan: Ah, truth, Jamie. Forgive me for interrupting—

Elizabeth: No, Nolan. Listen. Adopted, he said. Tell him yes. Tell him—

Nolan: I will handle this, Elli. Jamie, I am afraid the answers to your questions are for my niece's ears and not yours. That is for the family to know. Surely you understand family enough to know that you are not—

J.P.: Yes. But Alison is ready to know. She is ready for an end.

Nolan: I am saying that you are a Marquis. And whatever she is . . . I am saying you cannot step in and understand the bits of what you call truth on a weekend sojourn.

J.P.: You agree it is her truth.

Nolan: From where I stand it belongs to many. Some of us are still paying for that truth. But if she personally wants to claim her portion, I might have to give it to her. I am not a fan of truth. Is that the word? *Fan?* I try not to lie. My wife on the other hand, who knows her portion, is ready to lie. I am not as inclined as she to the lie, but—

J.P.: Stop.

Nolan: No. Let me say it again. I am not a fanatic about the truth. I also know that we know Alison better than you. That she has had problems, deep, hateful—

J.P.: And she is ready to take hold now. That is what I feel.

Nolan: No, that is what you want for her. And this family is not your family. And as much as I believe in truth, in history—

J.P.: Stop.

Nolan: —keeping the truth is also a part of history.

J.P.: Stop and listen—

Nolan: No, you stop, Jamie. Before you become a responsible party. There is a chance if *you* stop now. Take a bus home, to your family.

J.P.: I am getting tired of your tedious—

Nolan: Oh, there is still the anger, Jamie. Why don't you hop your taxi and we'll have us a chat—

J.P.: Just shut up. Give her—

Nolan: It is good the fire in your breath is being transformed to cool electricity over phone wires. Ah, Jamie, I still have that vision, cherished now, of a Marquis handcuffed to a Coca-Cola machine. Go home, Jamie. Go home to the hurts you comprehend fully.

J.P.: I am talking about Alison.

Nolan: And I am talking, Jamie. And I am saying . . . I am saying I have done my penance for years by watching over this family. I will go to any length—handcuffs, if I must. And I am saying . . . good day.

Suck Ice

(Molly, as you can see by the map and the photographs, the west side of Reverend Stillman Bowman's church parallels the Great Perpendicular. In 1963 this side, with its white-painted pine and its arched windows, faced the Palace grounds and what was left of the Palace. The front of the church, its two ten-foot doors and the long rectangular window above the lintel, faced and still face a street named Fort Bien. Across Fort Bien in 1963 stood a gray storefront. The storefront still stands, a pawnshop today, but when I made it to this point in the late afternoon on February 20, 1963, the sign on the storefront read Theriot's General Merchandise.

I remember the rain started as I knocked on the front doors of the church, and it might be important to note that I began or am beginning to notice the weather again, weather other than the general merchandise of false spring. Before I crossed the street to sit on the steps of the storefront, I tried opening the doors, but they were locked. I remember trembling under the eaves, counting the church steps, taking into my memory the square facade: the two towers on either side of the church, both sheered flat, were leaning right as far back as that day in 1963.

Do what you will, Molly, with these details and the tape recording I made of the owner of the storefront as the Fort Bien storm drain swallowed the last of the rain. But in my mind now, I see clearly what I should have been considering had I not been so damned content with myself at the time. I should have considered all the atoms in all the waves of circumstance that we Marquises liked to talk about at the table—the ripples and small waves of daily life, the larger waves that develop from these and from God knows where else, and then the rare but crushing mass of history in the larger sense. We couldn't reach an agreement at table, remember, about any of this, not with Dr. Einstein or Dr. King, but we all agreed that even as fools we were smart enough after the fact to be able to know when we had been crushed.

On that day in 1963 I sat and thought only of myself and Laurel and Alison and the gentle prick and chill of the water on my skin. But looking back now, I should have felt the first nudge.

But isn't it so like a Marquis not to see the patterns until later? And isn't it also a family trait to shake our heads and snicker at the family motto: Happy is he who knows the causes of things.

So do what you will, Molly, with this little transcription. I've probably put more time into it than I should, when one considers how much time has already been taken.)

The man talking to me from behind the screen door wore a plaid shirt with tails out, knee shorts, brown socks and sandals. The skin on his ankles was hairless, pale in the yellow light of dusk. He spoke with the local French accent.

Voice: You a bill collector, you? My boy's the chief of police in this town. You talk to him you collecting.

J.P.: Mr. Theriot?

Theriot: Yas. How you know that?

J.P.: Signs and things.

Theriot: That's funny. Are you being funny, you?

J.P.: Sure. What made you think I was a bill collector? The suit?

Theriot: What's that white box? Oh, I see. For evidence, huh. You a bill collector, all right. Why else would a white man be knocking on them doors? That there's a colored church. You can get out if you a bill collector. Find my boy.

J.P.: I'm not a bill collector. I'm a . . . when do you think Bowman will be in?

Theriot: I'll answer that if you a customer. You frequenting my business? How about a drink? I can bring it to you. You can't drink it on my premises—that's what the law says. My son's chief, him. But if you stay where you are, you ain't on premises. You a customer? Or what?

J.P.: Sure, why not. You have cognac?

Theriot: Cog-nack? Sure. Got something to celebrate? That ain't a call brand. I'll have to open a pint special. It'll cost you more cause it's imported. Sixty-five?

J.P.: Why not?

From the outside steps, I watched Theriot pour the drink. He stopped after half-filling a plastic cup, and walked to a side door. It was a dutch door open at the top; a piece of plywood made a counter of the closed bottom half. A Negro woman with a yellow umbrella leaned on the bottom half of the door. Without speaking, Theriot handed her a bag of groceries.

Back at the screen door, Theriot stood with the drink in one hand and three ice cubes dripping through the fingers of his other hand.

Theriot: You want ice?

J.P.: No, thank you.

Theriot: I got books in my store. Well, not on the premises, in a private room of mine. You can go look.

J.P.: Browse?

Theriot: That's it. Brow. Don't got to buy.

J.P.: White women?

Theriot: You know it. Don't worry. I got to make a living, but I got principle. No coloreds look at the books. Hey, why you throw that drink away? I ain't giving you your money back. Got to make a living.

J.P.: When is Bowman coming back?

Theriot: Didn't say, me, he was coming back. He's in there. But you can't use the front door. Bowman nailed it shut. He even got plywood over the windows so no light shine through. There's a door on the side. He make everybody walk in the side door. Sure you don't want to brow books? You ain't got to buy. They all show hair, lots of open shots. . . . Hey, wait, you ain't from here, is you. You come down to—

J.P.: That's enough.

Theriot: Bowman don't need help stirring them up. I can hear it through the plywood. You ever hear of a man that wants to be buried standing up? Behind them doors, behind them doors that always locked and glass that never shine, there's a man like that. Bowman. A nigger that wants to be buried standing up. You help stir them up and it will be your ass.

J.P.: Would you sell me another drink?

Theriot: Sure. I got principle. But I got to make a living.
J.P.: Suck ice.

Black!

The words *Powerhouse Hall* had been woodburned into the varnished side door, which divided horizontally like Theriot's. Both halves of Bowman's door were open. I made sure the tape recorder was off before I stepped inside into a pinewood foyer. I heard the sounds of a high-ceilinged chamber filled with people—soft mumbling, coughing—coming from the top of a short staircase to my right. An arrow on a woodburned Office sign on the foyer wall pointed left.

Turning left, I walked the dark hall until I was standing on the threshold of a room with no door. Inside, Bowman sat in silhouette behind a desk in the middle of the room, his small frame locked in the narrow breach between desk and wall, the top of his bald head capped with a fine arc of light that filtered softly through cheesecloth curtains.

"I am preparing," Bowman said.

"I'd like to speak with you."

"I know your voice. You are the lawyer I saw in Ozema's cell. Ozema has left, you know. And my lawyers who came all this way to free him. They have gone. Maybe it is best I am alone. Find the light. The switch on the wall there. It is close to time."

I patted the wall until I found the switch, flicked it up with my thumb. There was no light. Above us, the wood blades of a ceiling fan began to whirl slowly.

Bowman yelled, "Niggers," loud enough for those in the chamber to hear. He went on shouting, purposely changing his diction and pronunciation: "I told . . . tole you! When was it . . . short time, short time. I tole you it needed work. Needed changin'."

291

Bowman paused, then spoke to me, deliberately, calmly. "Are you surprised that I call them that? Call my children that? I can see your face plainly now in the dimness. Why didn't the word *nigger* in my presence startle you?"

"I've heard it before."

"From a colored man?"

"Yes."

"And a colored man calling another—his brother—a nigger. You have heard that, too? In your line of work or without?"

"Many places, many times."

"That must stop. That will stop. That gots to leave us! . . . Another question. Have you heard we should be calling ourselves 'black?' That is the word from the cities with the leaders. I have heard it on the TV news also. And in letters from my Philadelphia. I have been away a long time now from my . . . black. Have you heard this?"

"Yes. But I'm not sure if I've heard it yet in New Orleans."

"Well, you will be hearing it soon. Soon!" Bowman's last words had risen in intensity and rhythm. When he spoke again, softly, the rhythm remained. "I am preparing. I called them 'niggers' because they have been. I will be calling them 'black' even though they have been trained against both words. Soon. Because they have been, because they shall be. What is it you want?"

I told Bowman I had come for Prince Albert's legacy. He took a manila envelope from a desk drawer and slid it across the desktop. I told him that I had a few other questions, about the Palace and the Princess of the Palace, and that I would like to record the rest of our conversation. Before he gave me permission, he said the word *lawyer* to himself as though testing the feel of it on his mouth.

Bowman: Quickly. I am preparing.

J.P.: Do you know if there was a little girl living across the street, at the Palace, around '43 or '44? A girl that could have been adopted?

Bowman: Forgive my chuckle. You do not know about the Princess, do you? I know her. I fought her for years, as hard as I have had to fight the lions. Ah, but she deserved her name. No man, black or brown, made her spirit flinch nor dulled its crowning side. Though I felt she catered to the low side of her visitors, she did find many homes for many young children who might not have otherwise . . . *that gots to leave us!*

J.P.: But do you remember one, possibly? A white girl. Maybe with one Negro parent?

Bowman: Black!

J.P.: One black parent?

Bowman: Forgive me if I laugh to this, also. There were many of these. All shades. Most happy at the Palace, some sad. Most sad to leave the Palace. All children . . . *all.*

J.P.: Could Prince Albert have been the father of any of these?

Bowman: If I were not preparing, I would be laughing over and over on the floor, and I am not one inclined to . . . *that gots to leave!* Albert has a reputation on Landry. He is what they call a looker. He told me himself he never touched a woman. It is a fact everyone on Landry knows, so I am not disclosing something I should not be.

J.P.: And this legacy. Could you tell me about this legacy?

Bowman: You can view it yourself. Albert has given me instructions to give it to you. He has left, you know.

J.P.: I am talking about how you received it initially, the envelope.

Bowman: The Princess gave it to me. She used that word *legacy* and said that I should give this to Albert after she was gone. It is I who wrote the word *legacy* on the outside of the envelope.

J.P.: And this address written here. This Emerson address.

Bowman: You will see in a better light that the address is in another hand than mine. The Princess wrote that. The hand of the Prin— *in His hand!* . . . Have your eyes accustomed themselves to the light?

J.P.: Enough to see the envelope.

Bowman: And can you hear? Listen. Listen to them rustling in the chapel. They have been waiting for me for two hours now. There are legacies that are bigger than any legacy this envelope can enclose. You want to hear? Do you want to hear? Stay here if you like, and listen as I speak to them. When you hear me say, "Tonight I open the doors," you must leave. I will not speak again until you have shut the side door behind you.

I watched Bowman walk the dark hall to the ten-step stair. He ascended, on the tenth step halted, his palms against the door. He did not shove. The sounds behind the door decreased the longer he stood. When the door opened, from the other side, he dropped his hands but remained poised in the silence. In the glow of the low-wattage bulbs coming from the chapel, flecks of bronze on a synthetic robe; Bowman's small head, balanced on wide shoulders. After the door closed behind him, I listened as I recorded.

Bowman: I am the resurrection. . . . Nigger! Yes. Hear the quiet after the foul wind of that word. Hear it? Hear it? I treat you rough? I dare to foul the air with the wind of that word? Nigger! I treat you rough because you accept the foul wind so well. You stand bent and smiling at the side doors in the wind of that word, at side counters, your children watching. And lately I have made you stand also, have I not? Bent and smiling at the side door of the Lord. I've made you enter this holy place through the side door for how long now? Seven days? How long?

Voices: Seven days.

Bowman: I've had you sitting in here waiting for me. How long? Two hours? How long?

Voices: Two hours.

Bowman: Now you telling me you wants to stand?

Voices: Yes.

Bowman: You wants to stand? You tired of the side door? But you accept it so well, so well, calling your brother *nigguh* when you angry, *nigguh* when you joking. *Nigguh! Nigguh! Nigguh!* Now you telling me you are tired, tired of the side door?

Voices: That's right. What we telling, what we telling you.

Bowman: You tired of nigguh-hood? Tired of side door, bent-over-smiling, and standing in the front of your children eyes in the foul wind. Answer me then. Answer!

Voices: Yes!

Bowman: And I, too, say yes! I finally seen you standing straight. On a Sunday, seen you. I seen you standing while you singing to the courthouse walls. You were singing. Standing. I seen you standing. I want you to say yes to me now. But I want you to say it a new way. Hear it. Black! Say yes.

Voices: Yes.

Bowman: No! Say yes.

Voices: Black.

Bowman: Yes. Yes. Tonight I may open the front door. Say yes.

Voices: Black!

How the Lion Became a Weasel

The last light of the sun lit the sassafras and bay behind the Palace fence as I searched the ground for the matchbox. By the time I got to search inside the house, the sun had gone. I turned the lamp on in Prince Albert's room and left the door to Dugas' room open to try to discern the shapes on the table. I saw the makeshift candle, a beer bottle, but nothing else. Then the lamp in Albert's room went out and I stood in darkness.

(Molly, in those moments before the light went out I sensed the smothering closeness that Alison had described about the Palace. I smelled talc with its perfume gone, bloom of mold on beer, sweat and salt in bedding. After the light went out, the closeness remained and the smells combined to one. And I smelled—in my mind only, maybe, in the salt of my memory only, I do not know—I smelled the Fourchon: the Gulf, the marsh.

It was as though I were standing beside the Gulf again on the day I lost Abigail and Jane, beside the Gulf again but in darkness this time, in a darkness where my anger could not take direction from my senses. And without my anger, I felt the weakness at the core of my life, a small and frantic uselessness I had not felt since I was a child. And for the first time since I was a child, I knew what word to use. I was *afraid*.

I knew also, and know again now, that I had grown away from that word and into the world. I had felt just as small facing the Gulf, trying to find Abigail's voice in the green water. I had felt just as frantic, running in and out of and through that green. I had felt just as weak, falling with spasms to the sand. But I would not say that I was afraid, because I had my anger, had the blue between the clouds to raise my face and voice toward. There had been other words that day, just as there are now, to describe what I was feeling—torment, anguish—because there had been objects around me in the world to blame, to charge, to hate, to fall upon, to scream into. But had the Gulf, the sand, the light on and above the sea and the sand been taken away from me that day on the beach when I realized my daughters were dead, had I lain alone on that day too in a darkness with my smallness, my uselessness, my terror, I would have used the word then, too. *Afraid*.)

I could not remember what direction I had been facing when the room went to black. I heard what sounded like footsteps in the house with me, but the sounds came from all directions. I took a step toward the table to grab the beer bottle. I wanted the neck of it in my palm. I wanted anything I could call a handle in my palm. I took another step toward where I thought the table would be and tripped over what could have been a chair, bedstead, and while I sat on the floor my hand slid across the grime still seeking an object small enough to grip.

In that smelly void a red light suddenly hovered above me. The red had a mass to it, was not warm. Then above and behind that cold, solid red there popped into existence another light—white-yellow maybe. Floating in that light were patches of black, patches of lack of light that to me took shape, became the hollows of a visage.

(And, Molly, sitting in the grime, wasn't I feeling the purest fear, the cold red fear at every man and woman's center, what my grandfather called the "primal exploitable pitiable"? Wasn't I the unenviable, pitiable, alone, small human that you and I have both found recurring continually in our reading of the chronicles?)

I may have even moaned aloud. I say this because a sound like a moan also came from the visage, tones as deep as a visage should be expected to have. When this yellow, black face vanished, the red remained, hovering again, but no more than a moment before it fell downward.

I did not feel foolish until I heard the sound the red made on the floor. A sound I recognized, the bounce of plastic perhaps, but something identifiable as man-made. And then from the void the deep tones themselves took on the sounds foolish enough to be man-made—words. And those words became specified: "Shit goddamn, Jay Pee. Shit fuck goddamn!"

It was Lineman.

(Molly, Lineman and I did not laugh that evening in the Palace room, but I laughed with Lineman just today as we talked about that evening. He, too, had never been *afraid* since he was a child. We laughed at ourselves tonight. And I hope that you had a laugh from this, what can be called the greatest scare of this one Marquis' life.

Yes, Molly, I have gone to interview Lineman before my narrative reaches Mardi Gras Day. Lineman himself approached me about the interview. It seems that he is going to try to take some advice from Stillman Bowman on how to get some sleep. Years ago Bowman told Lineman's sister Angelle that Lineman cannot get satisfaction from sleep because of the black weight of *sin on his soul.* Lineman must counterbalance the black weight with the weight of *atonement*; if Lineman begins with *good works and good ways*, the tally will begin to add up, an ounce at a time, until one day Lineman's end of the scale will rise. I am part of what Lineman calls his "tonement tally." He will answer any questions I have about anything. Lineman hopes he will live long enough to do enough good to get the deep, long sleep he craves.

I will continue to work on my chronicle through tonight, but I may have to put it aside while I listen to what Lineman has to tell me.)

(Molly, speeding on now. A transcript of recording number 8—the evening in the Palace with Lineman, after the scare, when I solved the crime and answered the question, Who thrust the saber past Prince Albert's cheek into the Palace floor?)

Lineman: Shit, Jay Pee, I had to push you. I didn't know what you was reaching for inside your coat, you understand? Taping recorders don't fit inside coats. Guns do. I'm telling you I might've killed all over on you you go reaching like that.

J.P.: Lineman—

Lineman: No. I ain't Lineman, Jay Pee. Look here in the flashlight here—stole that flashlight from a man used to ush at the Grand Theater. You see a ring on my finger, man? I ain't the Lineman no more. I went back to being the Weasel, you understand? Call me the Weasel. What you here for?

J.P.: A matchbox. Prince Albert and Dugas gave me a matchbox in this room, and I was looking for it.

Lineman: A matchbox? With something rattling in it?

J.P.: Yes.

Lineman: Oh, man, Jay Pee. You don't have no idea what is significance about a matchbox with something rattling in it, do you? Here. Here's your matchbox. Found it right here on the floor by this table. And you know what? Call me Lineman again. Call me the Lineman. Shit, for a while there . . . what's that you see in that matchbox?

J.P.: A small piece of brass.

Lineman: Not gold?

J.P.: No.

Lineman: You sure, huh? Cause if it's gold and it look like a tooth, I got to go back to being the Weasel again. What that is, Jay Pee?

J.P.: It's something that tells me all that I need to know.

Lineman: Let me tell you something, Jay Pee. I own this place now, you understand. I been dreaming of changing the name on this place to mine for a long time. I come in here tonight, hoping to feel all like a lion, you understand, all conquer. But I feel something else. I feel there's things crawling around in here, on my skin, on my neck. Then I come on this matchbox here and the rattle inside the matchbox. I was sure, Jay Pee, sure, you understand, that I ain't alone in this place, that nobody ever alone. I took off my ring, my Lineman ring. Flung it at the wall. I changed my name back to Weasel, called myself Weasel out loud. And if you hadn't come along . . . now you telling me there's a explanation. God bless explanation. I can be a lion again. You want to help me find my ring? Where you going?

J.P.: I've got to make a phone call.

Lineman: No, you got to listen, Jay Pee. This is the Lineman again. I was a weary man there for a while. I need me some sleep, you understand. But that ain't nothing new. But I was weary of it more today, low on the floor. Some days, they like that. There's days I'd trade any name and any ring in for a full night sleep. I started taking cat's naps to stay away from my dreams. Now my cat's naps got control of me, kind of like . . . like even though I sleep most the time, but I don't sleep . . . like . . . like my eyes, they getting to be the color of the red on a movie-usher flashlight. You understand?

J.P.: What do you know about the Palace, its connection to Emerson Street?

Lineman: I don't answer to no questions, remember, Jay Pee. But cause your explanation saved me, let me tell you on the side, kind of, kind of away from your question. The Lion knows all. But he ain't telling, ain't messing with the riggin'. And I can't never tell cause that would give somebody a shot at stealing from me what's mine, you understand, my connection.

J.P.: You just said I helped you—

Lineman: Yeah, yeah. So listen while I equal that out with some advice. Listen. Things is peaking in this town. And Roussell tells me that even my kingdom in danger. Roussell told me you fuckin' around with the riggin' of the kingdoms. And I'll lean on you hard, Jay Pee. This is the Lineman again. You better leave town. No, don't go tapping that recorder like you trying to scare the Lineman. That's a lawyer way of trying to scare people. That don't work on the Lineman. So let me give you some advice. If you don't want to go home—and I got the feeling you don't—if you need to lose yourself—and I got the feeling you will—they tell me a man can do it round here by getting him a job in the oil patch. Go to Morgan City

300

and sign up. The boats leave every day. I can give you a name of somebody working the docks. Good money and long, lonely days over water. So let me get close to your pocket here and tell you. I'll lean on you hard you try to take from me what mine is. Everything mine that I want it. And that's the way the Lion going to keep it.

Bucked Up

(Molly, it's just about midnight, the midnight before I begin my Lineman interviews. And so, speeding on, tape number 9.)

J.P.: You're a son of a bitch.

Barron: Partner, is that you? Where are you calling from?

J.P.: From the phone booth outside the Cathedral Street drugstore.

Barron: I assume I am being recorded.

J.P.: You're damned right you are. And I'll use this tape against you if I have to.

Barron: Go on from there, partner. I have no qualms about being—

J.P.: It was you, all along. You tried to kill Prince Albert Willis.

Barron: Those are harsh words. I do not think I could kill anyone. Surely you do not think I am capable of such a thrust.

J.P.: You were there that night, at the Palace.

Barron: If you ask it that way, partner. Yes, I was there. Continue with the questions. I am sworn in, let us say. I promise to tell the truth, and nothing but the truth—

J.P.: Stop.

Barron: —but only if the question is properly phrased. Go on, partner.

J.P.: You tried to kill Prince Albert.

301

Barron: Objection. That is not a question. But to give you some help, partner: I already testified that I did not try to kill him. I am incapable, though not necessarily inculpable.

J.P.: Did you push the saber into the floor beside Prince Albert's face?

Barron: Yes. In a manner of speaking.

J.P.: Why didn't you tell me sooner? You were trying to protect yourself.

Barron: Protect. Maybe. Myself, maybe. Let me give you more than you ask for, partner. I pretended I was drunk at the Senator's party. Who would doubt that I was not, after what I have displayed in my life? My father brought me to his office to sleep it off. I went to the Palace on my own to scare this Prince Albert Willis. I did a good job. But kill, partner . . .

J.P.: He was on the floor when you got there?

Barron: Yes. Eyes glazed, staring up.

J.P.: You took his sword from him, raised it above his face?

Barron: Yes, partner. And he saw it. And it scared him.

J.P.: And you thrust it down, at his mouth.

Barron: That is stretching a bit. I have already admitted I wanted to scare him. Kill, I will not admit to.

J.P.: You son of a bitch. Why didn't you tell me this before I, before Alison, Laurel . . .

Barron: You seemed so content, partner. Traveling about. Who am I to spoil—

J.P.: Stop. Just stop. You were only trying to protect yourself.

Barron: Objection again, partner. There is a question of proof here. How would you prove this to a court? You have a motive. I have given you that. You have opportunity. I again have given you that. But proof? Aside from this tape and my admissions, what do you have?

J.P.: I have an eyelet from a boot. A brass eyelet with a hook. The kind of eyelet that is on the top of your flier's boot. You were sending your boots off to be repaired. You gave me the shoe box.

Barron: Forgive me if I laugh. I wish you were here to see me laugh. I have not done this in . . . from where was this eyelet, as you call it, taken?

J.P.: Prince Albert took it from a tooth from his dog. I figure the dog—

Barron: This is bountifully amusing . . . excuse me . . . laughter is—

J.P.: Am I correct?

Barron: I did not say you were mistaken, partner. Can't you see the absurdity of all this? Down to a dog's mouth, brass from a boot. Genocide, torture, all through history, and in Mondebon Parish we are down to an eyelet of brass and a dog's tooth. You are correct, as I say. But do you not see the humor? You will, no doubt, call as your final witness this Prince's dog.

J.P.: Stop.

Barron: Woof.

J.P.: Stop. For God's—

Barron: I'm collecting myself. Let us get ourselves serious then, partner. You and I both know your so-called proof will be scullery to a court.

J.P.: I have this tape.

Barron: A gift from me, partner. Take it. Use it. There are no charges pending. It is over, partner. Now you must stop. I suggest that you go on home now. Leave us to our—

J.P.: Don't say it. I'm going to tell Alison that it was you all along. The truth.

Barron: Listen to me, partner. You need to learn a lot about asking proper questions. And as for truth, you are seeing what you want to see. Ah, the benign blindness of the father. Take my word, you do not really want to see truth. And take my word, it is for the better. . . . Did I tell you I've decided to paint my sword gold?

J.P.: Go to hell.

Barron: Do not hang up, partner. I have a bit more to say. It is not irrelevant. And at any rate, I paid for the tape. My motive needs to be reiterated. You know, partner. You know what they used to tell me when they wanted me to buck up? "The war's over," they said. And I guess as an actuality, that statement is true. But can you imagine that, partner? Their thinking? Some things cannot be over. There are enormities so vast. You understand this. I saw it in your green eyes. And you know I am right to say this, am I not? Forgiveness, forgetting seems not in the scheme. . . . But I have bucked up. Yes, I have. Maybe the gesture, the holding of that sword above that Negro's mouth. Ritual, eh? Listen to me. I have bucked up.

J.P.: Go to hell.

Barron: With you defending me, I probably will be so sentenced. But one last thing. The sword. Below the hilt. I know what is written below. Would you like to know? . . . No?

Goat Cart

(Molly, after the call, I walked north along Main Street, retracing my steps from the bus station. I was going to buy a ticket that I could use to get back to you. I was angry still with Barron Roussell, but also I was content. I use that word, Molly, because you and I so often talked about the definitions of *contentment*, of *happiness*, of *joy*. And I use that word hoping that you will understand why I turned south again before I reached the bus station.

Hadn't I been lucky enough to find myself in a world

of Second Chance? Hadn't I helped my newest daughters? Found answers to their questions?

Why then, Molly, why wasn't I able to ascend to *joy*. The pain had been there, enough sadness had been there to give happiness the patina of joy. But why, Molly, why did I suddenly feel certain on Main Street in a town far away from you that a world of Second Chance would not be enough for me? Enough for me to face you with what we had to face.)

In the house on Emerson Street, I found Alison sitting in the dark at the piano. I turned on the lamp. She asked me to return the room to darkness. I did. In those seconds in the light I saw on her face a smile—her fine-edged lips tightened and her eyes creased at their edges—but there was no contentment or happiness or joy on her face. I also saw, as she brought her hands up to cover her face, that her nails were dirty and chipped, just as they'd been on the night I first saw her.

"It's over, Jay Pee. Isn't it?"

"I think most of what we wanted to know is, yes."

"I'm a child of the Palace, right?"

I showed her the envelope with the Emerson address. "Do you want me to show you this? I've already opened it."

"No, not yet. Give me time. First, tell me about what happened last Saturday night at the Palace. Is that over, too?"

"Yes. Do you remember your cousin . . . Barron . . . being there?"

"Barron? Barron was sloshed."

I played the tape for Alison, and when it was over we sat without speaking for a few minutes.

"Do you want me to remember for you?" Alison asked. "Or should I do that for myself later?"

"Not now. The tape's captured him. Why don't we wait until tomorrow with the rest of this?"

"No. Go on. I know more than you think now. But I'll explain. Go on for me. Before you tell me about the envelope. You must tell me: was that man, Prince Albert . . ."

"No. He wasn't your father. I can't prove that to you, but Reverend Bowman says he wasn't. I think he's right."

"Do you know who my father was, my mother, at the Palace? Will I ever know?"

"I can't say. The Princess knew."

"She's dead. . . . Show me."

I pulled a sepia-toned photograph from the envelope, showed Alison the back of the picture first.

"Words," Alison said. "I can't see well enough. No, don't turn on a lamp. Tell me what it says."

(Molly, I think now that I should have turned on the lamp again, to look into her face. Maybe I would have seen then. But I am thinking like one who has backtracked from the event.)

"There is a word, here. *Page*. And a date, 1944. I think Page is a name."

"And I'm this Page? Right?"

"Look," I started to turn the photograph over.

"No. Just tell me. Is it the same girl that's in the photographs in mother's room?"

"Yes."

"Are you sure, Jay Pee?"

"Yes. She—you—you're sitting on a cart, a cart being pulled by a goat. I've seen pictures like this before. Traveling photographers used to pose—"

"Go on, tell me about this girl."

"She's in front of the Palace. You were taken from the Palace in 1944 and brought here. The Princess knew you were taken here, and she put this photograph in an envelope with the Emerson address on the outside. Prince Albert got the photograph when his mother died. He came here, to the address on the envelope, saw the other pictures on your mother's shelf. He figured out the rest. Or enough of the rest to get some money from your family."

"He wasn't my father?"

"There may be some research we can do . . ."

"No, Jay Pee. Let's say that's over. But why I was brought here, I can know that if I want to, can't I? Uncle Nolan, Aunt Elli, they know why. He told me tonight at the party that he would tell me if I wanted to know. Do you think the answer's simple, Jay Pee? Something like a lonely, crazy woman named Bethany needed the warmth of a baby after her husband was killed? I can take the answer, Jay Pee. I believe I can. Look at how I've built on what happened at the Palace Saturday night."

"Barron called it a ritual."

"Yes, Jay Pee. Like some ancient rite. Like sacrifice. I can take any answer now. And on my own."

"What else did your Uncle Nolan tell you?"

"He gave me something. A paper. I'm trying to make sense of it."

"Let me see it."

"First take me to bed. You're cute, you know. But I'm tired. You're not my daddy."

"I know."

I went with Alison to her bedroom, in the darkness sat on the edge of her bed while she pulled the covers over herself.

"Like a child," she said. "Too tired to change myself."

"Shall I turn on the TV set for you?"

"No. Just sit. I put something in your pocket, Jay Pee, while we walked up the stairs. Kind of a surprise for you. Don't reach in there yet, okay. Later. Promise me."

I promised, and then she asked me if I still saw my daughter in her. Before I could answer, she asked me again if I had any idea why she'd been taken from Landry Street to Emerson. I told her I could make another promise, to help her find out, if she wanted to know.

"No, Daddy. It's up to me now. I don't need help. But don't worry. I can do it alone now. It's up to me."

"But I can help. I can try to get your Uncle Nolan—"

"No. He said he'd tell only me."

"I can still help, stay just far enough away—"

"I said it's up to me, Jay Pee."

(Molly, I knew that I would have to let her do as she should choose. But I thought that maybe I could compromise—just as I had planned to do with Abigail. I had been planning to offer to drive Abbi to college in the fall. She and I alone on a long trip to Berkeley, near a bay in California. I could watch, from a place not too far away, awhile longer.)

"You don't mind if I stay in the poolhouse," I said.

"It's all right with me. But Uncle Nolan . . . this is his house. I found that out at the dinner party tonight, too. He owns this place. He told me that I could stay here, that this house can be mine—but I'd have to ask you to leave. If I'm going to build on *me*, I've got to do it from here. You will leave, won't you? I'm not going to have to choose, am I?"

"You can stay with me in New Orleans. For a while. Then come back."

Alison turned beneath her covers and found my hand, held it. "No, Jay Pee. It's over. And I must be over for you, too. You dig? Leave me, please. Let me make my own sense of what there is to know. I don't feel I belong in many places, but at least around here I know where to stand if I want my picture taken. Leave me now. Leave this house. Leave us to . . . to us."

"One thing more. The paper your Uncle Nolan gave you. I left it downstairs. What did it say?"

"You won't quit, will you? Poor Daddy. And poor Daddy, you don't know about Laurel yet, do you?"

"Know what?"

"The dinner party didn't go well for Laurel either. She's had to stand up to sneers and looks. She's not a girl who can tread looks well. But she isn't a girl. A woman. She's talking to Bowman now about being Queen Zulu. And, Jay Pee—Zeema's with her."

M-A-R-A-N-O

Leaving Emerson Street with no direction in mind, I walked the town to the court square, where to this day one can see a pavilion of oak limbs and leaves covering the streetlights, and where the chance is good one will get to see azaleas blooming before the beginning of Lent. To this day also, one can buy a cigar at the same drugstore on the corner of Cathedral and Main.

That night the drugstore had closed early. When I lifted the receiver of the pay phone, it was with a deep desire to hear my wife's voice. Instead of calling her, I dialed Barron Roussell's number, for verification of what I already suspected I knew.

J.P.: . . .

Nolan: Is that you there, Jamie? My son and I had a feeling you would call back.

J.P.: I have nothing to say to you. I need to speak to your son.

Nolan: And he is my son now, Jamie. Returned to me from the dead. I am taking a step back, shall we say. As I prefer to do. I have done my work. History, Jamie. All coming together. It will happen without me. But I will delight in it because I know I have done my part. Do you—

J.P.: To hell with your history.

Nolan: Ah, now, Jamie. A Marquis saying such? What would your family say?

J.P.: Don't talk about my family.

Nolan: The bile will not leave you, will it, Jamie? I feel like the New Orleans judges. You need to be handcuffed for your own good. You have done too much in this town already. You have had your share of getting the story to where it is now. Step aside, Jamie. Or I will do my best to keep you away. Lineman will help me. There is much at stake. Leave us, Jamie. You have had your part. But you are not a part.

J.P.: Give the phone to your son.

Nolan: I am turning everything over to my son.

Barron: Partner? And you are recording.

J.P.: I have another question.

Barron: It must have taken courage to call me again and put yourself in that position. Is it a question of hope?

J.P.: The word on the sword I asked you about earlier . . .

Barron: I am surprised, partner. There are other questions you should ask, questions I am tempted to answer without your asking. Are you sure you do not want to ask me more about Saturday night at the Palace?

J.P.: Just tell me the word on the hilt.

Barron: Marano. M-A-R-A-N-O. Were you expecting another?

J.P.: . . .

Barron: Has Alison told you that you must be leaving the house? Really, partner. You are not a part, as my father says. And I sense that somehow now you understand you are not a part. Shall I spell it again for you, partner? N-o-h-o-p-e, Marano. Sorry it had to end this way, at any rate. Good-bye.

(Molly, had I really believed there would be etched into the sword the word *Marquis*? So perfect a word? So perfect a world? Had I really believed that a world had been made for me? How many of us are there, as Laurel said, who do believe this, who daily and pridefully use a metaphor as impetus to emerge, to damage, to save?

Marano.

Close, but no cigar.

An unforgivable cliché, dearest. Forgive me.)

The End of the Smaller Sense

I dropped myself down, erect but down, to sit on the concrete step at the front door of Theriot's storefront.

Before me, across Fort Bien Street, the sounds of an organ and of singing; over and above the organ and the singing, Laurel's voice.

At my back, a Closed sign on a closed door; behind those, the scuffling and scraping of an average citizen named Theriot.

I gave up then, for the second time in my life, one time more than my brother Berman. I let my new-world daughters go. I tried, though, with all the courage left in me to hold on to my other two daughters, to Jane Ann and to Abigail. I would not surrender them to the Gulf.

I believed that if I hated God enough, I could keep them. Keep them in me. I began to stand, to summon from myself with hate or with courage the will to stand, to lift an angry face up, up at a visage. To keep them. But before I could, I saw Zeema walking around the side of the church. When he recognized me, he crossed Fort Bien Street and sat beside me on Theriot's concrete step.

"I guess you can tell I'm back, Jay Pee. And I'm sorry, man. But . . . now how can I say this?"

"She's your daughter."

"Sounds like you're handing her back to me."

"Nobody hands Laurel back to anyone. I've learned that much."

"Well, thanks anyway, Jay Pee. But I should try to say, to explain—"

311

"No. I understand."

"Well, I'm glad one of us does. It can't just be that I'm a daddy made me come here. Or that she's a steal, like Lineman says, more than a steal. There ain't words. I'm back is all."

"Then we'll leave it at that."

"That's it, Jay Pee. That's always the issue besides Laurel. Leaving, staying. You know what's going on in that church? How can I take her away from that? Should I take her away from that? How can I deal us out of this one, Jay Pee? I don't want to lose more than I've already lost."

"You're asking the wrong man," I said. I should have added, *a man who can lose again and again and again.*

"No, Jay Pee, tell me. Your family been around the kind of stuff going on in that church. Answer some questions for me, damn it. Shouldn't the issue always be Laurel? When Bowman opens that door, Jay Pee . . . how can you grab on to and not lose a daughter to that hurricane?"

I had no answers, though in any court I would have been called and questioned as an expert witness—as a Marquis, as a father who's lost.

"What you feel, Jay Pee? Say it to me."

There, beside Zeema, I felt not a despair, but a yearning. I missed my wife and my brother and my daughters. But I could say nothing.

Across the street, the end of the smaller sense:

Hammer claws and crowbars at the plywood, sheet by sheet, until the glass arch blazes, amber, violet, amber, amber.

Out through the front doors, the choir, in gold and white. Then others, in hats, without hats. They descend to the sidewalk, sing.

Then Bowman and Laurel, both in bronze-colored robes. They stand together before they descend, into the song.

After the last of the crowd had turned the corner from Fort Bien, Theriot's red eave-light came on. Zeema stood. "Should I go, Jay Pee? And if I do, Jay Pee, how far behind her should I stay?"

I wanted to say, *a place never too far away*. But again I could say nothing.

Then Zeema left me alone.

Empty palm. . . .

(Early morning now.
To Lineman—
Will write soon.
Ah, the recrudescence of Spring,
Molly.)

Molly's History

(A.D. 15–29)

Taking the Steal

My husband did write me:

June 21, 1974
Molly,
    I have finished with Lineman now. I am sending those tapes to you, along with my other tapes and notes and research. The tape recorder also—my gift from Barron Roussell—I am sending to you. My chronicle is over for me. I must get along with myself now. I must wait until next Easter to try again to fulfill my promise.
    Isn't it for a Marquis always to keep a promise?
    Isn't it for a Marquis to know a truth from a conclusion?
    And isn't it also for a Marquis to never give up, to complete the task? Are Berman and I to be remembered as the only Marquises ever to leave a chronicle unfinished? And both of us left it for you to finish. Molly of the larger sense, he called you.
    What is left for me to write, Molly? You can do the job from here. What is left is your realm. Even the event itself is recorded for re-search in a photograph almost anyone would recognize. Trace the trail backwards from the photograph of the event and I am certain you will find that all the atoms in the climax of that event had come together by the time I sat alone under a red eave-light.
    And isn't that a fitting end for me? The climax of my life? My part of the damage done. The world of Second Chance gone. The world called De Plus En Plus fighting my design.
    Yes, Molly, there is a world called De Plus En Plus, but it is not connected to a world of Second Chance. Everywhere around us,

Molly, de plus en plus en plus. Wave after wave of always again, crashing, rolling. Atom on atom. Small events, larger events, the Event. The nothing-to-be *until the is. The atoms in frightful combinations and connections. And rather than attempting to help with its stop, we contribute our part by getting up again, moving, again and again.*

The war ended for my brother Berman, but he found it never ended. He brought what he saw and felt to our table. We ate together, beside him, digesting the small bits of his sorrow, a bit now and then of his joy. Then he walked away from the table. And he dived. And he ended. And he never ends for me. And I move, taking my atoms with me. Away. To this town, where others sit in the closest room of their own design. A different Gulf but the same sea.

What was the last line of the note Berman left in his car? I am a Marquis, but only partially. A Marquis does not give up, does not fail. I have given up but please God let me not fail this one time.

I too have failed, Molly. My problem, however, seems to be that I can not stay put long enough to put a stop to the again and again.

I gave up on myself after my daughters died. But I came to this town and began again.

I gave up again that night under the red light of Theriot's storefront, left town for Morgan City and a job over water. But I returned to town on Mardi Gras Day.

I gave up again, on the bridge over the Bayou Mondebon, after the event on Mardi Gras Day. But I started writing my chronicle again, to keep a promise, to know the story, complete and whole.

I am giving up again now, even though I know there is one interview left to do and other interviews your clear mind will find left to do. But God I hope desperately not to fail in my resolve to fail, to give up, to never take up pencil or tape again, to avoid the near occasion of being a Marquis again.

Lineman has made me an offer, dearest. An offer that helps him with his "tonement tally." A steal, he calls it. And I'm going to take it.

So for me dearest, complete and whole, Molly of the Larger Sense, finish a chronicle again.

The only again for me shall be to try to keep my last promise.

I miss you, Molly, but I know a truth from a conclusion. I can never see you again if I am ever to keep that promise.

Good-bye, my dearest,

Molly—

James

Molly of the Larger Sense

I have done as my husband requested, have interviewed, have read, have transcribed. And I am thinking closely now of my husband as I decide on how best to get what was once his narrative to Mardi Gras Day, 1963. I am certain now that my own account should take over where his story seems to end—that night under the red eave-light after Zeema left my husband alone. From there the trail can be followed for a while from day to day.

The Discarded Tape

According to my husband's notes, as he started to rise from Theriot's concrete step he looked up and saw Lineman standing in front of the church. Lineman and my husband approached each other, meeting perhaps in the middle of Fort Bien Street.

In his notes, my husband refers to this incident as "the stand-off on Fort Bien." Lineman suggested "more than strongly" that James Peter Marquis take a bus back to New Orleans immediately. If my husband refused, Lineman said he would "handcuff the Mar-kee to the nearest Coke box," which was a suggestion offered to him by "a certain member of a Main Street family."

At first my husband protested, then acquiesced on the condition that he get to pack his bags and say good-bye to Laurel and Alison. Lineman then told my husband that his bags had already been packed for him by "more than one member of the Main Street family, complete with tape machine and yellow paper," and that these belongings had been loaded onto a pickup truck Lineman had borrowed from his brother Emmon. The truck was parked in the darkness of the Great Perpendicular and was "waiting to take a Mar-kee to ticket booth or pop machine."

This standoff led to the first important compromise of what was left of that Mardi Gras season of 1963. In his notes, my husband does not say whether it was Lineman or he who mentioned the oil fields of the Gulf as a solution to the standoff on Fort Bien Street. The notes do indicate that my husband passed the rest of that Wednesday night with Lineman in a truck heading for the Morgan City docks, where with the help of a retired welder Lineman knew, my husband boarded the crewboat that took him to an oil-company camp in time for breakfast with the day-shift roughnecks.

My husband remained "offshore" five days and four nights. All that can be said about him during that period is that he spent much of his time catching up with his note taking, trying to recall with the "poetic accuracy of his memory" all that had happened to him in town since his last entry. Nowhere in those notes does he talk about the camp, the Gulf, or the thoughts he had living above the Gulf. My husband does say that he made a recording of the conversation he had with Lineman in the truck on the way to the dock, a "final tape, a farewell to the town." He also says that he tossed this tape into the water as Lineman watched the crewboat pulling away from the dock, an action "most unlike even the most partial Marquis."

I have spoken to Lineman about the conversation he had with my husband in the truck, and—historians everywhere forgive me—it is not difficult for me to reconstruct that conversation based on what Lineman told me and on what I myself know of the circumstances. It is not difficult for me to imagine the ride west along Highway 90.

Outside the truck, "clear black—the edge of the end of the world."

Inside . . .

"You ever been in the service, Jay Pee? In the war, I mean?"

"Yes. But I got to stay stateside. I had brothers in all theaters. I don't want to talk."

"We got a lot in common, Jay Pee. They couldn't find a uniform big enough for me to get killed in, and they filled up too many uniforms for your family. You think they had fabric quotas they had to meet?"

"I don't want to talk."

"Trip too long we don't talk. Name it, Jay Pee. What you want to talk about?"

"Nolan Roussell. Your connection with Nolan Roussell."

"My ticket, Jay Pee. He the one give me the key to my kingdom. I ain't saying I'm a man that likes Nolan Roussell, but I am a man that looks after himself. Roussell even give me a set of handcuffs to tie you down."

"What excuse did he use for that? Family? History?"

"Listen, Jay Pee. I don't answer questions, remember? You keep on forgetting that. But look outside. Be nice, wouldn't it, there was things all around us clear as that black air outside. You understand? This bad, this good. Who's to say? But we just all of us bumbling into each other. We need excuses, most of us, after we bumble bad."

"Tell me your excuses, Lineman."

"Some of us don't need excuses, Jay Pee. We stick around

and pick up for profit all the leavings of the bumblers. Some of us just can't wait till the end of the world to pick up on the leavings."

"I'm sure Roussell had other things he wanted you to tell me."

"He said you'd understand, you understand, that it was time to let things go their courses, to sit back, just like he's going to sit back. Both of you done had your effect, done done your damage. What's been started been started. What going to be going to be. You made the right decision, Jay Pee. After a point it ain't nobody fault what happens."

"Somehow I want to fight that belief with all—"

"I believe we both need some long sleep, Jay Pee. Not cat's naps, you understand. Sometime, like I said before, I think I'd trade my kingdom in for sleep deep and long. Know what the Reverend told my sister Angelle? She's a teacher, you know. He told her the only way for me to get a night of sleep is through something called tonement. After I tone enough, blam, I be sleeping with the lambs. I'd just have to make sure not to die before the scales level on up."

"Tell me how you would atone for kidnapping a lawyer five days before Mardi Gras."

"I'd give him a ticket. Tell him all about the past, when he's ready to know the real about the past."

"I'm finished for good with—"

"Come on, Jay Pee. You telling me you wouldn't like to get to Roussell? Know what I'd tell you to tell him—if I was tone-ing, you understand? Remember what I had you write on that letter for me? 'On Emerson there's a hole always open to the past.' Roussell, he's been toneing all his life to fill that hole. Yes sir, show me how a man's toneing and I'll show you how he's carrying his hell with him. That's another thing the Reverend says, Jay Pee. He says hell ain't burning. Hell's a eternity of what you most afraid of. Shit, Jay Pee, can you imagine a eternity of cat's naps? What hell is for you, Jay Pee? You believe what the Reverend say? Shit, man, speak up. It's a long way to Morgan City when men don't talk. Where your hell is?"

"I carry mine with me, too."

"Jay Pee, Jay Pee. In the dark there you sound like Zeema. Y'all too easy to figure out. Your hell got something to do with what you lost, and what you lose always got to do with people. Y'all put your bet on people. Y'all can't help y'allself, can you? You did, didn't you, Jay Pee? On people, didn't you? Sucker bet. Listen to the Lion, Jay Pee. If Zeema was here I'd give him the same advice. Don't never, Jay Pee, don't never put your bet down on people. Easiest way for me to get you's if I know who you love. Didn't you know that, Jay Pee? Show me who a man loves and I'll show you how to get to him. You understand?"

"Do you mind if I sleep?"

"Give me pleasure listening to you trying. Look outside, look. Something clear. The edge of the end of the world."

Im-Pee-Tuss

A Marquis once wrote, in the foreword of the *Fourth Chronicle*, a defense of such reconstructions as I have just attempted: "If the reader trusts me, this is more than conjecture."

My husband, it can be shown, would leave the offshore camp and return to town on Mardi Gras Day, 1963. The impetus of this action cannot be shown with any certainty. I have investigated the matter of his return as far as is possible.

But it is more than conjecture when I say that at some point during his stay offshore my husband remembered that Alison placed a "surprise" in one of the pockets of his coat, something she did not want him to look at until later. It was this surprise, I believe, that got my husband to board a crew-boat late on Monday, the night before Mardi Gras Day.

Meet Meet Meet

On the same Monday night that my husband left the offshore camp, the second important compromise of what was left of the 1963 Mardi Gras season was completed: the Mondebon Zulu Landry Street Carnival Club and the Mondebon Delos Main Street Carnival Club agreed to have representatives of their courts sit on the same reviewing stand during the Delos parade.

The meetings that led to this compromise are all part of the history of the time as recorded in biographies, autobiographies, texts, and journals. Other details can be taken from the public record: the findings of grand juries and inquests; reports by doctors, hospitals, and police. What is not to be found in these public texts can be gleaned from my husband's research—his notes and tapes—and from the research I did after my husband turned the task of completing his chronicle over to me.

What follows is a short history of the smaller events as they can be shown to have occurred.

Wednesday, February 20

The Krewe of Delos meets at the Parish Municipal Auditorium. Nolan Roussell announces to the members that he is stepping down as president of the club. He would like, he says, for the membership to elect in his stead his son, Barron Palmer Roussell, "for the sake of tradition, family, continuity." The members elect Barron Roussell president by acclamation. The Senator presents Nolan Roussell with a plaque. In a brief speech, the Senator says that some titles can be erased, some cannot; the title of "founder" will remain with Nolan Roussell forever, "like a crown of gold untarnished." A party follows.

Alison and Laurel walk into the party minutes after the band starts playing. They sit alone at a table on the east end of the hall. The Senator orders the music stopped. Barron Roussell tells Laurel that "for propriety and, if she chooses, for pay" she should sit with the band. Laurel goes to the stage. The applause is "sparse but polite" as she steps to the microphone. Before she leaves the auditorium Laurel says to the audience, "Y'all don't own all the world."

Footnote. Next day's headline, New Orleans *Times-Picayune*: NEGRO GIRL CHALLENGES BAYOU ROYALTY.

Later that night the Krewe of Zulu, meeting at the Powerhouse of Salvation Hall on Fort Bien Street, vote to remove Zeema Steeple as King Zulu and to replace him with a Queen Zulu, Laurel Steeple. Before suggesting that the coronation of the queen take place in the court square, Stillman Bowman tells the audience that he wants to be buried standing up because he has been "bowed too long."

Footnote. During an interview with the Senator at Municipal Auditorium, a photographer for a national news magazine is alerted to the court-square demonstration. This photographer, known professionally as Willi Q, arrives in time to snap a picture of Laurel standing on a bench with a makeshift scepter. In the photograph Laurel appears to be floating above the ground, the bench beneath her blending into the black tones of the ground shadows below and the oaks around and above. In his autobiography, *Hope Without Expectation*, Willi Q says that this picture is his least favorite of his "well-anthologized shots." When I interviewed Willi Q and asked him to elaborate on that statement, he said the picture is "an example of how development-lab chemicals as well as humanity can elevate the day-to-day into the surreal." He also told me that his magazine chose this shot over one that he asked them to print, a close-up of Laurel's face beside the "streetlight-on-foil" sheen of the scepter.

Arriving at the court square Barron Roussell, "representing the Krewe of Delos and for the sake of peace and order," asks the demonstrators to return to their homes. In exchange, the Krewe of Delos promises to meet with the Krewe of Zulu to preserve the order and settle all differences before Mardi Gras.

Thursday, February 21
The Reverend Stillman Bowman in several interviews says that all his attempts to telephone the Senator and the new president of the Mondebon Delos Main Street Carnival Club have "delivered him failure and humiliation." He announces that "the aim of the Mondebon Zulu Landry Street Carnival Club is still to be granted a license to parade on Mardi Gras Day. Nothing more." He also announces that there will be a meeting of the Mondebon Zulu Landry Street Carnival Club at 7:30 P.M. in Powerhouse Hall to discuss appropriate actions "even if appropriate actions mean jail time."

Barron Palmer Roussell, on the steps of the Senator's home at 5:30 P.M., tells reporters that Bowman's "nothing more" comment is the real issue. There is, Roussell says, more to consider than "certain elements" would like to be considered—namely, the written and established laws of government bodies, the common laws of tradition and decency of citizens of both the white and Negro communities. "There are methods established," he says, "methods even for getting parade licenses, that cannot be got rid of for the sake of calming the spasm of the moment." The police jury and the city council will be holding private executive sessions "among and between themselves and with these concerned citizens throughout the day tomorrow."

When Barron Roussell is asked if he can "produce Negro citizens who are concerned the way he is concerned," Roussell answers that the steps of the Senator's house are not "a proper place for this production," but that Negro citizenry will be forthcoming.

Footnote. In Willi Q's autobiography, he says the "most photographically articulate" of all the faces in his pictures is the face of the unnamed Negro citizen who stood behind Barron Roussell during Roussell's subsequent encounters with the press. Half of this man's face was as tired as a face could appear—"eye-bags like mail pouches, ivory eyeballs swirling with vivid madder." The other half of his face held a smile "of patience and sustained expectancy, of power and confident leisure—as though any outcome, even to the point of destruction, results in reward."

This man, of course, is Lineman.

At the Krewe of Zulu meeting that night, Stillman Bowman recognizes Zeema sitting in the audience and welcomes him back as the "prodigal king." Zeema refuses to sit beside the pulpit with his daughter and the officers of the Mondebon Zulu Landry Street Carnival Club. He asks if there is a method more dignified than "marching in grass skirts" to accomplish Bowman's goals. Bowman says that the club is going to "throw back what has been thrown at" his people. When Zeema tries to speak again, the jeers from the audience cover his words. After Bowman quiets the audience, Zeema points to Laurel and asks, "Isn't there a safer way?"

Footnote. Bowman's answer to Zeema's question appears in

the cutline of a front-page photograph in the New Orleans *States-Item*. In the photograph, Zeema and Laurel are embracing beside Bowman's pulpit. Caption: " '*Safety* means *beside*,' Civil Rights Reverend says as a royal family reunites."

In the last paragraph of the accompanying story, Zeema is quoted as saying, "I will continue to bet on compromise."

Friday, February 22

The Reverend Stillman Bowman, with from "fifteen to twenty of his local followers," goes from public office to public office trying to keep up with the unscheduled public meetings. This "series of smaller demonstrations" is extensively photographed.

At the end of the day, Barron Roussell meets with Bowman on the courthouse steps to tell Bowman that "progress is being made and patience is still the key to progress." Roussell also says that a license cannot be issued today because by law all parish and city offices must close at 4:30 P.M. and cannot reopen until Monday. After Bowman's questions and questions by reporters, Roussell admits that a special session of the city council could be called by the mayor and that the council could enact emergency statutes. The mayor, however, is out of town until Monday.

Footnote. From my own visits to the town, I can recognize in the photographs that record Friday's events most of the characters in my husband's chronicle: Zeema beside Laurel; Lineman behind Barron Roussell; Lineman's family—Emmon, Angelle—behind the Reverend Stillman Bowman; the Senator, the banker Stalker, both Theriots. Nolan Roussell, who stepped aside in favor of his son and quiet control, can be seen in several of the photographs. Even Roussell's wife, Elizabeth—in long sleeves, her head bowed and blurred—can be discerned in one of the photographs. Only two of the characters are missing. One is Mayor Poule. The other is Alison

Belanger, who seems to have disappeared from recorded history until Mardi Gras Day.

Saturday, February 23

A few lawyers and representatives of "national black-interest groups" arrive in town "to survey the seriousness of the situation." A CBS News producer with a sound and film crew also arrives; they all leave thirty minutes later when other members of the press corps having lunch at the busy five-and-dime across the street from the Roussell Building tell them that every town official is out of town or unavailable for comment.

Footnote: Most of the out-of-town reporters and all of the photographers except for Willi Q will leave town after the compromise of Mardi Gras eve is announced. The CBS producer and two other reporters will mention their respective departures as sources of regret when they discuss "the story that got away" in their memoirs.

At a meeting of the Mondebon Zulu Landry Street Carnival Club, public plans are made for "calling attention to the cause" by a peaceful demonstration during the Krewe of Istrouma parade, scheduled for 2 P.M. the next day. In his speech, Bowman says that the town "will be available tomorrow" at the parade, that "tomorrow will be our turn to comment," that Zulu will march on Tuesday with or without a license. "Freedom is every man's license."

The single member of the black national groups remaining in town is introduced to the gathering. He says that all men everywhere on the side of decency agree, and support Bowman's position. Handing Bowman a check for $500, he also says that "considering the relative seriousness of other matters developing in places like Birmingham," he will be able to remain in town only until the next morning. He asks that everyone present pray that 1963 will be labeled by historians as "the year of decency."

Sunday, February 24

At 10 A.M. the captain of the Istrouma parade receives a call from the Senator. The Senator tells him to "report in to police central" when his parade is ready to roll. The captain, Stanwood Ezelle, tells other members of the krewe that he believes the call is a practical joke, but at noon he calls anyway, using the number "the alleged Senator left." From the phone booth at the supermarket on the corner of the Great Perpendicular and Doug Canal Road, Ezelle reports that the floats and automobiles are lined up and ready to proceed. He asks to speak to the Senator personally. The Senator, he is told, is about to make a speech to the crowd gathered in front of the reviewing stand across from the Roussell Building on Main Street.

Footnote. My husband and I both interviewed Ezelle, who was present at many of the private sessions that involved the licensed Carnival clubs. Ezelle also wrote and self-published in 1973 "The Senator Called Me Personal and Other Vignettes on Mardi Gras in Mondebon."

On the reviewing stand, the Krewe of Istrouma and guests are standing by in costumes coordinated by Nolan Roussell, the theme Style Through the Ages: false switches and chignons; stomachers; houppelandes; mob caps and turbans; the Worth look; Edwardian satin; turn-of-the-century Sears, Roebuck; flappers with bobbed hair; Coco Chanel. In the crowd below, Bowman's "demonstrators" also await.

At 1:30 P.M. the Senator arrives, begins his address to the audience by quoting Shakespeare—*There is a tide in the affairs of men*—and Abraham Lincoln—*now we are poised*. The Senator reminds the audience that although many of them speak French, they are still part of the "vast heritage of southern

America." Across the South, men of decency have already said that they will stand to bar and block the doors of institutions held most dear, in order to protect the "treasures of tradition" behind those doors. It is time, he says, for "Acadian and creole southern America" to stand with "the sword of decency in hand to protect their treasures as well."

The Senator goes on to cancel that day's Istrouma parade. After an empty whiskey bottle is tossed at him, he is escorted from the reviewing stand by a state trooper.

Footnote. Although texts of the Senator's speech are to be found in many sources, there are no accompanying photographs. Willi Q told me that he was there, but in trying to get close to the stands he "got into a dispute with a celebrant dressed in playing cards and moss, a dispute that led to a cracked lens and swollen ankle." In my interview with him, Willi Q contends that Bowman's part of the crowd accepted the cancellation of Mardi Gras quietly. Willi Q remembers one comment from a single "black reveler in yellow Indian feathers," who said after the cancellation of Mardi Gras, "But all we want's a license, man."

On the stand, however, again according to Willi Q, there was "vocal and physical shoving from the Krewe of Istrouma." Stanwood Ezelle agrees, saying that the many members of his family who were present on the stand that day "were more than a lot upset that their parade had been put on hold for the sake of some speech or other."

At sunset the state police report to the Senator's secretary that the streets are peaceful. After midnight the Senator is driven to Moisant Airport, where he boards a flight for Washington, D.C.

Monday, February 25
Throughout the day, Bowman and Roussell exchange words through representatives of what is left of the press

corps. At a 5 P.M. press conference at Municipal Auditorium, officers of the Krewe of Istrouma vent their outrage at having been canceled after a year of preparation; members of the Krewe of Delos say they will "fight in the streets before their parade is canceled." It is at this conference that Barron Roussell stands and uses the word *compromise*. Over the protests of the krewes, he invites the Reverend Stillman Bowman and the members of the Mondebon Zulu Landry Street Carnival Club to a meeting with the Mondebon Delos Main Street Carnival Club at 10 P.M. in an empty courtroom in the courthouse.

At Powerhouse Hall, Stillman Bowman publicly refuses to compromise when the reporters bring the offer of a meeting to him. After an impromptu meeting with Zeema Steeple, Bowman says that he will meet with Roussell, but only to listen, "not to be hosed and watered down."

Tuesday, February 26

At 3 A.M., on the steps of the courthouse, the Reverend Stillman Bowman, Laurel Steeple, Zeema Steeple, and Barron Roussell stand together. After photographs are taken, Roussell announces the compromise: Both parties have agreed to work within the order. The Delos parade will roll, the Zulu parade will not. In exchange, the king and queen of Zulu will be allowed to sit with members of the Krewe of Delos on the same reviewing stand. Mayor Poule will bring a parade permit for the following year with him to the stand, and after King Delos' float arrives at the stand, Poule will rise to present the permit to the king and queen of Zulu.

Footnote. Only Willi Q remained to question the people on the steps of the courthouse. None of his questions or the answers to his questions were ever published, but he related these to me in my interview with him.

When asked by Willi Q if members of his krewe were

332

happy with the settlement, Barron Roussell answered that "in a compromise everyone loses. My own people have decided to trust me. And with that word *trust* I say adieu."

When asked if members of his krewe were happy with the settlement, Bowman answered: "No. Compromise is just another way to hose down the truth."

When asked why he accepted the compromise, Bowman answered: "Zeema Steeple again. He pleaded his case for safety, the safety of his little girl."

When asked if she was Zeema's little girl, Laurel Steeple answered, "Just this one last time."

When asked if he could guarantee the safety of those who would gather on the reviewing stand, Roussell answered, "No man who is armed will be allowed on the reviewing stands—not even the police. All that will be done will be safe and symbolic. You have my word on that. I do not lie when I say the order will be preserved, history served."

Footnote. In my interview with him, Stanwood Ezelle says, "Everyone in every legal krewe objected to Barron Roussell's idea for the compromise. All along, though, he insisted, him, that he had an idea and that his idea would have more of a far-reach than any one Mardi Gras. Still, everyone said, *no way*. Then his—Barron Roussell's daddy—called me on the phone and said that his boy should be given his chance. And how do you say *no way* to that?"

Two Clichés

Sometime after the compromise was announced, my husband boarded another crewboat. His hasty notes, probably written while he was on the boat, mention a midnight argument with the captain of the trawler *Two Pookies* and a predawn bribe with the captain of the jo-boat *T-Bud*. My husband, as close as I can tell, did not get to the Morgan City docks until late morning on Tuesday, February 26, 1963. I can conclude that his subsequent trip back to town was an effort for him: although Morgan City is only fifty miles from town, he did not arrive in town until late that afternoon.

As I said, I can also conclude that at some time on Monday he had discovered in his pocket Alison's surprise. It is only supposition on my part, however, when I say that this surprise was my husband's own bottle of green pills that had been buried along with a backpack, a pistol, and bullets. It is only supposition also when I say that my husband's attempt to get back to town resulted from his having realized that Alison had been digging in the orchard behind the house on Emerson Street shortly before he left her alone that Wednesday on his way to the standoff on Fort Bien Street. Thus, I have come to believe—although I have no way of knowing—that my husband's return to town was a struggle to get back to Alison. I have also come to believe that he wanted to get to her before the Delos parade began.

I say all of this now from the historian's position, tracking atoms of circumstance back now from the event on the reviewing stand on Mardi Gras Day. From that position there is such a word as *inevitable*. From that position *inevitability* becomes an embarrassingly simple truth.

Yet I cannot help but ask myself, as my husband often did, the rotting question: What if one atom . . . what if my husband had arrived in time to prevent Alison from going to the reviewing stand?

There is, of course, no way of answering. And it may be a waste of time, for physicist and historian, to attempt to list *what can be shown to have had the possibility of occurring.*

Thus, at this point in my history, am I left with two unforgivable clichés:

1. I am delaying, as my husband also had, the inevitable.

2. My husband, according to his notes, did not make it to Main Street until a few minutes before 5 P.M. on Mardi Gras Day in 1963, hours after the streets had been cleared by the state police. So close, my dearest, but no cigar.

Willi Q And The Mossman

The best eyewitness account of the event on the reviewing stand on Mardi Gras Day, February 26, 1963, comes from the photographer Willi Q—from his testimony at the coroner's inquest, from an interview that I had with him in New Orleans in 1981, and from the chapter "Chance and Proper Lighting" in his autobiography, where he describes how he happened to take a famous photograph.

The Krewe of Delos rolled at the scheduled time, noon, after having gathered and arranged itself, at the supermarket parking lot at one end of the Great Perpendicular, into the lengthy configuration—the marching bands, the escort cars, the tractors and floats—that have come to be known as a Mardi Gras parade.

Dressed again as a silver space-traveler, Willi Q with two cameras at ready snapped pictures of what seemed to him to be the "organized mayhem of preparation." For these shots he used only the camera that contained the 36-shot roll of color film. He wanted to save the long, bulk-loaded magazine of black-and-white film and the camera with the motor drive for the "more newsworthy to-do" scheduled for the reviewing stand in town.

At "what well might have been precisely noon," Willi Q took what felt to his fingers to be the last shot on the color roll—the king, "in ersatz ermine and alkyd gold," taking his command by "rising with his robes from the papier-mâché, drawing gold sword from gold scabbard, ordering all behind him forward by pointing in the general direction of the red tractor assigned by God knows what lot to towing the throne."

Willi Q had estimated that it would take the parade about an hour to reach the Main Street reviewing stand—plenty of time, he thought, to pack equipment into his Jeep and drive through the tunnel and along the Great Perpendicular to Landry Street, where he would park and walk the last five blocks to Main. The three-block walk from the corner of Landry and Main would take at most fifteen minutes. Or so he also estimated.

Because of the crowd, Willi Q had to abandon his Jeep at the corner of Fort Bien Street. He drank what he now estimates to be two cans of beer with "insistent well-wishers" before he reached a point where he could see the Landry streetsign. On Main Street his "trek through a mass that took two hundred *excuse me*s to part each of five dozen times" began after 1 P.M. As the Roussell Building finally came into view, Willi Q could also see the lime-greens of the columns surrounding the throne on the king's float.

Willi Q cannot explain how he traversed the final hundred yards to a position in the crowd—"a mass immune to a million-million *excuse me*s"—gathered at the foot of the reviewing stand. He is certain that King Delos had already made his toast to his queen, "that pretty girl in emerald-green" by the time the bulk-loaded camera was lifted overhead. He is certain also—because of that first picture, the one black-and-white photograph that would survive—that the reviewing stand had been cleared of all but three other people "besides the green queen and the cops": the mayor, Zeema Steeple, and Laurel Steeple.

336

After taking that one picture, Willi Q made it to the red tractor, and he is certain that while climbing to the top of the tire nearest the reviewing stand, he saw the following: as planned, Mayor Poule presented a license to parade next year to Zeema Steeple; as planned, Steeple accepted the permit. Then, standing atop the tractor tire, Willi Q saw King Delos draw his sword and jump onto the stand, heard King Delos shout, "Not as long as tradition stands."

In the moment that followed those words, in the moment before the mossman yanked Willi Q by the ankle from the tractor tire, Willi Q switched his camera to motor drive and brought the viewfinder to his face. Willi Q is certain he saw Zeema taking a step in front of Laurel. Willi Q also thinks, but can never be certain, that before he fell he saw Zeema move toward the king and the sword.

Willi Q fell backward to the concrete of Main with his finger on the shutter release. What he witnessed of the rest of the event on the reviewing stand he saw during his struggle with the "man covered with moss and playing cards." Four times Willi Q managed to climb back onto the tractor tire. Three times the mossman yanked him down to the concrete below.

The first time back on the tire, Willi Q saw Zeema and King Delos scuffling, "rolling on the plywood and in the bunting," and saw a local policeman "in local-cop blue attempting to separate the two men"; the next time up, he saw the king and Zeema being restrained by "local-blue and khaki-brown."

During the first fall to the pavement, the mossman held Willi Q's finger to the shutter release until the motor drive had expended most of the film. The rest of the film went after the second fall when the mossman tore the camera from Willi Q's grip. Willi Q says that it was after his third fall, while fighting with the mossman to reclaim his camera, that he heard the gunshots—two. And these gunshots, he says, made him surrender his camera to the mossman and climb the tire for the last time.

Exhausted, Willi Q sat. Instinctively, he says, he reached for the camera of color film still hanging from his neck—realizing even as he did so that in the crush of the crowd he had "unforgivably neglected" to rewind the old roll and load a fresh one. Nevertheless, he lifted the camera neck-high and—perhaps with his eyes closed—pressed the shutter release. By chance, he says, there was one frame left on the roll.

"And there you have it," Willi Q told me. "Chance and proper lighting, right? But what do you have? On Kodachrome, everything a festive . . . and let me ask you to be honest and innocent, like you don't know the history behind the scene or the history of the time, like you discovered this picture eons from now and you don't know a thing from a thing about what went on with us. There you have it, a wash-blur of colors except for two faces, each looking at the other as though nothing else is going on around them, as though they had just met after being apart a year maybe, a day, you don't know. Maybe meeting in a train station or a backyard garden. But meeting, not leaving. Father and daughter, maybe— but you know that from history—but you can't tell, not really, not from just the picture. And you can't tell either just from the picture that the father has the daughter in his arms on the floor of a Mardi Gras reviewing stand. Not really. Just that look, each at the other and nothing else around. And then on the yellow dress, a small wash of red. A flower? But history tells you, so you know. And it's hard to be innocent and honest when history talks so loud. Blood on a yellow dress. And what do you have?"

According to the coroner's report, Laurel Steeple died at 3:06 P.M. at Mondebon General on February 26, 1963.

Conclusions

My brother-in-law Geoffrey Marquis mentioned the photograph of Zeema and Laurel in his *Southern Chronicles*. He linked what happened on the reviewing stand on Mardi Gras Day to "other examples of violent outcomes during a time in our country's history known as the Civil Rights Movement." And so it has been linked, justifiably I believe, in footnotes in bottom boxes in a number of studies and treatises and dissertations.

The photograph of the event and the event itself, however, fit well into any Marquis chronicle, especially those parts of such a chronicle where the family attempts to speculate on decency, on good and evil, on history in the smaller sense and its connection with history in the larger sense. My husband, had he the remaining desire, would have gone on to do just that, skirting the edge of what is known as "objective history" with his "Garden District gossip."

I, one hired to create bottom boxes for the Marquises precisely in order to form that objective link, ironically am left with the job of deciding how best to end Jay Pee's chronicle, to get to the present, which—as any Marquis would say—is eternally mine. I hope the Marquis family will forgive me if from my bottom boxes I "betake myself to poetry, speculation, judgment, and opinion." But I must speak for them, for my husband, and for myself. The Marquises have long ago forgiven me for my having labeled myself *historian*. I have long since forgiven them for their lack of objectivity. Perhaps, in my struggle to get this chronicle toward *today*, there is a case for, a need for, a merciful blend.

Even so, let me begin the end by attempting to relate only what can be shown to have occurred, hoping as I do that by now the reader trusts me. And with that trust, one remove from faith . . .

No one in eyewitness testimony ever disputed that Alison and Mayor Poule touched the gun, "the paint-splattered .22," that killed Laurel Steeple, nor did anyone doubt that Mayor Poule was holding that same gun when it discharged the bullet that struck Chief of Police Theriot in the head. Based on that same testimony—including that of Zeema Steeple, Barron Roussell, Mayor Poule, and Willi Q—a coroner's inquest concluded that both shootings were accidental and that a reasonable account of the actions on the stand could be constructed as follows.

After Barron Roussell jumped to the Mardi Gras stand, he and Zeema Steeple fought. A small group of town police and state troopers attempted to separate the two men. No more than fifteen to thirty seconds later, Chief of Police Theriot stepped away from the group, pulled a pistol from "somewhere inside his uniform," shouted "Halt," and raised the pistol over his head as though to fire into the air. He was then knocked down to the stands, and his pistol skidded across the reviewing platform to the feet of Mayor Poule. Poule, who had urged Alison to move with him to the railing when the confusion began, picked up the pistol. The fight was apparently under control when Poule also lifted the pistol into the air and shouted, "Halt." Theriot, who had climbed back to the platform, admonished the mayor, walked toward Poule, and grabbed the gun. The gun fired—accidentally, according to the findings of the inquest and the grand jury—and Theriot collapsed.

From here the testimony gets muddled. People from the crowd had by now started to climb onto the stand. Many of these people joined the group gathering around the wounded chief of police. No one—not even Zeema, who was walking toward his daughter—seems to have seen Alison bending over to the pistol, which had landed at her feet after Theriot was shot. Only three people—Willi Q, Mayor Poule, and a fourteen-year-old girl who had been standing on the roof of the Roussell Building—could testify that they saw Alison with the gun in her hand. Two of these, Willi Q and the fourteen-year-old, did not see the firing but did see the gun fall from Mayor Poule's hand after the weapon discharged the second time.

Mayor Poule in his testimony took "all blame for all the horrible outcomes." He had tried to do good, "but ended up clumsying into the bad." He ran to Alison, he said, to take the gun from her and to end the "terribleness he had begun."

"I took the gun from that poor girl," Poule said. "I take all the blame for all that happened. The gun was in my hands then, too. I still feel, me, the sound of the shot in my hand. I can only hope that I can embarrass myself away from this tragedy."

The coroner ruled the second shooting accidental, mentioning in his findings "everyone's attempt to use the weapon benevolently in an attempt to stop the violence." It was fortunate, he added, that Alison Belanger, who suffered "ensuing severe mental trauma as a result of the mishap," did not also meet with "a worse harm."

Perhaps Geoffrey Marquis most accurately summarized the historical importance of the event when he wrote in his second-to-last *Southern Chronicle:* "On the local level, both the Mondebon Zulu Landry Street Carnival Club and the Mondebon Delos Main Street Carnival Club issued statements to the press that they agreed with the coroner's conclusion, but each blamed the other for initiating the violent outcome. National supporters of both groups also concurred with the coroner, and on this 'national level,' intermittently even to the present, Laurel Steeple's name is used by both sides as an example of what can happen when supposedly decent men struggle for deep-kept views of their worlds."

Landry Street Blues

My husband in his own notes wrote one line as a way of mentioning the proceedings that followed the shootings. That line was in the form of a question—*How did Theriot get the purple-flecked .22?*

Testimony revealed that one of the stipulations of the Mardi Gras compromise was that everyone who had access to the reviewing stand was to be unarmed. The chief of police himself agreed to this stipulation. Indeed, Theriot did not wear his holster to the parade that day. The inquest could find no answer as to why he decided to conceal the weapon. Although Chief of Police Theriot lived ten years past Mardi Gras, he had to be cared for by his father and never regained his ability to speak.

Of course, no one at the coroner's inquest had read my husband's chronicle, which often mentions the pistol as one of its atoms of circumstance. Anyone reading his chronicle would have known that the person to ask was Alison Belanger. But even then she would have been unavailable, having been taken by ambulance to the state mental hospital in Jackson hours after Laurel died.

My husband's research into the event and the aftermath of the event answer most of the other questions one might ask. I believe that the one interview he says he had left to do was to be with Alison. I believe also that my husband remained in town for over thirteen years waiting to do that interview. I do not believe, however, that my husband would have been *capable* of doing that interview even if Lineman had not offered him "a steal."

But I am getting ahead of myself. I am also getting ahead of (as many a Marquis has often told me) the sense of balance that I crave from chronology.

As close as I can tell, my husband spoke to two people the evening of the day Laurel died: Stillman Bowman and Zeema Steeple. I have my husband's notes on one of these conversations. I have a tape the label of which suggests the existence of the other conversation. I believe that my husband erased this tape soon after it was made.

The first person my husband talked to was Stillman Bowman, who explained as my husband took notes all that had occurred in town while my husband was offshore. After talking to Reverend Bowman, my husband visited Ozema Steeple, still in his cell in the Mondebon Parish jail. I know my husband visited Zeema because of the tape label: "Zeema and I, jail cell, 11:00 P.M., February 26, 1963." That is the tape that was erased. A hiss covers what might have transpired between these two men.

I can picture the two there, alone, perhaps sitting on the cot beside each other in the darkness. One might assume that there were questions they posed and tried to answer, questions of fatherhood, responsibility, the true nature of the world called De Plus En Plus, circumstance, chance, repetition, shared regrets, and hell.

But I have come to believe that the hiss covers twenty minutes and thirty-seven seconds of thorough silence.

And I have also come to believe that it was during that silence that Zeema reached into his pocket to give my husband a gift, a sheet of paper. Many years later, I found—in parts, as though it had been opened and closed again and again—this gift in my husband's last notebook.

And here, for the sense of balance chronology makes, are the fragments of that gift:

The First Letter

If my estimates are correct, my husband left Zeema's cell before midnight. From there, as close as I can tell, he walked the streets of the town until 2 A.M. on Ash Wednesday. At that hour he sat alone in the poolhouse behind the house on Emerson Street and wrote his first letter to me, a letter that he never mailed, a letter that I also found in the same coat pocket of his suit:

2:00 A.M., Ash Wednesday
February 27, 1963
the poolhouse, Emerson St.

Remember, Molly, Berman's last words to us at the table the night he died were in the form of a question, a question I now understand.

Remember, Molly, we had all returned from the Shakespeare festival—ten of us that night, I think—and were having a late dinner. We talked about right and wrong, about there being no right or wrong but that thinking, everyone's thinking, makes it so. That notion was horrible to contemplate, we agreed. We ended up clinging to our religion, even to the extent of accepting the idea of a God that we Marquises despise—the Old Son of a Bitch Lord. Even He is better than the everyone's-thinking-makes-it-so notion. And we, all of us but Berman, were laughing, I remember, as we usually did, clinging to our laughter much as we did to our religion.

Then Berman rose. He said he now believed in the Notion. *And if the Notion is correct, if the world works itself that way, shouldn't we let the world go rather than live with that comprehension?* Let the world go, *he said.*

I remember no one spoke for a while, not even my father, who would later regret his silence. Then you rose, Molly. You reminded Berman of his work with the United Nations War Crimes Commission, of his work left to do on the International Court of Human Rights. You spoke about the Marquis quest to define the word de-

345

cency, *of the need to continue that struggle. No matter how defini-*
tively transient that word has been through the ages, you said, there
is a need for a definition, universal and timeless.

All of us sat a bit stunned by your attempt—you a Marquis-in-
law—to tell a Marquis how to be a Marquis. And how long did you
and Berman face each other in silence before Berman finally sat
again? He still said nothing after he sat, but you did not sit until he
spoke again. And when he spoke, his words formed the question:
"For the jump?" Then you also sat. No one answered Berman, but
we all knew what he meant. If everyone's thinking does make it so,
why indeed go on? Even you admitted that the definition of decency
changes with the ages. Why try at all to pit silver ideas against ideas
that seem black when all ideas are equally valid, all the meted and
same silver-black in the end? Just for the struggle? Just for the jump?
Doesn't it follow that struggle defines life? And who can compose
himself after learning that? Who?

Forgive me, love, for my errant poetry, for this moment of thor-
ough and undivine despair. But I wanted you to know, to share with
me what I carried with me besides a suitcase full of notes and tapes
as I walked the streets of this town.

About an hour ago I stood alone on a bridge. I told myself I would
not walk from that bridge and return to the dilemma of our age: We
must forgive one another to get along with life, but there are enor-
mities so vast they should not be forgiven by any decent man. I
would not walk from that bridge and return to the anger I needed to
get along with my one life, to that monumental hatred never ending
to the never . . .

I went so far as to hold the suitcase over the railing. But I couldn't
let go. I dropped it to the bridge grating and I cried. I cried for
someone named Laurel as I hadn't cried for my daughters, in a most
undignified way, on the bridge over the dirty Mondebon, my hands
clutching the back of my head, my hands pulling my head to my belly
and knees.

And so a question for you, Molly. Why did I walk from the
bridge? After I have seen existing on a smaller scale what Berman

saw in the larger sense after his war, why? Why do I go about the living? What atoms malfunction in me? Why de plus en plus en plus do I walk from the bridge?

I am afraid now to stop writing, afraid any word will be the last word before the end of the world and will go on forever as an epitaph—

And more terrible still, alone now in lamplight with a pool somewhere outside, I cannot help myself from feeling a sense of joy as I mutter your name and the names—

You Molly I long for and love.

Please God do not send me hope.

Not Profiting Overly

I know from my own interview with Zeema that Laurel's body was released at the end of that week, after most of the official investigations into the happenings on Mardi Gras Day were completed. I also know that my husband made the trip with Zeema by bus and by train to a town in central Mississippi, where Laurel was buried. According to Zeema, while my husband was in Mississippi he decided to accompany Zeema on a trip to Birmingham to participate in the marches and demonstrations. But when Zeema left for Birmingham in late March or early April, my husband was no longer with him.

Footnote: A vivid picture of that "heaving spring in Birmingham" can be found in Geoffrey Marquis' *Southern Chronicles.*

Footnote: Zeema told me in my interview with him that he went to Birmingham in April of 1963 to fulfill a promise that he had made to Laurel and to Stillman Bowman to get them to consent to the reviewing stand compromise on Mardi Gras Day. Bowman and Laurel agreed then to give up the Zulu parade if Zeema promised to "lend spirit and name to the Birmingham crisis"; Laurel also promised to return to school

347

if Zeema made it to Birmingham "and made it with her wherever they were needed after Birmingham."

Bowman was there to meet Zeema at the bus station in Birmingham, as were over 500 other people. According to Zeema, this trip produced the first of what he called his "rediscoveries." As he explained to me, "That's when record sales go up for no reason of your own talent. Hell, probably 250 of the 500 jamming the Birmingham station were agents and other platter buzzards."

Zeema remained in Birmingham for two weeks, believed for two weeks that perhaps he was "contributing, fulfilling more than a promise." During those two weeks, Zeema received the wound that gave him his permanent limp. Zeema is certain that the bite on his leg that gave him the limp came from the same "human-trained German shepherd" that paralyzed Bowman's left hand.

"Regardless," Zeema told me, "that wound promised me bigger sales still. In fact, someone close to me, a teenager in a black jacket in the emergency room bed next to mine, said just that, said I deserved the rise in reputation considering what I was *contributing*. Then while I was leaving the hospital with Bowman, a reporter asked me how it felt to be in the forefront of the movement. Same reporter mentioned Laurel's name in the same breath as his question. Me and Bowman both caught on then. Bowman himself let me out of his side of the promise I made, saying there was *something* impure going on around me. That something's something, ain't it? Bowman decided I could give to the cause best by doing what I do best, leave town. I was on a bus by midnight headed . . . headed, I don't know, that time north. I've been spending my life fleeing easy wounds and the lies of my rediscoveries now for years and years, still singing songs other people wrote. But maybe that's what I'm purest at . . . not profiting overly from songs other people sung."

My husband returned to town in April of 1963 and visited Nolan and Barron Roussell. It was then that my husband made his "social contract" with the Roussells.

From then, my husband passed his time by holding the Roussell family to their part of the social contract and by researching the town and trying to write his chronicle. My husband remained in town for over thirteen years. And the rest—as the family I married into delights in saying—is history.

Footnote: My own research supports what Jay Pee's chronicle shows about James Peter Marquis' life in town. Very slowly, my husband retraced the atoms of circumstance that led to the event on the reviewing stand; very slowly also, my husband began to get along with himself.

My husband was employed for most of those thirteen years as what has become known in our place and time as a "social worker," first for the diocese Catholic Charities, then for the state Department of Health and Human Resources. He had to be moved often by supervisory mandate from position to position because, according to his employment files, his "outward personality did not match the needed objectivity required for the task at hand." Through phone interviews with three of my husband's supervisors, I have learned that this statement, which appears eleven times in my husband's DHHR file, means that although my husband requested working in "crisis management" with those cases involving abused and neglected children, he found it "difficult not to physically attack the parents and adults accused of doing the abusing and neglecting." Eventually, my husband seemed to do well in a position the state had found hard to fill: working with children who were placed in hospitals as a result of injuries, whether of birth or accident or abuse— children who "more often than not died during their institutional stay."

As Jay Pee's chronicle shows, my husband by 1975 was getting on with himself by slowly, very slowly, getting on with others around him, those he met on the streets of the town. I am convinced that he had managed, by the time he gave up on his chronicle, to concentrate his hate in one direction, toward the heavens, and that he was on the verge of forgiving his God—as he had promised Laurel he would do—because he was daily being reminded less and less of his sorrow.

Because I understand what I have just written as true, it is difficult for me to answer the question: why did I go to town for my husband? I knew in 1975, when I received the last of my husband's chronicle, that if I went to town for him, he would have a terrible choice to make. It is true when I say that I loved him enough to stay away, that I believed that I would be overly profiting from my love if I went to him.

Question: why then did I go to town in the summer of 1975 and again just before Easter of 1976?

Answer: because I finally understood a word.

Still Always Night

I brought my questions, my yellow notepad, and my husband's tape recorder with me that summer of 1975 as I boarded the Greyhound bus that took me south to the watery part of the world, to the town circled in red ink on one of my husband's maps. I exited the bus under the hackberry trees that grow along the natural levee where the Landry Street Bridge crosses Mondebon bayou, and I walked Landry until I reached Lineman's place, which was still functioning and standing with the same signs and benches, but with the tin siding now painted a brick-red.

As I said before, I found a Lineman eager to answer my

questions about the holes I had found in his tapes and about other details I knew to ask him about.

When I asked what had happened to the Zulu parade after the Mardi Gras of 1963, Lineman answered with a short history of the town since that time.

Mayor Poule shot himself dead in his garage on Christmas Eve of 1963.

Stillman Bowman never did resurrect Zulu, finding himself involved in "more important demonstrations," among them, running for town council and trying to keep open his "orphan/transient facility," which he operated from mobile homes in the field behind his church despite the "forces trying to shut him down for the so-called civilized reasons— sanitation and public-nuisance ordinances."

Nolan Roussell "stepped back from all the kingdoms" and took care of his wife, who died of a skin disease in 1969, "the same night—or so the headlines said—that white people stepped in silver shoes on the silver of the moon." Roussell died of cancer the year after. Roussell's son, Barron, showed his head on occasion, "testing the waters for candidate-cy and office." But he never "tried to actual run or to amount to nothing you could count for no reason nobody could figure."

The town had embarrassed itself completely away from the 1963 happenings on the reviewing stand. Few people had been known to bring the event up in conversation, unless of course a television camera or microphone had been pointed toward them. The parish had taken eight more years but finally got around to integrating the schools.

The question that delighted Lineman the most concerned the deal, "the steal," he offered my husband after they had completed the Lineman tapes.

"My best attempt ever at my tonement tally," Lineman answered. "I kind of suggested to Jay Pee, you understand, that the two of us make a bid to buy the old post office building that went up for sale on Main Street. Kind of, you understand, moving Landry to Main. We had us this brave kind of scheme to save the crumblings of downtown by tempting the tourists down from New Orleans. We'd buy us the place and kind of import a big-name jazz star down here to attract the tourist dollars. I was suggesting that me and Jay Pee, we could manage the place together. Can you imagine, you understand, a Mar-kee and a man used to be a Weasel. . . . Anyways, man, Jay Pee he went at that with all his soul. Took out money from his stocks and bonds. Got us another silent partner. Never did tell me his name.

"So, well, anyways, Jay Pee went along with my idea, but not until after he made me promise to donate the old Palace grounds to Reverend Bowman for Bowman's orphanage. Shit, I mean hell, I figured that would get me a night's sleep for sure instead of my naps because, you understand, that was a hell of a lot of good and sacrifice . . . took every cent I had me. And a lot of good that did me. I'm still toneing, as you can see by the snores you hearing."

When I asked Lineman who this big-name jazz star was, he sat back in his chair and, smiling, he answered: "Zeema. We went and rediscovered Zeema."

In minutes Lineman was on the phone to Zeema, who was the manager of the Main Street Jazz Club. Within the hour Zeema had joined Lineman, me, and my questions under the tin-hole stars of Lineman's place, where days and nights were still always night.

I had one question left to ask, and as we sat I sensed that the two men were trying to steer me away from the asking by volunteering to talk about those things they rarely spoke of. Zeema told me about his last day with Laurel, without divulging the details—"those things," he said, "that was the mystery of us two." He did use the word *tender* once, and both men looked down uneasily at the table, searching for a deck

352

of cards perhaps. I felt that they had offered me that word as a gift, hoping that I would leave them after that, leave their table a winner.

"And my husband?" I asked. "Jay Pee?"

As Lineman sank away into his abrupt slumber, Zeema answered: "He's gone. The oil patch probably. Turned his share of the jazz club to me. Said he wasn't coming back."

"But what could make him do that after all these—"

"She's back in town."

Delight on Emerson

I found Emerson Street by myself, walked the street from one end to the other trying to locate Alison's house by what I had imagined it would look like. I tried to find it at one point by looking into backyards, but I could not see from the street any signs of an orchard or pool. I finally chose one house with red shutters and knocked. The child, a girl of about eight who answered the door, told me that the house I wanted was "further down, about three houses." That off-white, well-cared-for, farther-down house had no shutters; a six-foot cedar fence blocked any view of the backyard. Again I knocked.

The tall man who came to the front door was dressed casually in slacks and a blue-and-white polo shirt. He looked younger than I—in my fifties then—even though his hair was completely gray. I started to excuse myself, certain that I had again knocked on the wrong door.

"I am looking for someone named Alison Belanger," I said.

"You're in the right house," he said. "May I ask who's calling?"

"Yes. The wife of James Peter Marquis. I would like to speak to her."

"Ah, this is delightful indeed. Your husband told me about you. I am Barron Roussell."

"I am Molly—"

"I know, I know. Say no more. Please come in. You are welcome here."

He led me through the entrance way into the room that must have been the living room my husband described in his chronicle. Just as I expected, it was a room of open curtains, sunlight through prisms of glass. But the piano I expected to see was not there; in fact, all of the furniture had been removed, replaced by three desks of the kind one might rent from an office-supply store—black enamel on steel, chrome legs, wood-grained Formica tops. A breeze from the open double doors on what I guessed was the northern wall softly lifted the edges of stacked papers and posters.

"I must apologize for my work area," Roussell said, his back to the double doors. "But I am running for district attorney. I've had to scurry to get myself in the race. Of course, you know of all this. Your husband told me that he sent you everything, that you were, in effect, custodian to the Marquis research. You know, too . . . but by the look on your face, you do not know all."

I explained to him that I had come to town to finish my husband's research and to see my husband.

"And do you know," he asked, "that I am the last person your husband spoke to before he left town? He shall not be returning, I'm sure."

"Did my husband interview Alison?"

"Interview? No. The last words he said before he walked from that door—before he told me to continue taking care of Alison—were 'I do not want to be reminded.' He's finished for good with us, I'm afraid. And you must trust me when I say there is no need for you to continue either. Did you know of the great social contract your husband drew up between my family and him?"

"No. And I do not think I will be here long enough—"

"Oh, quite so . . . are you here also to judge?"

354

"I do not judge," I said.

"Your husband, though, could be quite judgmental, couldn't he? An avenging angel. But he released me from the contract, as I said. Would you follow me to *my* patio, through these doors here? We could be more comfortable. I have made a patio for myself here, behind me here. Alison is sitting at her patio at the back of the house. But before you see her, we have much to discuss. Please."

At first, I declined Roussell's offer even though there were questions I had planned to ask him. Perhaps because I did not know if I could trust him. Perhaps because my husband probably did want the chronicle stopped. Perhaps because I had begun to realize I would not see my husband.

And I was tired at this point, frustrated and tired. I now wanted to make quick end.

"I will just speak with Alison," I said.

"But that will take you some time. You must refurbish yourself with lemonade."

I thought of Lineman's gift to Zeema and to my husband— one question. I would ask Alison one question: how did the gun get to the reviewing stand? The answer to that question would be enough to end my husband's story. Then I would leave.

As I walked away from Roussell, I did not think of my husband's description of him, of the connection my husband had made—Barron Roussell and Berman Marquis. But with my back to Roussell, when I heard him say *Please* again, I suddenly remembered that description, and I hesitated, for a moment only. I now feel that it was fortunate for me that I did, for this chronicle that I did. I was not one question away from the end of the story.

"That's better," he said. "Follow me."

I did follow him, sat with him beneath a yellow-and-blue umbrella on *his* patio. I don't remember having ever been as thirsty in my life as I was that afternoon. Roussell and I sat without speaking for several minutes as I drank, a bit lustily perhaps, two glasses of his lemonade. In his chronicle, my husband mentioned Roussell's lack of laughter. Roussell laughed deeply that day as he watched me drinking. He used the word *delightful* again. And with that word I, too, made the connection, without wanting to, with Berman Marquis. It was then, too, that I realized that I had fully become a character in a Marquis chronicle. I was about to realize that this chronicle was mine.

The First Molly Tape

Barron: I just knew you had your husband's tape recorder in that valise. It was a gift from me, you understand.

Molly: I know.

Barron: But of course you do. Do you know also that you cannot purchase tapes for that recorder anymore? They had not standardized the size of the cassettes then.

Molly: I have two left.

Barron: Did you bring both with you?

Molly: Yes.

Barron: Would you mind, then, recording me and Alison on separate tapes?

Molly: I don't understand.

Barron: You will.

Molly: May I ask a question, then?

Barron: Yes. Delightful. Let's see if you do better than your husband.

Molly: I assume my husband saw you after the events on Mardi Gras Day, 1963. How long after?

Barron: After he left town. He left town soon after that with the singer, with Steeple. When your husband returned to town, he paid me a visit. He found me in my apartment. In the throes of my last binge. I still had on remnants of my

Delos costume, a modicum of fur, my sword. Must have smelled enough to prorogue the legislature. He roughed me up without touching me, your husband. Standing there, across the bar from me. He told me to buck up.

Molly: To compose yourself?

Barron: Exactly. He said that we—he and I—had things to do, for the town and for ourselves. I, of course, told him to go to hell. He told me that he was going to see my father and that he was going to propose a contract. The terms? My father would retire. I would take my father's place, running the business, taking care of Alison. I would have a quiet life, he said, aiding him in town projects of his own design. And all the while I would not be allowed to run for public office.

Molly: Did he tell you he was going to use his chronicle as blackmail?

Barron: No, that would have made no sense to me. But he did say he was going to become that self-righteous Marquis avenging angel. He put much responsibility on my shoulders and my father's for what happened. He said that I had deceived the singer Steeple into thinking everything was going to be safe on the reviewing stand. That I had planned all along to jump to the reviewing stand with the sword. That I had done all as a personal gesture—to resurrect myself, as it were, rather than doing anything as a symbol of a southern ideal. And again I told him to go to hell. I would finish my drink, I said, and resurrect myself any damn well time I felt like it. And we sat there, thrusting and parrying responsibility. I parried by telling him that it was he who had forced the outcome more than I. I told him that if he had not entered the town limits, perhaps things would have gone differently. Back and forth we went, thrust, parry, riposte.

Molly: Another standoff.

Barron: A quaint, delightful, and apt expression. Yes. A standoff. But he came at me. Over the bar. Roughed me up with more than his words. You know what he said? "I want

357

that goddamn sword," he said. I told him my father wanted the sword. Well, to make . . . your husband left with the sword. If ever you hear from your husband, I would like you to ask him for me what he did with that sword. I've foraged around the grounds here looking—.

Molly: Did he go to see your father?

Barron: Oh yes.

Molly: And it was then he said he would use the chronicle as blackmail?

Barron: Oh yes. Do you know the story of the burial in the orange grove?

Molly: Every detail.

Barron: I do not think your husband knew the full story at the time. He knew enough. At any rate, he faced my father, a duel of a different sort, I heard. Told my father that my father was to continue in his retirement. My father tried to match thrust for thrust for a while. He told your husband that what was going to happen was going to happen without a James or a Nolan being around.

Molly: History? Quiet control?

Barron: Ah, you know us too well. Yes. My father asked your husband to think of how many hands the gun went through before—

Molly: Your father agreed to go along with this contract?

Barron: Yes. Your husband told him—and these are the exact words—"On Emerson, there is a hole always open to the past." And that did it. My father visited me that same day. Cleaned me up. Told me about the incident—19 . . . 44, was it? Yes. My father said that we were to go along with the contract. That I was not to run for office. That, in effect, we were to remain quiet. I had a feeling my father would never earn enough in his lifetime to pay for a debt that began in 1944. But he never said this to me. Never apologized, either, for asking me to continue the payments. He did mention the family name.

Molly: And you went along with this?

Barron: Oh, minimally. I tried a few times to run for office. Your husband would make a subtle appearance. I would find him present, for instance, in the clerk of court's office when I attempted to qualify for a race. He told me to write a letter to the police jury whenever Bowman's soul-slum was about to be condemned.

Molly: Are you the silent partner on Main?

Barron: Pardon?

Molly: The post office building on Main. Did my husband ask you to invest?

Barron: Your husband never *asked* me to do anything. And I'm sure you'd never be able to use the word *partner* when referring to me around him. Yes, I had to invest. The "new connection," your husband called it. Landry to Main. He also asked me soon after to give for a project of remodeling the Palace, some orphanage or other. And so, thus, for all these years . . . I fell into cadence with the contract. Paying both my father's note and mine at the same time. I began feeling rather good about it, like leaving the church after confession on Saturday, stepping into the oaks and breeze. Then Alison returned. Your husband paid me a visit. He sat here with me on my patio. Didn't speak much. Waiting just as you to see Alison. What would he have asked her, do you think?

Molly: He told you about me?

Barron: Yes. He said it was finally over for him. That he was releasing me from the contract. That he would see to it that the chronicle was not published. Are you going to put it away also?

Molly: I've not been told anything.

Barron: Vigilant, you Marquises, eh? . . . And your husband's twelve years in town. He did penance also. He's done quite a lot of good. Good works. But I have a feeling your husband does not think there is a penance big enough for him. Do you agree?

Molly: I'm asking the questions, remember?

Barron: Yes. Delightful. At any rate, here we were, my father, your husband, me, our sins exposed. We all have our excuses for everything, but we do our time anyway. Doing our time for twelve years. Then she returned a few weeks ago.

Molly: Alison.

Barron: Yes. And it's as though your husband had set that date as a limit of some sort on the contract. But he would have botched it up, wouldn't he?

Molly: What do you mean?

Barron: His blindness. He would have asked her the wrong questions. He always did when it came to Alison. No matter what I tried to warn him about . . . do you see?

Molly: Enough. Yes. But possibly no more than he.

Barron: But if you are to finish the story for your husband, you must ask the right questions. The questions he did not ask. I will not lie. Ask me.

Molly: I do not understand.

Barron: What would *you* ask me about Alison? You have no doubt studied the bits of the story. So, to get the story . . . what? What would you ask me? Think.

Molly: I would ask you about a cat.

Barron: A cat?

Molly: A detail. Something Lineman and Zeema saw when they first encountered Alison. The way she was holding a cat, the way she—

Barron: And without knowing what you're talking about, I would tell you that you are on the correct line of questioning. Can you see it? I, on the stand, sworn to tell the truth, as I am. You bring up the way Alison holds a cat. I shift a bit in my seat.

Molly: I have always wondered, from what you told my husband about the night Prince Albert was—

Barron: Yes. Excellent.

Molly: What really happened that night at the Palace?

Barron: Yes. That question. Your husband was blind to it. That night. Alison was in the room with Prince Albert. She saw me outside the window. I was outside dodging that accursed dog. She unlatched the window. I crawled inside. In the room, I came up with an idea for scaring the hell out of the Negro on the floor. I took the sword, held it over his mouth, threatened him. Alison beside me said, "Dark daddy, dark daddy."

Molly: The drugs . . .

Barron: Yes, I know. Drugs. Another excuse. We may never know the depth of *their* involvement. She used the statue. It was she who hammered the sword into the floor. Not once but twice, that statue came down on the knob of the sword. My God, do you know how close she came . . .

Molly: Why didn't you volunteer this information to my husband? It would have changed—

Barron: *If.* I still feel the vibration of the handle in my hand. *If.* If your husband had pulled away. If the Negro blackmailer had told your husband what really happened. He, that prince of a fellow, saw her, I'll tell you. *If.* But don't you think your husband suspected?

Molly: No. I don't.

Barron: Why did he leave this house then, the other day, without seeing her? Don't you think—

Molly: No. That's a different story completely.

Barron: It's your story now, isn't it?. Rather a tragic figure, your husband. But I wouldn't tell him that. Come at you over the bar, you see. . . . And you'll have to judge her.

Molly: I didn't come here to judge. Does Alison remember doing what she did at the Palace?

Barron: I tried to test her the day after it happened, questioned her. And I've put her on the stand again for redirect almost every day since she's returned from the state hospital. I have to take care of her, but . . . she may be telling the truth when she says she doesn't remember. But I can't tell. I asked her the other day again if she remembered me standing with the sword in my hand. She told me only that your husband told her years ago that I had confessed to that. . . . I have a feeling that she lies, just as her mother and stepmother . . . that she knows . . . but I just can't tell.

Molly: I remember she scratched Prince Albert on the cheek.

Barron: I did not know that. A deep scratch, deep scratch. . . . You know, I've been reading some of the Marquis chronicles while I did my time. The word, in the Marquis chronicles . . . *mean*. That doesn't describe any psychological . . . and, after all, she has excuses. She lived with Bethany, after all.

Molly: Are you saying that she wanted to hurt someone else?

Barron: I can't say anything. I've questioned Alison about it. Don't want to redirect any more. You'll have to judge.

Molly: I'm not here to judge.

Barron: I believe there won't be an answer after all. That you won't be able to find a question that will give you the answer that ends the story. That your story won't close as easily as you had hoped. Throw in one liar or one madman and there's always . . . a hole.

Molly: I don't like calling it a story. And I'm not here to judge.

Barron: You're a Marquis, aren't you? They do just that in their chronicles, don't they? I've done my research too over the years. I've read the chronicles, as I said. They—the Marquises—always take time out to judge.

Molly: Regardless, Alison's also served her twelve years.

Barron: Perhaps. And isn't it strangest of all—I've thought about this, too, for twelve years—all the ideals gathered on the reviewing stand—

Molly: It's all the smaller sense.

Barron: Pardon?

Molly: . . .

Barron: Are you going to tell your husband the truth about the Palace?

Molly: I believe he won't ask the question.

Barron: Well, welcome, my dear.

Molly: Molly. My name is Molly.

Alison II

I had entered the house with the faith of my expectations, expectations built on my husband's chronicle. I had expected to see a piano in the living room. My not finding the piano had not disturbed my faith. As I had begun to walk to Alison the first time—before I hesitated and followed Barron Roussell onto his patio—I had expected to find a woman as tired as I was, a young woman who looked my age, a covering of sunglasses and makeup, perhaps, to hide the strains of the trip. When I left Barron Roussell, I had lost all faith in my expectations, but I was still surprised at what I saw through the screen door of the kitchen.

The person I saw sitting at a wicker table and reading a news magazine was beautiful. I have never felt comfortable using that word before, nor can I remember ever seeing it used in any of the most poetic passages in any of the Marquis chronicles. But in every sense, the Alison I saw that day was beautiful: dark eyes alert; thick hair colored and curled, auburn in the highlights.

I expected also to see her in a green shade, the shade of translucent panels molding with age in the patio roof. Instead, she sat in bright sunlight in front of a cedar fence that hid all the green of the backyard from my view.

I introduced myself before I opened the door.

"How delightful," she said. "Please join me."

After I sat, I explained what I had come for. Some questions, I said.

"And I'll bet . . . yes, Jay Pee's tape recorder. How—but let me put this magazine away. I have been trying to catch up on my tan and my news. But you know the story, right? To be honest, I've been expecting your husband. I will never forget his kindness."

Sitting back, she crossed her legs under her sun dress and folded her hands over her lap.

"Will he be joining us ever?" she asked.

"I can't answer that. You don't mind then if I record us?"

"Mind? After all your husband did for me? And this is pleasant in a way. Now that I'm back . . . to, you know, start again where I left off. Kind of like a sequel to a movie. *Alison II.*"

Her laugh was what I would call genuine—no, more so. I found myself smiling back at her health, demeanor, recovery.

The Last Molly Tape

Alison: Where shall we begin? You know, you said you had questions. Like what?

Molly: Questions about Mardi Gras, 1963, if it's not too difficult.

Alison: Put that word out of your mind. Difficult is gone. Questions like what?

Molly: Do you know, for instance, how the pistol that was buried in the orchard made it to the reviewing stand?

Alison: You've come to the right person. Yes, I know. And Barron, too, I've told him. He knows the answer to that. But you must have others? It's like the questions test my fortitude, you know. And I'm doing well. Barron will tell you.

Molly: The others may be more difficult for you.

Alison: Like *Why?* I'm ready for that, too. All the *why*s. It's the least I can do to repay your husband's kindness. But where shall we start? You must help me there.

Molly: That Wednesday before Mardi Gras. There was a Krewe of Delos ball. You and—

Alison: Let me say her name first. Laurel. There, that might help you see I'm all right. Ask away.

Molly: You told my husband—that Wednesday that you and Laurel attended the ball—you told my husband that your Uncle Nolan gave you something.

Alison: Yes. He certainly did. You see, your husband— may I call him Jay Pee?—Jay Pee and I had figured out, or so we thought, everything about my past up to that point: that I was *adopted* by Bethany Belanger, that I was really born at the Palace. But I have a feeling you know more than I do, right? I went to that party sure of who I was. Then Uncle Nolan handed me something and I no longer knew who I was.

Molly: And what was that?

Alison: A birth certificate. He gave me a birth certificate. Your husband and I could not find one in this house. You know? Follow? That's how we came to believe that I was transplanted into this house from Landry Street. Then Uncle Nolan gave me a birth certificate with my name . . . Alison's . . . on it. He gave me Alison Belanger's birth certificate. Can you imagine what that did to me? Yes, I'm sure you can. I mean, the questions. The birth certificate said December 27, 1942, 7 pounds 4 ounces, 4:14 A.M., Alison. But that date was long before Jay Pee and I had figured that I was brought here to Emerson from Landry. Well, it made no sense.

Molly: Unless you know about . . .

Alison: Don't be afraid to say it. The orchard. The burial in the orchard. Shall we take a walk? Through the orchard?

Molly: No. Please, go on.

Alison: My uncle would tell me the truth, of course, about what happened in the orchard. I demanded all along that he tell me.

Molly: Did he tell you the night of the ball, when he gave you the birth certificate?

Alison: Oh, no. Later that week. Much later. I'm not sure exactly when. But not that night of the ball. Wednesday, right?

Molly: Yes.

Alison: Maybe he started to tell me the truth the night of the ball, but other things happened . . . with Laurel. And I had to try to figure out what that birth certificate meant. It didn't fit at all with the dates on the photographs in my mother's room. Alone, I had to do that, make sense. And all of this is my . . . state of mind . . . which will make sense when . . . state of mind, you know. How they like those words at the facilities. Hospitals, you know.

Molly: You had to make sense of the birth certificate based on what you understood at the time. But surely you guessed that what my husband and you had surmised about the past was not entirely correct. Why didn't you tell him then, after the ball when you saw him again?

Alison: That's a *why* I know also. He had other things on his mind—Laurel, mostly. But I wanted to stand alone. I believed I was strong enough. Are you following?

Molly: Yes. How did you make sense?

Alison: Oh, every whichaway. For a while I even guessed I was a twin. That explanation made sense to me at the time.

Molly: In what way?

Alison: Like my twin sister and I had been born here on Emerson, and then we were separated. I was brought to the Palace, you know, then brought here again. Or we were both born at the Palace. I don't know. Nothing I could come up with fit the photographs. But I kept trying.

Molly: Did you try to get to your uncle?

Alison: Yes. I called. But things were really happening by then.

Molly: Why, though, did you conclude you were a twin?

Alison: Of course, we know that is not the truth, but in my mind, then . . . my state of mind . . .

Molly: But what made you conclude—

Alison: Oh, I see what you are getting at. My mother, Bethany, told me once she had a tumor removed from her ovary, her left. The doctors told her they found hair and fingernails on the excised ovary. They told her she should have been a twin. I always felt, I guess, I should have been a twin, too. So I latched on, do you see, to that idea, to make sense? Isn't it funny, even knowing what I know, I still call Bethany my mother. . . .

Molly: You must have been very confused at this point. Did you still believe you could handle all of this alone?

Alison: Yes, still, all along I thought myself strong enough. But my state of mind must have shown. Laurel even suggested once that I move away from this house to Uncle Nolan's house in the subdivision. But I was content to be where I was, here.

Molly: With Laurel?

Alison: Yes, she stayed with me in the house. Even in my confused state of mind, Laurel was calming. She talked about the details of Mardi Gras, all the meetings. I listened, but all that time I was trying to make sense . . . you see?

Molly: Going back to Wednesday night, may I ask now what it was you put in my husband's pocket—the surprise— before he left you.

Alison: Surprise? I can't . . . I remember giving him something before he left, yes. But I can't say. I remember digging in the orchard before he came to me that last time. Oh dear. I say I was in control of myself, and then I say things like, "I was digging in the orchard." Isn't it funny, though, even before Uncle Nolan told me the truth about the burial in the orchard, I was digging in that dirt, just as I'd seen my mother— Bethany—doing. She's the one who always made me feel like a twin.

Molly: So you don't remember what it was you gave my husband?

Alison: No. But I can try. If I try to remember what I buried out there . . . let's see: towel . . . would you like me to—

Molly: Not just now.

Alison: That may have been when I dug up the pistol. Yes. It was in there, you know. In the ground. I know I got my hands on it eventually. It may have been that same night Jay Pee left. I'm still a little confused about that. Of course, after my uncle told me the truth about the orchard, I dug in the orchard then, too. My nails were always caked. I understand my mother's digging now, I guess. But I'm still . . .

Molly: Your state of mind. Go on.

Alison: Yes, good. All the while I was trying to make sense, life was like going on around me: Mardi Gras, Laurel. I remember listening to Laurel. I remember getting scared she was in danger. That she and Zeema shouldn't go up on the stand after they told me about the . . .

Molly: Compromise?

Alison: Yes. Well, you *do* know the story. I was worried for their safety. I even offered Zeema the pistol, to protect himself in case . . . but it was like I couldn't get out of myself for trying. I couldn't do my making sense and at the same time get totally *into* the rest of life that what was going on around me. I made a mess of things, I'm afraid.

Molly: The gun . . .

Alison: Yes. I offered it to Zeema when he came to the house with Laurel once. For protection, as I said, you know. I remember that made sense, too. Like, there was the gun. It had to appear for a reason, right? Why else would it be there? Everything had to be there for sense if I could find the sense for everything.

Molly: Zeema didn't carry the gun onto the reviewing stand.

Alison: Oh, no. I'm afraid I'm responsible for that. I'm responsible for digging it up and for carrying it with me that day—in my muff, a white fur muff. And why? Did I want to offer it to Zeema again, for protection, for him and for Laurel? That makes sense, doesn't it? I was concerned still for their safety. I carried it with me to the stands. A police officer found it on me before I went onto the reviewing stand. I'm afraid I was very confused by then. Still trying to make sense. And then somewhere in there—my goodness, what a jumble, like—but this is a good re-creation of my state of mind, you know. But let's back up. Somewhere in all of this, Uncle Nolan got to me and told me all about the real Alison, how Bethany had smothered her poor little daughter. You said you know that story as well?

Molly: Yes.

Alison: Well, can you imagine my state of mind after that? All of this would drive a Stoic nutso. And all the while I was carrying on outside, you know, making my way through Mardi Gras, with Laurel, Zeema. I made it to the stand, after all, didn't I? Changed into my costume. So I must have been functioning in that world, too. Outside, you know.

Molly: Trying to make sense. Yes, I can see. Then the gun was taken from you—

Alison: No, let's stop there. I don't want to ruin that moment. I've had to accept some responsibility, you know. And that has seemed to be what everyone at the hospital wants me to accept. They at the hospital . . . feel . . . you know . . . that I have blamed myself all along for Laurel's death because I carried the gun with me. But let me say some things . . . may I say these things, trusting you . . .

Molly: Go on.

Alison: I'll end up telling you how I can sit here now, after all that's happened. But first let me tell you . . . I've never said this aloud before. I was very confused until the gun made it to my feet. Then everything came together. Sense was made *for* me by the world outside. Why else would the gun make it to my feet? I looked down at the gun. I looked up and saw Laurel. And I must look at it this way. I picked up the gun. I looked at Laurel again. Now, follow me with this, please—it may sound like madness, and it was, it was, I admit it. Laurel looking to me, to see if I was all right, smiling. That was Laurel, you know, like a sister. I saw Laurel, my sister, my dark twin. I told them at the hospital I saw me, too. My state of mind, remember.

Molly: Are you telling me you thought of killing Laurel when you picked up the gun?

Alison: I told them at the hospital that when I looked at Laurel I saw myself, my twin all at once. They said I may have been thinking of killing myself. That makes sense to them. And I told Barron that just the other day. I saw myself as my twin. I suspect Barron thinks I'm lying. And *responsibility*. I said that, too, to him and to others. But I can tell you this now. I can't lie to you or to Jay Pee. I can return his kindness, I guess. All along, I knew it was Laurel I was looking at.

Molly: Please, I must understand. I see your confusion. See the . . .

Alison: Madness? Yes, call it that. I can call it that now.

Molly: But you're saying you thought of killing Laurel when you picked up the gun?

Alison: I'm saying that went through my mind, yes. But I'm just saying it to you and Jay Pee. There, it's been said. And that's what really drove me wacko. That's why I've had to spend my time away. Can you see? Going up there with the gun. Having it taken away from me. Having it go through all those hands. Landing at my feet. Picking it up. Considering killing Laurel. Having it taken away from me. Having it . . . in someone else's hands do what the gun seems to have been made to do . . . from the outside. Like the sense of it was being made from the outside. Do you see? I am going to have to use another word I knew better than to say before, at the hospital: I believe now that Laurel's sacrifice—

Molly: Sacrifice?

Alison: No, you're right. I won't use that word, even now.

Molly: No, go on. Is that how you've brought yourself to sit here now?

Alison: It's part of my secret. It took me awhile to deal with what happened. But I've come to accept what happened as Laurel's gift to me now, that I was rather destined all along to survive. Otherwise, no good comes out of this, and Laurel's life is wasted. Look, don't get me wrong. I'm not going to look for excuses—my state of mind, you know, excuses like that. Say that Laurel took the blackness of my life away. Say the blackness smiled and stood before me. Then it was gone. For me. What it took to save me . . . she gave me that. I can live again because of Laurel.

Molly: But something doesn't seem quite . . . are you saying that you live with the remorse by . . .

Alison: And something doesn't seem quite right with what you just said. That is why I never mentioned it before. All this brings her life down . . . down . . . I won't have that. Turn that thing off!

Molly: Do you remember what happened at the Palace? Did you plan to hurt someone—Laurel—when you approached the reviewing stand with—

Alison: Off!

Time Out

Let me say at this point that I went on to investigate something that Alison told me in her interview:

Before I left town, I asked Zeema if Alison had ever offered him the pistol for protection. Zeema's answer, his *no*, was definite. He said that the first time he saw or heard of the pistol was on Mardi Gras Day, when he "saw and heard its harm."

And I investigated something that Barron Roussell told me in his interview:

Two months later, I found Prince Albert Willis at the Bronze Star Bar on Burgundy Street in New Orleans. Though Prince Albert refused to answer my questions, his head shook affirmatively when I put forth Barron Roussell's description of what really happened at the Palace the night saber pierced floor.

Let me say also that I was guilty on that day I interviewed Alison of doing something Barron Roussell had said I would do, something that I have criticized the Marquis family of doing again and again in their chronicles:

I judged Alison.

But I did not judge her for anything she said before I turned the tape recorder off.

Alison wasn't finished speaking. I must deliver here the rest of what she said, as I remember it, as objectively as I can. But I must confess that as I sat there listening to her, I judged her as a Marquis would judge her.

In all of their chronicles, the Marquis family never apologize for speculating freely about the characters under their scrutiny and how the beliefs that these characters profess fit into the Marquis notion of good and evil. As early as 1886, Catherine Walden Marquis wrote of what the family liked to call the "definitive and etymological" explanation behind this Marquis notion.

Barbarians, she said, are brave, rushing headlong into battle without mind, but they display no courage. *Bravery* becomes *courage* only with contemplation. Courage, in other words, for a Marquis, is one level above bravery, and that level is made possible by mind. (I have taken some liberties here. Catherine Walden Marquis also used the word *heart* as being interchangeable with *mind*, but that does not translate completely into the vernacular.)

To a Marquis also, any human at any time in any age can also be mean—"headlong and low, animalistically mean." But when humans begin to contemplate their meanness, then, then one is getting to the mindful level above mean, which is evil. For a Marquis, she said, there can be no good or evil until there is contemplation. Thus a Marquis believes that only when people in any age contemplate with delight their meanness, only then are they entering the realm of evil. And when these same people try to give name to their delight, they invariably look to the good of their age for labels.

All of what I have just summarized is of course a ponderous abstraction. Marquises admit to this. Marquises over the generations have looked to the characters in their chronicles to exemplify these abstractions. Just as Barron Roussell said, the reader can expect to find a Marquis taking time out from the narrative flow to do this. This time out vexes some, enrages critics of history. I myself have spoken out against the practice at after-dinner gatherings in the closest room on many nights, but not so much against the notion as against the judging, which I have called "elitist" on some occasions, "presumptuous" on others. When I have said, "Let history judge," every Marquis down to a man and a woman has laughed and told me that this is the same as saying "Let no one judge," which to a Marquis is reprehensible.

And here am I, struggling to finish a Marquis chronicle, my chronicle now, finding myself taking time out to attach the Marquis abstractions to the actions of what have become my characters. But I do this freely now as I remember Alison's last words to me after I turned off the tape recorder.

"Let me tell you the other part of my secret," she said, "how I can sit here now after something so horrible hap-

pened. This anyone will understand. My age believed   and
I still believe—life is good. Anything that comes from life
therefore must be good. That is the one clear truth we must
all accept if we are to live with ourselves after . . . after things
so horrible happen."

In this chronicle—forgive me—the character of the mossman is mean. In this chronicle, I am afraid that Alison, the
Alison I interviewed in the summer of 1975, is one level above
the mossman.

Understanding a Word

The second time I went to town, during the Easter season of
1976, I did not bring with me as much of the faith in my expectations as I had brought with me in 1975. But I did bring
with me my brand of stubbornness and effrontery that fit so
well into the Marquis family. I felt certain that my husband
would show up for confession at the cathedral in town even
though he had said he would not return. I felt I knew my
husband. I was betting on that knowledge, on that faith,
which is one level above trust.

Without entering the church, I asked penitents in hats and
tignons the schedule for the confessional on that Good Friday. There were two "rounds," one from 3:00 P.M. to 5:00
P.M., the other from 6:30 P.M. to 8:00 P.M.

I did not know what my husband would look like after
thirteen years, both of us now well into our fifties. I remember we had laughed often in bed about how we would age,
but it was the laughter of those too young to imagine with
any accuracy the marks in the strata of a contingent future.
We were too young then to even take into consideration the
simplest of natural laws: the pull of gravity on the skin beneath the eyes, on the breasts and chin, on the round of the
back; or the pleasurable inertia an aging body feels as its bot-

tom rests on the ledge of a molded concrete fountain beneath oaks that are beneath gargoyle spouts on the copper gutters of a cathedral in a town south of New Orleans.

I walked the grounds of the cathedral square, the concrete buckled by oak roots, for two hours, studying those who walked from church, hoping, I believe, to see my husband again. I watched the custodian making his evening rounds, turning off the fountain, skimming debris from the water with his palm, rolling up his shirt sleeve before immersing his arm for coins. I sat on the ledge of the concrete fountain from five o'clock to five thirty, the half hour when no one entered or left the doors. During that time, I caught my reflection often in the still surface of the pool: Eyeglasses still, metal rim—had I changed the style? My dress, flowers—was it the same style, full-pleat, I had worn when my husband left? Was it or any part of my covering in style at all? Had I been too busy writing my own books, doing my own research, maybe, to get involved with style, with fashion? Maybe I had frozen myself without intending to into the exact picture of myself that I had been when my husband left. But I did not know. I knew I was feeling the excitement of the wait again, the wait I had felt in the garden, in the amber light. . . .

I walked the streets of town for an hour after I left the square in front of the cathedral. Behind the jazz club and the Roussell Building, I strolled the new wooden walkway along the natural levee of the Mondebon Bayou. After having a supper of fried fish and french fries in the five-and-dime across the street from the Roussell Building, I walked the Great Perpendicular to Lineman's place. On this trip, I noticed that the Palace had been completely razed. Only a white-shell parking lot remained. And that lot seemed small to me, considering the angles of my husband's chronicle, the many stories and balconies, the sassafras and bay of my husband's chronicle.

I found Lineman behind the bar of his place, the same

signs, the same brick-red paint from the year before. But Lineman's face, even in the dim purple of the black light, seemed to have pulled itself up somehow, away from continuous gravity. I smiled at him, and he smiled back as he recognized me, "Mrs. Jay Pee."

He put a beer in front of me, but "not on the house."

"There ain't, you understand, no on the house, even for saints. And they lying if they say th'opposite."

I asked him about his eyes—why the red had turned to ivory-white, where the pouches had gone. He told me that what I saw was "more than Visine eyedrops and good tonement," that he had been to a doctor who identified his sleeping trouble as a form of narcolepsy, and that he was being treated with drugs. He slept all night now, not the satisfying rhythms of "normality sleep," but a long sleep with "short, silly dreams."

"Does this mean that you are finished atoning?" I asked.

"Habits, baby. Don't know. When I think of all the good I did all these years . . . "

"Is that why the Palace is gone? The orphanage?"

"No, I give the Palace up to Bowman, remember? But Bowman give it back to me when he was flat-out sick in his last bed. A gift. Bowman said it was up to me to decide what I was going to do with the Palace. I told him, you understand, about my doctors and drugs and all-night sleeping. He asked me, 'How you know it wasn't the tonement scale rising after all those years of trying good?' Well, I don't know, you understand. But I tore down the Palace. That got nothing to do, you understand, with tonement or not-tonement. That was a project. Projects is left to certain types with project brains. I ain't project-brained, you understand, like Bowman and your husband. And now Zeema and his silent partner on Main with their lovers' walkway behind the jazz club. Hell, Bowman's dead. Buried him standing up, 'cross the canal. And

Jay Pee, he ain't round to hold me to project deals. But I wonder, you understand. Was it doctors or all my toneing got me my nightfuls of sleep? Like Zeema said, you understand, half magic, half sense."

I asked Lineman to tell me more about Zeema. Zeema was still playing jazz for tourists in the club across the street from the court square, still making the investment work. Lineman had pulled out of his own part of the investment, but the silent partner and Zeema and what was left of Jay Pee's capital were still "making business."

I asked also if Barron Roussell had won the race for district attorney. He had not, but Lineman expected him to try again.

"Roussell's face be the most common you see on the telephone posts," Lineman said. "He don't even take the posters down, you understand. Like them people that keeps up they Christmas lights around they porch. They just turn them on when it's time to light up again."

Before I left for the cathedral square, I asked Lineman about his plans.

"White man's bet," he said. "But habits, you understand. I been trying to figure out what I could do and still be kind of toneing and kind of taking the steal at the same time. Got it figured. School board. I be running for school board. What a good fuckin' steal."

At sunset, I saw my husband walking from church. I recognized him by his erect Marquis frame against the shadows in front the arched doorway—his erect Marquis frame. But what I saw when he stepped into the remaining light of that day surprised me. James was wearing a checked polyester coverall, the garb perhaps of an oil-rig man fresh from the first bath of his off-shift days in town. As I stepped closer, I saw that he looked older than I, older even than I might have imagined: his hair completely gray, combed in waves straight back over a shining scalp; and above his top lip—a moustache, a thin moustache of the kind we had laughed at together many times, the "racketeer-trying-to-be-Clark-Gable moustache." Would we ever laugh again, together, at ourselves?

He said, "Excuse me," as he stepped out of my path.

"James," I said.

When he turned, he let his eyes glance at my face, and then he looked quickly away. I stepped closer and held his hand. He would not say my name, nor would he look into my eyes. I looked into his, past the "ruck and rivel" into the lively green.

"Why?" he asked.

"Come home with me, James."

"I've still got things to do. "

"Your promise to Laurel. I know. Did you keep your promise?"

"No. Please . . . you understand. I know you do."

"Yes. My bus leaves at eight thirty."

I asked James to escort me back to the bus station, and he agreed. We walked the streets of town together, without touching, without talking.

Under the hackberry trees along the levee, in the blue beam of a lamp that lit the Landry bridge and the back lot of the bus station, James turned to me, and looking over my head, he said, "I'm sorry."

"Hold me, James."

"We can't."

"Say my name, look into my face."

"I can't. "

"Tell me, James. You tell me. Why?"

James looked at my face, held me so that he would not have to look again.

"Why are you going to force me to make a choice?" he asked me. "I did not expect it of you."

"Tell me, James. Why?"

"Because I don't want to be reminded."

"Tell me. Say my name and tell me."

"Because *they* were us, Molly."

James pulled me closer. I remember one of his hands, soft on my shoulder, rubbing me there. And I remember the other hand, on the small of my back, above my ovaries, that hand hurting me. I remember wanting that softness and that pain.

"Marry me, James."

"We are married, Molly."

"No. Marry me."

There, under the hackberry, I think James finally understood a word.

The Merciful Blend

(A.D. 31–*circa* Yesterday)

Shaping Our End

Two years after he returned to our home, James began going out with the family again. One of those times, attending another version of *Hamlet* at the Shakespeare festival, James nudged me during the lines, "There's a divinity that shapes our ends, / rough-hew them how we will."

That night, late into the night, James and I had our first argument together since his return. We disagreed somewhat on the words *There's a divinity*. James's interpretation suited his needs, mine suited mine. James, still considering himself a Roman Catholic, cited the Nicene Creed. I told him that my sense of the divine went beyond the face of his God, into a universe only expressible by opposites like *all-nothing, everywhere-nowhere*.

"At least there is something for you to believe in," James said.

"Believe in. I don't know if I'd go so far as to use—"

"Sometimes, Molly, I think you're hopeless."

"I know I wouldn't go that far."

What we disagreed on thoroughly were the words *shapes our ends*. James needed to believe in the shaper. He clung to the hope that he would someday have his time in divine court, and just before being rushed to hell, he would deliver his summation, on the record, concerning "mismanagement and unjust enrichment."

James and I argued, settled on nothing. At one point he called me a "damned existential humanist," and I called him an "equally damned Papist." It was then that we laughed at ourselves for the first time. With the laughter still in the room, I asked James to shave his moustache. He complied.

James and I argued like this often, settling on nothing. We went about a marriage as it was for people with our knowledge in our station at that time and that place, arguing into the night, making love in what was left of the night, settling onto and into nothing but ourselves.

Gumbo Bay

It took James a great while longer to walk through the back doors of our house into the courtyard to sit beside the brick pond he had built with our daughters. The day he did this, he pulled the curtains apart and stared through the window at the pond for what could have been an hour. Then he named the pond.

"Gumbo Bay," he said.

Then he walked outside.

I think sometimes that after we made love, James held my face in his hands and felt the joy, the purity of nonthought, just the sound of our breathing, like the sound of the Gulf in the dark. Slowly through our years together, James allowed me to move my chair closer and closer to his, until finally our chairs were touching. Sometimes during those days when we sat together beside the pond, I sensed in him what must have been that same purity we shared after our lovemaking. We got to the point also where James would turn to me and would signal me with his green eyes that he was about to sink away, into his thoughts and the silence we could not share.

During one of these times sitting together beside the pond, I told James that I had bought a computer and was going to try to put his chronicle together as a single document. He said

384

that suited him as long as I understood that it could not be published and that he did not want to speak of the details. I did not tell James that I now considered the chronicle mine and that I would have finished the project without his permission.

When I asked him if he would grant me one question, he smiled.

"One only," he said.

I thought for a long while before I asked, "What made you return to town after you left for the oil fields that Wednesday before Mardi Gras?"

James grabbed the pocket of his shirt and shook the fabric. "The surprise she put in my pocket," he answered.

"What was it?"

"That's two questions."

"What did you do with the Marano sword?"

"That's three, Molly. And I will save the answers, for a sense of mystery. We will die with our mysteries about us."

I thought of the Marano sword, the flash of lamplight on bronze above the knob of the sword, the flash again.

"That we will," I said.

Then James said my name, *Molly*, which was followed by silence, and before he got quiet again he said, "And I have a question for you. Would you answer for me?"

"I can try."

"Why, Molly? Why do I come back again and again, de plus en plus, when my brother did not?"

"I don't know. But I suspect that defines you both. Defines us all, for what it's worth."

"And what, Molly? What do you believe in?"

"That's two, James."

"Do me a favor, will you. If you ever get around to finishing the chronicle, put that in there for me. Answer that question for me. And when you do, for God's sake, be a Marquis. Do try to be poetic."

So, for you, James, now, an answer to your last question, as best I can:

I, Molly Marquis, believe in the music of Landry and Main, of the Avenue where we Marquises live, of the water in me. I believe in putting movements to the music. I believe in what-is after what-is springs from the Event. I believe in giving up some of my atoms to possibility before the Event, again and again.

I long, just as you, for a visage above the waves and for my daughters. But I do not watch from the sand. I do not visit a grave.

James Peter Marquis died on July 10, 1985. Until then, my husband daily sinned the bravest sin. And I believe his God withstood it.

On the night he died he lay beside me without touching me. I remember that he kicked once in his sleep. I like to think he had, with some power unknown to us in our waking lives, the strength to lift the weight of a car from his belly, one kick. One kick. Then he turned, and he rolled in the sand, and he lifted himself to run at the Gulf.